Franzeska C

MORE GEESE THAN SWANS

𝒮wansong

2 Craighouse Square
Kilbirnie
KA25 7AF
U.K.

© Franzeska Ewart 2023

The Silver Swan

*The silver Swan, who, living, had no Note
When Death approached, unlocked her silent throat
Leaning her breast upon the reedy shore
Thus sang her first and last, and sang no more:
"Farewell, all joys! O Death come close mine eyes!
More Geese than Swans now live, more Fools than Wise."*

*Orlando Gibbons
1583 - 1625*

ACKNOWLEDGEMENTS

I am indebted to Jacqueline FitzGibbon, Karen Strang, and Moira Kinniburgh for their editorial advice, and to my partner Adam McLean for his invaluable technical assistance.

The cover was designed by Brian McCluskey, and his interest and advice, as well as that of his partner Claire Paterson, was a great help and support.

Thanks are due too to the staff and congregation of St Columba's Parish Church, Largs for the help they gave me in my research, and to Mike Duncan for allowing me to visit his hives and experience firsthand the pleasures and pains (mostly pains!) of bee-keeping.

I would also like to acknowledge the various inspiring young women over the years who have been my models, in particular Raquel Aragon and Nasim Luczaj, and the contemporary artists of Scotland for the ongoing inspiration their work gives me, in particular through the Facebook group *Women in the Arts in Scotland*.

1

Ella Blyth trundled her case very slowly up the path to the big blue front door of 22 Beech Avenue. She walked slowly because her hip was stiff and sore from driving, but also because she didn't want the chains she'd draped over her shoulder to clink. It was important not to draw attention to herself.

There was a smell of sea in the air, and as she walked she took long deep breaths of it, knowing from her other visits that it would soon fade and, like the seagulls' cries, become commonplace. Half-way up the path she stopped to reposition the chains and take a wary look at the house windows, but they were black blanks in the morning sunshine and if any of her three new neighbours were looking out at her she wouldn't have known. Nevertheless, as she turned the shiny Yale key and shuffled her way inside, she reflected that if anyone *had* been watching her arrival, they might well be wondering what on earth this new occupant was doing with fifty feet of steel-alloy chain draped over her left shoulder. She should have asked the B & Q man for a bag.

The entrance hall was dark after the sunshine, and for a while she stood at the foot of the curved stairway, blinking her eyes clear and savouring the scent of polished wood from panelled walls, and rainbow-coloured light filtering through Art Nouveau windows, and the wonderfully elegant sweep of the staircase that led to the two upstairs flats. It reminded her of Gran's house, though it had been nothing like as large or as grand, but even so, as she climbed the stairs and stood, key poised, outside her new front door, she felt as though she was coming home.

She pulled the case through the wide hall into the big front room she'd chosen to be her studio and dumped it and the chains on the wooden floor. Desperate now for a coffee, she went into the kitchen, switched on the brand-new red kettle, and set off back down the stairs to fetch the carrier bag containing a jar of coffee, a spoon, and a sachet of powdered milk. Before she pulled the front door shut she made sure the house keys were safely in the pocket of her dress, and as it slammed solidly behind her it occurred to her that for thirty-odd years she'd lived in a house with a mortice lock, and now she'd have to be careful not to shut herself out. Later, she'd get some more keys made.

The carrier bag was just visible between the feet of her easel, and as she tried to persuade it out she realised that actually everything would be less awkward without the easel, so before she had that coffee she'd take it into the house. The easel – a big paint-encrusted thing that had been her mother's – was what she most dreaded hauling up the stairs, so if she accomplished that she could enjoy her coffee knowing that everything else would be straightforward.

She opened the back of the car and, leaning in as far as she could, pushed boxes and bags aside then took hold of the easel's feet and pulled. It slithered easily enough off the mountain of luggage on which it was perched, and when she let go it tumbled out onto the road and she walked it, like an ungainly dancing partner, to the pavement. She went back and grabbed the bag of coffee things, and then she locked the car, slipped the keys back into her pocket, picked up the easel, and heaved it up onto her shoulder. The old wood snagged at the thin material of her dress and the edges bit painfully through the sleeve, and as she manoeuvred her way through the gate she felt a tearing kind of pain across the back of her neck.

Putting the easel down on the path she shrugged her shoulders to check she hadn't strained something, then raked back the drift of white-gold curls that always managed to escape from whatever ribbon or hair-tie or clasp she tried to secure them with, and began to walk it along the path to the front door. How she'd manage to haul it up the three stone steps, let alone the entire staircase, she'd no earthly idea, but she'd cross that bridge when she came to it and hope none of the neighbours was around to see. As she reached the steps and stood recovering her breath, however, she realised there was a woman watching her from the ground floor window on her left.

It was difficult to see the woman because her own slim bedraggled reflection got in the way, but when she took a step closer and narrowed her eyes she saw that she was probably in her seventies. She had wispy grey shoulder-length hair and milky eyes and was sitting so still, staring out at the overgrown garden, that she hardly seemed to breathe or blink. Her expression was completely blank, and even when Ella raised her eyebrows at her in what she hoped was good-natured exasperation she made no response, and she wondered if the milkiness of her eyes might be due to cataracts, and that perhaps she was blind.

Giving up on the wraith-like woman, she clunked the easel up the three steps, unlocked the door, and managed to persuade the thing into the hall. She'd have killed for a coffee now and was sorely tempted just to go and make herself one, but the easel was blocking the hallway and there was nothing for it but to grit her teeth and get it upstairs.

She dragged it across the carpet and began to climb the stairs backwards, pulling it up step by step. Her heels kept catching in the hem of her dress, so she tucked it into her pants and, praying no-one would come out of either of the ground-floor flats, managed to reach the point at which the stairway began to curve.

She took a short break, and was on the home straight when she heard a key being turned in the front door and, hastily pulling the dress free, she sat down on the step beside the easel just as a man in a smart navy suit, carrying a black leather briefcase, marched in. Arranging the dress over her knees in decorous folds, she gave the man what she hoped was a polite and suitably contrite smile.

"Sorry about this," she said, and she got up and made a show of pulling the easel up to the next step. "I'm finding it a bit awkward ..."

The man frowned up at her. "Don't you have a man to do that?" he said and then, reddening slightly, added, "A *trades*man I mean? Far be it from me to ask personal questions ..." and then he put down the briefcase, climbed the stairs to join her and, reaching over the easel, extended a hand. "I'm Paul Wetherby. Top flat on the left."

Ella shook the hand, which was unpleasantly moist. "I'm Ella Blyth, top flat on the right," she said, "and I really am most terribly sorry to inconvenience you. I don't suppose

...?" but Paul Wetherby already had the easel in his arms and was hefting it up the stairs. Ella anchored her hair again and, picking up his briefcase and her carrier bag, trailed meekly up behind him, and when she reached the top landing she saw, much to her surprise, that the door to her flat was wide open and both Wetherby and the easel had disappeared.

Somewhat bewildered, she walked through the hall and there they both were, standing in the big front room, beside the suitcase and the pile of chains. Wetherby was holding a keyring, from which he was removing a key.

"I should not have held onto this," he said as he twisted and turned the metal ring. "I ought to have given it to the rental chappie after Flick went, but I'm afraid I never got around to it. I'm most terribly sorry ..." and he pulled it free and held it out to Ella.

Ella took the key and handed Wetherby his briefcase, and for a few moments they stood facing one another in awkward silence. Then Wetherby began to back towards the door. "I'll leave you to it, then," he said jovially. "Welcome to number 22!" and he swung his arms up and down stiffly, as though unsure what to do next.

Clammy with heat and embarrassment, Ella muttered her thanks, and it was only when he was out on the landing unlocking his own door that she remembered her manners and, hobbling out, held up the carrier bag and shook it so that the teaspoon and jar rattled together.

"I was just going to make myself a coffee," she said. "Would you like one?" and then, before Wetherby had a chance to answer, "Who's Flick?"

It took Wetherby some time to consider Ella's questions, and as she waited she took a good look at this new neighbour of hers. He was a stocky man, about the same height as herself and probably in his late fifties like her, though the suit and the neat greying hair and balding temples might make him look older than he was. He had remarkably bright and piercing brown eyes and a round, not unpleasant but rather nondescript face, and he smelt of sweat and cologne.

The over-riding impression Ella got from him, however, was one of sound common sense and solidity, and having lived with sound common sense and solidity for over thirty years, she was rather disappointed to have it popping up again so soon. Although actually, she told herself as Wetherby disappeared inside his flat and reappeared minus his jacket, sound common sense and solidity might be exactly what you looked for in a neighbour. She'd never had one before, so what did she know?

"I tell you what" - Wetherby rolled up his sleeves - "on this occasion I'm going to say 'no' to your kind coffee invitation, because I'm actually up to my eyes in appointments this afternoon, which is why I popped back home for an early lunch, but it just occurred to me you might have other unwieldy objects to carry upstairs, and if so I'm more than happy to oblige ...?"

Relief flooded through Ella. "That's extremely kind of you," she said. "I've got a bit of a sore hip you see, and there's one suitcase I'd find difficult to get up the stairs on my own, so if you're sure you've time?" and she led the way back down to the car and indicated the suitcase, and when Wetherby had hauled it out she went up the path ahead of him and held the door open for him. The woman with the milky eyes was still at the window, and Ella noticed she'd turned herself round a little so that she was looking directly out at them, but when Ella flashed her a smile she still didn't react.

"Now, what about all those boxes?" Wetherby said when they were back in the studio. "Can I give you a hand with them?" Ella, however, assured him none of the boxes was particularly heavy and added that, unlike him, she didn't have any pressing appointments today, and then she thanked him for his help and moved towards the door. She expected him to rush off, but now he seemed in no hurry to go, and he kept looking at the easel, then over at the window, as though trying to work something out. There was a difference in his demeanour too, as though his earlier confidence and bluster had drained away, and Ella prayed he wouldn't notice the chains.

"So, you must be an artist?" he said at last, and when Ella said she was he gave a little gasp. "But that's uncanny. Really quite uncanny ..." and he turned towards her with an expression she couldn't place.

"Why?" she said. "Why's it uncanny?"

He didn't reply immediately, and as she waited Ella decided the look on his face could best be described as one of awe, in which case perhaps Paul Wetherby wasn't all sound common sense and solidity after all.

"It's uncanny," he said at last, "because Flick was too. This was her studio, and over there" – he pointed over to the bay window, the floor of which, Ella now noticed, was flecked with paint marks – "was where she had her easel."

Ella walked into the bay of the windows and stared down at the paint marks. They formed a broad rainbow of smattered colours, and she could see where Flick must have stood or sat because the floorboards were darker there and almost completely clean. She let her eyes drift upwards then, and looked out at the view, and suddenly it dawned on her that it was quite different from the view she remembered from her earlier visits. How on earth could she not have noticed? Like the paint marks, it was so obvious.

"That really is quite a coincidence," she said. "I mean, this is exactly where I've been planning to put my easel too, but then" - she turned round to face Wetherby, whose face still bore the remnants of its awestruck expression — "it's the obvious place, isn't it, where the light's strongest. So, what kind of art did Flick do? Was it seascapes? And did she exhibit?"

She was careful to make her tone light and conversational, but Wetherby gazed grimly out of the window as though seeking an answer to some hugely complex riddle. "She did exhibit, yes," he said after a while. "In fact, she was an extremely fine artist and could have had her pick of galleries. And as for what she painted, I'm not sure what you would call it. Fantasy art, perhaps, which I'm afraid is not to my taste, but there you are. Art is a very personal thing ..."

Ella nodded. "It most certainly is. 'One man's meat', as they say," and she gave a little laugh to which Wetherby responded with a good-natured grunt. "So," she went on, "did Flick move far away? I mean, would I be able to see her work here in Largs?" and once more she waited for an answer that was a long time coming and, when it did come, wasn't really worth the wait.

"I have no idea where Flick is now, Miss Blyth," Wetherby said rather primly. "She didn't leave a forwarding address," and, turning abruptly away, he walked over to the door, and Ella could see the subject of Flick was well and truly closed. He stepped out into the hall, then stopped and came back in, and when he spoke again he was back to his bright breezy self.

"I do apologise, Miss Blyth," he said, beaming at her. "It really was quite unnecessary, harking back to the past like that and getting upset about it. It doesn't do, does it, dwelling on days gone by? *You* have taken Flick's place, and I'm sure I speak for all the residents of number 22 when I say we are happy to have you in our midst, and if there is anything at all any of us can do for you, please don't hesitate to ask."

For the first time in months Ella felt a small surge of well-being, and it was so unexpected and so pleasant it made her suddenly quite light-headed. Putting her hand in her pocket, she took hold of the key Wetherby had returned and turned it over and over in her palm. Then, throwing caution to the winds, she held it out to him.

"You're very kind, Mr Wetherby," she said. "And I'm so grateful for your help. Perhaps you wouldn't mind keeping this for me? And if you like, I could keep one for you?"

Without a moment's hesitation, Wetherby took the key. "I'd be so grateful if you would," he said. "Since Flick went, I've never felt I wanted to ask any of the other neighbours, and I'm afraid I can be a dreadful duffer with keys. I'll have one cut as soon as I can, and pop it in to you. And please do call me Paul, won't you? And perhaps I might call you Ella?" And when Ella assured him he might, he straightened his back, wished her good luck with the rest of the move, and marched briskly into the hall and out.

As soon as the door closed Ella headed for the kitchen, made herself the longed-for coffee, and took it through to the studio. Her floor cushion was still in the car, and the only seats in the flat were two kitchen stools and a large red settee which she'd put in splendid isolation in the sitting room opposite, so she lowered herself very carefully down onto the floorboards and, sitting on the arc of paint marks, turned all her attention to the view.

Now she understood what was so different about it. The sky, and the Firth of Clyde with its hazy maze of mauve islands, had all but disappeared, replaced by a curtain of green leaves from the huge beech tree that grew outside the window, so close to the glass you could have reached out and touched its upper branches.

It was hugely disappointing. For over thirty years, she'd lived in a neat bungalow in Highgate, cloistered by manicured hedges and red brick walls, and on her first visit to number 22, way back in November of last year, it had been those wide wonderful sea views that had made her choose this flat. Being so high up made her feel like a bird, or a queen in her clifftop castle, but of course, now she came to think of it, the view had never, even in deepest winter, been an unimpeded vista. Everything, even then, had been criss-crossed by the beech tree's delicate topmost branches, but the spaces between them had been so wide she'd hardly noticed them.

In the spring, however, the tiny spear-like leaf-buds had unfurled, and over the summer had widened and darkened until now, in place of the sky into which she could imagine soaring, there was a great green sheltering arbour hemming her in.

The sun was high in the sky now and shadows of every shade of greenish-grey flitted this way and that, and by afternoon the whole studio floor would be daubed with them, as would any canvas she put on her easel, and as Ella sipped her coffee she felt the hollow, hopeless feeling she'd hoped she'd left behind in Highgate threatening to seep back.

This room was to have been the perfect studio. She'd chosen it above the other public room because it was bigger and had a large walk-in cupboard, but mainly because its three bay windows made it lighter and airier; but perhaps she'd made the wrong choice. Now, she'd either have to change her plans and use the living room as a studio, or measure up for blinds and arrange for them to be hung.

Reaching up, she released the catch on the nearest window and pushed it open and, leaning back against the window ledge, took big deep breaths of the moist green scent that wafted in. She closed her eyes and continued to breathe deeply, and as her body relaxed she became aware of soft, chattering birdsong. The tree was fragrant and full of life, and when she looked up into its canopy she saw small shimmers of movement from within its branches which might have been caused by a breeze, or perhaps birds.

Drowsy now, she focussed all her attention on the kaleidoscope of greens as leaf overlapped leaf and, despite the coffee, felt herself drift off into sleep; and when she jolted awake and stared up, she saw to her delight that Flick had already solved the problem of the leaf-shadows. Above each of the three windows was what looked to be a perfectly serviceable fitting for a blind, so all she had to do was check the drop and phone a blind company. And since all her working life she'd preferred to work under daylight simulation bulbs rather than unpredictable natural light, the arrangement would be perfect.

Full of energy again, she eased herself up and went downstairs and, after several slow and increasingly painful trips bearing boxes of painting equipment, lamps, the floor cushion and a large tin of white floor paint, the car was empty. The boxes were stowed away in the walk-in cupboard, the kettle was on, and a packet of egg-and-cress sandwiches sat on a plate beside the floor cushion, so after lunch the real work could begin. And, as she'd meticulously planned during innumerable sleepless Highgate nights, it would begin with the white-out.

2

A mile or so away, as the crow flies, from Beech Avenue, Jinty McVey stood on the path at the foot of Haylie Brae, gazing in horror at the scene of the massacre. Behind her, the Gogo river gurgled happily in the dappled sunshine, but all Jinty heard was the roar of engines and the scream of saws, like a thousand demon dentists drilling in unison.

"Hey you!" a man was shouting at her from the seat of a yellow JCB. "Clear off! You're goin' to get yersel' hurt!"

Jinty didn't move and, switching off his engine, the man jumped down from the vehicle and walked towards her, huge arms swinging and fists clenched. He stopped for a moment to wave over at the two men in the field opposite the JCB, and when the saws stopped screaming he swiped off his white plastic helmet and let his headphones fall around his neck. Then he marched on till he was right in front of Jinty and glared down at her, red-faced, sweat-streaked, and colossal.

"You deaf, pal?" he asked, and when she assured him she most certainly was not, he pointed in the direction she'd come. "Then would you move yoursel' before a chunk o' this tree falls on you and cracks yer skull and yer brain oozes out" - he thumped one enormous fist into the palm of the other and ground it back and forth, making squelching sounds with his cheeks – "like it was strawberry trifle. *Then you'll be flippin' deaf, so you will* ..."

He put his helmet back on and began to re-seat the headphones, but Jinty still didn't move. Leaning back, she fixed him with as withering a look as she could muster.

"That's a first-class tree youse are sawing to bits," she said, aware there was a tremor in her voice and hoping the man wouldn't notice. "It's the best tree in the entire forest in fact, so I hope youse've got a good reason ..."

The man raised his eyebrows, and Jinty saw the sides of his lips twitch, but she held her ground. "Have youse?" she demanded. "A *valid* reason?"

The man squatted down so that his face was level with Jinty's. "We do," he said very quietly. "We have a very *valid* reason. This tree was leanin' so far over the track it was a danger to the public, and if we hadn't of chopped it down, it'd 'ave fell down, and I don't think you'd of liked it if it'd fell down on yer head, or yer mam's head, now would you?"

Jinty considered this. "Couldn't youse have supported it?" she said. "Couldn't youse've put in poles and lashed them to the trunk with ropes ...?"

But the man had had enough. "Believe me," he said, straightening up, "it's hurtin' me as much as it's hurtin' the tree, and you can take that any way you like. Now, do us a favour pal, and get lost," and he signalled to the men with the saws, swung himself back into the JCB, and revved its engine so hard Jinty's ears sang.

"You haven't heard the last of this!" she shouted over her shoulder as she stomped away. "I'll write a letter to the council, so I will ..."

She walked until the sound of the machinery was bearable, and then she climbed over the fence and ran down to the edge of the river Gogo. She took off her trainers and socks and dipped her feet in, and for a while sat very still, focussing all her attention on the cold lick of the water and the bell-like music it made as it trickled its way over the stones. The summer had been so hot the river was almost dry, its music so faint you had to strain to hear it, but even so its water was ice-cold.

It was downright criminal that they'd chopped down the tree. In fact, it was a tragedy, particularly as she'd only found it a couple of weeks ago and was just getting to know it, and now there it was, gone. It was the most perfectly climbable tree she'd ever set eyes on, and it had taken her till now to find it because, strictly speaking, she wasn't supposed to go that far into the forest. Mam said it was too near the main road and there could be people wandering about that you didn't want to meet. So far, however, Jinty hadn't seen anyone she didn't want to meet - apart, of course, from the man in the JCB.

She knew, however, that things did happen in the forest — mysterious and deeply undesirable things she preferred not to think about — because once or twice she and her best friend Shabs had found small milky-white objects that Shabs recognised. She'd fished one of them out of the undergrowth with a stick once, and held it up for Jinty to see.

"It's a very dull colour for a balloon, isn't it," Jinty had said, but Shabs had shaken her head knowingly.

"It's not a balloon," she said. "It's a grown-up thing."

"What sort of a grown-up thing?" Jinty asked, part of her wanting to know and part of her not.

Shabs had looked all around to check there was no one lurking in the undergrowth, and then she edged closer to Jinty and lowered her voice.

"You know when women have their period they have to wear what are called 'sanitary towels' inside their knickers, because if they didn't they'd drip blood all over the place?"

and Jinty nodded, because Shabs had already told her, in graphic detail, about periods.

"Well," Shabs continued, "it stands to reason men must have periods too, so *they* have to wear things on their penises to stop *them* dripping blood all over the place, but they can't wear sanitary towels, so they wear these balloon things instead. I know because I saw one once in our upstairs bathroom, floating in the toilet pan. So my daddy must've been having his period."

She'd gone on to take the white object, still speared on its stick, down to the river, where she dipped it in and held it under till it filled with water. "See?" she said, holding it up. "It's exactly the size and shape of a grown man's penis, isn't it?"

Jinty had hesitated before nodding, because she hadn't the foggiest idea what a grown man's penis looked like. Her daddy never visited long enough to have tea, let alone his period, whereas Shabs' mum and dad were both doctors, so she knew a staggering amount about the workings of the human body. She was also more than a year older than Jinty, having been put in a younger class when her family arrived from England, so she tended to use words and expressions Jinty didn't understand.

At the time, Jinty had listened to Shabs' explanation in stunned silence, and after Shabs had pushed the male sanitary towel into a hole in a tree root and covered it with leaves she'd changed the subject, but that night in bed a hundred questions chased themselves round her head, each more worrying than the one before.

There was, for example, the whole question of how *much* blood there was when someone had their period. Was it just a few little spots, or was it a deluge?

A few days later she asked Shabs, and Shabs tossed her hair back casually and said, 'Oh, there's loads. You positively *gush'*, which was not at all what Jinty wanted to hear. In the weeks that followed she found herself gazing at people's crotches, imagining what horrifying load might be concealed within, and in school, during Art, she'd find herself looking at Mrs Nwapa and wondering if even *she* might be having her period, and she'd tell herself that Shabs must have got it wrong. She *must* have.

Mrs Nwapa couldn't possibly be walking round the classroom in her lovely tight dresses, looking more beautiful and smelling more fragrant than anyone Jinty had ever known while secretly gushing *loads* of blood. It was inconceivable, because Mrs Nwapa, as everyone knew, was completely, utterly perfect.

Far in the distance, a church clock chimed four and, jumping up, Jinty checked the back pocket of her jeans to make sure the five-pound note Nan had given her to buy ciggies was still there. Then she ran like the wind down the steep hill that led into Largs.

As she ran, she tore the scrunchie from her hair, scraped back her pale brown mouse-tails, and re-tied it as tightly as she could, and when she reached the main road she stopped and took off her glasses. She spat on each lens, gave them a good clean with the hem of her tee-shirt, and ran across the road to the newsagents where Mam worked.

"What time d'you call this then?" Her mam took the note and handed over a packet of Players and the change. "Shove them in your pocket quick," she added, "before anyone sees. Is your nan OK?"

Jinty nodded. "Can I buy a notebook with the change?" she said, pointing at the box. "Nan would let me, cause my old one's full and I need it for research. They're only 20p," and she held out one of the coins.

"Oh would she now?" Mam said. "Says who?" but she reached over to the box, asked her if she wanted red or blue, and handed her a red one. "Now you run home this minute, and for goodness' sake gie your face a wash, and clean your specs too. I don't know how you can see through the stour.

"And make your nan a cup o' tea," she shouted at Jinty's retreating form, "and mind and gie her what's left o' her change!"

When Jinty reached the bridge at Gogoside Street she slowed her pace to a crawl. These days, she dreaded going home to the cramped little house with its stale cigarette-smoke smell and stuff lying around all over the place. She was always wary in case Uncle Chris was there, with his beery breath and the looks he sometimes gave her when he managed to get her on her own, and these days she didn't look forward to seeing Nan either.

They'd always been the best of pals, she and Nan, but in the past year or so Nan had changed, and now she just wasn't herself any more. She hardly spoke, and when she did it often didn't make a lot of sense, and most of the time she was fast asleep in her chair with her head back and her mouth wide open, looking like a corpse.

If she was asleep, she wouldn't wake her. She'd check she was still breathing, then she'd leave the ciggies and the change on the table beside her chair and go up to her bedroom. She'd copy the picture she'd drawn the other day, of the poor massacred tree, into the new notebook so that when school started she could show Mrs Nwapa just how good it had looked.

There were still two weeks of holiday left, but it was better to do it today while the memory was fresh, and at the thought of going back to school, Jinty felt the familiar lump of sadness swell in her throat, because when school started, there was no guarantee Mrs Nwapa would be there.

It was just a rumour of course, but people had been saying Mrs Nwapa was going to have a baby so she might not come back after the summer holidays, and if that was true Jinty honestly didn't know what she'd do.

She'd told Shabs that, but Shabs hadn't been very sympathetic. She'd said it was only to be expected, that Mrs Nwapa was getting quite old and it stood to reason she'd want to start a family while she still could, and that Jinty should be happy for her.

But Jinty wasn't in the least bit happy for Mrs Nwapa, and when Shabs said her mum would soon find out if the rumour was true because there was a School Council meeting coming up, it made her feel even worse. As hard as it was not knowing if Mrs Nwapa was coming back, at least when you didn't know you could hope she was. Once you knew for sure she wasn't, you'd nothing but a big hole where the hope had been; and the thought of that big hopeless hole made Jinty want to cry.

3

First thing on Tuesday morning Ella prised open the tin of white paint, stirred briskly, and dipped the brush in, but she didn't start to paint immediately. For a few minutes she sat in the window bay, staring at the white-tipped brush, summoning up the courage to make the first mark.

It was sacrilege to cover over those beautiful old floorboards, she knew it was. It almost amounted to an act of deliberate vandalism. One day, when she was dead and gone or sitting in an eventide home, mind addled like her mother's had been, some nice young couple would stand on the threshold of this room, shaking their heads at the desecration. Then they'd ring a company that rented sanding machines, and spend the next week laboriously rasping off Ella's handiwork.

Desecration or not, however, the painting of the studio floor had to be done for her vision to be accomplished, and as Ella began to lay the paint on in earnest it occurred to her that the need for this total white-out had other reasons besides the purely aesthetic. It was a rite of purification, an erasure, not only of the house's past life with Flick, but also of her own dreary existence, in The Moorings, with Derek; and the thought of this fresh new beginning energised her, like the sea air had, and the scent of beech leaves, and the birdsong.

Not that she could properly erase all signs of Flick's presence. Not without giving the walls the same treatment as the floor, and as she put the paintbrush down and stretched her legs to take the strain off the grumbling hip joint she saw that now, against the white floor, those walls were actually an unpleasant yellowish-grey; and the more she looked, the more she saw that the yellowish-grey wasn't uniform.

There were echoes of the past everywhere – oblong strips of the original white where tables or desks had sat, rectangular ghosts of paintings, a rounded shape in the middle of the marble mantlepiece where a clock had once stood, and a large triangular shape on the wall opposite the fireplace she couldn't place. With school starting in two weeks, it was impossible to paint them all out. She'd just have to learn to live with them until she'd more time.

Heaving herself to her feet, she turned to face out towards the tree and rolled her head gently from side to side, easing the ache in her neck. Then she stood on tiptoe, stretched her arms above her head, and breathed in and out steadily, and as she watched the flicker of sunlight on the leaves and the constant change of their light and shade, she felt the earlier calm return.

It was all going to be fine. For the time being, she'd hide the echoes of Flick's life behind her own preliminary sketches, and by the time she had to face the looming horror that was Seavale Primary, she'd be well on her way to making that vision of hers a reality.

By the end of this morning the first coat would be on the floor, and this afternoon she'd leave it to dry while she went to Glasgow. And *that* would be fine too, because last week she'd made an appointment, so she knew she was expected, and she had a map, so she knew exactly where she had to go.

She'd made the call from her mobile with its brand-new SIM card, after putting the old SIM in an envelope and burying it, under earrings and necklaces and her wedding and engagement rings, in her jewellery box, and she loved the feeling the new SIM gave her of being completely adrift, her whereabouts unknown.

Derek was away on one of his frequent business trips and had probably been ringing her old mobile number when she hadn't answered the landline, and by yesterday evening he'd be wondering where on earth she was. He might even be worried enough to be trying her number again now, during his coffee break, and he'd probably try again after lunch, before he set off back to London.

Whatever he was doing, Ella didn't want to think about it. She didn't want Derek, and his feelings, to occupy her thoughts, partly because she wanted to forget the past and concentrate on the now, but mainly because it struck her as profoundly sad that after thirty years of marriage she'd not the faintest clue *how* he'd be feeling.

Would he be angry with her? Or absolutely frantic with worry? Or not in the least concerned because he'd assume she'd gone off on some jaunt or other? She hadn't the slightest idea. These days, Derek was an enigma she'd given up trying to solve.

Surely by Monday evening he'd have been concerned enough to phone someone though, and that someone would almost certainly have been Carys, who was their oldest friend and the very model of good sense and practicality. And Carys would doubtless have suggested he ask a neighbour to go in and check Ella wasn't lying on the floor with a broken leg or dying of a heart attack, but even when Ella imagined *that* nightmare scenario, she was surprised to find it didn't overly worry her.

It would, of course, be cringingly embarrassing, and especially so if the neighbour found the note she'd left and offered to open it and read it to Derek, but - in the great scheme of things – even that was of minor importance, and as she began to paint again she directed every ounce of attention to deciding what time she'd have to leave the house to get to the station and catch the two o'clock train to Glasgow, and when she got to Glasgow where exactly she was to go, and what she was going to say when she got there.

By midday the floor was covered apart from a narrow strip at the far end and, checking there was no paint on the soles of her trainers, Ella made her way along the unpainted strip and out into the hall; and as she passed the front door on her way to the kitchen she saw an envelope lying on the floor. It was white and had her name written on it in small neat capitals, and when she picked it up it was heavy so it must be Paul Wetherby's key, and she took it into the kitchen and put it on the work surface to deal with later.

She ate lunch in the kitchen perched on a stool looking out over the back garden which, like the front, was divided into two by a path and low box hedge. The garden on the left - presumably Wetherby's - was almost exclusively given over to neat rows of vegetables, the taller ones staked to stand shoulder to shoulder in military precision, and at the end of the garden there was an apple tree heavy with fruit, and beside it a well-creosoted shed.

The garden on the right, however – Ella's garden - couldn't have been more different. It too had a shed, but its shed was painted sky-blue, and on its right-hand side there was a mass of pink roses that grew in profusion round what was presumably a window. The garden itself was a wild tangle of flowers and weeds, but Ella could see that underneath the chaos there were signs of paths and borders, and once again a rush of unexpected pleasure filled her with new energy.

One of these days, before the summer was over, she'd tidy up the garden enough that she could use it. She wouldn't go overboard – she wouldn't have time – but she'd get rid of the worst of the weeds without losing the charm of the unruly tangle, and when she was out there sipping her wine in the evening sunshine she'd enjoy that feeling of wildness all around her, so unlike anything she'd ever had before.

She looked at her watch, gave a little gasp, and slid off the stool. Dumping the dishes in the sink, she took the quickest of showers, then went to the bedroom to dry her hair and put on the dress she'd chosen for this afternoon's appointment.

It was a simple but expensive one in cream-coloured linen, fitted but not too tight or too short so that it showed off her trim figure but hid her knees, and she'd ironed it last night and put it on a hanger and hung it on the back of the bedroom door with the large arty necklace she'd chosen to set it off.

The bedroom had no mirror yet, but there was quite a large one above the wash-hand basin in the bathroom so, slipping on her white sandals, she went to give her top half an inspection and put on a little make-up.

The mirror was still steamed up from the shower, and as she wiped it with a face flannel she took a better look at its frame. Like everything in the bathroom it was white, and she'd already noticed its sinuous lines but now, when she looked more closely, she saw that it was carved into the shape of two swans, their dipped heads lightly touching so that their necks formed the shape of a heart, and she wondered why, when Flick went, she hadn't taken such a beautiful thing with her.

She stood for a while, fiddling her earrings into place and checking the long silver triangles hung level, their brightness just visible through the mass of faded gold curls, bouncily girl-like now after the shower. It was the first time in years she'd worn those earrings, and now she remembered she usually put her hair up into a bun when she had them on so, taking great handfuls, she pulled the curls back and twisted them into place, high up on her head. Then she turned her head from side to side, wondering if she should fix them in place for today's meeting.

It would certainly make her neck look longer and even more slender, and the overall effect would be of an elegant and sophisticated woman who was perhaps more likely to be taken seriously, but, after a few moments' consideration she decided that actually, today she preferred to look as young and carefree as possible, and she let the hair go and bobbed it back into shape.

Then she rubbed her face with moisturiser and applied a hint of green eye-shadow to emphasise her eye-colour and just enough mascara to make her pale eyelashes show, and as she stepped back to examine the overall effect she tried to remember the last time she'd dressed herself up like this.

Could it have been Christmas? Could it have been that awful, interminable, Christmas Day, when Carys had arrived and kept wanting to know what was going on? Because of course Carys had noticed the minute she'd stepped into the hall that something wasn't right with Ella. She always knew when something was amiss, no matter how hard you tried to hide it from her, and that day, before she'd even unpacked, the enquiring looks had started, and the tirade of questions began.

Why was Ella so pale and jittery? Was she anaemic? And surely she'd lost weight, which she couldn't afford to do? And why weren't there any new commissions on the easel? On and on she'd gone, firing one awkward, unanswerable question after another till Ella was reduced to a state of nerves so crippling she couldn't think straight.

Mercifully, Derek had eventually emerged from his home office to ply them both with sherry and she'd drunk far too much, and then far too much wine. She'd slipped off to the bathroom then and sat on the chair beside the bath, trying to pull herself together, and then she'd slathered on a ton of make-up to disguise the dark circles under her eyes. And when, eventually, she'd reappeared, Carys, bang on cue, had asked her, yet again, if she was *quite sure* she was all right ...

That day she'd come dangerously close to confessing the whole thing, and it still amazed her that she hadn't; and as she looked in the mirror at her wide green eyes and the creamy softness of her skin that showed scarcely a wrinkle in the bathroom's kindly light, she was surprised at how much her reflection pleased her.

It was the reflection of a woman who'd reached breaking point but somehow hadn't broken, the reflection of a woman with – at long last - somewhere to go to talk about important, exciting things; and, giving herself an approving smile, she fluffed up the curls again, patted the arty necklace so that all its bright geometric shapes sat neatly against the linen, and ran back to the bedroom for her handbag.

It was as she was taking her key from the hook by the door that she remembered the envelope still lying on the kitchen work surface and - because there might, she supposed, be a note along with the key that required some sort of response - went back into the kitchen and tore it open.

The key had a small white label attached to it, with 'P. Wetherby' written in tiny writing, and behind it was a piece of card on which, in the same neat capitals as the envelope, was the message: 'MANY THANKS, PAUL. P.S. LOOKING FORWARD TO THAT COFFEE.

She added the key to her keyring, dropped the torn envelope and card onto the floor, pushed the map of Glasgow city centre into her bag, and ran downstairs and out into the searing afternoon heat.

At the station, she parked her car and, safely aboard the Glasgow train, sat back to enjoy the journey. The previous day, driving up from the Lake District motel in which she always broke her journey, her brain had been too deadened by hours of motorway driving to give the sea and its islands more than a passing glance. Now, however, as one familiar vista after another appeared then vanished behind trees and hedges, all those blissful childhood Largs summers came back to her, and she could almost feel her five-year-old self, nose pressed excitedly against the glass, and Gran sitting, straight-backed, beside her, pointing and naming each island as it flashed by.

First came Great Cumbrae, so close it didn't even look as though it was an island, and then Arran, huge and armoured, like a sleeping warrior, and finally Ella's favourite, the tiny cap of Ailsa Craig, which Gran called 'The Dumpling' and which, she said, would one day disappear entirely under the Irish Sea because of all the granite they were hacking out of it to make curling stones for posh people to play with.

There they'd sit, the two of them, day after glorious day, in their crisp summer dresses and whiter-than-white cardigans that, despite their best efforts, always ended up crumpled and streaked with ice-cream and raspberry sauce; and sometimes they'd get off at Ardrossan, and sometimes Saltcoats or Fairlie, whichever took their fancy, and every day, every single day, was sunnier, and more gloriously adventure-filled, than the last, and when the evening came and the ice-cream shops and arcades closed, they'd ride home, sleepy in the sunset, their faces sticky with rock and their pockets filled with sand and shells and barnacled pebbles.

The train left the familiar coast then, and the view opened out to sheep-studded hills which Ella hardly remembered because Gran never liked the fuss of taking her to the big city in summer; but as, slowing, they clattered over the Clyde and she saw the Glasgow skyline, she felt again the thrill of the rare treat. Clutching her map, she fought her way through the surge of people, searching for the right exit from Central Station and, for one tiny moment, felt herself reach out for Gran's reassuring old hand.

The agency was in Bath Street, and it had seemed on the map to be quite close to the station, but as Ella began the uphill climb she could see from the numbers on the buildings that she was nowhere near the address she was looking for. Worried now, she checked her watch and saw that she had less than five minutes to get there and, jostled on all sides by distracted shoppers and fast-walking business people, she forced herself to walk more quickly.

The further she walked, the more multi-storeyed office buildings there were and the fewer shoppers, but even so, the heat and the noise and the tall glass-fronted buildings made her feel increasingly uncomfortable. Somehow she'd imagined Glasgow to be smaller and less crowded than central London - which she hadn't dared visit for well over a year - but Bath Street was every bit as nightmarish.

Finally she found the building – a big office block with a door entry system on which a dozen companies were listed – and pressed the button beside *Angels Castings,* on the fifth floor. A tinny voice asked her name and where she wanted to go, and when the door clicked open she pushed herself into a mercifully cool and empty hall. The clock on the wall showed five past three, and as she ran into the lift she could feel her chest tighten with panic and a thin tickle of sweat run down her spine.

The lift, to her dismay, was mirrored on three sides, and even though she tried to concentrate all her attention on the door, she couldn't help but see out of the corner of her eye that the stylish linen dress was now clinging to her inner thighs and showing off every inch of those knees of hers, the big arty necklace had wound itself round her left breast, and the girlish curls were soaked in perspiration and unflatteringly flattened. There was, of course, no time to find a Ladies, so before stepping out she pulled everything roughly into place, wiped the sweat off her brow, and re-tousled her hair. Straightening her back, she marched resolutely towards the pistachio-coloured door marked *Angels Castings.*

"Ms Blyth?" A smart young woman with a halo of black hair detached herself from a desk – also pistachio-coloured - and walked towards her. "I'm Almasi," and she held out a perfectly-manicured hand with long pink nails. "We spoke on the phone. Do have a seat, and would you like some water?"

Ella sat down opposite Almasi, whose pink talons were already hovering over her laptop keyboard. "I'm so sorry I'm late," she said. "I haven't been to Glasgow for years, and it was more of a walk than I thought. And yes, I'd love some water ..."

"Two ticks," Almasi stood up again. "I'll get you one from the fridge," and she disappeared.

Ella looked around nervously. *Angels Castings* was bigger and more impressive-looking than she'd expected. Its walls had broad vertical stripes of pink, pistachio and cream, and its big windows were made of frosted glass, adding to the ice-cream-parlour atmosphere. It was filled with rows of pastel-coloured desks behind which a host of beautiful young people answered phones and tapped away on laptops and called out gaily to one another.

The walls were hung with portraits of sulky-looking girls, macho-looking boys, and several visions of loveliness whose gender was impossible to pinpoint, and every now and then the door would open and in would walk yet another breathtakingly beautiful young thing. It was all rather intimidating, especially as Ella was easily old enough to be the lovely young things' mother, if not their grandmother. She wondered what on earth Almasi must think of her, and wished she'd chosen the 'sophisticated bun' look after all.

"So, Ms Blyth" - Almasi eased herself elegantly back into her chair and thrust a bottle of ice-cold water at Ella – "you're looking for a model? Male, female or other?"

"Female," Ella said, and she took a gulp of the water. "And preferably slim, pale and fragile-looking," and she watched as Almasi, frowning slightly, tapped in the information. When she looked back at Ella, her face wore a dubious expression.

"We've got literally hundreds of slim pale fragile-looking girls, Ms Blyth," she said. "I hope you don't mind my asking, but what would you be wanting your model to actually *do*?" She glanced down at a notepad beside the laptop. "You said you were an artist, so do I take it you'd be wanting 'nude'?"

Ella took a deep breath in and held it for a moment. "No," she said. "Not entirely. I mean" – she squirmed round in her chair, preferring the blank window to Almasi's eyes – "I don't intend to actually depict her naked. I have white chiffon to drape over her, but obviously in order to see the details of her flesh tones and musculature I would have to ask her to remove her clothes. Which, naturally, she would do behind a screen," and she turned back to Almasi, whose face was still expressionless. "That's how most figurative artists work," she added. "I do assure you."

Without a word, Almasi swivelled the laptop round for Ella to see. A perfect face, framed with perfectly straight golden hair, pouted out at her.

"This is Eve," Almasi said. "She's been very popular this season with the perfume companies, in fact we're just waiting to hear from London if she's going to be the face of 'Double Jeopardy'. She currently charges £500 a session, which of course includes our agency commission." She narrowed her eyes at Ella. "Any good?"

Ella picked up the bottle of water and dropped it into her handbag. "I see," she said, and she smiled her best smile at Almasi. "I'm afraid I wasn't aware of your rates. I should have asked on the phone. I do apologise for taking up your time." She stood up, and immediately sat down again as a sudden intense pain shot from her hip down through the back of her leg. Slowly and carefully, she eased herself up again and hobbled away.

She'd almost reached the door when another spasm of pain made her stop, and this time it was so severe she let out a cry, and for a while all she could do was cling onto the side of the nearest desk, biting back tears. The young man at the desk stood up and, coming round to her, put a hand gently on her back.

"Are you OK dear?" he said. "Here, let me get you a seat," and he wheeled one round and lowered Ella gently into it. "Just you sit down for a minute and catch your breath, and don't you worry, my gran's got what you've got. It'll be a slipped disc nipping your sciatic nerve, so it will. Can I get you some water?"

Ella gritted her teeth and assured the young man she was fine, that she had a bottle of water in her bag, and then she added that actually, what she'd really, really like was a cup of strong coffee if, that was, she could manage to get herself to a café.

"Don't you worry," the young man repeated, and he pointed to a door on their right marked 'Cafeteria'. Placing a hand under Ella's arm, he eased her up and guided her towards it. "There's a toilet in there too," he said as he lowered her down at the first table, "if you need it. Have you got a mobile?"

Wearily, Ella opened her bag, handed him her phone, and watched as he did some deft finger-work. "There you are," he said. "Give me a wee ring if you need any help. My name's Adrian," and he spun round on his heels and was gone.

For a while Ella sat very still, looking round the empty cafeteria with its coffee machine in one corner and its snack dispenser in the other, and felt her spirits sink perilously close to rock bottom.

Why in God's name hadn't she found out about models *months* ago? Any sensible person would have checked out agency prices and then, when they turned out to be vastly too expensive, made a search of the colleges in the area in which you could advertise for a life model with less lofty financial requirements. It was madness to have left something this important to chance, particularly when she'd planned all the other details of her flight so meticulously.

Perhaps she was suffering from some awful menopausal delusion. Perhaps the whole idea of cutting herself loose from everything and everyone and re-inventing her art was the product of an unsound mind. Her body was certainly a lot less sound than she'd thought, judging from the sickening ache in her hip and the pins and needles that still tingled in her leg, and she wondered how old Adrian's gran, with her slipped disc and nipped sciatic nerve, must be. Sixty? Sixty-five? Adrian, bless him, probably popped in every other day to see she was all right, and it was a fair bet he'd always ring her before he left work to see if there was anything she'd like brought in from the supermarket.

Who would look after *her* when she was old and unable to walk? Not Lucy, that was for sure. She'd no idea where Lucy even was, and as she felt herself being drawn into that particularly agonising train of thought she focussed all her attention on rummaging inside her bag for her purse which, when she found it, only contained some small change and two £20 notes. Beaten, she put her elbows on the table, sank her head into her hands, and breathed slowly in and out.

A loud thud, followed by a series of lesser thuds, interrupted her meditation, and she sat up in alarm as a tall slender girl, wearing a black tee shirt with something indecipherable written across the front, stormed into the cafeteria. The girl pushed a coin into the coffee machine, and when her coffee was delivered she threw herself and her plastic cup into the farthest away table. Drawing her legs up to her chest, she sat with her chin on her knees like an angry angular foetus, and every now and then, in between gulps of coffee, she sighed ostentatiously.

Ella sat watching her for a minute or two. It was obvious from the theatrical sighs that the girl wanted attention and Ella was in no mood to give her any, but when she showed no signs of stopping she leaned over and said, "I'm sorry to bother you, but would you happen to have change of a £20 note? I'm absolutely gasping for a coffee ..." and to her surprise the girl immediately unfurled herself, stood up, and proceeded to empty the pocket of her jeans onto the table.

She picked up a handful of coins and three £5 notes, sauntered up to Ella's table, and dumped the money in the middle. Then she took Ella's £20 note, shoved it into her pocket, and went back to her table, and when Ella still didn't move she stood up again. "Want me to get you it?" she said

Ella held out a couple of the pound coins. "I'd love you to. I'm afraid my hip's rather unreliable today. And I'll have a chocolate biscuit too, please," and she watched as the girl fetched the coffee and then moved to the other machine to examine the biscuits.

Her legs were amazingly long and she moved in an elegant, dancer-like way, and when she turned to ask her whether she'd like a Penguin or a KitKat, Ella saw that her almond-shaped eyes were a darkly piercing brown, like Paul Wetherby's but infinitely more beautiful.

"Thank you so much," Ella said as the girl returned to the table with the coffee and Kitkat. "I'm Ella, by the way, and I'm most terribly grateful."

"I'm Arlene," the girl said, "and I'm most terribly pissed off. Do you mind if I join you?"

Without waiting for a response, she fetched her coffee and backpack and sat down and, rather to Ella's surprise, flashed her a smile, and Ella was startled to see that those almond-shaped eyes of hers really were most unusual. They were big – far too big for her face – and so dark it was hard to make out where her pupils ended and her irises began.

There was a crescent of white below each of the brown-black irises too which, even when she smiled, gave the girl a look of extreme melancholy which, combined with her slender neck and aquiline nose, reminded Ella of the suffering saints at the foot of the cross in an Italian church painting. Gulping down her coffee and munching her Kitkat, she stared in wonder at her, imagining those haunting eyes without their caking of dark eye-shadow and mascara.

"I'm pissed off too, actually," she said at last. "I came here looking for a girl to paint, but I can't afford any of them. Do you mind me asking what's pissing *you* off?"

Arlene looked her up and down with amused interest. "This bleeding agency is," she said. "It's the third one I've applied to this week, and it's always the same old story. My mouth's too big, my nose's too big, my eyes are too big, my feet are too big ... Christ! All they want is pretty pretty pretty, and I don't *do* pretty pretty pretty" – she pulled her features into a grimace that showed a mouthful of perfect teeth – "I do *fierce*!" Then she drained her coffee, hurled the empty cup adroitly into the bin, and walked to the door.

She was pulling it open when Ella stood up. "Wait a minute, Arlene," she said, and she took a tentative little step towards her. "I was wondering, could you and I have a little talk?"

4

When Ella got home from her afternoon at *Angels Castings*, the first thing she saw when she opened the door was Paul Wetherby's note lying on the floor beside the torn envelope. Stepping over both, she went into the studio to check the progress of the floor paint.

It was dry and, as she'd suspected, it was going to need at least one more coat, and ideally that coat should be applied tomorrow because Arlene, they'd decided, was to come for a 'taster' session on Friday. Before then, a chair would have to be bought and painted white, and the lighting arranged and an additional lamp purchased. In addition, the white chiffon she'd brought with her had to be fashioned into some sort of loose garment for Arlene to drape round herself, so she'd have a quick rest, and then she'd finish off the painting, and when that was done she'd go to the retail park. At least by that time it would be cooler.

Despite the pain in her leg, which had eased considerably after Arlene had run to the chemists to get her some paracetamol, Ella felt a thrill of excitement at the thought of that first session. Now that she'd bitten the bullet and booked the girl, she was more and more sure that Arlene, with her remarkable eyes, and the insectile angularity of her long limbs, was going to make a far gutsier model than the fragile pretty one she'd always imagined she'd find. Fragile pretty models, after all, were - as Arlene had pointed out - ten a penny, whereas *she* was thoroughly unique, and as they'd drunk a second cup of coffee together, Arlene had been at pains to point out the various elements of that uniqueness.

Those 'heroin chic' looks of hers, she assured Ella, were 'cutting edge', and her double joints (and Ella had winced as Arlene demonstrated their mobility) enabled her to adopt any pose a photographer required, however bizarre. It was, she said, just a matter of time before she was snapped up by some state-of-the-art agency, but the trouble was that all the *really* state-of-the-art agencies were in London, so her plan was to save up till she could afford to stay there for a few days and go to castings. Then, hopefully, she'd land some high-end work that would finally get her noticed.

Ella had been enthralled by the whole 'cutting edge' thing, because of course that was precisely what she wanted her new art to be, and the fierceness and double-jointedness had all sorts of exciting possibilities too. She hadn't, however, been so keen on the 'heroin chic' which, for a number of personal reasons, she'd found worrying.

She told herself, however, that, at £15 an hour plus £3 to cover travel, Arlene was at least affordable and, if nothing else, the taster session would give her the opportunity to test out her studio set-up and get back into the way of painting from life. And if, in the end, things didn't work out, she could always look for someone with rather less challenging looks and attitude.

Ella fetched herself a coffee. She dragged the floor cushion into the window bay and sat looking out at the wall of dancing leaves and the flickering shadows they cast on the newly-whitened floor. The blinds were coming tomorrow, and although it was a real shame to shut all this glistening greenery out, she comforted herself with the thought that she'd only have to pull the them down when she was working. The rest of the time, the view was hers to enjoy.

Revived by the coffee, she went to change out of her dress and put on her painting clothes, and this time the sight of Wetherby's discarded card pricked her conscience enough that she picked it up, and when she was back on the cushion she gave some thought to the matter of the invitation. Why, she wondered, did she not want to accept it?

It was more than simply the sense of 'out of the frying-pan' that the invitation gave her, though it *was* annoying that her hard-earned solitary existence had been taken away from her before it had even begun, and that by a man who, in several troubling little ways, rather resembled the man she'd only just left. There was something else that bothered her, something other than Wetherby's rather strident, pedantic manner, but she couldn't put her finger on what it was. Sitting with her back against the window-sill, she let her thoughts drift back to their meeting, and in particular to his reaction when he discovered she was an artist ...

It had been an odd reaction. Sure, she and Flick both being artists was a bit of a coincidence, but surely not such an overwhelming coincidence as to cause tears to fill Wetherby's eyes, and his cheeks to drain of colour, at the mention of her name? There might even have been traces of fear in his face, or perhaps Ella had just imagined that, but however you looked at it, his discomfort when he talked about Flick, and his evasiveness when asked where she'd gone, surely weren't entirely rational.

It made Ella wonder whether his relationship with Flick had been more than simple neighbourliness, and as she binned the card and, going through to the kitchen, rubbed the brittleness out of the paintbrush's bristles, she decided that this hint of a possible romantic connection between the two of them was probably the real reason she preferred to keep her distance.

There was something else about that meeting with Wetherby that made her uncomfortable though, and as she knelt down and began to apply paint to the unfinished strip of floor she cast her mind back to the reluctance he'd had to tell her why Flick had left. It had puzzled, and slightly annoyed, her.

Why had he more or less refused to answer when she'd asked him what was, after all, a straightforward question? He'd fobbed her off by saying, 'She went rather suddenly, without leaving a forwarding address?' which surely had a kind of melodramatic, cloak-and-dagger feel to it, but why not just tell her where she'd gone and why?

And why, come to that, had he said 'when Flick *went*' rather than 'when Flick left', or 'when Flick moved'? Was there something sinister and final about the word 'went', or was she just being paranoid?

Perhaps she was. Perhaps the fact that her new life hadn't really begun yet made her even more insecure and vulnerable than usual, and therefore over-sensitive. She certainly had an uncomfortable sense of being in limbo, of trying not to dwell on thoughts of what she'd left behind, yet having nothing solid with which to replace such thoughts.

Perhaps, under the circumstances, it was understandable to be paranoid. She'd always had a vivid imagination, after all, and in the past her mother was forever saying she allowed her imagination to run away with her. Come to think of it, hadn't Carys regularly done that too?

That was probably what it was. She'd far too much time to dwell on things and blow them out of proportion. Once she started painting Arlene and teaching at Seavale, everything would be better.

Calmed by the thought, she finished off the last few floorboards, then took brush and tin back to the kitchen, and as she was standing at the sink washing the brush she looked down at the wilderness she would one day tame and suddenly, despite herself, she thought of Derek.

That garden would have appalled Derek. The minute he'd seen it he'd have done what he did when first they moved into The Moorings, which was to phone some hideously expensive Landscape Gardening outfit and get them to come and clear everything out and then draw up a meticulous plan of how it should look. And when, weeks later, the garden was finally finished it was the tidiest, most tamed and sterile garden in the whole of Highgate, and - of course - it was solidly Derek's domain.

He hadn't even liked it when, one spring, she'd put a terracotta planter at the back door and planted it with a mass of bright purple and pink petunias. He'd said he worried they were a tad too garish, that they clashed with the rest of the planting.

Her garden, she reflected as she swished the brush bristles back and forth under the tap, would be as garish as it was possible for a garden to be. It would be filled with bright clashing colours and tall straggly sweet peas and big blowsy roses, and it would look, and smell, utterly divine ...

She went to the bathroom, peeled off her painting clothes, and gave her face and hands a thorough wash, but no matter how hard she tried to keep her thoughts focused on Arlene and the paintings she'd do of her, and on the lovely garden she'd one day create, she just couldn't shift Derek from her mind.

Yesterday, he'd have arrived home. He'd have let himself into The Moorings as he always did, but he wouldn't have gone straight upstairs to change, because he'd be worried, or upset, or curious, or angry, at not having been able to contact her.

However he felt, though, he'd be sure to search everywhere before raising any kind of alarm, and the first place he'd have gone would probably be the tiny spare bedroom at the back of the bungalow which she used as her studio.

But would he even notice that her easel and spotlight were gone, and the shelves where she kept her paints and solvents were almost bare? Probably not, because these days he hardly ever came to the studio, except to poke his head round the door to ask if dinner was ever going to appear, and possibly make an anodyne comment about the current painting (also anodyne) on the easel.

He'd check the bedrooms in the roof extension next, and when she wasn't there either and their bed was neatly made, surely something approaching panic must have set in? He'd almost certainly have gone back to the living room then to get himself a brandy, and once he'd had a couple of mouthfuls he'd check the kitchen, where he'd find the envelope with his name on it, propped up against the kettle.

He'd rip it open, read the note inside, and how he'd feel then she couldn't - she really couldn't - allow herself to think.

Pulling the painting clothes back on, she unhooked her keys, ran out to the car, and drove as fast as she dared to the retail park, where she bought another tin of floor paint, a small tin of white gloss, and a simple wooden chair, and when she got home she put the first coat on the chair then began to plan the making of the chiffon garment, and after she'd eaten she sat on the red settee and sewed the sides together as neatly as she could.

The action of sewing was soothing after all the physical work she'd done that day, and as she worked the needle in and out, trying to make each stitch as even and tiny as the one before, she noticed her earlier panic had subsided. Gathering up the half-finished garment, she draped it over the back of the settee ready for Friday, when Arlene would slip it on and she'd see how much of a hem it would require.

Then the two of them would get down to the real work of planning the first pose, and surely then, when she was finally making her vision a reality, all these awful, intrusive, thoughts of Derek and Wetherby would fade into insignificance, where they belonged.

Neither man, after all, had anything whatsoever to do with her reasons for being here, or her hopes and plans for the future; and Derek, she reminded herself as she took a leisurely shower, had only himself to blame for every worry and anxiety her leaving might now be causing him. She'd absolutely nothing to feel guilty about, or to regret.

Her only regret, in fact, was that she'd given Wetherby her spare key ...

5

By Friday morning the white blinds were in place, the chair and floor were flawlessly white, and the chiffon garment was ready for a fitting. Arlene's stage was set.

Ella had decided to position the chair facing the windows, and she'd found an eight-panel screen made of white cotton in the retail park, which not only formed a backdrop that hid the cupboard door and Flick's ghosts on the wall, but also gave Arlene a private place behind which to change. She'd draped the chiffon garment over the screen and, in a neat little silver pile beside the chair, she'd laid the chains.

Her easel, with one of the kitchen stools, stood in the window bay, and she'd prepared several large pieces of grey paper, one of which she'd taped to a drawing board and set on the easel ledge. On one side of the easel there was a spotlight, and on the other a low table with sticks of charcoal of various thicknesses, two boxes of pastel crayons, and her camera. Another, much stronger, spotlight stood to the right of the white chair.

The arrangement was that Arlene would arrive just before eleven, and Ella had a tray with coffee mugs and a plate of biscuits in the kitchen in readiness, with a small brown envelope containing her fee propped up against one of the mugs, just in case it slipped her mind to pay her; but by five past eleven there was no sign of Arlene, and Ella's insides were tight with anxiety as, perched on the stool, she looked around the studio, checking that every last detail was in place.

Over the past days she'd done a number of sketches she hoped would help Arlene adopt an appropriate pose, using a book of Egon Schiele's life studies from her Art School days. She'd particularly liked one study, entitled 'Female Nude with Black Stockings', and had spent a whole evening copying it in China ink then colouring it with gouache paint.

The painting showed a woman, almost certainly a prostitute, wearing black stockings and red garters. Her elbows were tightly bent and she had both hands behind her head, which was demurely averted from the viewer. She had dark red hair, pale pendulous breasts, and a smudge of dark pubic hair. Several folds of loose skin hung round her stomach, and it was clear she was no longer young. It was also clear the artist had no wish to flatter her.

Ella had liked the flagrant confidence of the woman's pose and the down-to-earth details of her anatomy, but the demure face was not at all what she was after. She wanted Arlene to stare straight at the viewer as the models did in so many of Schiele's other studies, so she'd chosen three whose expressions were frank to the point of arrogance and had them photocopied at the library.

She'd stuck all four images on the fireplace wall (covering, to her intense satisfaction, two and a half of Flick's ghosts), and when Arlene arrived the first thing she planned to do was ask her to look at them and decide what expression she might assume, and how she might sit.

By quarter past eleven, however, Arlene had still not arrived, and Ella sent her a text to ask where she was, which Arlene immediately answered to say she was sorry, she'd missed the bus, but was now on the next one and would be with her 'in 5'. Relieved, Ella went and switched on the kettle, and as she waited for it to boil she looked out of the kitchen window, wondering where she'd begin the clearing of the garden. The kettle had just begun to whistle, and she'd turned to pick it up, when she noticed a small movement and realised there was someone in her garden, at the near end, just below the window.

She leaned across the sink and peered down and there, directly underneath her, was a khaki-coloured hat with a very broad brim and fine netting stretched across it. The hat's wearer, clad head to foot in a loose suit of the same khaki colour, was bent over some small wooden structures, pumping a thing that looked like tiny bellows from which smoke was emanating. Ella was about to fetch one of the kitchen stools to stand on for a better look when the doorbell rang, and she ran downstairs as fast as her hip would allow.

When she opened the front door and saw Arlene, she hardly recognised her. As requested, she'd applied no make-up, which made her eyes, freed from their thick black outlines, seem even more stunningly mournful than before. Her skin was pale to the point of translucency and the area below her eyes was violet, which darkened at the inner corners to deep purple, like a small bruise. Her cheeks glowed softly pink and her hair hung loosely over her shoulders, its mousy brown replaced by a vibrant damson red.

Ella held the door wide, but Arlene remained on the doorstep. "What's up with her?" she said, jerking her head to the right. "She keeps staring at me, and her eyes look funny, like she's not really seeing you. Is she blind, or has she got dementia or something?"

"I'm not sure," Ella whispered, and she put a finger to her lips and motioned to Arlene to come in. When she'd closed the door and was leading the way up the stairs she said, still in a whisper, "She stares at me too, and I must admit I find it quite disconcerting but the thing is, if she *is* blind, she may have very good hearing, and the last thing I want to do is offend her," and she showed Arlene into the flat and shut the door as quietly as she could. "I've only just moved in," she explained, "and I'm attempting to keep as low a profile as I can.

"Now," she said, ushering Arlene into the studio, "why don't you have a seat, and when you've got your breath back maybe you could have a look at the drawings on the wall? They're copies of an artist called Egon Schiele" – she said the name slowly, pronouncing each syllable separately as one would with a child – "and they're roughly the kind of thing I'm after. Can I get you a coffee?"

Arlene obediently dumped her backpack, sat down on the white chair, and directed all her attention to the four drawings. "Schiele's one of my major influences, actually," she said. "And black please, no milk, and two sugars."

Back in the kitchen Ella scoured the cupboards for sugar and searched her memory for any hint Arlene had given, when they'd had their coffees in *Angels Castings*, that she might be involved in art herself, but could find none. Perhaps she'd forgotten though, because the whole afternoon had been a bit of a blur, what with the heat, and the pain in her hip, and the disappointment of those agency prices.

She added a crumpled paper bag containing some sugar to the tray, but before she went back to the studio she stole a quick glance out of the window to check the progress of the khaki hat. The figure, however, was no longer visible and the smoke had cleared and now, when she looked again at the small wooden structures, she saw that of course they were beehives, and she wondered who the bee-keeper might be.

It seemed highly unlikely that smartly-suited Wetherby would keep bees, and even if he did he'd surely keep the hives in his own garden, and it was even more unlikely that the possibly-blind woman at the ground floor window did, so the figure in the khaki hat must be her downstairs neighbour. And since he or she must own the front garden which was in almost permanent shade from the big tree so that the only flowers were those in pots and hanging baskets near the front door, Flick had probably given permission to house the hives in her garden.

That was it, she decided as she nudged open the studio door with her foot, and the thought that a nice nature-loving man or woman might be her downstairs neighbour made her feel, all of a sudden, wildly cheerful. Then she had another thought, which was that if Flick had given the man or woman permission for the hives, they must have been pretty close friends which meant that, given time and tactful questioning, she'd eventually be able to elicit more information about Flick from them. She might even discover the nature of her relationship with Wetherby and where, and why, she 'went'.

As she deposited the tray on the table beside the easel she was surprised to see that Arlene had already removed her trainers and was in the act of pulling off her jeans. Her feet, Ella was pleased to note, were large, with long, very red, toes, and her toenails were pale mother-of-pearl mauve with stunningly white menisci. They looked like the shells of tiny bivalves, and she loved the incongruity of their delicacy alongside the red of the skin, and as Arlene kicked her jeans to one side she saw that her legs were perfect too - long and slender and muscled.

She'd been a bit concerned about the possibility of tattoos, because Arlene had struck her as someone who might sport several, and was relieved to see her embellishments were limited to a rose on her left shoulder, a bat on her back, and a couple of small reptilian creatures clinging to each of her upper arms. If her breasts turned out to be small, Arlene really would tick all the boxes.

"So you like Schiele?" She handed her a mug of coffee and the bag of sugar with a teaspoon stuck in. "Sorry there's no bowl ..."

Arlene spooned in the sugar and stirred her coffee. "I don't *like* Schiele," she said. "I mean to say, who in their right mind *likes* Schiele? He was an arrogant prick who treated women like dirt. But I love his flowing lines, and when he paints himself I respect how honest he is."

Then, in answer to Ella's look of surprise, she added, "When I left school I went to Art College, but I dropped out after my first year. Mental health issues" – she waved her free hand vaguely in the air – "but that's a long story that, trust me, you do not want to hear."

She took a few gulps of coffee then put the mug down on the floor and, before Ella could offer her the privacy of the screen, stripped off her tee-shirt and bra so that all she was wearing was a skimpy pair of black pants. Her breasts were pert and tiny, their areolae a stunningly deep purple from which sprouted perfect pale pink nipples.

"So you want me completely naked then?" Arlene said, and she pushed her fingers into the waistband of the pants. "Only I thought you said you didn't, so I haven't shaved ..." and before Ella could answer she removed the pants and laid them, with the bra and tee-shirt, on the chair. As she did, the pile of chains caught her eye. "So are we going to do something kinky here?" she asked, matter-of-factly.

"Not really," Ella said. "In fact no, not at all. 'Kinky' is the last thing I want, which is why we've got this white thing to cover you up, so if you wouldn't mind ..." and as Arlene obligingly swathed herself in the material Ella turned away and, suddenly nervous, hid behind the easel and pretended to be doing something.

After a few moments, when Arlene said she was ready, she came out, switched on the spotlight, and gazed in wonder at her. Perched on the edge of the chair, every muscle taut and ready for action, she looked like a lioness preparing for the kill.

"May I?" Ella said, and, taking great care not to let her fingertips touch Arlene's body, she rearranged the chiffon so that the lines of her scapula bones were visible. She made a light pencil mark where the hem should be, and then she arranged the rest of the material in folds that draped elegantly over, but didn't completely cover, her legs.

"Could you sit right back now and bring your feet up so that the toes are hanging over the edge of the chair?" she said, remembering the foetal position Arlene had thrown herself into in the café. "And then I'd like you to curl the toes very tightly, almost as though you're hanging on by your toenails. I'll be painting out the chair, by the way, so that you'll look as though you're floating in a white space," she added. "I want you to appear to be floating or flying in all the poses, which is why I painted the floor white."

She watched as Arlene shuffled her feet into position, and waited till her long toes were curled tightly over the chair edge.

"Perfect," she said. "Now I need you to raise your arms above your head while I position these," and she picked up the chains and stood facing Arlene, waiting.

"Right above my head?" Arlene repeated. "Like this?" and she stretched both arms high in the air like a ballerina.

Her hands were as pink as her feet, the fingers so deeply red they looked as though they must hurt, and tiny scales of dead skin clung to the sides of her nails, which had been bitten down to the quick.

"Could we just try something for a minute," Ella said suddenly. "Could you tense your fingers for me, make them look like birds' claws? Think of when you were little, pretending to be a wicked witch."

Arlene hesitated. Then she brought her arms back down and examined her hands in disgust. "My eczema's really bad just now," she said, "and my nails are hideous. Do you want me to get false ones for next time?" and Ella shook her head vehemently and assured Arlene that both her hands and her nails were exactly, precisely, what she wanted.

"I'll explain the point of the project in a minute," she said, "but just for now, please let me assure you that these things you see as imperfections are absolutely the opposite.

"The woman in this series of paintings has to look as though she's suffering; in fact I'd go as far as to say her suffering is the whole point of the paintings, so once I've tied the chains round you, if you could possibly stretch your arms out towards me and position your fingers as though you wanted to claw my eyes out, it would be fantastic. Just as long as you don't hurt yourself," she added, and she waited again as Arlene stretched her arms up out of the way before coiling the chains as tightly as she dared round her chest and the back of the chair. As she did, she noticed the old scars on her arms and the faint brown lines that ran alongside her veins. and wished she hadn't.

"That's not too tight, is it?" she asked when everything was secured. "Can you breathe?"

Arlene took a couple of trial breaths in and assured Ella she was as comfortable as possible under the circumstances. "Now should I stretch my arms towards you and do the 'claw' thing?" she asked, and Ella nodded.

"And what I'd like to see in your face is a mixture of fear of, and intense hatred for, your captor. Probably more hatred than fear, actually. Think of a tiger caged," and as Arlene experimented with her arm and hand positions, all the while pulling her face into an array of animal-like facial expressions, Ella moved the spotlight back and forth till the shadows of her features were suitably accentuated.

"I'm planning a series of four or five large canvases depicting the stages of imprisonment and eventual release of a woman," she explained, "and as the series evolves I'm hoping to show her slowly realising her purpose in life and beginning to strive to realise it. Because the chains, you know, are almost entirely of her own making ..."

Turning her back on Arlene, she withdrew to the window bay to survey the whole scene from the easel. Her heart was pounding now and she could feel small beads of nervous perspiration gathering on her forehead. It had been years since she'd sketched from life – probably more than twenty – and the idea of a real person being in front of her instead of a photograph was daunting.

What if she couldn't find a likeness? What if she'd lost the skills she used to have, of finding the angle she wanted and then, keeping her eye trained on it, picking out the areas of greatest light and deepest shade? And what if Arlene hated what she drew?

Telling herself not to be so stupid, that it was merely a question of concentration, she picked up a piece of white chalk and turned it over and over. Her hand was trembling now, and when, at last, she dared to look over at Arlene, she was surprised and upset to see that tears were sitting, unshed and brightly illuminated, in the pink looseness of the girl's lower eyelids.

6

"Are you OK?" Ella asked Arlene, and she reached over the table for a tissue, but Arlene shook her head furiously and nodded towards the camera.

"Might be an idea to take a picture before I dry up," she said, and she flashed Ella an ironic smile. "I'm good, but I can't do tears on cue," and as Ella came out from behind the easel and picked up the camera, she bared her teeth and leaned towards the lens with hands outstretched in a position that was a subtle mix of fury and supplication, the chains biting painfully into the white skin of her breasts.

Ella fired off a volley of shots from different angles, then put the camera down and told Arlene she should stop posing now, and Arlene duly sat back on the chair and examined with satisfaction the red wheals the chains had left behind.

"You should take some more shots that show the red marks," she said, "before they fade. It's a bit of a shame there's no blood. Do you want me to get some fake stuff for next time?"

Assuring her that wheals were more than adequate, Ella did as she was told, and when the chains had been replaced and she began to sketch on the pale grey paper with the white chalk, she saw that her hands were still trembling slightly.

"It's been ages since I sketched from life," she confessed to Arlene, "so this might take me a bit of time, but your pose and expression are perfect, and if you can just hold it all for a bit longer I'll let you know when I've done your face."

For a while Arlene was silent as she concentrated on maintaining the intensity of her facial expression, and Ella felt herself relax a little as she sketched in the overall proportions of her body. Then she began to pick out the details of the face, carefully copying the play of light and dark that gave life to her model's extraordinary features.

"I'm doing your body now," she told Arlene, "so you don't have to bare your teeth any more. Don't want you getting lockjaw, do we!" and she laughed as Arlene pulled her mouth this way and that till her face settled into a neutral expression. To Ella's relief, she seemed to have cheered up again, and she wondered what had evoked the sudden unshed tears.

"Don't you usually do portraits then?" Arlene said, and Ella shook her head.

"Not much, these days," she said as she continued to sketch, "and almost never of adults. Mostly, I paint flower studies, which I'm quick at and which sell well. I particularly like roses actually, but I do get the occasional commission to do children or dogs, neither of which are capable of holding a pose for more than thirty seconds, so I always use photos. To be honest" – she laughed again – "it's been decades since I actually did anything from life and I'd forgotten how much I used to enjoy it. You get a much more powerful result," and she took a sanguine crayon and began to pick out the subtle shadows that gave the small swell to Arlene's breasts.

The chiffon had slipped down now, exposing the breasts, and when she'd finished the shading Ella added a small bright white highlight to the side of each nipple so that they appeared to project out from the paper; and when she was satisfied with the body, she took a sharp white chalk and, leaning heavily, traced the edges of the chiffon.

Later, when she painted the picture in oils, she'd go through a similar process with Titanium White, and as she imagined wrapping these wonderful chiffon folds, lightly opaque and delicate as lily petals, round Arlene's jagged, tortured form she felt, for the first time in years, the electric thrill of an image suddenly coming to life and defying expectations.

Stepping back from the easel, Ella assessed her work. Then she replaced the drawing-board with a large rectangular canvas, but before she began to draw again she held the sketch up for Arlene to see, and was gratified to receive a solemn thumbs-up.

"And now, if you'd go back to the initial pose please," she said, "I'm going to sketch the whole composition roughly out on the canvas. It shouldn't take terribly long, so don't worry about catching your bus, and if you'd like something to eat I've got some cheese sandwiches. I don't suppose you'd be able to come back tomorrow?" and she concentrated on choosing her crayon so as not to pressurise Arlene. "I start a teaching job next week, you see, and it would be nice to feel the project was properly underway before then, but I know tomorrow's Saturday, and it's very short notice …"

She looked shyly up, and was relieved to see Arlene nod. "I'm fine with that," Arlene said. "Weekends are a bit flat these days. And this time I promise I'll be on time," and she arranged herself into such a good copy of the initial pose that Ella didn't have to tweak a single detail.

"I really love your work," Arlene said as they were eating their lunch, "and the whole concept you've got for the series is incredibly 'now'. It's like, OK we've got all these rights we didn't have before, but actually there's still one hell of a lot of stuff stopping us from doing what we really want to do. I know a load of women who'll relate to your series. *I* certainly do," and she stared down at the sandwich. "So," she went on, "are you living here on your own? I mean, have you got a husband or something? If you don't mind me asking."

Ella thought for a while before answering. She was surprised at how much she did mind. "I have a husband, yes," she said, and, after a pause, "Who I've left."

Arlene frowned. "Did he ... I mean ... was it an abusive relationship? Or was he just shagging someone else?"

Ella paused again. Neither of these questions had a simple answer, but now Arlene was looking at her expectantly. "Let's just say he didn't abuse me physically," she decided on. "He'd never do that," and she looked over at the pastel sketch, giving herself some more thinking time. "He was – he *is* – a very kind and gentle man, but sometimes, over time, people change and that makes relationships change, and now" – she began, rather brusquely, to pile up the plates – "it's high time you went for your bus."

She picked up the small brown envelope, and when they were at the front door she handed it to Arlene. "Thank you very much for all your hard work," she said, "and I'll look forward to seeing you tomorrow," and she watched as Arlene loped down the path and stopped at the gate to turn and wave, first at her and then at a point just to her right. Following Arlene's gaze, Ella saw that the woman with the milky eyes was smiling out and waving back at her.

She was about to go in again when she noticed, high up to the left of the door and partially covered by Virginia creeper, a set of labelled bell-pushes. At the top left, plastic-covered and in bold typewritten letters, was 'P. Wetherby' and opposite a rather faded 'F. Hunter'. Below it, on a green plastic strip embossed with white, was 'H & M Flood', but when she tried to read the last label, it was so old and weather-worn she could make out nothing at all of the milky-eyed woman's name and, pushing the door open, she went inside and waited while her eyes accustomed to the hall's dim light.

The door to her right must be the Floods' door, and presumably either H or M was the khaki-clothed beekeeper, so the flat to the left belonged to the indecipherable old woman, and she walked up to it and peered close at its polished brass plate. It was embossed with 'J & M Oliver', and for a few moments she stood staring at it, torn between ringing the doorbell and opening herself up to another potentially awkward relationship, and scurrying back upstairs to deal with the multitude of tasks that awaited her.

The multitude of tasks won. There was, after all, all the time in the world for her to find out more about J, or M, Oliver, and all the time in the world to strike up a conversation with H, or M, Flood too. For the time being she had much more pressing concerns, because sitting in a pile on the kitchen work surface, virginally crisp and clean, were seven empty folders marked 'Lesson Plans' each of which, in a few short days, had to be filled with stimulating, educational art activities suitable for every single class in Seavale Primary, including – horror of horrors – the Reception Class whose members, she knew from past experience, might not even possess sufficient motor and cognitive skills to pull up their own little knickers.

She climbed the stairs slowly, and when she'd tidied away the pastels and pinned up her first sketch of Arlene, she made herself another coffee and, perched on the stool with the camera, looked through the series of photographs she'd taken. Later, she'd tackle the first lesson plan, and then at least she'd feel she'd made a start, but first she'd go to the library and get them to print out the best photographs of Arlene, and sometime soon she'd buy herself a printer, and a nice comfortable chair for the studio.

She looked at each photograph in turn, and when she'd got the choice down to four she cropped and enlarged them to see which had the best detail, and was left with two images. One was the very first she'd taken of Arlene in chains, when her eyes were filled with tears and her expression was at its fiercest, and the other was the one that best showed the red wheals on her breasts. For a while she sat, studying each in turn.

For the time being, she'd call the first image 'Arlene Chained' and the second 'Arlene Unchained' and the more she looked at them the more she felt her body ripple with creative energy. She especially loved how soft yet vibrant Arlene's tear-filled eyes looked, and the tender way her pale arms reached out pleadingly to the viewer, magenta fingertips almost quivering in their desperation to be free.

Of the two, however, it was the second she found most affecting. With the chains lying loosely in the folds of the chiffon it should have suggested a hint of release, yet the livid red wheals were, if anything, a more potent symbol of captivity than the silver metal had been. They were the living embodiment of the woman's imprisonment.

Laying the camera to one side, she fetched the folders, took them through to the living room, and spread them out on the bare floorboards. Right at the bottom of the pile was another folder, marked 'Source Material', and over the past months she'd been filling it with examples of various famous paintings – Munch's 'Scream', a couple of Mondrians, a variety of examples of Impressionism and, especially for the Primary Twos, a brace of Jackson Pollocks for them to emulate with poster paints. The thought of the latter made her feel nauseous with apprehension.

She chose which paintings would be most appropriate for which stage and filed them away, but before she began the task of actually planning 'Pointillism for Primary Four' she decided she needed another coffee and went to the kitchen to make it. As she walked past the sink, she heard a low scream coming up from the garden and, looking out of the window, saw the tail end of the khaki figure running away from the hives while swiping the air furiously, and as it turned into profile she saw it had a beard. Mr Flood, she presumed, having an altercation with his bees, and she marched herself briskly back through to the living room with the coffee. He no doubt knew what he was doing and didn't require assistance, and if he did he had 'C' to ask. There were to be positively no more distractions.

When the first lesson plan was finished and the photographs of Arlene pinned to the studio wall, Ella fetched herself a glass of red wine, pulled up the blinds, and sat on the floor cushion watching the sunlight flicker between the beech leaves. The few remaining ghostly marks Flick had left were all but hidden now, and all she was conscious of seeing were the images of Arlene, and the big canvas on which their journey together would soon begin.

7

Jinty stood in the centre of the tree circle and listened hard. It was so hot the top of the cliffside behind her was covered in haze, and even the seagulls seemed stunned into silence. Here among the trees it felt like standing inside a big cool cathedral, which was usually a lovely thing to do on a boiling-hot day, but today, for several reasons, it wasn't.

Shabs was late. She was supposed to meet Jinty here at three, but the church clock had chimed three ages ago and there was still no sign of her. Now Jinty was upset, and she was also thirsty, because the arrangement was that Shabs would bring two cartons of orange juice and Jinty would provide the crisps.

She walked to the top edge of the tree circle where she and Shabs had built their den, pulled aside the sheet of corrugated iron that served as a door, shuffled her way in, and sat on the carpet of dry pine needles with her legs in the sun and her backpack beside her. She took a pencil out of the backpack and added some more branches to the tree she'd been drawing, but her heart wasn't in it.

She hated it when Shabs was late. She always imagined she'd forgotten they'd planned to meet, and the idea that she could just forget made Jinty want to cry. She, Jinty, would never, ever forget an arrangement with Shabs, because meeting up with Shabs was, apart from Art with Mrs Nwapa, the very best thing she did.

Shabs, however, often *was* late because she led a very complicated life, and there had been times – several times in fact - when she really had forgotten. Sometimes, when that happened, she'd apologise profusely and go on to tell Jinty just exactly *why* she'd forgotten – the time of her dance lesson had moved, or her mum had an emergency meeting with the school about her big brother, or one of the menagerie of hamsters was at death's door, and so on - but there were also times when she didn't apologise, and those times were even worse, because they meant their arrangement was so insignificant she'd forgotten it entirely.

If it turned out Shabs had forgotten today Jinty didn't know what she'd do, because today she desperately needed to talk to her. Taking a stub of brown pencil out of the backpack, she began to colour in the trunk of her tree, looking up from time to time to see where to lean harder so that it looked as though there were shadows on the bark, and as she did she strained to hear the crack of a twig, or the creak of a gate, or the faraway call that would announce Shabs' arrival; but all she heard was the scrape of crayon on paper and the odd chirp of a bird.

The tree she was drawing was the tallest of the three ashes in the tree circle, which was quite a good tree in that it had one very large thick branch sticking out from the trunk at about waist height, and no jaggy branches lower down that could snag at your legs, so it was great if you just wanted a place to sit and look down at the river. It was nowhere near perfect though, because once you'd reached that first branch, the next was far too high up to reach, which was very frustrating.

It was nothing remotely like the wonderful tree that had got chopped down the other day which, with its stout branches that grew at just the right angles all the way up into the canopy, really *was* perfect. If you climbed to the top of *that* tree – and Jinty's biggest regret was that she never had – who knew how far you'd be able to see? Arran and Ailsa Craig, definitely. Perhaps even further. Perhaps Ireland.

Jinty scraped back the rats'-tails of hair that had escaped from her plait to hang limply over the lenses of her glasses and pulled them as straight and long as she could, then tucked them behind her ears. She knew they wouldn't stay though, because the plait wasn't tight enough, and when the plait wasn't tight the loose ends annoyed her all day.

Usually, before breakfast, Mam brushed her hair hard back – so hard sometimes that Jinty imagined it coming out at the roots – and then she divided it into three strands and twisted the strands together, weaving one on top of the other so firmly not a strand escaped, but these past few mornings she'd hardly seemed to have the strength to brush the hair, far less weave it into a plait.

She'd kept yawning and groaning and dropping the elastic band, and when, exasperated, Jinty asked her to please pull more tightly otherwise it wouldn't stay, she'd thrown the brush across the room and yelled at her to stop complaining or she'd just leave it hanging.

Now, what with the loose plait and the dirt on her glasses, she could hardly see a thing in the distance, so she took off the glasses and breathed hard on each lens so that minute droplets of fresh spit formed, then rubbed them dry on the hem of her tee-shirt, and as she put them back on she saw a flash of pink near down by the river and stood up to follow its progress. Then she shouted, "Hey! Shabs!" and as the shape wheeled round and, in a series of wheeling pirouettes, began to move up the hill towards her, she felt her heart race and she ran to stand at the edge of the tree circle in readiness.

The field was dotted with molehills, and she watched Shabs run round them, one after the other, taking tiny dainty steps and holding the skirt of her pink dress out on either side so that it floated around her legs like a great sparkling saucer. Her pink ballet shoes were tied onto the strap of her Pocahontas backpack, and as she spun they danced around in their own little arcs, their pink satin ribbons rippling in the air like tiny banners.

At last she reached the tree circle and, with a final spin, sank down beside Jinty. She slipped off her backpack and took out not only the two cartons of orange juice, but also two dark chocolate Bounty Bars. "You are not going to *believe* what's just happened," she said as she punched a hole in her carton with the plastic straw. "It is beyond my wildest dreams ..." and she swept the long dark waves of her hair up onto the top of her head and leaned back, eyes closed and an expression of utter rapture on her upturned face.

Jinty took out the crisps and laid them beside the Bounty Bars. "Sorry they're flattened," she said. "I fell off that stupid tree" – she indicated the ash – "and landed on my back." She punctured her carton and gulped the juice down noisily, and then she looked at Shabs. "I thought you weren't coming. You're ever so late."

Shabs opened her deep brown eyes wide and gave Jinty the puzzled, slightly aggrieved, look she always gave when she knew she was in the wrong. Then she ripped open one of the crisp bags and poured its powdery contents into her mouth. "I like them when they're crumbs," she said, smiling a saltily beguiling smile at Jinty. "It brings out the flavour. Aren't you going to ask me what's happened then? They told me to be sure and keep it a secret, but I couldn't wait to tell you. I ran all the way ..." and she moved so close Jinty could smell the crisps on her breath.

"Go on then," she said. "Tell me," and Shabs inhaled dramatically.

"You know Mrs Epstein always puts on a special show for us to perform in September, with parts for all the children from *Top Steps*, including the seniors?" she said. "*Well*, this year it's a modern take on the Teddy Bears' Picnic, but it's *so* not babyish. It's set in the future and it's about this little girl who goes into the woods and finds these teddy bears having their picnic – only the teddy bears aren't cutesy and fluffy, they're like robot teddy bears from a distant planet and they're going to have really sharp outfits - and guess who she's picked to be the little girl?" She paused, like a compere on a games show. "*Me!*" and she scrambled to her feet, picked up the hem of her skirt, and gave Jinty a slow and elegant curtsy.

"Can you imagine, Jinty?" she said. "And the *very* best bit is that the leader of the teddy bears is Aryan Hassan, who's auditioning for the Royal Ballet School next year and is the most utterly amazing dancer, and he has to pick me up and run round and round with me on his shoulder, and he did it today and I am not kidding Jinty, it was like *flying* ..."

Jinty let the information sink in slowly, and when she got to the bit about Aryan Hassan she felt the itch that sometimes happened right at the back of her eyes when she was about to cry, which was silly because Aryan Hassan making Shabs fly was beyond amazing, and should make her feel proud and happy.

Aryan Hassan had once come to their school to help with the Cycling Proficiency Tests because he was doing his gold Duke of Edinburgh's Award, and once, when they got to the part where you had to steer your bike through a line of traffic cones, he'd put his hand on Jinty's back to steady her, and when he bent close there was a waft of some kind of scent from him that made Jinty feel so lightheaded she almost fell off. She closed her eyes now, and tried to imagine what it would be like to be picked up by him and made to fly. "Oh my god," she breathed. "*Really*?"

Shabs gave a little squeal of pleasure. "Really," she said, and she unwrapped her Bounty Bar, and Jinty unwrapped hers, and for a while the two of them sat, mouths full of sweetness and heads swimming with ferocious passion.

"Congratulations," Jinty said at last. "I'm so pleased for you," and she tried very hard to make it sound as though she really was. Then she let a respectable time pass, and asked the question she'd been dreading asking.

"Did your mum hear anything about Mrs Nwapa at the Parents' Council meeting? *Is* she coming back?" She stared at the ground as she spoke, trying to sound as though her entire happiness didn't hinge on the answer, but when she dared to look up at Shabs, she could see the news wasn't good.

"I'm afraid we were right about the bulge," Shabs said. "She's pregnant."

The word thudded into Jinty's head like the very knell of doom. "She won't be back at school for ages," Shabs went on. "In fact if you ask me she'll want to have other babies, so she may not come back for years.

"But you know Jinty" – she leant over and tapped the back of Jinty's hand the way Mrs Nwapa did when she wanted to drive a point home – "it might turn out to be for the best, because apparently Mrs McMahon's fought tooth and nail to get a replacement Art teacher and who knows, she might be even better than Mrs Nwapa. 'She' might even be a 'he', which would be brilliant," and she took a packet of moist wipes out of her backpack and removed any trace of stickiness from each of her fingers. Then she jumped to her feet and put the backpack on.

"Want to go down to the river?" she said. "See if we can see any sticklebacks?" and she walked out into the sunshine.

Jinty didn't follow. "But what about our Commonplace Books?" she shouted at Shab's back, and now she could hear something cracking her voice. "Mrs Nwapa said she'd give them back to us after the summer holidays. She gave us her Solemn Word ..."

She jumped up and ran out to where Shabs stood, took hold of her arm, and shook it hard. "Didn't you hear her say that, Shabs?" she said. "Didn't you hear her give her Solemn Word?"

"Of course I heard her," Shabs said. "And we all know when Mrs Nwapa gives her Solemn Word she never breaks it," but all the time she was speaking she kept looking down towards the river, and then suddenly she broke free of Jinty's grasp and was gone, wheeling and flying round the molehills in a great whirl of sparkling pink joy.

Jinty closed her notepad, threw it into her backpack, and stomped away to the farthest corner of the tree circle. She crawled inside the den, right to the very back where it was cold and damp and almost dark, and then she clawed the floor like an animal, feeling the soil fill her nails and the needles dig into her palms.

She'd set her heart on getting that Commonplace Book back. All the tree drawings she'd done in her notepad that summer, all the notes she'd scribbled below the drawings detailing approximate height, number of branches, angles at which branches grew from the main trunk, all that was destined to be copied carefully into the Commonplace Book.

And then of course, once term started again there was going to be so much more, because the thing about

Commonplace Books was that they had entries about absolutely anything; so there'd be poems about trees, and myths about trees, and drawings of birds and animals that lived in trees – even recipes for apple turnovers and pear melba, because apples and pears grew on trees - and everything would be written, or drawn, on the beautifully smooth white pages they'd spent so long sewing into what Mrs Nwapa called 'signatures', before gluing on the cardboard covers.

They'd even gone as far as staining the covers with coffee to make them look more like the leather covers of the real Commonplace Books Mrs Nwapa had printed out from the internet to show them, and for days after their classroom had smelt like Nardini's café down by the pier, where Mum had once taken Jinty on her birthday. Jinty couldn't wait to finish the covers and fill her book with all the things she'd prepared. She'd been looking forward to it all summer long.

But now there was to be no Mrs Nwapa, and no Commonplace Books, and for a long time Jinty sat at the back of the den, hands covered in soil, sobbing silent tears. Then she dragged herself out, heaved her backpack onto her back, and trailed home.

8

Seavale Primary wasn't far from Beech Avenue – a ten minute walk, or fifteen if you went along the sea front - but on Friday Ella had so many plastic boxes and rolls of paper she needed to take that there was no choice but to drive.

Her teaching days at Seavale were actually Mondays and Tuesdays, but Friday was an In-Service Day and she felt she shouldn't miss it. She'd been told that after the morning's staff meetings the teachers would be given time to organise their classrooms, and as she saw the low outline of the school appear in the distance the thought of running the gauntlet of a new staff room made her stomach heave.

She'd taught children before of course, away back in the early days of her marriage before Lucy came along, but those girls in Highgate, with their neat school uniforms and demure straw hats, bore little resemblance to the playground tumult she'd fought her way through on her interview day. Many of the Seavale children wore smart blue blazers, but quite a lot didn't, and the behaviour of both girls and boys seemed much less inhibited than anything she'd been used to. Their voices too, as they called to one another, had a rougher, more worldly, edge to them, and it had all been rather overwhelming.

Steering her car very carefully into the playground, she reminded herself that today was not the awful interview day when, for a whole variety of reasons, she'd been a complete and utter nervous wreck. Then, her head had spun with conflicts and doubts and hurts about leaving Derek and she could hardly think straight, whereas now that she'd actually done it and had her wonderful studio and her equally wonderful model, she was much calmer and more grounded.

And actually, when she came to think about it, even on that first nerve-wracking day, once she'd escaped the playground and was inside the school she'd been struck by how well-ordered it all was, and how pleasant and welcoming. Today, she told herself, would be fine. Everyone would be nice and helpful, and even if not all of them were, it would soon be over, and tomorrow there was another session with Arlene to look forward to.

There were already several cars in the playground, and she parked in one of the vacant bays, took out three of the plastic boxes, and carried them, one on top of the other, to the main entrance. She rang the bell, and when the door was released she went to the office where a young woman greeted her cheerfully and handed her a piece of plastic with her photo on, with instructions to hang it round her neck and use it in future to scan for entry. Then she walked down the short passageway to the staffroom and steered herself and the boxes inside.

There were three women in the staffroom, and as soon as Ella went in two of them stood up, introduced themselves and, taking the boxes from her, stacked them on the floor and led her over to where about twenty blue armchairs were arranged in a square round a collection of coffee tables.

"Since you're Grace's replacement" – the tall elegant one called Yasmin indicated a chair at one corner of the square – "you might as well have Grace's seat," and as Ella sat down, Yasmin turned to the other two and laughed.

"Not that anyone could ever really fill Grace's place, could they?" she said, and the one called Yvonne laughed too and agreed they certainly couldn't, and added that when they made Grace Nwapa, they sure as hell broke the mould.

"Oh come on you two," Joanne, the third and largest, butted in, "give poor Ella a chance! It's her first day for God's sake," and she smiled over at Ella. "Don't you listen to them," she said, and she took a swig from her mug. "OK, yes, Grace *was* brilliant, but nobody's irreplaceable, and the bottom line is we're bloody lucky to've got another Art teacher at all. I didn't think we would, you know, and honestly, the thought of twenty-five Primary Ones with loaded paintbrushes is enough to bring on one of my heads. Have you got more stuff in the car, Ella?" she asked. "D'you want a hand in?"

Ella nodded and stood back up, but Yasmin motioned to them both to sit down. "Wait till after lunch, then Aminah can show her where the base is. The base, by the way"- she turned to Ella - "is a glorified cupboard which you'll be sharing with Aminah Usmani, the Bilingual Support, so I hope you've not got too much more stuff. Tea or coffee, and did you bring a mug?" and when Ella shook her head and said she hadn't but she'd have a coffee, Yasmin jumped nimbly over Joanne's legs and bounded into a small kitchen area. She returned with a large mug emblazoned with a cartoon face with cross eyes and wild hair.

"Here," she said. "You might as well have Grace's mug too." Then she raised her own and said, "Welcome to the madhouse that is Seavale Primary, Ella. Long may your sanity last!"

All this time the staffroom had been filling up, and as each new arrival put their handbag or backpack – or, in the case of the man, his briefcase - by their chair, Yasmin took it upon herself to introduce Ella to them as 'Grace's maternity leave', to which almost every one made a comment to the effect that Grace was a hard act to follow; so when at last Mrs McMahon, the Head Teacher, walked in, she was more than a little relieved.

Clutching Grace's terrible mug with both hands and resolving to bring in one of her bone china ones next week, she sat back to listen to the long list of Mrs McMahon's hopes and dreams for the coming year. Despite the length of her speech, Ella couldn't help but feel moved by her obvious fondness and pride for the school, and as she began to make the odd amusing remark and one or other of the teachers responded with their own witticisms, she allowed herself to think that perhaps working in Seavale really wouldn't be so bad after all.

When Mrs McMahon's welcoming speech was over and the teachers were queueing up in the kitchen area for more coffee, Ella stayed where she was and looked through the notes she'd scribbled down, matching names to faces; and later, when they'd split up into groups for departmental meetings, she was pleased to see that Aminah Usmani was sitting directly opposite her.

Ella, it had been decided, would spend her first month doing her 'own thing' and only later, when she'd settled in, would she start planning with teachers about how she'd support their classroom activities, so once she'd filled in her timetable the meeting didn't really concern her, and she found her mind drifting back to the studio, and the canvas on the easel, and Arlene's tear-filled eyes and subtle flesh tones.

As time went on and lunchtime approached however, she noticed that some of the teachers, notably Yvonne, began to make more and more snide comments about Mrs McMahon - who they referred to as 'Molly' - which the others obviously found very entertaining. Aminah, however, remained poker-faced, and Ella noticed that each time a derogatory comment was made she looked over at her and, hiding her face with her hands, frowned and gave her a conspiratorial little wink.

The more she did this, the more Ella found her eyes drawn back to the handsome young woman, with her thick blue-black bob of hair and her dark fiery eyes, and the third time Aminah winked, she winked surreptitiously back. It reminded her of being a child at school again, pulling silly faces behind the teacher's back then trying not to giggle and, bending down, she took a tissue out of her bag and pretended to blow her nose. When she looked back over at Aminah, she saw she was heaving with suppressed laughter.

When the meeting was finally over and everyone was filing back to the staffroom, Aminah fell in step with her. Up close she was surprisingly small and slim, and her blue-and-white striped tee-shirt and knotted red scarf gave a her a jaunty, nautical air that made Ella smile.

"I'm *so* sorry, Ella," Aminah said, and she gave Ella's arm an apologetic squeeze. "I'm awful for doing that in meetings, but they go on *so* long and they're *so* tedious and Yvonne can be *such* a bitch ... You'll have seen our horrible little cubby-hole by the way?" and when Ella said she hadn't but she'd heard all about it, Aminah steered her round and, with a mock flourish, pushed a door open to reveal a tiny windowless room with two desks.

"It's officially known as 'the base'," she said, "but personally I call it the Black Hole of Calcutta – though obviously not out loud because it might be construed as being racist - but really, it's a ridiculous workspace. It would be too small for one person, let alone two. Do you fancy bringing your stuff along before we have our lunch? There's always such a blooming fuss in the staffroom at the beginning of break, as though the toaster and the urn might sprout legs and run away ..." and as Ella followed her in she took a cloth from one of her desk drawers, climbed up onto Ella's desk, and began dusting the shelves.

Ella looked approvingly at Aminah's perfectly ordered desk with its 'in' and 'out' trays, and the shelves above it, all neatly arranged with carefully-labelled files. "I'm pretty obsessive about tidiness myself," she assured her, "so maybe the two of us'll be OK. I'll go and get my boxes," and she went to the staffroom to retrieve them.

"It was *so* much worse when Grace was here," Aminah said as Ella dumped the boxes on the desk, and when she saw her look of surprise she smiled. "I know, I know, Grace was a fabulous teacher who could do no wrong. Well yes, she *was* a fabulous teacher and I love her to bits but boy, was she chaotic! She was forever bringing in armfuls of branches and boxes of soil with worms in and flowerpots for the kids to grow beans and stuff, and of course it all ended up in here. Once, she even set up an ant colony" – she gave a little shudder – "can you believe it? It was like an island made of plaster of Paris with a sort of moat all round it which was meant to keep the ants in, except it didn't. I was bitten alive, and eventually Maura had to get Environmental Health in."

"Maura?"

"Oh, that's Mrs McMahon's real name. They just call her Molly because they think it's funny. Anyway, Grace never threw anything away either, so as time went on it rotted and stank to high heaven. It was like working in a midden ..."

She broke off with a laugh. "Don't tell anyone, Ella, but when Grace announced she was pregnant, I was *so* happy; and just between you and me, I don't think she'll be back any time soon. Apparently Max – that's her husband - wants a huge family, so with any luck this is just the beginning ..." and she put one empty box inside the other and took the lid off the third.

"Do you fancy going for a coffee after?" she said when the last box was empty. "There's a café down the road that does excellent jam doughnuts – do you like jam doughnuts? - and it'd be nice to have a chat somewhere where you're not always looking over your shoulder to check no one's listening," and she stopped and looked rather anxiously at Ella.

"I'd really like that," Ella said. "Thanks!" and Aminah's face relaxed into a delighted smile.

"Great," she said, and she pushed the empty boxes under Ella's desk and together they walked round to the staffroom, but when they reached the door Aminah stopped abruptly and gestured to Ella to do the same. A heated discussion was taking place inside, in the course of which Ella distinctly heard the word 'paedophile'.

Aminah raised her eyebrows. "It's Yvonne," she whispered. "On her soapbox again," and when Ella gave her a quizzical look she explained. "We sometimes have a problem with men hanging around the gates. They're probably just crackheads or lonely old guys, and of course you can't take any chances when you're dealing with children, but the thing is, our Yvonne just loves a good drama, so you can take everything she says with a big pinch of salt ..." She opened the door and they slipped inside and into the kitchen area, and as Aminah topped up the urn, Ella turned to the seated area where Yvonne, a half-eaten sandwich in her hand, was holding court.

"I was so worked up I didn't get the bastard's registration number," she was saying. "All I know is he was driving a big black car, which might have been a Ford, though I'm a bit hopeless when it comes to makes, but it was definitely black, and what struck me as really odd was that he was wearing a hat, and it wasn't a sunhat. I mean, who wears a hat in a car in this weather, unless they're trying to disguise themselves? Anyway, I couldn't really see his face, but I did get a good look at the hat, and it was like one of those felt hats old men wear – brown, with a small brim. Or maybe green ..."

At this point the door swung open and Mrs McMahon marched in. Her face was flushed and its expression severe, and as soon as she appeared Yvonne stopped talking. "Could I see you in my office, please, Yvonne," she said brusquely. "This will all need to be logged and the correct procedures adhered to," and she waited in silence as Yvonne put down what was left of her sandwich and walked meekly out. Then she gave the entire staff a minesweeper of a look.

"You know girls, and Gordon," she said, "I have said over and over again that matters pertaining to the children's security should on no account be bandied about at volume in the staffroom. *Anyone* might be listening, for goodness' sake," and she glared at the door through which Yvonne had disappeared, then back at the teachers. "Do I make myself clear?"

Everyone nodded and made mumbled apologies, and only when the door to Mrs McMahon's office was heard to shut did anyone dare to speak.

"Molly's quite right," Joanne said firmly. "Yvonne's way too mouthy. It's a piece of nonsense talking about paedophiles – or should I say *hypothetical* paedophiles – the way she does. Christ's sake ..." and she buried herself in her magazine, and for the rest of the lunch break everyone sat very quietly, immersed in their own thoughts.

"See you in the Black Hole," Aminah whispered a little later as she passed Ella's seat, and she gave her a little wink which made an unaccustomed ripple of pleasure creep lightly up her back.

9

The café, which turned out to be a small pizzeria, was in one of the narrow lanes that branched off the main street, and Ella let Aminah guide her to a parking place nearby then followed her through a maze of side-streets to a rather shabby building with a neon sign, unlit and dusty in the sunshine, that spelled out 'ENZO'.

"This is actually my local," Aminah said, "which is very handy when you fancy the odd late-night pizza," and she held the door open for Ella, who was relieved to see that, despite its unimpressive exterior, the Italian-themed café was bright and clean and welcoming.

"So," Aminah said when they'd both got their coffees and jam doughnuts and were sitting at a green table with bright red trimmings, "how was your first day?" and Ella smiled mid-sip and said it had been a great deal better than she'd been expecting, and that she already felt quite at home.

"I can see Maura's a bit of a dragon," she added, "but I like strong leadership in a school, and I get the impression she's a good judge of character."

Aminah bit into her doughnut and nodded thoughtfully. "She sure is," she said. "I've never met a more perceptive woman," and she glanced round the café to make sure no one was listening. "I'd go as far as to say," she went on in a low voice, "that she more or less saved my life," and when Ella raised her eyebrows she stared into her coffee mug and waited a while, as though rehearsing her lines.

"I don't normally talk about this, Ella," she said at last, "and no one on the staff has the slightest idea, except Grace of course, because we're good friends. But since you've taken her place I'd like you to know. I mean, I know we've only just met, but somehow I get the feeling I can trust you. Maybe it's because you're older," and she bit her lip and gave Ella a look that made her want to lean over and hug her.

"When I first came to teach at Seavale I was in quite a state," Aminah continued. "I'd been more or less disowned by my family, and I'd got myself into an awful, one-sided relationship – the usual shit, you know, where I liked the guy more than he liked me. I always knew, really, that he was seeing other girls but he always denied it, and I thought I was in love" – she licked out some of the doughnut's livid red stickiness with the tip of her tongue – "so I let myself believe that if I kept ignoring it he'd finally change his ways." She sighed and smiled over at Ella. "I really did think I could change him. Which never works, does it?"

Ella tore a tiny piece off her doughnut and steered it carefully into her mouth. It tasted atrocious. "I know it's a terrible cliché," she said, "but I do think the only person one can ever change is oneself," and she laughed. "Which unfortunately," she added, "doesn't always work either."

Aminah had abandoned her coffee and doughnut now and was staring at the mess of crumbs, her hands lying limply among them like two small brown birds. She looked so distressed that it was as much as Ella could do not to take the hands and hold them, but instead she said, "So, would you like to talk about it?" and Aminah nodded.

"Maura came into the Black Hole one day and found me on my own. I'd had a particularly bad night, and I was sitting at my desk, presumably looking like death warmed up, and she took me straight into her office and when I told her what was happening she made me promise to go to the doctor. The doctor put me in touch with a therapist, and gradually" – she rolled her eyes – "*very* gradually, I began to see how all my life I'd let people tell me what I should do and how I should feel.

"I dumped the guy, got myself a better place to live, and I'm actually planning to go back to Uni to study Psychology when I've saved up enough. And I know Maura's always there if I want to talk, and Grace too."

She gave Ella a frank look. "So, how about you?" she said. "Are you on your own, or married, or what?" and when Ella didn't immediately answer she added, "I'll understand if you'd rather not say."

Ella let a few moments pass as she mentally decided what she could confide to this sensitive young woman, and what she couldn't. "Until very recently, I was living with my husband in London," she began, and she was aware of choosing the words as carefully as she chose her colours, "but I left him. I left him because, for a whole variety of reasons, I could no longer bear to live with him, and I deliberately didn't tell him where I was going, which was probably extremely cowardly and unkind of me. His name," she decided to add, "is Derek, and he is a good, kind, man, and part of me feels very guilty that I've done this to him, but nevertheless I have."

She stopped then, and looked at Aminah's beautiful face, and as she watched her digest what she'd told her, she heard the gurgle of the coffee machine and the soft thrum of people's voices and felt a peacefulness she hadn't felt for a long time.

Aminah released the lip she'd been biting. "Why did you come to Largs?" she asked, and she moved fractionally closer to Ella, head to one side, ready to listen again. There was a row of small marks left on her lower lip from the pressure of her teeth.

"I used to come here every summer, when I was little," Ella told her. "My gran – my mother's mother - lived here, and we were very close. We had such good times together, paddling about on the beach and going round all the tacky souvenir shops, like a couple of kids," and she smiled at the memory. "I was much closer to Gran than I was to my mother. My mother was an artist too, and a very good one, but somehow she never quite let me into her life, ever."

"And your father?"

Ella shook her head. "He disappeared before I was born and I assume he'd no interest in knowing me. I could never get my mother to tell me about him. She died last year, after a long illness," she added, and she drained her mug and clattered it down on the table more loudly that she'd meant to. "So that's it," she said. "I'm a free spirit, for the first time in my entire life!" and as she smiled over at Aminah a rush of utter elation flooded through her and she suddenly felt that anything – *anything* - was possible.

Aminah sat in silence for a while. She looked as though she was mentally sifting through everything Ella had said and saw no reason to hurry to answer, and when she did she spoke very gently and thoughtfully.

"I don't think you were cowardly to leave your husband the way you did," she said. "I mean, I'm sure you had your reasons, and maybe you were trying to spare his feelings by not telling him them. And I suppose leaving someone, however you do it, is always unkind - but sometimes we just have to, for our own sanity. I mean, *my* relationship sucked all the life and energy out of me so that, in the end, I felt I was just going through the motions of living. So I guess even if your husband didn't mess you about like my boyfriend did, maybe he made you feel that way too?"

Ella didn't respond immediately, but those words 'going through the motions of living' struck home. She let them settle in her mind, wondering if she should add something more, when there was a loud tap at the window and Aminah jumped up and looked round. A tall young man with a beard and ponytail, holding a small blue table in one hand and an angle-poise lamp in the other, was gesticulating in at her with a certain degree of urgency.

She gave a little gasp. "I'm really sorry, Ella," she said, "I'm going to have to go," and she took out her purse and handed Ella a £5 note. "It's Sergei, one of my neighbours, and I promised I'd help him move some of his stuff …"

Ella pushed the note forcibly back into Aminah's purse and, as Aminah thanked her and began to move away, she picked up one of the red- and green-striped napkins and handed it to her. "You have a rather large blob of raspberry jam on your nose," she said, and she laughed as Aminah spat on the napkin, gave her face a thorough rub, then sidestepped between the tables and out onto the pavement. When she reached the door she turned and poked her head back inside.

"I gather from the folder on your desk it's 'Pointillism for Primary Four' on Monday?" she shouted across the café. "Should be a blast!" and Ella pulled a face then grinned.

Ella drove home slowly, savouring the light on the sea and the delicious feeling of being alone at last. It was the first time in longer than she could think that she'd spent an entire day surrounded by people and now, in the muggy heat of the late afternoon, she realised that the feeling of calmness she'd had when she was talking with Aminah in

Enzo's was still with her; and as she steered the car into Beech Avenue, the calmness was joined by an equally pleasant feeling of anticipation. Despite all her earlier expectations, she was actually looking forward to Monday.

Back in her studio, she began to prepare her colours for tomorrow, and as she laid out the tubes in a neat row of Titanium White, Magenta, Purple Lake and Rose Pink, it struck her that the anxieties about starting school weren't the only ones that had disappeared. Paul Wetherby and his little mystery about Flick no longer seemed remotely important and, suddenly ravenously hungry, she hurried into the kitchen and filled a saucepan with water.

She tipped in some frozen peas and put them on to boil, and as she fetched the colander from the sink she noticed that the bee-keeper was standing right below her window, looking directly up at her. He'd removed the veiled hat to reveal a shock of tousled greying hair and a rather pleasant bearded face, and as he raised his hand in greeting she noticed that the top half of the beard was dark reddish-brown while the bottom half was brightly white, like Derek's had recently become. Then she realised he was beckoning to her to come down, so she leant over the sink, tugged the window up, and, standing on tiptoe, leaned out.

"Hello there!" the man called up at her. "I'm Harry – Harry Flood. Have you got a minute?"

"I'm Ella Blyth," she called down, "and yes, I'll just turn off my peas," and she turned down the gas and ran downstairs to join him in the garden.

"I do apologise for all this," she said, waving her hand around the expanse of wilderness. "I mean, I really do intend to put it in order, but I've just started a new job and everything's a bit chaotic ..."

Harry smiled good-naturedly. "Don't you worry yourself about it, Ella," he said, and he spoke in a soft voice with an

Irish twang Ella found reassuring. "It's far better for the bees this way, so it is, so please don't you give it a second thought. In the autumn, or maybe come next spring, I can give you a hand to clear things up, if you like."

Ella began to thank him and assure him that she was looking forward to the challenge of tidying the garden herself, but as she spoke she noticed Harry's smile had faded and now he was looking very seriously at her.

"I promise I'll not keep you a minute, Ella," he said, "but ever since you moved in I've been meaning to check with you that it's all right for me to keep my hives here. I mean, Flick was OK with it – in fact she said she liked the bees, though sometimes I wondered if she was just being nice – but it's not everyone that does. And if they do bother you, you absolutely must say, and I'll move them round the front." He gave the roof of the nearest hive an affectionate tap. "Though I'm afraid, bees being bees, they'll still come round here, being as how nothing much grows in our garden on account of the tree," and he looked even more anxiously at Ella.

"I'm fine with the hives, honestly," she assured him. "And maybe" – she gave him a look that felt more coquettish than she'd intended it to – "you'll give me the odd jar of honey? I love the idea of eating honey made from my own flowers."

Suddenly aware she was blushing, she looked down at the narrow platform by the hive entrance, where a number of bees were performing what looked like a little dance. "They wouldn't sting, would they? I mean, don't they die if they sting?"

"They'll not sting if you leave them alone, no," and now Ella noticed Harry kept glancing sideways and seemed rather distracted. "Flick only got stung once, but it was shortly before she went and she was in a bit of a mood.

Bees can pick these things up, you know," he added, and he moved a little closer to Ella and dropped his voice. "She didn't notice one'd landed on her arm and she moved a bit too fast and that was that. We'd to get the sting out with tweezers ..."

He tailed off and took a step back as a slim woman wearing white trousers and a pale blue tee-shirt came round the corner. She had a neat cap of short, perfectly straight, blonde hair in which nestled a pair of expensive-looking sunglasses, and her honey-coloured skin glowed as though freshly moisturised, and when she saw Ella she came to an abrupt halt and stood looking at her. The expression on her immaculate face was anything but welcoming.

"This is Ella, Caroline," Harry said, and he avoided eye-contact with the woman as though suddenly shy. "She's just after moving into Flick's flat, and she says she doesn't mind a bit me keeping my hives in her garden, so that's good now, isn't it?" He smiled broadly at Caroline but, rather than smiling back, she seemed to be even more displeased. "Ella," Harry continued, turning to her, "this is my wife Caroline," and he looked eagerly from one to the other.

"I'm very pleased to meet you," Ella extended her hand, which Caroline took then immediately dropped. "I was just apologising to your husband about the state of the garden and assuring him I'd be clearing it up soon," and when Caroline smiled politely but didn't make any further response, she side-stepped towards the path and, muttering something about checking on those peas, gave an awkward little wave to both Floods and beat a retreat.

Back in the kitchen she drained the peas at the sink and as she did, she took a furtive look down into the garden. Through the mist of steam, she saw Caroline give Harry's shoulder an angry push, then turn and walk away. She couldn't be sure because of the condensation on the pane, but she had the idea Caroline might have been crying.

10

It was Monday morning, the first day of a new school year, and Jinty and Shabs were sitting on the low wall beside the bicycle sheds, watching the arrivals. Shabs was kicking the heels of her new sparkly pink sandals against the wall and waving cheerfully at people coming through the school gates, but Jinty sat very still.

This morning, Nan had got up earlier than usual and gone out into the garden where Jinty had found her, barefoot and in her nightdress, pulling the tops off the long grasses and muttering something about 'dead-heading the roses'. Her fingers were wet with dew and purple with cold, and when Jinty went to tell Mam, Mam was so sound asleep she refused to wake up, so Jinty had taken Gran back inside and helped her shower and dress, by which time Gran was exhausted and didn't want any breakfast.

Jinty had settled her in her chair with a cup of tea she knew she wouldn't drink, and then she'd got herself a bowl of cornflakes; but she hadn't felt like eating either, so now her stomach was filled with emptiness. It gave her a horrible fluttering feeling, as though there were bees buzzing about inside which might decide all of a sudden to swarm together and fly out through her mouth.

It was still early, but a few of the teachers had already arrived and parked their cars. Mrs Nwapa's space, however, was still empty, and even though she knew it was a forlorn hope, Jinty found herself imagining the sleek bottle-green sports car, its cloth roof down, purring into the playground and Mrs Nwapa climbing oh-so-elegantly out, with her big red-framed sunglasses pushed back on top of her head, and her tight, bright dress, and her shiny red shoes with their giddily high heels.

It could happen, she told herself. It was not, as Shabs would say, outwith the bounds of possibility, because before she'd had Jinty, Mam had lost two babies, one after the other, and that was called 'having a miscarriage', so maybe – just maybe - Mrs Nwapa would've had a miscarriage too.

Jinty had mooted the idea of Mrs Nwapa's miscarriage to Shabs, but Shabs had immediately poo-pooed it. Women only had miscarriages when their babies were so tiny they looked like little fish, she told Jinty, and Mrs Nwapa's bump had already been showing when school had broken up for the summer.

She went on to explain that these little fishy things weren't even important enough to be called 'babies', they were just 'foetuses', and often the ones that came out as miscarriages were damaged in some way, which meant that actually miscarriages were a good thing. They were Nature's way of making sure damaged foetuses didn't get to become poor crippled little babies.

Jinty had, of course, been deeply disappointed by Shabs' revelation that a miscarriage wasn't on the cards. She'd tried her best to comfort herself with the thought that those two foetuses of Mam's might not, as she'd always imagined, have grown into healthy older brothers or sisters for her to play with, but might instead have been horribly disabled and not had nice lives, but it hadn't really worked. And now, as she and Shabs watched a pale, slim woman with untidy yellowish-white hair and a worried expression emerge from the grey Morris Minor in Mrs Nwapa's parking space, her spirits plummeted to rock bottom and the bees in her stomach buzzed more ferociously than they ever had before.

For a while the pale woman stood with a hand on the roof of the car, bending and straightening one of her legs as though it had somehow got stuck. Then, leaning on the car for support, she went round to the boot and pulled out two big clear plastic boxes and a large roll of paper. She put her handbag over her shoulder, piled the boxes one on top of the other with the roll of paper on top, closed the boot, and headed shakily for the main door.

Shabs and Jinty watched her progress in silence for a while and then, in a soft and utterly disapproving voice, Shabs said, "Holy shit, Jinty. She's *old*. She's about the same age as my *Gran* ..."

Jinty watched the woman put the pile of plastic boxes down and then fish around inside her cardigan, searching for the piece of plastic round her neck she had to scan. The stiff, awkward way she struggled with her clothes reminded Jinty a bit of *her* Gran, although of course her Gran was very much older, and infinitely more stiff and awkward, than the new Art teacher. Nevertheless, the way she was struggling to scan the plastic and then pick up the boxes and the roll of paper made Jinty long to jump off the wall and run over to help her. She knew if she did it would really annoy Shabs though, so she stayed put.

"I think it's ridiculous, employing someone that old," Shabs was saying. "I mean, my dad says there are so many young teachers looking for jobs and they don't get them because of all the old people," but she'd already lost interest in the progress of the new teacher and was giving all her attention to a group of older girls gathering at the gates. Soon she slipped down off the wall and skipped over to the older girls, who had been joined by two boys round whom they were arranging themselves.

The girls were all giggling and pushing one another and playing with their hair, vying with one another to impress the boys, but when Shabs arrived they all stopped and gave her exuberant hugs and exaggerated air kisses. They drew her into the circle, and soon Shabs was playing with *her* hair too, while the boys watched and nudged one another. It made Jinty feel odd, as though somehow it wasn't quite right, and she looked back at the Art teacher, who was now half-in, half-out of the main door and trying to steer one of the boxes inside with her foot. With a final glance over at Shabs, Jinty jumped off the wall and ran over to the door.

"Please miss," she said, and she smiled a wide smile that showed two very large front teeth, "I'm Jinty McVey. Want me to help you in?" and the Art teacher smiled down at her and said, "How very kind, Jinty McVey. I'm Miss Blyth, and I'm going to be in Primary Four's classroom this morning, so maybe you could show me the way?"

Jinty picked up the roll of paper and handed it to Miss Blyth. Then she marched off with the three boxes in the direction of the classroom, stopping from time to time to make sure she hadn't left her behind. "I'm actually in Primary Four now," she told her as they reached the classroom, "and I'm very interested in Art. In fact I'd go as far as to say Art's my favourite subject. Want me to help you put stuff out?"

She looked anxiously up at Miss Blyth, but Miss Blyth was scanning round the room, nodding her head as though counting. After a while she stopped nodding and said, "We need to rearrange the tables into six groups of four. What's six times four?" and when Jinty replied promptly that it was twenty-four, she went on, "And there are twenty-five in the class, which means we'll either have to have a group of five or someone sitting on their own." She raised an eyebrow at Jinty. "What do you think, Jinty? Five, or one?"

"One," Jinty said firmly. "Definitely one," and before Miss Blyth could argue she dragged one of the tables apart from the others. Then the two of them arranged the other tables, and Miss Blyth gave Jinty a box of felt-tip pens and asked her to put a selection on each table while she laid out paper, and when everything was ready, she thanked her and told her to run along so as to be ready for the bell to ring.

Jinty, however, had no intention of running along. Extracting a paper hankie from her backpack, she took off her glasses and breathed on their lenses. Then she began, very slowly and carefully, to polish them. "See the table on its own, Miss Blyth?" she said, speaking as casually as she could. "Can I sit there? Only when I'm doing Art I prefer to have plenty of space." She put on the glasses and squinted up at the teacher, her eyes large and watery-blue. "I also don't like it when people talk when I'm working," she added. "It ruins my concentration."

Miss Blyth gave the slightest of nods, but Jinty could see she wasn't really listening. She was looking up at the clock, which showed five minutes to nine, and all of a sudden she gave a little gasp and rushed out of the room. When she returned a moment or two later with two folders in her hand she looked surprised to see Jinty was still there.

"*Can* I?" Jinty said, and when Miss Blyth looked blankly at her she repeated. "Can I sit by myself so I can concentrate?"

Miss Blyth gave Jinty another quick, distracted, nod and walked over to the big teachers' desk, opened one of the folders, and took out a sheaf of pictures, which she began to lay out side by side. Jinty was about to check that the nods had meant it really was OK to sit at the single table, but now Miss Blyth was up at the whiteboard writing in large black capitals, and the bell was ringing, so she slipped into the seat and, taking her pencil-case and water bottle out of her backpack, assumed ownership.

The large black capitals on the whiteboard spelled out a long word that began with 'point' but then got very complicated, and while Mr Shaw, their new class teacher, gave them a 'welcome to Primary Four' speech then took the register, Jinty sneaked surreptitious glances at the back of the classroom, where Shabs was sitting. What she saw was deeply troubling.

Shabs had chosen to sit beside Tracy Bell, and Tracy Bell was notoriously the worst-behaved child in the class. She always sat as far away from the teacher as she could, and she was never out of trouble for insolence and lack of attention. She had a very unpleasant older sister, who was one of the girls in the group that had been messing about at the gates, and everyone knew Tracy was desperate to be accepted into the group too and was forever doing things to try and impress them. Rumour even had it she'd been spotted with cigarettes and a lighter on the last day of term, and although the rumour remained unsubstantiated Jinty knew that if Shabs had made a friendship with Tracy Bell, things were really going to change. The thought made her feel even more awful than she already did.

Turning away, she concentrated on Mr Shaw, who was looking at the word on the whiteboard and stroking his chin. "Doesn't that look interesting, boys and girls," he said, though Jinty didn't think he sounded the least bit interested. "I'm sure you're all going to have a lovely morning with your new Art teacher," and he darted a smile at Miss Blyth and left.

As soon as Mr Shaw had gone, Miss Blyth told them all that the word on the whiteboard was 'Pointillism', and she began holding up pictures from her folder one by one while telling them what exactly 'Pointillism' was.

She explained that, quite a long time ago, there were painters who decided to experiment with exciting, modern ways of painting. They wanted to find new ways to give the impression of lots and lots of light in their work, and she held up one of the pictures to show what she meant.

The picture showed a lot of people in old-fashioned clothes beside a river on a lovely sunny day. Some of the people were sitting on the grass under the trees watching boats sailing by, and others were strolling about with umbrellas up to shade them from the sun. There was a man playing a trumpet and a little girl in an orange dress dancing around, and she looked a bit like Shabs, and there was another girl with a bunch of flowers, sitting beside a woman who Jinty thought was probably her mam.

Jinty particularly liked the girl with the flowers and, glad that her seat was right at the front, she squinted hard at her, imagining she was the girl, sitting in the sun beside her mother, smelling her flowers and listening to the trumpet music and hearing the splash of the boats.

Miss Blyth explained that the painting was called 'A Sunday on La Grande Jatte', and it was by a very famous French artist called Seurat, and she asked them to look closely and see if they could see how he got everything to look so bright and sunny.

"It's hard to see in this small reproduction," she said, "but if we were in an art gallery looking at the real painting we'd be able to see that everything in it is made up of tiny dots, or 'points'. and that is what 'Pointillism' is. And today, we're going to make our own 'Pointillism' pictures, using Seurat's for inspiration."

She stuck the Seurat picture on the whiteboard and said that, if they liked, they could copy some of it, but that they could also add people of their own, and animals, and she pointed out that Seurat had put two dogs in. "And if you look here, in the foreground," she said, "there's even a monkey." She turned her back on the class to find where the monkey was, and it was then that the sound of giggling from the back table, which had been growing steadily from soft sniggers to outright laughter, grew in volume till it could no longer be ignored. Jinty watched anxiously to see what Miss Blyth would do.

Mrs Nwapa would have nipped the soft sniggers in the bud. She'd have stood as still and silent as a statue and given Tracy Bell and Shabs one of her looks, and if that didn't shut them up she'd have told them to stand.

Then she'd have narrowed her eyes and given them an even worse look, and if she spotted even the slightest hint of a smirk from either of them she'd well and truly let them have it. Not that she'd shout – Mrs Nwapa never raised her voice in the classroom – but the softness of her words had an effect like a spider's lethal venom, paralysing whoever it touched and reducing their insides to pulp.

Miss Blyth narrowed *her* eyes, and glared at Tracy Bell and Shabs. "What are your names?" she asked, and when they muttered them under their breaths she shouted, "Speak up please!" and waited till they said them fractionally louder. Then she told them that, since they obviously couldn't be trusted to sit together, they were to come out to the front and she'd find them other places to sit.

As the two girls stood up, scraping their chairs along the floor as they did so, and made their way sullenly to the front of the class, Jinty bit her lip till it hurt. Every fibre of her being longed to ask Miss Blyth if she could go and get Miss

Usmani, because surely Miss Usmani should already be here, sitting with one or other of the bilingual children; but of course to do that would be utter folly. And as Miss Blyth ordered Tracy to sit beside squeaky-clean Shazad Haq, while Shazad Haq's squeaky-clean neighbour William Hay went to the back of the class, Jinty offered up a prayer to Jesus and the multitude of the Heavenly Host that she wouldn't ask Shabs to change places with *her.*

In the event, however, Jesus and the multitude of the Heavenly Host didn't deliver. "And as for you, Shabana Ahktar," she heard Miss Blyth say, "I'd like you to sit here at the front on your own, and Jinty - you may join William."

Quick as a flash, Jinty put up her hand. The bees had finally out-buzzed her. "Miss Blyth," she said, and then, when Miss Blyth didn't immediately look at her, she stood up and began to move towards the door. "Please, Miss Blyth," she repeated, breaking into a run. "Can I be excused? I'm going to be sick," and she rushed out.

11

In *Enzo's* later that afternoon Ella sat opposite Aminah and marvelled at the vigour with which she was tackling her jam doughnut. She was shocked at how badly her head ached and how exhausted she felt.

"It wasn't so much Primary Four's 'Pointillism'," she confided, "so much as Primary Two's 'Abstract Expressionism'", and she shuddered as she remembered all those tiny, uncontrollable people with their straws, blowing liquid paint everywhere but onto the gigantic pieces of paper she'd provided. "Remind me never *ever* to do Jackson Pollock again."

She glared over at Aminah, who was shaking with mirth. "And there I was, all on my own too," she added accusingly. "It shouldn't be allowed ..." and she grinned. "So, what did you say to Shabana Ahktar when the two of you had your 'little chat' this morning? She looked suitably chastened when she came back in."

Aminah frowned. "I was beyond angry when you told me what had happened," she said. "You know that way, when you're acting furious but actually inside you really *are* furious? I mean, Shabana Ahktar – brilliant, focused, talented Shabana Ahktar - teaming up with Tracy Bell and the two of them giving you attitude? What's that all about?"

She shook her head. "I know what it's all about, actually," she went on. "Bloody peer pressure. Wanting to be in with the 'it' girls, the cool gang. I'll tell you something, Ella," and she leant in close, "that dance school – *Top Steps* or whatever it's called – has a lot to answer for. They want to be careful what they're doing, casting young kids like Shabana with streetwise guys like Aryan Hussain. Anyway" – she sat back and picked up her doughnut – "I don't think you'll have any more trouble with her. I'm well in with her mother, and the two of us can be quite persuasive when we're riled …" and she took a bite of doughnut and washed it down with a large gulp of coffee.

"On a lighter note," she said, "I was wondering if you'd like to come round to mine after school on Friday? Grace Nwapa's coming for coffee, and I thought maybe you two would like to meet?" She narrowed her eyes. "Or not. Just say if you'd rather not …"

Ella sat back in her chair and considered Aminah's invitation, and as she did, the image of Jinty McVey's earnest little face flashed into her mind. "That reminds me," she said. "Do you know anything about 'Commonplace Books'?"

Aminah frowned and nodded. "Oh my god yes. The Black Hole was full of them for months, dozens and dozens of pages that had to be sewn together, and of course Grace and I had to do most of the sewing, because kids these days don't know one end of a needle from the other. And then there was the smell when they painted the covers with cheap coffee to make them look like leather. It was *rank*, and it lasted for weeks … Anyway, have the children been asking?"

Ella waved over at the man with the red-and-green hat behind the counter. "Jinty McVey did when she came back from the medical room," she said. "She asked three times actually, even after I'd insisted I didn't know. She's such a poor little soul, isn't she? And so *earnest*. My heart goes out to her.

"She said Mrs Nwapa had given them her solemn word they'd get them back after the holidays, and that Mrs Nwapa never, ever broke a solemn word. She was nearly in tears ..." She stopped as the man arrived at the table, ordered herself a second coffee, and asked Aminah if she'd like one too. "And yes, I'd love to come on Friday, thank you. I need to meet the legend that is Grace Nwapa!"

"I think you'll like her," Aminah said. "I mean, I know I've done nothing but moan about her messes, but she *is* as charismatic as everyone says. She's got a fantastic studio too, in the Dennistoun area of Glasgow, and she paints big wild pictures and makes the most amazing clay sculptures. Her husband's Max James of *Max James Fine Art* in Glasgow," and she looked questioningly at Ella, who shrugged. "It's an incredibly classy gallery in the Merchant City – at least *I* think it's incredibly classy, but you probably went to loads of much classier ones in London. Did you? Did you have lots of exhibitions?"

Ella shook her head. "Never had exhibitions, no," she said. "At least, not in the last twenty years or so. And I didn't go to galleries either, classy or not classy," and when Aminah said nothing but looked at her expectantly she fiddled with her napkin, waited while the coffees arrived, then finally spoke again.

"Before our daughter was born," she said, "things were quite different. Derek and I did all sorts of things together, and even though Derek had zero interest in art, he quite enjoyed going to exhibitions with me, and listening to me chuntering on about the Pre-Raphaelites, and Salvador Dali, and Leonora Carrington, and Goya. Especially Goya, actually" - she gulped down some of the fresh coffee and felt the ache in her head ease a little – "in fact on our honeymoon we went to Madrid, to the Prada, to see his work, and we had a great time. I came back pregnant, actually, and we both liked the fact that our baby had been conceived in Spain ..."

She stopped and let herself drift back to those balmy Spanish evenings when, young and strong and brim-full of hope for the future, they'd sat at a table for two outside their favourite café, eating *tapas* by candlelight and drinking thick red wine from a bottle with a plastic bull round its neck.

She still had that bull. It was in her jewellery box, along with the discarded SIM card and the discarded rings.

"I should go," she said suddenly. "It's Picasso with Primary Seven in the morning, so gird your loins." She stood up and was surprised to find her head still throbbed. Her face was glowing with a ferocious heat too and, desperate, suddenly, to be outside, she took out her purse and stood up, and as she did, another, stronger, wave of heat enveloped her. It was ages since she'd had a hot flush. She thought she'd finished with all that.

"Would you mind settling up, Aminah?" she said. "I hadn't realised the time ..." and she handed her a five pound note, popped fifty pence under her saucer, and picked up her bag. As she did she felt, for the briefest of moments, the ground fall away from under her feet.

"It's just a headache," she assured Aminah as she sat back down, "but I don't want it to develop into a migraine because that can really floor me," and when Aminah's concerned look continued, she went on to explain. "After my Gran died, when I was about ten, I started getting migraines. I'd usually got them when I was at school, and they scared me because they affected my sight too, which meant I couldn't see to write. And you know how it is when you're a child – I was too embarrassed to tell anyone. Anyway, they wore off eventually, and for years I hardly ever got one. But this last year's been so stressful, I've started having them again. It's probably my hormones," she added, grimacing. "Isn't everything!"

Aminah nodded and laughed. "Don't mention the dreaded hormones," she said. "When I'm premenstrual I could kill someone. Off you go home and lie in a darkened room with a couple of paracetamol, and don't worry about paying" – she handed back the note – "it's my shout today," and they both moved towards the door.

"Thanks for listening to me going down Memory Lane," Ella said as they parted. "And see you tomorrow!"

As she'd done after the In-Service day, Ella drove slowly home, and as she crawled along the sea front, windows down and breathing in the salt air, she felt herself revive and began to relive the various little conversations she'd had that day with the children, smiling now and then at the funny things they'd said.

Even the Primary Twos, in the odd calmer moments when they weren't blowing paint into one another's ears, had been very sweet, and it surprised her how nice it was to have, after all these years, young children back in her life. Their trust, and their openness, warmed her heart.

She'd been particularly moved by Jinty McVey though, who'd followed her around all day like a skinny, freckled puppy, gazing up at her through the crooked turquoise-framed glasses that magnified her watery blue eyes, pleading to be allowed to help her.

She'd been moved by her general air of neglect too, by the grime behind her ears and the stains on her clothes which should have been freshly washed and ironed for a new term, and now she made a note to herself to ask Aminah tomorrow if she thought they should arrange a home visit; and even when she'd parked she remained sitting in the car, thinking about the little girl who'd run out of the classroom with her hands clamped to her mouth.

She hadn't, in the end, been gone long - thanks to William Hay, who'd offered to take her to Mrs Vance, the auxiliary – and as soon as she'd re-joined the class had thrown herself into her 'Pointillist' painting with gusto, and at the end of the morning Ella was delighted with the standard of work the children had produced.

She'd handed their paintings in to Mrs Vance to be mounted, and asked her for some large sheets of card to take home, and this evening, headache permitting, her plan was to write headings for them, and for the four huge, and reasonably convincing, 'Jackson Pollocks'.

She got out of the car, opened the rear door, and pulled out the sheets of card, relieved to feel the fresh breeze blowing up from the sea, cooling her head. Making sure the card remained flat, she walked carefully up the path, and as she reached the door she saw, or thought she saw, a strange flash of white streaking by in the window on her left. Clamping the pile of card firmly under her arm, she unlocked the door, and when she was safely inside she laid it out carefully on the hall floor. Then she went back out for another look in at the window.

Had she imagined the pale, lightning-fast, movement? Was it perhaps just the elderly lady, Mrs Oliver, moving across the room while staring sightlessly out of the window? But surely she couldn't move that fast? And there had been something taut and sinewy about the movement too. It had a sort of wildness about it Ella couldn't place.

Mrs Oliver was nowhere to be seen, and Ella stood for a minute or so peering in at the room, but the reflections on the glass made it impossible to make out anything much of the interior except two large winged armchairs and a settee. She was certain, though, that no one was in there unless, of course, Mrs Oliver had fallen and was lying behind one of the pieces of furniture, so she clambered over the box hedge and, blinkering her eyes with her hands, stared into the big dim room.

The armchair where Mrs Oliver always sat, with its two plump cushions, was just a foot or so from the window, and Ella could see the indentation of her small back in one of them. She could also see a book, open and face-down, as though she'd left the room and would soon return to resume her reading. Inclining her head, she read the title. It was 'The English Madrigal', and it was written in golden letters with an image below, this time in silver, of a swan playing a small harp. Its beak was open, as though it was singing along to the music.

The garden was very still and quiet and, telling herself not to worry, that Mrs Oliver was probably just in the kitchen, and the strange shape had probably been a reflection of her white card, Ella turned to go back in. Then she heard, softly but quite distinctly, a low-pitched moan coming from deep inside the house, and she hurried back into the hall and up to the Olivers' door.

She rang the bell and waited, and when nothing happened and the moan, louder and higher and much more insistent, came again, she rang it once more. Still no one answered and, more than a little alarmed now, Ella ran to the Floods' door. She gave the bellpush several jabs, and then she thumped the door as hard as she could, and eventually it opened and Harry Flood stood looking at her in astonishment.

12

Harry Flood was smartly dressed in neat grey slacks and a pale lemon shirt, and he looked so different from the previous times she'd seen him that when he said, "My goodness Ella, you look as though you'd seen a ghost. Whatever's the matter?" it took Ella a moment or two to answer.

"I think something's happened to Mrs Oliver," she said. "She's not in her chair and there's a terrible moaning sound coming from the hall ..." and, to her surprise, Harry threw back his head and guffawed.

"It'll just be Cally, Maeve's cat," he said when he'd recovered. "She can howl like the very devil sometimes, so it's no wonder you got a fright. Come on, and we'll check anyway," and he stepped back into the flat and re-emerged with a bunch of keys.

"Cally's an Oriental, and they're noisy little buggers," he explained as, carefully sidestepping the pile of white card, he led the way across the hall, inserted one of the keys into the door, and tiptoed in. "Maeve often doesn't hear the bell," he explained, "so she's used to me letting myself in. Mind you don't let the cat out."

Ella followed Harry into Mrs Oliver's hall. It was filled with big heavy furniture and smelt of bacon, and as soon as the door closed behind them the moaning began again, very much louder, and gradually Ella made out a white shape in the semi-darkness. Moving closer, she saw it was indeed a large creamy-white cat which, seated high up on carved table, looked so regal and elegant it could have been mistaken for a marble statue.

Harry stopped to stroke the cat's dog-like nose and it immediately leapt up and landed lightly on his back where, purring rapturously, it rubbed the side of its head on his hair and beard. He grinned over at Ella. "She's got a right thing about my beard, has Cally," he said. "I reckon it's a testosterone thing," and, with the cat balanced across his shoulders, he walked towards the kitchen door.

"Are you in here Maeve?" he called, pushing it open a crack. "Are you cooking your tea?" and sure enough, Maeve Oliver emerged with a spatula in her hand.

"Oh, it's you, Harry," she said. "Trust you to smell food. Would you like a bacon roll?"

Harry, however, shook his head. "No thanks, Maeve. Not today. I'm on my way out to the Drama, but I've someone I want you to meet," and he deposited the cat on the floor, took Maeve by the elbow, and steered her out into the hall.

Ella was surprised to see that, apart from the floral apron, she was elegantly dressed in a navy shift dress with a stylish white shirt and a pink silk scarf tied loosely round her neck. Her white hair was twisted elegantly on top of her head, and her fine-featured face was flushed and animated and - in striking contrast to the wraith-like presence who'd stared sightlessly out of the window - she was, in fact, an attractive and rather distinguished-looking woman.

"This is Ella Blyth," Harry told Maeve. "She's just after moving into Flick's flat and she heard Cally doing her singing, and didn't know what it was." He winked at Ella. "She was worried you'd maybe had a turn."

Maeve frowned up at him. "I'm afraid you'll have to speak up, Harry," she said. "I haven't got my hearing aid in. Who did you say this young lady was?" and when Harry repeated what he'd said, she moved closer to Ella and looked up at her, a worried little frown on her brow.

"So you've moved into Flick's flat?" she said, and she wiped her eyes with her free hand. "You'll have to excuse me getting a bit emotional, dear, but I was very, very fond of Flick, and the whole business upset me terribly. Flick was an artist, you know. A wonderful artist, and a most beautiful singer too."

She put the spatula into the pocket of her apron, grasped Ella's hand, and squeezed it with both of hers. "I do hope you'll be happy living here," she said. "We've had our differences" – she glanced sideways at Harry – "but on the whole we're quite a close-knit little family. It's lovely to meet you, dear, and I hope you'll visit me sometimes."

Brightening up, she indicated the door on the left. "Why don't the two of you come in now, if only for a moment. I know Harry's always terribly busy but …" and she grabbed Harry's arm and led them both into the living room.

"Just a couple of minutes then," Harry insisted. "You know if I'm late for Lady Windermere's Fan there'll be hell to pay, and I gather from the pile of stationery in the hall Ella's brought work home with her." He turned to Ella. "What is it you do, Ella?"

"I've just started teaching Art two days a week in Seavale Primary," Ella began, but before she could elaborate Harry smiled broadly.

"I'm a teacher too," he said, and he gave a little grimace. "English and Drama, for my sins. So how do you find teaching the little ones? Bit of a handful, I imagine?"

"A bit, but it's only two days a week so I'll probably survive," and she hesitated for a moment before continuing. "Actually," she said, "I'm a professional artist too," and, propping herself up on the arm of the chair by the window – the one on which the Madrigal book was lying - she watched Harry's reaction with interest. "I'm a painter."

Harry stared at her, mouth slightly open. "You're a *painter*?" he said. "Really?" and he bent down to shout into Maeve's ear. "Did you hear that, Maeve? Ella paints too. Now, would you credit it!"

His tone, when he spoke to Maeve, sounded as though he was deliberately making what he said sound conversational and not terribly important, but Ella could see that the information had a profound effect on the old lady. Lowering herself down onto the settee she sat very still, almost as though she couldn't believe what she'd just heard. For a while nothing was said, and to break the silence Ella picked up the book on the chair and held it up so that the swan and harp were visible.

"This is such a beautiful illustration. Do you like music then, Mrs Oliver?" and as she spoke she realised that the back of the room was almost entirely taken up by a baby grand piano, its top crowded with white busts of composers and lines of photographs of orchestras and choirs. To the side there stood a series of carved wooden music stands, each holding an open music book.

Maeve smiled a wistful smile. "I was a piano and singing teacher for nearly fifty years," she said. "But sadly I've had to retire because of my hearing, so now I only play and sing for my own enjoyment. Oh, and do please call me Maeve."

Brightening, she gave Ella a mischievous look. "You look tired dear, and ever so hungry. Couldn't I just tempt you to a bacon roll and a nice cup of tea?" and Ella thought for a minute, then said that actually yes, she probably could, but that she'd take her stuff upstairs first before someone tripped over it.

To her surprise, given the hurry he'd said he was in, Harry insisted on coming upstairs with her and, before she could argue, began to gather up the card and bound up the stairs ahead of her, the card flapping like white paper wings; and as she watched him round the bend in the staircase Ella was suddenly reminded of Derek, because in the early days of their marriage Derek had bounded everywhere too, like a puppy desperate to please its owner.

She followed Harry up slowly, and when she reached the landing and stopped to take out her key she heard the front door being opened and heavy footsteps coming up the stairs. It had to be Paul Wetherby, and she neither wanted to meet him nor, for some reason, have him see her showing Harry Flood into her flat, so she hurried to unlock the door and motioned to Harry to go in first. Half-way through the door, however, Harry dropped one of the pieces of card, and by the time he'd rescued it Wetherby had reached the landing.

Ella gave Wetherby the polite-but-distant smile she'd been preparing for such an eventuality, and he smiled back and turned away to unlock his door, but at that moment Harry re-appeared and the two men's eyes met. Ella watched with interest as Wetherby gave Harry a rather forced smile and said, "Evening Harry," and Harry merely nodded back.

"You've met Paul then?" he said when Wetherby was safely inside his own flat, and Ella said that yes, they'd met, and he'd been extremely helpful, and then she thanked Harry for carrying up the card, pulled the door shut, and began to walk back downstairs. She fully expected him to run on ahead of her and away but, to her surprise, he followed her down, and when they reached the hall he still didn't rush off but stood moving his weight from foot to foot, as though he wanted to say something but couldn't decide if he should.

"Thank you again, Harry," Ella said, and she pushed Maeve's door open and began to go inside, but Harry took her arm and pulled her gently back into the hall.

"I was just wondering, Ella," he said hesitantly, "you being an artist and everything, whether you might like to see the painting Flick gave me and Caroline? She did it specially for us, because of the bees."

Ella smiled and said of course she'd love to, and when would be a good time, and Harry thought for a bit more and then, quickly and rather breathlessly, he said, "Well, Caroline's going away tomorrow for a few days, to her sister's in Wales, because she's got breast cancer – I mean her sister's got breast cancer, not Caroline thanks be to God - so any time after tomorrow would be fine," and, before Ella had a chance to answer, he went on, "I was wondering about this Sunday coming, actually. We could have afternoon tea, and I'll make bread, and we could have it with honey from the bees ...?"

His voice petered out then, so Ella gave him another bright smile and said that would be lovely and would three o' clock be a good time, and Harry said three o' clock was the perfect time for honey and tea, and wasn't there even a poem about that, and then he turned and bounded over to the front door and away, leaving a somewhat nonplussed Ella to go and eat her bacon roll with Maeve Oliver.

Maeve had laid out a tray with embroidered napkins, rose-patterned cups and saucers, and two gigantic bacon rolls, and as she poured out the tea Ella was pleased to see she'd replaced her hearing aid. For a while, as they munched companionably together, they chatted about generalities, and Ella told her about the dreadful Jackson Pollock art lesson and Maeve told her about a concert she'd given where a four-year old had fallen off the piano stool, and by the time the rolls were eaten Ella could hardly believe that Maeve, with her witty conversation and insightful observations, was the same woman who'd stared vacantly out of the window at her.

There were, however, times when she seemed, quite suddenly and for no reason, to drift down into herself, and during these times her face reverted back to the familiar expressionless mask. It reminded Ella of her mother in her last years, and she wondered whether Maeve might be in the early stages of dementia, and as she went back upstairs she made a mental note to ask Harry about it on Sunday. She'd ask him about the 'whole business' with Flick too, the one that had upset Maeve terribly, and at the thought of Sunday's bread-and-honey tea her stomach turned over in an uneasy combination of nervousness and anticipation.

Her headache was almost gone now and, despite the bacon roll, she was still hungry, so after she'd taken the sheets of card into the studio she threw something into the microwave, took a half-full bottle of red wine out of the fridge, and sat down on the floor cushion, and as she ate she surveyed the two paintings – the finished 'Arlene Chained', and the 'Arlene Unchained', which was still on the easel.

The 'Arlene Unchained' was almost complete, and everything Ella had hoped to express was there. The fierce, almost savage, expression of rage and release in the face contrasted beautifully with the vulnerability of the outstretched hands with their raw red fingertips; and those hands, thanks to the excellent depth of field her camera allowed, were as crisply in focus as the body behind, giving the viewer the feeling that any minute now they might reach out of the canvas and claw them in. It was as powerful and confrontational as she'd dared to hope it would be, and it was proof – if proof were needed - that her flight from The Moorings was, after all, justified. A painting like this could never have been done in the prim confines of Highgate.

The little chinks of sky between the beech leaves were pale pink now, and the wine had made her pleasantly drowsy, and as she relaxed back against the wall she recalled how strongly Harry had reminded her of Derek as he bounded up the stairs. Up till now, anything that made her think of Derek had been so painful and complicated she'd pushed it away again, but now, in the pink of the evening, she felt, for the first time, secure enough to confront her feelings.

For it wasn't just Harry's puppy-like eagerness that had made her think of the young Derek, was it? There was also the musky, slightly gingery, smell of his aftershave as it wafted down the stairs behind him, because Derek had taken to wearing aftershave again these past months.

In fact, the comparison of Harry with the Derek she used to know had already begun when they'd met in the garden and she'd seen his two-tone beard. At the time, she'd merely found the similarity interesting, but then today, when Harry had opened the door in his yellow shirt and smart slacks, and grinned at her with those grey schoolboy eyes of his, she'd definitely felt more than a simple shock of familiarity.

Bizarre though the idea was, there was quite definitely something more, and as she sipped more wine and gazed out at the darkening sky she remembered her talk with Aminah in *Enzo's*, and the wonderful closeness of their sharing, and the glorious realisation came to her that everything – absolutely everything – had changed. She'd shed her past life like a snake sloughing off its dry old skin, and now she was actually free to do, and feel, whatever she liked.

That sharing with Aminah had been such a blessed release and relief, and in particular she'd been grateful to her for giving her the space to talk about Derek, and how she'd left him.

For weeks and months she'd tortured herself about the cowardly and unkind way in which she'd chosen to leave her marriage, but hadn't Aminah been right when she'd pointed out that leaving someone was always unkind? And, in the end, hadn't she, Ella, chosen the kindest way she could think of to do *her* leaving?

She hadn't, of course, told Aminah the full story about her and Derek. She'd felt she shouldn't, for two reasons. Firstly, Aminah was very young – older than Lucy, but easily young enough to be Ella's daughter – and secondly, though they'd become close quickly their friendship was still very new. She couldn't risk being completely honest yet, but one day, when they knew one another better, she'd tell her what Derek had done.

She'd tell her the whole story from start to finish, and then Aminah would understand that, in his own quiet, unassuming way, Derek had been every bit as unkind as *she*'d ever been ...

Ella swallowed the last of the wine, then hauled herself to her feet. Thankfully, the headache hadn't, after all, developed into a full-blown migraine, but her head still wasn't quite clear, and though she'd had every intention of writing captions for the children's pictures, surely she'd done more than enough for today and the captions could wait till later in the week? She deserved an early night for once, with a mug of cocoa and a book.

She showered, put on her nightdress, and went through to the bedroom. Like the studio, its floor was bare and its walls white, and so far the only splashes of colour she'd got around to introducing were a small rainbow-striped rug beside the bed, and a bright Tiffany lamp on the bedside table, which cast a magical glow over the room but was useless to read by.

The rug and the lamp had come from Gran's house, and Ella rather liked how they stood out in the sparse, high-ceilinged room. Compared to the cosy, cluttered little bedroom she'd shared with Derek, however, with its Morris-design wallpaper and curtains, and row upon row of the best of her rose paintings, the room was decidedly characterless. With just a little effort, it could be quite stunning and, sitting up in bed, she began planning how, when time allowed, she'd decorate it.

She wouldn't spoil its elegant simplicity by filling it up with furniture, but would keep it as plain as she could. The ceiling, and the wall above the picture rail, could remain white, and the walls she'd paint a nice subtle duck-egg blue, and get a duvet set to match; and, one of these days, when the dust of her departure had well and truly settled, she'd go back to Highgate and rescue some of those rose paintings she'd spent a quarter of her life painting, and hang them from the picture rail on the wall opposite her bed. Derek wouldn't mind if a few went missing. He'd probably never noticed they were there in the first place ...

She'd run up some cream-coloured curtains for the new bedroom too - heavy French lace ones with white linings - though actually there was no need for curtains at all at the back of the house. She didn't mind the sun waking her in the morning, and at night no one could see in anyway, unless they were in the habit of gardening by moonlight, and the thought suddenly popped into her mind that the day after tomorrow, if the weather stayed fine, she'd start the clearing of the garden.

She'd start at the far side, where the sheds were. She'd get rid of the weeds and cut back the roses, and then she'd clear the area round the wooden bench and fill it with new compost, so that next year the plants would be even more luxurious than they'd been in Flick's day, and when all that was done she'd gradually work her way towards the house, where Harry had his hives.

Throwing back the bedcovers, she went over to the window and looked out over the greyscale garden, imagining it all. From the bedroom window you couldn't really see the part of the garden where the hives were, but as she moved closer and looked down she just made out the corner of one of the little wooden roofs, shiny in the moonlight. And as she peered down she had a sudden memory of Harry's wife, standing down there beside the hives, crying.

13

Wednesday morning was, as Ella had hoped, bright and sunny and, not bothering to shower, she pulled on her painting clothes, washed down some toast and marmalade with coffee, grabbed her yellow rubber gloves and the big kitchen scissors, and went downstairs.

She headed straight for the shed, where she put on the rubber gloves and clipped and tore down the worst of the roses. The gloves were uncomfortably sweaty and unyielding, and the scissors woefully inadequate, and as she eased the little door open she crossed her fingers that, if nothing else, she might find gardening gloves and secateurs inside. What she did find inside, however, was not at all what she expected.

The shed wasn't laid out like any garden shed she'd ever seen, in fact apart from a bright blue trowel and a fork hanging from nails on the left-hand wall and a small pair of equally bright blue Wellingtons on the floor below them there was nothing in it that remotely pertained to gardening. On the wall to her right, as she'd guessed, there was a window, but it was covered by pink gingham curtains so that the only light came from the door, and before she stepped inside and pulled the curtains open she stood for a while on the threshold, taking in the strangeness of the scene.

It was more like a grown-up Wendy House than a garden shed. There was a chest of drawers against the left-hand wall, with tins and jars and vases on top, and in the corner a low, armless chair with a blue furry cushion and a neatly-folded blue furry throw, on which lay an ancient teddy-bear and a floppy white rabbit. To the right of the chair was a large leather trunk, and above it was pinned a huge array of art reproduction postcards, their drawing-pins red-brown with rust and their edges curled with damp.

Ella took a couple of steps in. Despite the hot weather, there was a dampness in the air and a smell of dust, decay, and ancient cigarette smoke, and when she stepped her way carefully over to the window, avoiding the mess of books and papers and over-spilling ashtrays, and drew back the curtains, she saw that everything was covered in a filthy skein of cobwebs and mould.

The mould grew in great green mottles on the cushions and blankets, and the curtains and chest of drawers were swathed in dark lace webs on which hung tiny leaves and twigs and small living things that scuttled away from the light, and when Ella tried to open the window it was stuck so fast with creeping tendrils from the roses it wouldn't budge. She took the trowel and fork off their nails but, as she turned to step back out into the fresh air of the garden, the swans stopped her in her tracks and she stood stock-still, gazing at them in utter wonder.

There were two of them, almost life-sized, flying across both wall and door, and they were as white and as clear against their cloudless blue sky as the day they'd been painted. Each wore a jewelled crown, and the jewels in the farther-away swan were blue and in the nearer pink, and their expressions as they flew towards the window were of infinite calmness and serenity, as though wherever they were going was exactly where they needed to be.

A small grating noise from outside startled Ella, and when she looked out she saw Paul Wetherby moving one of the wheelie-bins that stood against the house wall. She darted back inside the shed, but even as she flattened herself against the flying swans she knew she was too late. Self-important footsteps were coming towards her, and then a shadow appeared outside and Wetherby looked in.

"Good morning, Ella," he announced, "and what a fine morning it is!" and he looked round the shed, sniffing the air with distaste. "I see you've found Flick's little smoking lair."

Ella watched him survey the mess. He was obviously upset as he looked from one dust-covered corner to the other, and his eyes kept being drawn back to the little chair in the corner, with its pile of soiled cushions and mildewed blankets and grubby soft toys. Guiltily, she wished she'd thought to open the shed door before now and clear everything up.

"I'll fix it," she assured Wetherby. "I promise, I'll make it all nice again. As soon as I've cut back the roses, I'll open the window and let the air in, and then I'll take everything out, and throw away the ashtrays and wash the cushions and blankets, and when Wetherby said nothing but continued to stare at the little chair, she had to stop herself from putting an arm round his shoulders and holding him.

Instead, she indicated the back wall. "I got such a surprise when I saw the swans," she said, smiling at him. "They're absolutely exquisite, aren't they. I presume Flick painted them?" and, when there was still no response, "She seems to have been very fond of swans. Did she put them in her paintings too?"

Wetherby turned slowly round and stared at the flying swans as though he'd never seen them before. Then he straightened his back and took a deep breath. "She was, yes," he said, "and she did." He paused, then, and looked down at his feet, and Ella waited in silence, praying he wouldn't hide behind another platitude and then take his leave. His face, she noticed, was redder than before, and a small vein pulsated dangerously on his temple. When he found his voice again, it was choked with an emotion that might have been anger.

"Flick could be extremely child-like at times," he said, and for the first time he looked directly at Ella, "which was a very endearing quality and one which others found most attractive. Sometimes, however, she took it too far ..."

He turned round then, and began to walk towards the house with big purposeful strides, but Ella followed. "I was wondering, Paul," she said as she caught up with him, "if you could possibly lend me some proper gardening tools? Secateurs maybe, or shears? It's a bit of a jungle out there and there's nothing very helpful in the shed," and she laughed, keeping it light.

Wetherby stopped, then spun round and marched up to his shed. He unlocked the padlock, went in, and emerged with secateurs and shears and a pair of leather gloves. "They'll be a bit big for you" – he said as he handed her the gloves - "but it'll save you getting thorns in your fingers. And it doesn't surprise me there's nothing helpful in the shed," he went on, "because Flick didn't bother with these kind of practical things. She got Harry Flood to do her dirty work for her," and he looked straight at her again and raised his eyebrows.

Ella took the gloves and tools and waited while Wetherby fastened the padlock. She could see, from the way he fumbled with the lock, that he was impatient to be away, but she knew if she missed this opportunity to learn more about Flick she'd regret it.

"I was wondering whether perhaps you have any of Flick's paintings?" she said and when, after a pause, he said he did, that Flick had given him one, she took a deep breath and said, rather more loudly and exuberantly than she meant to, "Oh, that's wonderful! I'd absolutely love to see it, and I know you're probably terribly busy but I wonder, could you possibly spare the time to have that coffee? I promise it won't take long," and when Wetherby said, gruffly but not unkindly, that he could as long as it really didn't take long and to come up as soon as she was ready and then strode off, she put down the gloves and tools and hurried upstairs to change into something respectable.

As she fumbled about with sleeves and zips and fastenings, clumsy in her wish not to keep Wetherby waiting, she wondered what kind of painting she was about to be shown. Judging from the bright blue garden tools and the soft toys, Flick certainly seemed to be in touch with her inner child, so would it be some naïve seascape, with red-sailed yachts bobbing on azure waves under cotton-wool clouds, or an impenetrable abstract in garish primary colours? If it was either of these, it would be painfully embarrassing to search for something positive to say about it, and the last thing she wanted to do was give offence.

But then it occurred to her, as she ran into the kitchen to grab a packet of Custard Creams from the cupboard, not everything in Flick's shed was childish, was it? There was the wonderful 'flying swans' mural, that had taken her breath away. It showed real artistic ability, and even though it was illustrative rather than painterly, it wasn't the least bit naïve, and, somewhat comforted by the thought yet clutching the Custard Creams nervously, she rushed out onto the landing and rang Wetherby's doorbell.

Wetherby smiled graciously as he opened the door and showed Ella into a room that was the mirror-image of her studio. "Do have a seat, Ella," he said, and he took the Custard Creams with a nod of thanks and indicated one of the two green velvet armchairs that sat on one side of a coffee table, opposite a green settee. There was a large crystal vase on the coffee table, full of pale flesh-coloured roses, and as he put the biscuits down he gave a cluck of disapproval and swept up the pile of petals that lay beside it.

"The Queen of Denmark," he explained as he headed for the door. "It's one of my favourites, and it has the most heavenly scent, but this one, I'm afraid, has come to the end of her reign. There are still plenty of blooms though, and you're more than welcome to pick them if you'd like to. They're at the far side of the shed. Do you take sugar?"

Ella declined the sugar and perched on the edge of the chair, and as she waited for the coffee to arrive she looked around the room, marvelling at how completely different it was from hers, and how much smaller it looked. Its décor, unsurprisingly, was deeply conventional, with pale grey fleur-de-lis wallpaper, some large oil paintings of ships on stormy seas, a couple of bookcases, and a few silver ornaments. In the middle of the mantelpiece there was a large and ostentatious clock with a heavy marble base and little gold columns, and to either side of the fireplace were two alcoves with slightly darker grey wallpaper. A small painting hung in each, with a rectangular brass light above.

Ella looked at the nearer painting – an insipid watercolour seascape - with little interest, but when she stood up and went to the alcove beside the window bay and saw the painting it contained, her heart skipped a beat. There was no doubt at all that it had been done by an experienced and highly talented artist.

It was an oil painting, and as Ella leant close to examine its minute brushstrokes she could hardly believe how intricately detailed it was, and how skilfully painted. It showed a bucolic scene with mistily distant hills in the background and the figure of a man in the foreground. The man wore a golden crown and a long red tunic and stood solemnly facing three birds, one of which Ella recognised as a peacock. She also noticed, floating sadly on the surface of a little lake at the foot of the misty hills, a lone swan.

The colours of the painting were so intense they leapt out of the canvas, and even though on first glance its style was reminiscent of one of the Medieval masters, on closer inspection there was a certain abstraction in the way the figures were portrayed that marked it out as modern, and when Ella stepped closer and narrowed her eyes to read the signature in the bottom right corner she saw, in minute capitals inside a tiny blue lozenge, the signature 'F HUNTER'.

"This is the painting Flick gave you, isn't it?" she said as the door opened and Wetherby deposited a tray on the coffee table. "It's wonderful. I'd no idea she'd be anything like as good," and she waited while he joined her at the alcove.

"Oh, she was good all right," Wetherby smiled grimly. "I mean, I don't have much time for modern art so this is not to my taste, but the fact remains Flick's work was first-class, and if only she hadn't been so strong-willed and obstinate she'd be earning thousands by now. I did try to keep her on the straight and narrow," he added. "God knows I tried ..." and he turned away. "Shall we have the coffee before it gets cold?"

Ella, however, stood her ground. "What's its title? It looks like one of these Greek myths, but I'm afraid I'm not very knowledgeable?"

"Its title is 'Juno and the Peacock'," Wetherby told her, "and yes, it's one of these Greek myths. I'm afraid I can't remember the precise details, but the nub of it is that the peacock complained to Juno that his song was less tuneful than the nightingale's, and Juno told him in no uncertain terms that his gift was not harmony but great beauty, so he should be grateful for what he'd been given rather than complaining about what he hadn't."

He broke off then and went and sat down on the settee, and when he patted the space beside him Ella felt she'd no choice but to join him. "I'll let you help yourself to cream," he said as he poured the coffee, "in case you're watching your figure. Shortbread? Or one of your Custard Creams?" and when Ella had settled herself on one of the chairs he broke open the packet and put some on the plate with the shortbread.

"So, was there a reason Flick gave you that particular painting?" Ella helped herself to a large piece of shortbread and a generous amount of cream. "I mean, have you a special interest in Greek myths?"

Wetherby stirred his coffee thoughtfully. "I have, I suppose, a certain academic interest in mythology in general, but that was not Flick's reason for giving me this particular work." He took a few sips of his coffee, then put the cup and saucer down and leaned back.

"I don't know if you are aware of the parable of the talents?" and Ella nodded non-committedly. "Well, at the time she gave me the painting, I was writing an article about that particular parable for an eminent theological publication. Flick made a connection between the myth and our Lord's words: 'For he that hath, to him shall be given; and he that hath not, from him shall be taken even that which he hath', and decided I'd like the Juno painting."

He popped a small corner of shortbread into his mouth. "It was a kind and generous thought, and I'm sure she meant it as a token of her gratitude for all I'd done for her, but of course the poor girl had no idea about Holy Scripture, nor any interest in it. There is, in fact, only a very tenuous connection …" and he refilled his cup and topped up Ella's.

After several minutes of awkward silence, Ella sneaked a look at the ostentatious clock and saw it was after eleven. "You said Flick sometimes went too far and you tried to keep her on the straight and narrow. In what way did she go too far?" and she fixed Wetherby with a purposeful look. Wetherby, however, gave the look and the question a dismissive shake of the head. Then he stood up and went over to the door.

"It's been delightful, Ella," he said, "but now I really must be getting on," and he opened the door. "Let's just say Flick could, on occasions, be hot-headed and impulsive in what she chose to portray, which was not good for her career," he added as he ushered Ella out. "Thank you so much for coming, and bringing the biscuits. It's been an absolute pleasure talking to you."

For a few minutes Ella stood outside her own door, key in hand, silently fuming. Even in the shady landing, the air was hot and oppressive, and she wished she'd time for a walk along the sea front. Despite her earlier sympathy towards Wetherby, the way he'd just treated her like an over-inquisitive child annoyed her.

Surely she had some kind of right to know what had happened to Flick? She was, after all, surrounded by memories of her, and wasn't she just about to spend the next hour clearing up a shed that looked like the remains of the Marie Celeste? Surely it was natural to want to know why it had been left like that?

She let herself in, changed back into her painting clothes, grabbed a roll of black plastic bags, and went down into the garden where she put on Wetherby's gardening gloves and picked up his shears. Mustering all her pent-up anger, she let rip on the roses, gathered the clippings into a pile, and dumped them on the compost heap by the side of his shed. She filled one of the plastic bags with Flick's detritus and crammed all the salvageable things into the other, then threw the first bag in the bin and took the second upstairs to deal with later.

Back down in the garden again, she laid the gloves and shears outside Wetherby's shed door, and went off with the secateurs in search of the Queen of Denmark. She picked a sizable bunch, making sure there were buds as well as full-blown blooms and then, feeling altogether better, she took them inside, put them in a jar of water, and carried them through to the studio.

She stood for a while, moving the jar this way and that, examining the roses from all angles until she was satisfied with the way the light hit their petals. Then she picked up her palette, squeezed out dots of Rose Madder, Naples Yellow, and Mixing White, and mixed herself tiny mounds of every shade of pink the colours could yield. She pulled down the blinds and, sitting at the easel facing 'Arlene Unchained', she began to paint roses on the floor by Arlene's feet.

To begin with she painted the fuller blooms, whose pollen-rich hearts had been ripped and broken by bees and, back in her comfort zone at last, she worked quickly, pleased at how easily she was able, in just a few strokes of thick paint, to give the impression of delicate petals stretched back to expose unruly stamens.

Then, when she judged there were enough blown roses on the ground, she added a single tight bud, positioning it on Arlene's lap where her unshaven pubic hair darkened the chiffon, and when she stood back to check the overall effect she could have wept with joy. The blown roses, their sex flagrantly exposed and violated, was the perfect symbol of female vulnerability, and now the painting was well and truly complete.

She took her time cleaning her brushes, every now and then allowing herself a glance at the painting to check the composition was just right. Then she pulled the blinds back up, sank down on the floor cushion, and closed her eyes. The studio was warm, and outside the window the leaves of the beech trees hung almost motionless. Face bathed in late afternoon sunshine, Ella comforted herself with the thought that the morning, despite its various frustrations, hadn't been a complete waste of time.

Wetherby had at least deigned to show her Flick's painting, and even though, in the end, he'd refused to be drawn on the finer details of what had happened between them, she did know more than she had before. More importantly, she knew that Flick was an artist of great vision and talent, and that knowledge made her more intrigued than ever to know what had happened to her.

14

When Ella arrived at Aminah's flat on Friday afternoon, she was given a hasty kiss on each cheek then steered into the tiny kitchen and a bowl of mud-coloured butter icing thrust into her hands. Aminah, she noticed, was looking decidedly flustered.

"I am *so* sorry Ella," she said breathlessly, as she took the potted plant she'd brought and thanked her profusely, "but could you possibly ice these things for me" - she indicated a tray of charred buns on the table – "while I go and change? I was meant to do them last night, but I was so late home ..."

For a moment she seemed about to elaborate, but then she dumped the plant on the counter and ran out. "If Grace arrives," she poked her head back in to say, "push the button and let her in, and, by the way, do *not* let me forget to ask her about Primary Four's Commonplace Books!"

Ella busied herself with the buns, and as she was smearing the last one the intercom buzzed and she released the entry system, waited till the sound of footsteps reached the door, and showed Grace Nwapa in. Grace, and the huge bouquet of flowers she was carrying, filled the entire hallway.

"You must be Ella," she said, and she threw her arms round her, and when they were both in the kitchen they stood on either side of the table, taking one another in.

Grace was tall and broad-shouldered, with black hair cut close to her scalp, and she wore red hooped earrings and a tangerine-coloured skin-tight dress with a bright red scarf. Her shoes had extraordinarily high heels and were the same red as the scarf, and her bump was neat but quite prominent. "I've been so looking forward to meeting you and hearing about your work," she said warmly. "Aminah tells me you're a painter too?"

Ella took the bouquet and laid it carefully in the sink among the pile of unwashed dishes. "I've been looking forward to meeting you too. I've heard so much about you. And yes, I paint," and she hurried to pull one of the kitchen chairs out from the table.

Grace thumped herself down on the chair and rubbed the perspiration off her forehead with the back of her hand, and Ella moved the buns to one side and sat opposite, watching her. She'd never seen a woman with a presence so majestic nor a smile so wide, and she had the impression that even when she was at ease, Grace's face would bear the imprints of a lifetime of smiles.

"I do hate it when people say 'I've heard so much about you'," Grace said, laughing, and Ella hastened to reassure her that it was all good.

"The children really miss you," she went on. "They talk about you all the time. In fact" – she looked round as Aminah came running in – "I feel a bit like the poor substitute. I'm sure my lessons aren't anything like as much fun as yours were."

Aminah gave Grace a hug, then turned to Ella. "Of course you're not the poor substitute! Ella's doing the most incredible stuff," she told Grace. "You should see her wall display in the hall. There's Pointillism, and Abstraction, and paper cut-outs, and even gigantic Jackson Pollocks, which reminds me" – she ran over to the kettle and began to fill it – "have you got Primary Four's Commonplace Books? Jinty McVey says you gave your *solemn word* they'd get them back after the holidays?"

Grace gave a huge gasp and clamped both hands over her face. "Holy shit," she breathed, and then she parted her fingers and peeped through the gaps. "I clean forgot. I'd planned to come and visit you all on the In-Service Day, and I'd laid them out ready to take, and then I had the most awful night of sickness and I was so wiped out I just couldn't. I'll bring them in next week, I promise ..."

She shot a furious look at each of them in turn. "I'd like to know, by the way, who came up with the term *morning sickness*" - she spat the words out - "because it sure as hell wasn't a woman. Without a word of a lie, I have vomited my guts out all day, every day, for the past five months, which is why I keep forgetting things," and she took a handkerchief out of her bag and rubbed her face again.

Making sympathetic noises, Aminah brought a small teapot and a cup and saucer across to the table and then she handed out plates and napkins. "I've made you and me coffee, Ella," she said as she gave her a large mug, "and that's your mint tea, Grace, if you'd like to help yourself. And there's home-made cinnamon buns, and jam doughnuts from *Enzo's*, so please dig in.

Grace took one of the buns and nibbled round its circumference. "So how's Jinty doing? Or should I say, how's her *mother* doing? Tell me she's not still with that wanker she was seeing last year? The one that pumped her full of heroin and then knocked her senseless?" and when Aminah said that unfortunately she was indeed still with that wanker, she sighed and shook her head.

"Zareen did a home visit yesterday," Aminah went on, "and found Jean McVey with a black eye and – surprise, surprise – significant evidence of drug use in the home. And as for Jean's mum, she's definitely needing to be assessed for a Dementia Unit. Apparently Jinty's caring for her in a way no child should have to." She cut her doughnut in half and licked out the jam. "My heart goes out to that little girl, you know. She's so intelligent and creative, but what chance has she got with all that going on at home? If her mother doesn't come to her senses soon, she'll end up being put into Care again."

Ella listened as Aminah and Grace went on discussing Jinty, and as she did she found herself watching Aminah and wondering what it was about her that was different. Despite the seriousness of what she and Grace were discussing, there was a definite glow to her face she'd not seen before, so when they'd drunk their coffees and Grace had apologised for having to leave early and pulled herself up out of her chair, she followed her and Aminah out to the hall but left her bag in the kitchen.

At the door Grace gave her another warm hug. "I was just wondering, Ella," she said, "would you be in tomorrow morning if I was to bring the Commonplace Books to you? I've a few free hours, and I'd be happier knowing you had them for Monday. And if you've got time maybe I could see your studio too …?" and when Ella said that would be fine, she'd be free till eleven, Grace asked her to text her the address, and she'd see her about ten.

Back in the kitchen, Aminah made them both another coffee and then, as Ella suspected she would, she sat at the table opposite her and, hands clamped round her mug, leaned eagerly towards her. "You'll never guess, Ella. Sergei asked me out!"

"Is Sergei the man with the chair?" Ella said, and Aminah nodded and grinned.

"I've fancied him for absolute ages, but I'd no idea he liked me, so when he phoned me to say would I go to the cinema with him, I was completely gobsmacked." She beamed over at Ella, her cheeks pink and her eyes glowing. "We had *such* a good time, and I really like him," she said. "I mean, I know it sounds crazy, but I've never felt such a connection with a man before. It's like I'm in a dream …"

Ella smiled over at her. "That's lovely, Aminah. I mean, I only saw him through the café window, but he looked really nice."

Aminah continued to smile, and then she said, "I've never, ever, been 'in love', you know. I mean, I've had the odd crush, and then of course there was the guy I *thought* I was in love with who turned out to be a total shit, but this is different. I mean, it feels right. It feels like it could go somewhere. Like I *want* it to go somewhere, and it's the first time I've ever had that feeling. Do you know what I mean?" and she gave her such an intense look Ella felt obliged to say something other than a platitude.

"I do know what you mean, yes," she said. "When I first met Derek there was something about him I'd never seen in a man before. He had a kind of depth to him, and it made me feel he really might be the one for me."

She stopped, drank some of her coffee, and forced herself to think back all those years, to the shy twenty-something she'd been. "I suppose" – she stared into the coffee mug - "it was what they call a 'meeting of minds'. Derek wasn't like other boys I'd dated, who'd prattle on inanely, trying to impress me. He was quiet and serious, and not very confident, and he had a gentleness about him I liked, and an honesty. Do you know what I mean?"

She looked up then, hoping that Aminah wouldn't notice the tears she'd felt gathering in the brim of her eyes, but of course Aminah did. "So what changed?" she said. "Oh no, sorry, I shouldn't ask …"

Ella picked up her bag, but she didn't move to go. "Basically, I suppose, all those qualities I most loved in him became the things that most annoyed me, and I'm sure it wasn't his fault. I mean, he's really always been the same; it was me who changed, particularly after Lucy was born," and she hugged the bag close.

"Actually, it started long before Lucy," she decided to say. "It started when I had two miscarriages, one after the other, and after them we were advised to stop trying for a baby." She paused, thinking back. "The miscarriages completely devastated me, you know. The grief of them was unbearable, and yet they didn't completely devastate Derek. He was disappointed, of course, and very concerned about the way I was taking it, but it wasn't the end of the world for him, whereas for me it was, and I don't think our marriage ever recovered from that. From him not caring as much as I did ."

She raised her eyes to look over at Aminah and saw that she was holding onto her lower lip with her teeth, digging them hard into its softness. Her upper lip, she noticed for the first time, was as neat a Cupid's bow as she'd ever seen. Smiling at her, she stood up.

"You have the most wonderful features, Aminah," she said, "and such beautiful skin and eyes. One of these days, when I've finished the 'Arlene' series, I'd love to paint you. Would you be up for it?" and Aminah, releasing the lip and jumping to her feet, said of course she would, that it would be an honour, and together they walked into the hall.

"It must have seemed like a miracle when you got pregnant with your daughter and had a healthy birth,"

Aminah said as she opened the door. "Did it somehow make up for the miscarriages?" and when Ella hesitated and dropped her gaze to the floor, she added gently, "I've heard it doesn't always …"

They stood for a while at the door in silence, and then Ella said, "No, it doesn't always," and then she turned and gave Aminah a grateful hug. "Thank you for a lovely morning, Aminah," she said, "and for introducing me to Grace, and for letting me talk about things. I never have before, you know, and it does help," and she stepped out of Aminah's embrace and began to walk carefully down the concrete stairs, hanging onto the metal handrail.

When she reached the first landing she looked up and saw that Aminah was still there, arms resting on the balustrade, hair hanging like wavy blue-black curtains on either side of her face, smiling down at her. "It helps me to talk to you too, Ella," she called down, her words echoing back from the walls. "See you on Monday!"

Ella got into her car and turned the key in the ignition, but instead of the usual healthy purr of the engine there was a dull grating sound which sounded as though it could be serious. She tried again, and this time the car coughed into life, but as she drove through the town traffic there was an ominous clunking sound coming from somewhere under the bonnet.

She found a garage, talked to a mechanic, and booked it in, and then she drove carefully on past the harbour, slowing to avoid the bustling crowds that poured out of the Cumbrae ferry and jostled into the street, and even when she was past the crowds and the road widened she continued to drive slowly.

Outside number 22 she parked in a patch of shade, wound down both windows, and sat on for a while, thinking. Today was the first time she'd ever spoken to anyone about the aftermath of the miscarriages, and it had brought home just how profoundly they, and then Lucy's birth, had affected her, and her relationship with Derek.

Because that 'miracle' birth had not, as everyone around her assumed it had, made up for her losses. It had, in fact, come between her and her need to mourn those two tiny, unrecognised, lives, and because she couldn't find words to explain how she was feeling, she felt further and further apart from the people who were supposed to care about her; people like Carys who, distracted by Lucy's charms, could only think of celebration, as though the two children who'd come before had ceased to matter.

But then, Carys, as far as Ella knew, had never had any sort of lasting relationship with anyone except, perhaps, her mother. What could Carys have understood about the mysterious ferocity of maternal love? Or the agony Ella felt when she was unable to love Lucy as deeply and selflessly as she felt she should?

In the end, as Lucy grew out of babyhood, a pleasant enough bond developed between mother and daughter, but despite that Lucy always remained a little separate from Ella, just as Ella's mother had been distant from her. The strong parental bond was always between Lucy and Derek, and when, suddenly and chaotically, Lucy disappeared, Derek and she were left together, but completely and utterly alone.

Next morning, at ten o' clock on the dot, Grace arrived. She was dressed much more casually than the day before, in trainers and a pair of blue-striped dungarees, with a bright pink scarf wound round her head, but still managed to look every bit as stylish.

Ella took two of the three bulging plastic bags she was carrying, led the way upstairs, and showed her into the flat.

"What a weight!" she said as they dumped their bags on the hall floor. "You should have texted me and I'd have come down to the car," and she stretched the ache out of her arms.

Grace laughed and assured her that, as a part-time gallery owner, she was well-used to carrying heavy loads. "Please don't feel obliged to do anything with the Commonplace Books, by the way," she added. "I mean, I know you'll have your own lessons planned, so you could just give them back to the children and let them take them home. I have a feeling, though" - she opened one of the bags and rummaged about inside - "that Molly might ask about them at some point. There are rumours of an HMI inspection in December you know, and this sort of thing ticks a whole load of National Curriculum boxes, if you get my drift."

She rummaged through another bag and finally found what she was looking for. "This is far and away the best one," she said, and she opened it for Ella to see, and flicked through its pages. As she flicked there was, Ella noticed, a distinct smell of rancid coffee. "I mean to say" – Grace stopped at a page and handed the book to Ella – "is that not the most beautiful work you've ever seen? It's just as good as the real ones I found on the internet to show them. The print-outs I made of them are in there too, by the way," she added, "in a folder."

Ella took the Commonplace Book and gazed at the pages Grace had chosen. Each was covered with intricately detailed drawings of trees, their light and shade so carefully observed they looked three-dimensional. The trees were carefully labelled with their names in tiny writing, and beside each was a diagram showing the angles between trunk and main branches. Below, in bright red, there was what looked like some kind of 'star rating'. None of the trees, Ella noticed, had been awarded five stars.

"It's almost unbelievable that a nine-year old could be capable of work like this," she said, "and I bet I know who that nine-year old is," and she closed the book and looked at the cover. Sure enough, the title, printed in perfect capitals formed from tree branches, was 'The Commonplace Book of Jinty McVey'. She flicked through the other pages, but apart from an illustrated recipe for apple crumble and some half-finished drawings of blossom and beech-nuts, most of them were blank.

"I'm afraid Aminah and I spent far too long making the covers and sewing in the signatures," Grace said apologetically, "but I felt it was important the kids appreciated the way these books were made. It worries me that children have less and less interest in real books these days. In fact" - she smiled her wide smile - "children and how they learn's a bit of an obsession of mine."

Ella slipped Jinty's book carefully back into the bag. "I'd definitely like to go on with them," she said. "I love the freedom they give you to explore art and science and poetry and all sorts." She took a step towards the kitchen. "Would you like a coffee? Or a tea, though I'm afraid I don't have mint? Have you time?"

Grace nodded. "I'll risk a milky coffee," she said, "and I'd love to see your work. Aminah's told me about it and it sounds very exciting. If you're sure I'm not keeping you back?"

"My model's not due for another hour, and she's sometimes a bit late," Ella assured her, and she showed her into the studio and went to the kitchen. When she came back with the coffees Grace was standing in the window gazing at 'Arlene Unchained', and for a moment the juxtaposition of this majestic, pregnant woman on her backdrop of beech leaves beside the twisted, tortured image of Arlene made Ella stop in her tracks. She would have liked to have taken a photograph, but was too shy to ask.

"This is a series, right?" Grace said. "Exploring the idea of the ways in which women are imprisoned? And those overblown roses" – she pointed to the freshly-painted array of Queen of Denmarks lying at Arlene's feet – "are so flagrantly sexy, aren't they? They remind me of women lifting up their skirts to lure men in."

"I'm glad you get the reference," Ella smiled. "It came to me a couple of days ago, and now I love the idea of including the different stages of the rose, from tight bud to blatant openness. And I'm much more secure painting roses than people, because I painted almost nothing but for years!"

Grace stepped back from the paintings and studied them again. "You know, Ella, I find your work enormously affecting. Especially now," and she placed a hand on her bump and rubbed it in small circular movements, caressing the unborn child within. When she looked back at Ella, however, her smile had gone. "I get the feeling the woman in your paintings has had her chains imposed on her," she said, "but often we make our own, don't we?"

She took the coffee Ella held out to her. "Max is quite a bit older than me, and he's reached that age when he wants to start a family. And he wants lots of babies," she said between sips. "He swears blind he'll put in just as much as I do in terms of rearing them but honestly, Ella, he won't. I know he won't. We've got two galleries, one in Glasgow and one in Edinburgh, and there is no way on earth he's going to compromise his vision and take an equal share in childcare. Know what I mean?" and she gave Ella a wry look over the rim of the mug.

Ella perched herself on the stool beside the easel. She wanted to say she certainly did know, and that, in her case, all the compromising she'd done hadn't even produced a loving daughter, but she didn't. "I'm sure you'll be assertive when the time comes," she said instead. "More assertive than I was. I've never been great at standing up for myself, but" – she smiled at Grace – "I'm determined to get better at it."

Grace raised one eyebrow but said nothing more, and as she drank her coffee she walked around looking approvingly at the sketches and photographs of Arlene. "Your model is wonderful," she said. "Just look at those mournful eyes, and those expressive hands ..." and when Ella agreed and told her about Arlene's extraordinary double joints she gave a squeal of delight.

"Oh my goodness, what could be better! I just can't wait to see what the two of you come up with next," and she drained her mug and handed it to Ella." You must come and see the Glasgow gallery" - she winked – "soon, before the baby arrives. I'll text you. And now I'd better fly ..."

They were half-way down the stairs when Paul Wetherby's door opened and he clattered down behind them. He was wearing a smart straw hat with a dark band, wide white trousers, and a nattily striped blazer with a gold-emblazoned badge on the top pocket and, as he squeezed past them both, Ella noticed Grace give him a quizzical look. She also noticed that, as Wetherby overtook them, he tugged the brim of the hat down, as though not wanting Grace to see his face.

"I take it he's your neighbour?" Grace asked when the front door slammed behind him, and when Ella said he was, she frowned. "I'm sure I've seen him before, you know, and I think it might have been in the gallery. What does he do?"

"I don't really know, but I get the impression he's some sort of minister. He's certainly very religious. Did you get the impression he was avoiding you?"

Grace frowned and nodded. "I've got an uncomfortable feeling about him, you know. It was a while ago, but I'm sure he came to the gallery with a young woman and there was some kind of row. I'll ask Max as soon as I get home …" and she stepped out into the sunshine then turned to hug Ella. "Thanks for the coffee" – she gave her a peck on the cheek – "and be sure and let me know when you've got some more gorgeous paintings to show me!"

15

To Ella's surprise, Arlene arrived five minutes early, and as soon as she opened the door she could see she was in high spirits.

"I've done it," she said as she led the way upstairs. "I've booked a place to stay in London, and I've got my train ticket, and I'm going at the beginning of October" – she stopped to beam round at Ella – "by which time I'll have saved enough to pay for my food and accommodation. I sent my photo – the one you took - to fifteen agencies and twelve of them gave me casting appointments. Can you believe it, Ella? *Twelve!*"

She ran on into the studio and began peeling off her clothes and Ella, who'd completely forgotten the shots she'd taken of Arlene at the end of one of their sessions, smiled and congratulated her. Then she went to the easel and asked her to adopt the pose for the 'Arlene Unchained' painting.

"This'll be the last session on this one," she said as she adjusted the folds of the chiffon. "I just need to do some more to your face and hands, and adjust the shadows and *then,* young lady" – she breathed in through her teeth – "you are going to have to fly, though heaven knows how," and when Arlene looked enthusiastically up at the light fitting she smiled and shook her head.

"I'm going to get a ladder and attach you to it somehow, and then I'll use shadows to give the illusion of you floating in mid-air. That's why I needed the studio to be white box - so I could play around with space. When you're a supermodel," she added, laughing, "you'll get to do all sorts of aerial acrobatics, but right now my ceiling's not ready for a trapeze," and she took her place at the easel and began to intensify the shadows around Arlene's nose.

By lunchtime they were finished, and as Arlene got dressed and Ella put her brushes in white spirit, an idea occurred to her. From what Grace had said, there seemed little doubt that Wetherby had had some sort of altercation in their gallery, and the more she thought about what he'd said about Flick and galleries, the more likely it seemed that she was the young woman Grace remembered. Now Wetherby was safely away in his natty blazer, presumably at some bowling green somewhere. When Arlene left, maybe she'd do a bit of snooping ...

Arlene, however, was in no hurry to go. "I've done some pen and ink drawings I'd like to show you," she said rather coyly, and she took a thick roll of paper out of her backpack, unfurled the drawings, and laid them out on the floor. "What do you think?"

There were five drawings in all. They all had harsh desert backdrops and very dark blue skies, and were filled with images of bodies skewered to the ground by gigantic thorns, with acid-green snakes writhing in and out of their various orifices. They were far too violent and brash for Ella's taste, but she could see Arlene was an excellent draughtsman with a vivid, if macabre, imagination.

"They're very well done," she said. "Actually, they remind me of tattoos," and immediately Arlene's eyes lit up.

"That's exactly what they're meant to do," she said. "My plan is to make a pile of money with my modelling, rent a shop, and run the coolest tattoo parlour in Glasgow. Or in London, who knows?" She gathered up the drawings, stuck them back in her backpack, and took the envelope Ella handed to her. "OK," she said, "see you next Saturday, and thanks," and she was off.

Ella looked out of the living-room window to check Wetherby's car was still gone. Then she ran across the hall, unhooked her keyring, and hurried out onto the landing. She stood for a moment outside Wetherby's door with the key poised and then, before she had the chance to tell herself this was a perfectly dreadful way to behave and she mustn't even think about doing it, she inserted the key, turned it, and headed straight for the living room. After another guilty glance out of the window, she took Flick's 'Juno and the Peacock' painting off the wall and turned it over.

Sure enough, the back of the painting had a label stuck to it that read: 'Juno and the Peacock', Felicity Hunter, 2004, and underneath was an elegant gold sticker with 'Max James Fine Art, Glasgow & Edinburgh', and two phone numbers.

She turned the painting back over and, freed from the confines of Wetherby's presence, examined every bit of it closely, marvelling again at Flick's depiction of Juno's rippling muscles and the birds' jewel-like plumage. Again and again, however, she found herself drawn back to the tiny swan floating on the surface of its faraway little lake. Small as it was, Flick had positioned it dead centre, just above the peacock, so that the viewer's eye was drawn to it. She'd curved its neck and angled its head so that its gaze was downcast and sad, and painstakingly painted the details of its beak and plumage with a brush so tiny it could surely only have had one bristle. There was no doubt that this swan was as important as any of the other birds in Juno's menagerie, and Ella recalled the flying swans in the shed, and the mirror in the bathroom with its two swans, necks entwined.

Carefully, she replaced the painting on the wall and began to make her way back out, but before she left she couldn't resist taking a look at the other public room, and when she opened its door she saw it was laid out as a library and study. Panelled in dark wood, it had bookcases lining two of the walls from floor to ceiling, and in front of the window there was an imposing mahogany desk on which sat a simple wooden cross. She crept in to take a closer look at the books, and saw that almost all of them were theological texts.

There was, she thought, something oppressively holy about the room. Even the smell – a mix of wood polish, paper, and Mint Imperials - reminded her of the church she and Gran had gone to every Sunday. She could swear she smelled Wetherby's cologne too, and as his invisible presence made her feel more and more uneasy, she hurried back out of the flat to prepare herself a late lunch.

By the time she'd eaten, then washed out her brushes with warm soapy water, it was nearly three. Her plan for the afternoon had been to go to IKEA to search for a comfortable chair for the studio, but lunch had made her sleepy and the thought of a longish drive on a warm Saturday was less and less appealing. In the end, she took a drawing pad and some pencils into the living-room and began to sketch out the next painting – the one in which Arlene would break free from her chains and fly.

She sketched a rough outline of the ladder, then experimented with various positions in which she could place Arlene without actually endangering her life, and as she drew she was reminded of the image of the stark wooden cross on Wetherby's desk.

That was it. The next painting would be a prelude to the rising, with Arlene's broken body, bound by chains, hanging as though from an invisible crucifix. It would be a strong, emotive image not only of imprisonment but also of self-sacrifice, and for a brief heady moment she allowed herself to imagine Grace's reaction when she saw it. Then she began to picture the walls of 'Max James Fine Art' covered with her paintings, and Aminah and Grace and Arlene in their smartest clothes, with their glasses of champagne, admiring them.

Shaking the fantasy away, she sat down with her sketch pad to think about the details of the third pose. The shadows on the blinds were hazy and ill-defined now, a sign the sun had already dipped down low in the sky, and she pulled them up and stood looking out at the beech tree. The summer sheen was gone from its leaves now, and soon their greens would start to show signs of the autumn browning. Despite her earlier elation, Ella felt a tiny hint of the sadness the season always brought with it, and she moved into the living room and, feet up on the settee, watched the passers-by on the pavement below.

Wetherby's car still wasn't in its parking space, and she wondered vaguely how long a game of bowls took. Maybe it went on all afternoon and into the evening. Maybe there were cups of tea and cucumber sandwiches afterwards.

She relaxed back in the settee and tried very hard to think about the next 'Arlene' painting rather than worry about tomorrow afternoon's bread-and-honey afternoon tea with Harry Flood, and she was beginning to drift into sleep when a noise from the street woke her and, kneeling up, she saw a car nearing the house. It was travelling slowly, and she assumed it was Wetherby home from the bowling green, but when it came to his parking space it didn't stop but continued to crawl, ever more slowly, by.

Blinking her sleepiness away, Ella stood up. She stared down at the car, and before it gathered speed again she saw that it was not Wetherby's after all. His was grey, and this one was black, and it was being driven by a man wearing a brown hat with a small brim.

16

Ella was a bag of nerves from the moment she woke on Sunday morning, after a more or less sleepless night, and as she cut up a grapefruit for breakfast and waited for the kettle to boil she teased out the various reasons for that nervousness.

One reason was the glimpse she'd had yesterday of the black car with its brown-hatted man creeping slowly past the house, and ever since she'd been telling herself not to be ridiculous, that black cars and brown hats were ten a penny, and even though it did sound like the car and the man Yvonne claimed to have seen, there was sure to be a perfectly innocent explanation.

Even if it *was* the same man who'd hung about outside the school - it was children he was interested in. He'd no reason to stalk one of the teachers, and how could he possibly know where she lived? It was all just a coincidence but all the same, Ella knew that every time she left the house she'd be looking from left to right, checking to see if he was there.

She took the coffee and grapefruit through to the studio and, glad of the protective curtain of leaves, sat down on the floor cushion and addressed the other reason for her agitation which was, of course, the impending afternoon tea with Harry Flood. And *that*, she told herself impatiently, was something she really must put into perspective.

It was all very well to drink half a bottle of red wine and fantasise about the first man she'd found attractive in two decades, and it was perfectly justifiable to tell herself that she was a free woman now and could do whatever the hell she wanted, but when she thought about it in the sober light of day, the whole thing was completely impractical and could only lead to trouble.

Harry Flood was a married man and - if those tears of Caroline were anything to go by – he might be a bit of a philanderer. If she were stupid enough to let herself be drawn into something with him, she'd land herself in a horribly complicated situation for which she didn't have the time or the energy. And besides, she wasn't a silly romantic little girl, she was a serious artist with an exhibition to put together, and she mustn't – she absolutely mustn't - let herself be side-tracked.

She finished her coffee, showered, then concentrated on making captions for the Commonplace Books display, but when that was done and she went on to the more brainless task of mounting Grace's photocopies of antique Commonplace Books onto black card, the butterflies began to gather in earnest, and by lunchtime she felt so sick she couldn't eat a thing, which made the butterflies worse.

Eventually she took herself off to IKEA and bought the comfortable chair for the studio, and then she had another shower and chose what to wear and finally, on the dot of three, she presented herself at Harry's door and was shown into the living room, which was the room directly below her studio. The room had pale yellow walls and generous scattering of pastel-coloured gingham cushions, and almost all the furniture was scrubbed pine, all of which combined with the homely smell of freshly-baked bread to give the place a thoroughly wholesome, happily-married feel.

"Have a seat," Harry said as he took the pot of miniature roses Ella had chosen for him, "and these are lovely, thank you. The painting's over there" - he pointed to a rather dark corner over by the window - "if you want to take it down and have a look while I make the tea. It's called 'Aristaeus and the Death of the Bees', and you'll have to excuse the dust," and he went off to the kitchen; and as Ella took the painting down and examined it in the light of the window it occurred to her that, judging from his flushed cheeks and damp hairline, Harry might be even more nervous than she was.

The painting was the same size as Wetherby's, and the sky and grass the same vivid blue and acidic green and, like the 'Juno and the Peacock' picture, everything was painted in exquisite detail. In the foreground, seated on the stump of a tree, was a long-haired woman wearing a gauzy pink dress out of which hung one ample breast. She had an expression of utter despair on her downturned face, and when Ella looked down she saw that the reason for her distress was the slender green snake that gripped one of her ankles in its fangs. In the background, and apparently oblivious to the unfolding drama of woman and snake, a bearded man holding a bell-shaped beehive was staring down in horror at the stream of dead bees cascading out of the beehive's doorway, to lie in a dark pile on the ground below.

"Here we are now," Harry came in with a big tray loaded with jars and plates and teacups and a great mound of thickly-sliced brown bread. Grinning proudly, he set the tray down on a low table and turned to walk out again. "I'll just go and fetch the teapot and then, while the tea's infusing,

I'll tell you the tragic story of Aristaeus and Eurydice - what I can remember of it, that is."

Ella looked back at the painting. This time, she looked past the distraught figure of Aristaeus with his dead bees and the agonised Eurydice with her writhing little snake and saw, above Flick's signature, a small pond on which floated the familiar form of a downcast swan.

"Did Flick always put a swan in her paintings?" she asked Harry when he returned with the teapot and joined her at the window, and he peered at the painting as though seeing it for the first time.

"To be honest," he said, "I've no idea. I never saw any of Flick's other paintings, though I do remember her saying they were all inspired by Greek myths." He stopped suddenly, as though he'd run out of steam, and Ella noticed that his damp hairline was now beaded with perspiration. "Anyway," he wiped his brow then scraped the hand through his hair, "as far as I recall the woman's Eurydice, and the reason she's getting bitten is because she ran away from Aristaeus, who was hell-bent on trying to rape her."

Something in Ella's memory stirred. "Is that not why his bees died? Wasn't it a punishment?" and Harry nodded slowly.

"Yes, of course – yes, that was what it was. And was the punishment not all down to the nymphs?" and he turned and gave her an impish look. "I'm pretty sure that was the kind of stuff nymphs did back then. I mean, I've not read any Greek myths since Uni, but I seem to remember they were heavily into the old crime-and-retribution thing."

He squinted closer to the painting, and Ella caught the spice scent of his aftershave. "I never noticed the little swan before though," he said. "He looks pretty miserable, doesn't he? As though no-one's paying him any attention," and he laughed, rather too loudly. "Caroline couldn't stand the painting," he went on, "which is why it's banished to the corner. Now, how do you like your tea?"

They'd gone over to the settee then, and Ella sat down on it while Harry took the big armchair opposite, and as they tucked into the bread and honey Ella rehearsed the questions she'd planned to ask him about Flick. She didn't, however, ask anything right away. The botched interrogation of Paul Wetherby had taught her to take her time and tread warily.

"I really enjoyed meeting Maeve Oliver," she said instead. "She's a lovely person, and we had such a good chat, but I did notice from time to time she seemed to sort of lose concentration and become quite" – she paused to think how best to describe it, and noticed that Harry was nodding slightly – "absent, you know, which made me wonder if she might have the beginnings of Alzheimer's? My mother recently died of it, you see, and I remember it starting like that. Have you noticed too?"

Harry gave a more definite nod. "I'm not sure about Alzheimer's," he said, "but I know what you mean about the absences, and I'd say they started after her husband died, a couple of years back. I'd imagine she misses him although, just between you and me, I never liked the man. I thought he had a cruel streak, you know. Before he retired he was a banker, but in his spare time he basically slaughtered anything that moved."

Ella looked at him in alarm. "What kind of things?"

"Pheasants, rabbits, hare, deer, all sorts. The farmers got him to shoot crows and pigeons too, and Caroline and I had to pretend we were veggies so's he didn't keep bringing us awful carcasses," and he picked up the butter dish, which was filled with neat little curls of butter, and leant over to offer it to Ella. As he waited for her to remove two of the curls, she noticed that he was watching her carefully, and she hoped she wouldn't drop anything.

"Has she any children?" she asked, spreading the butter thickly on her bread, and when Harry didn't immediately answer she looked up and saw his brows were furrowed.

"She has a son. His name's Nathan, and from what I've seen of him he's a bit of a strange, distant individual. Apparently Maeve had her heart set on him studying Music, but he dropped out and I'm not sure what he does now, other than loaf about and visit his mother once in a blue moon. As you'll gather, I don't have a lot of time for him ..."

He grinned over at Ella. "Are you managing all right with that honey, Ella? It's helluva runny in this hot weather, isn't it just. Hang on and I'll get you a serviette ..." and he bounded out of the room, reminding her once again of the young, awkward Derek, then returned with a handful of paper napkins.

He handed one apologetically to her and she made to take it, but somehow both her hands had become impossibly sticky, and as she struggled to open it out he took it back and, very carefully and tenderly, laid it on her lap and smoothed out its creases. As he smoothed, he looked down at her, and when she dared to meet his eyes she saw there was a tenderness in them that made her blush, and she was glad when he handed her another two serviettes and sat back down.

"I got the impression that Maeve was extremely attached to Flick," Ella said, "and that she misses her terribly. Was she? I mean, were they very close?" She made sure she looked at her hands rather than Harry, and that she spoke in a casual, conversational way, but she could see his face had become grave again.

"We all liked Flick," he said, and then, after a pause, "and we all miss her, but yes, you're right, Maeve and she were particularly close. They shared that love of music, you see, and Flick was a beautiful singer." He looked over towards the painting, and when he spoke again his tone was thoughtful. "I'd never thought of it before, but she was probably the daughter Maeve never had, and maybe she made up for her son. She used to accompany Flick on the piano you know, though of course Flick herself was a very good harpsichord player ..." He raised his eyes up to the ceiling, and Ella pictured the big triangular shape on the wall opposite the fireplace that had puzzled her.

"Caroline and I would sometimes hear her practising," Harry went on, "and sometimes she'd sing, and occasionally you'd hear other voices too, and something that sounded like a flute. Would you like a top-up?" He leaned over and poured some tea into Ella's cup, and as he did he smiled down at her – a strange, wistful, little smile. "I must say I rather liked the singing myself, but Caroline wasn't keen, so she always cleared off to Waitrose. Still, each to his own."

For a moment Ella had the feeling he was going to say something else, but then he seemed to think better of it. "Would you like to come and see the hives?" he said instead. "See where your honey started life?" and when Ella said she wasn't sure that she did, that she wasn't keen on bees up close and *en masse*, he looked quite deflated.

"You did tell me Flick got stung," she reminded him, "and you said it was because she was upset, so maybe bees are like horses and smell your fear," and, rather guilty at having disappointed him, she took another slice of bread, smeared it thickly with butter, and dribbled more honey on top.

Harry, however, wasn't so easy to deflate. "I'll make sure you don't get stung," he said. "I've a veiled hat and some gloves you can wear, and I'll use my smoker to calm them down, just to be on the safe side. I'd really love you to see them, you know. I mean, they're in your garden so they're partly yours ..." and he waited while she finished the slice then leapt up so enthusiastically she felt she really couldn't refuse. In any case, she remembered as she followed him into the garden, she needed to ask him if he'd a ladder he could lend her.

When they were in the garden, Harry opened the door of a large lean-to shed and, peering in over his shoulder, Ella saw that there was, as she'd hoped, a tall aluminium ladder leaning against the wall at the far end. She waited while he gathered up a pile of equipment, and when he'd handed her the veiled hat and a pair of thick leather gloves and helped her put them on, she squinted through the mesh and watched as he lit a little metal device with bellows attached. When he was satisfied it was belching out a strong enough stream of smoke, he pulled on his own hat and gloves, lifted the lid off one of the hives, and pumped smoke in. The garden filled with the acrid smell of burning paper.

"The smoke makes them drowsy," Harry explained as he lifted out a comb seething with what didn't, to Ella, look like particularly drowsy bees, "but actually these little fellows are workers so they're usually pretty laid back anyway. The smoke's more of a precaution against the guard bees, because sometimes they take it into their heads to protect the hive" – he brushed a couple of bees off his trousers and grinned when Ella winced and backed away – "and that's when you want to make a sharp exit because, believe me, they are lean mean stinging machines!"

He rolled up his sleeve to reveal a line of livid red marks. "See?" he said. "They had a field day yesterday. The problem with them is when they decide to go on the rampage they emit an alarm pheromone that attracts other guard bees, so it can end up being a bit of a stinging frenzy," and he replaced the comb and lifted out another. "I'd just love you to see the queen," and, quite oblivious to Ella's growing discomfort, he turned all his attention to turning the comb this way and that. "There's a wee daub of green paint on her back," he muttered, more to himself than Ella, "so she should be easy to spot …"

Ella stood very still then while Harry told her all about how he marked his queens, and how he organised his hives, and how and when he collected honey, and she tried her best to pay attention and ask intelligent questions, but the veil of her hat was covered in a swarming mass of bees now, and the noise of the buzzing was growing louder and more determined. Harry's trousers were crawling with bees too, and she was terrified some of them would find their way onto her bare legs, and the more he talked, and the more bees he brushed off his clothes, the more nervous she became. Eventually it all became too much for her, and she stepped back from the hives.

"That was very interesting, Harry," she said, politely but firmly, "but I'm afraid I'm going to have to have to forego the queen for today," and she walked briskly up the path away from him, pulled off the hat and gloves, checked them carefully for stray bees, and went into the shed. She sat down on Flick's little chair and sank back, savouring the silence.

The other day, while she was removing the mouldy blanket and cushion, she'd noticed books on top of the trunk against the walls and now, in the light from the window, she saw there were two of them lying, covers upwards as though Flick had stopped reading and wanted to keep her place. One was a book of Sylvia Plath's poems, and the other a book of Greek Mythology which had been left open at a coloured illustration of the legend of Leda and the Swan, and for a few moments Ella sat reading the myth, glancing back and forth at the image of the beautiful woman being raped by Zeus in the shape of a swan.

It was, without doubt, a distinctly shocking – even disgusting - image, and yet Leda didn't look one bit as though she was being subjected to a bestial assault. Quite the reverse, in fact – the expression on her face as, head thrown back, she accepted the amorous swan's kisses, was positively orgasmic, as though an erotic game was being played out in which both capturer and captor were complicit. Much to her surprise, Ella found the idea of it more than a little arousing and, still holding the book, she sank back in the chair, closed her eyes, and, suddenly pleasantly drowsy, put herself in Leda's place as she was chased along the waterside by the lustful swan-god.

Squeezing her eyes tight shut so that none of the sunlight from the window filtered through, she imagined the terrible cracklings of branches as his wings flapped up and down and the wingtips brushed against the trees, and the deep, lustful hissings that came from his throat as he stretched out his neck to catch her hair, and how, holding up the hem of her gossamer-thin dress, she ran for her life, bare feet bruised and scratched by stones and thorns.

The sun's heat caressed her skin, and she could feel herself on the brink of sleep but, more than a little aroused now, she stuck with her fantasy, imagining herself looking over her shoulder and realising the great white bird was gaining on her, till at last he was so close she could smell his fishy breath and see the froth on his beak and the lust in his deep black eyes.

On and on she ran along the side of the pond, knowing that, in the end, there was nowhere to go, that in the end he must catch her; and when, finally, she tripped on a tree-root and crashed to the ground and he was above her, his outstretched wings beating over her, she felt herself give up the struggle. In the rank feathery darkness, crushed tight to his huge sweat-drenched breast, she opened first her lips, and then her throat, to his stone-hard kisses. Arching her back, she wrapped her legs around the great girth of him, and as he entered her she threw back her head and, moaning in pain and ecstasy, submitted to his wild thrusting.

When the fantasy was over, it took Ella a few moments to shake herself back to reality, and even when she'd stood up and walked to the door her legs still trembled with the newness of the feelings it had evoked. For a while she stood breathing in the scents of the garden, and as her heartbeat slowed the realisation filtered into her consciousness that this was the first time in years she'd felt sexual; that sexual fulfilment was just another of the things she'd forced herself to accept had gone forever – things like happiness, and self-worth, and hope for the future; and the more she kept hold of that long-lost feeling of joyful abandonment, the more she felt something timeless – primeval, almost – begin to release itself from the chains she'd wrapped around it and fly, triumphantly, upwards.

Out in the garden she could hear the shed door being opened and, laying Flick's book back on the trunk, she gathered up Harry's gloves and hat and hurried out to join him. She apologised for having had to leave, assured him she was fine, and asked him if she might possibly borrow his ladder. Then she let him carry it upstairs for her, but at the door she told him she was perfectly capable of taking it into the studio herself and, to her relief, he handed it over and loped off downstairs.

Two minutes later, however, he was back. "I meant to give you this," he said, holding out a jar of honey. "It's last season's finest, and actually it's rather good mixed with whisky, if ever you fancy a nightcap," and he raised one eyebrow at her, in an unashamedly flirtatious way.

Blushing, Ella took the honey. She held it up to the light, remarked on how wonderfully golden it was, and thanked him again for the lovely afternoon, and then they stood at the door looking at one another, neither knowing what to do or say next.

"I really hope the bees weren't too much for you," Harry said at last. "I've a tendency to forget that other people don't find them as fascinating as I do, and I'd hate to think you were traumatised?"

Ella said nothing. She was aware of the blush rising into her cheeks and something that felt like a tiny bubble of laughter gurgling up into her throat, and she dipped her head and looked down at the space between them, not trusting herself to meet his gaze.

"You weren't, were you, Ella?" Harry whispered, and when she dared to glance up she saw his lips twitch as though he too might be on the point of laughter. "Tell me you won't be having nightmares tonight," and when she looked down again he put his index finger very lightly under her chin and tipped her head back up so she'd no choice but to face him.

For a moment, before she stepped back and, laughing rather too gaily, assured him her dreams would be as sweet as his honey, she knew he was going to kiss her. And later, safely back in the studio, she found herself imagining, over and over again, what would have happened if he had.

17

On Monday morning Ella was surprised, and very relieved, to find not only Jinty McVey but also Shabana Ahktar waiting for her in the teachers' car park, both desperate to help her heft her various bags and rolls of paper out of the car and along to the classroom.

Since Aminah's 'little talk' with Shabana the previous week there had, apparently, been a significant improvement in her attitude, and as Ella steered the two girls into the school she was pleased to see they seemed to be the best of friends again, and Tracey Bell was nowhere to be seen.

It didn't take long for Jinty to realise what was in the bags, and as soon as they reached the classroom she began to pull out book after book, demanding to know where Ella had got them, and if she'd seen Mrs Nwapa, and if Mrs Nwapa was going to come back and see them, and eventually Ella told her that yes, she *had* got the books from Mrs Nwapa, and that Mrs Nwapa had said to tell them she was very sorry she'd kept them longer than she meant to.

Jinty had gone on pressing for more and more information however, till finally, in desperation, Ella said she was sure that after Mrs Nwapa's baby was born she'd come and see the finished books which, though not strictly true, seemed to satisfy Jinty, who took her Commonplace Book to her table and pored over its pages as though reunited with a long-lost friend.

Shabana picked out her book too and laid it at her place, but her reaction was more polite than enthusiastic and she didn't bother to open it. Instead, she helped Ella distribute the rest of the books, then handed up the captions for her to pin on the wall, and by the time the bell rang and everyone filed in, all Grace's photocopies of antique Commonplace Books were on display.

When Aminah arrived, she and Ella put jars of flowers and small beech twigs on each of the children's tables, along with some well-sharpened coloured pencils, and explained that today they were going to work on their Commonplace Books by doing botanical drawings then writing poems about them. It was a mercifully peaceful lesson, and as Ella walked up and down the rows of tables, pointing out stamens and pistils and the veins of leaves, her thoughts kept drifting back to Harry Flood, standing on the threshold of her flat, tipping back her head and looking down at her with those confoundedly attractive grey eyes of his.

Did she step back into the safety of her hall simply because she was afraid of Harry's wife finding out? Or was it more than that? Was it shame at the thought of having an affair with someone else's husband, because never, in her entire life, had she thought herself capable of such a thing? Or – and she suspected this was the main reason – was it because she was terrified of the strength of her feelings for him, and where those feelings might lead them both?

Her thoughts were interrupted by more and more of the children announcing they'd finished their drawings, and when the playtime bell rang and she and Aminah were on their way to the staffroom, Aminah took her aside and whispered, "You know Social Work's visiting Jinty's house this afternoon? Maura's sure they're going to insist the grandmother's moved to a Dementia Unit, and I've got a feeling Jinty's got wind of it. She's been quite subdued this morning, don't you think?" and Ella agreed that she had.

Aminah pushed the staffroom door open then and was about to go in when Ella suddenly stopped and gasped. "Oh heavens," she said, "that's just reminded me. There was a man in a black car outside my house on Saturday. He had a brown hat on, like the man Yvonne said she saw, and he was kind of loitering. It's probably nothing, but I wondered if I should mention it to Maura. What do you think?"

Aminah stepped back out, closed the staffroom door again, and gave Ella a concerned look. "That's weird," she said. "I mean, if it was the same man, how would he know where you live? And why would he want to stalk you anyway? It's children he's into, surely?"

"That's exactly what I thought," Ella said. "I mean, it gave me a shock at the time, but the more I think about it the more I think it probably wasn't the same man. Anyway, I think I'd better go and tell her anyway, don't you?" and when Aminah agreed it was best to be on the safe side, she asked her to grab her a coffee, and hurried over to the office.

After break, when the children were busy writing their poems on scrap paper, Ella headed up to the back of the class. She knelt on the floor beside Jinty, who was sitting open-mouthed with a pencil loosely held between her teeth, so deep in thought she seemed hardly to notice she was there. At the top of her piece of paper she'd written the word 'Leaves', which she'd decorated with tiny sprigs of beech.

Ella looked at the jar on Jinty and William's table and then at the drawing Jinty had done in the Commonplace Book, and was astounded at what she saw. Today's drawing was even more detailed and lifelike than the ones she'd seen yesterday, with every contour of every leaf so carefully drawn and shaded it looked as though you could pick it up. There were even tiny scallops on the edges of some of the leaves, where they'd been nibbled by insects and, all in all, it was the drawing of a much older child.

Jinty had turned to look at Ella then, though not with any particular interest. Her freckles were more prominent than usual against the paleness of her skin, and her face was veiled with long strands of greasy hair she kept pushing back behind her ears. Her spectacles were cloudier than ever, but Ella could see her eyes were dull and sunken and there were deep purple marks beneath their inner angles, like the ones Arlene had when she was tired.

"You know, Jinty," she said, "you're an extremely gifted artist," and then she cupped her hand over her mouth so that only Jinty could hear. "Maybe one day you'll go to Art School, like Mrs Nwapa and I did. Do you think you'd like that?" and she waited, hoping for more of a response than she got.

For a while Jinty said nothing, and Ella wondered if she'd actually heard the question. Then, taking the pencil out of her mouth, she yawned and rubbed her eyes. "I can't think of words today, miss," she said wearily. "Usually they come to me just like that, but today it feels like they're all fast asleep. Can I please take my Commonplace Book home? I promise I'll get the poem done by next week …"

Ella hesitated. Then she said, "All right, Jinty. I'm sure you'll look after it, won't you? Come and see me when the bell goes, and I'll give you a plastic bag to keep it clean." She leant on the table, ready to stand, but Jinty hadn't finished.

"See tomorrow morning, miss?" she said. "Can I help you in with your bags again?"

"That's very kind of you, Jinty," Ella smiled at her, "but tomorrow I won't have any heavy bags, because I'll be walking to school. Someone's coming from the garage tonight to take my car away to repair it because it's been making a funny noise. But next week, when it's all fixed, I'm sure you can help me again," and she hoisted herself up.

Jinty continued to watch her. "One day, miss, your legs'll be so stiff you'll have to get a stick, won't you?" she said. "That's what happened to my nan, and now she can hardly walk. I'm afraid," she added solemnly, "it's all part of the aging process," and she picked up her pencil and began to write.

Later that afternoon, in *Enzo's,* Aminah banged down her coffee mug and heaved with laughter.

"She actually said that? 'It's all part of the aging process'? Well, you know where she got *that* from, don't you?" and when Ella shrugged she said, "It sounds suspiciously like one of Shabana's pearls of wisdom," and she sighed and shook her head. "I'm all for being frank with children and answering their questions honestly, but I sometimes think that child's parents go into far too much medical detail. And of course Shabana's quite a bit older than Jinty, so she takes in everything she says.

"Anyway" – she took a bite of her doughnut, picked up the mug again, and gulped down its contents – "how was your weekend? Did Grace like your paintings? And did you go to tea with the dishy bee guy?"

Ella fiddled uncomfortably with her teaspoon. She'd forgotten she'd mentioned Harry to Aminah in such glowing terms. "Grace seemed to approve, yes," she said, and then, "actually, *yes* - she liked them, and she said she wants to see more, so I'm hoping when she went home she told her husband, and maybe one of these days he'll ask me to bring them in to the gallery …"

"And the bee guy?" Aminah leaned over, eyes wide. "How was that?"

Ella tore a corner off her Danish Pastry and pretended to eat it. The base of her neck was wet with sweat, and she could feel Aminah's keen eyes watching her every move, and she forced herself to give her a wide smile. "It was really interesting actually," she said brightly. "He showed me one of Flick's paintings - one of her Greek myths, about a man who kept bees, whose name of course I've forgotten - but it was a remarkable piece of work. And what I find very curious is that" – she was aware of talking more and more quickly now, not leaving space for Aminah to interrupt – "in every painting of hers I've seen, there's a tiny swan somewhere in the background, and – did I tell you? – she also painted a couple of swans on the wall of her shed, and there's a beautiful swan mirror in the bathroom too …"

She paused for breath then, aware that her face must be glowing. "Anyway, after that we had a fabulous afternoon tea, with home-made bread and his own honey, and he'd even made the butter into little rolls – I mean, who does that? And afterwards, he showed me his bees," and she frowned over at Aminah, daring her to laugh.

"He showed you his bees, did he?" Aminah gave a little smirk. "And how was that?"

Ella took a deep breath. "Not great, actually. I had to wear a hat with a veil and I hated the buzzing, but the most irritating thing about the whole experience is that in the end I didn't find out anything more about Flick, apart from the fact she hated bees too," and she sighed. "Paul Wetherby wouldn't tell me anything either when I tried to fish for information. He just skirted around it. It's all *so* frustrating."

She picked up her coffee mug and hid behind it, but she could still feel Aminah looking at her and she was sure she was going to ask another leading question. Aminah, however, had other things on her mind. "Why, do you think," she said, "is it so important for you to know what happened to Flick?" and then she turned and gesticulated at Enzo, who scurried over to take her order.

Ella let the question hang in the air between them, and even after Enzo had gone to fetch more coffees, she sat in silence for a while, gathering her thoughts and waiting till her breathing became steadier.

"There's a couple of reasons," she said at last. "The main one is that ever since I moved in I've felt I've been living in the aftermath of something I don't understand, and Paul and Harry's reluctance to tell me anything about it makes me more and more uncomfortable. And the other reason is because of Lucy," and she looked at Aminah, checking she remembered who Lucy was. "She always had issues with her mental health, and even when she was in her late teens and early twenties she was rather childlike and easily led, and about a year ago she disappeared and it worries me dreadfully.

"I get the impression Flick was childlike and vulnerable too," she went on, "and that's why I identify her with Lucy, as though she's my surrogate daughter and I somehow need to know she's all right, which is pathetic I know ..." and she leaned back in her chair and looked out of the window, sightlessly watching the passers-by.

Aminah leaned over and put a hand on her arm. "It's isn't the least bit pathetic, Ella," she said, giving the arm a squeeze. "It's what people do. I'm sure Maura's my surrogate mum, and if I really wanted to upset myself I'd say the arsehole I wasted most of last year with was a surrogate dad. Maybe, you know"- she gave a tentative smile –

"you're a bit of a surrogate auntie to me. I mean," she hastened to add, "not an auntie like *my* old stick-in-the-mud aunties - a right-on, super-cool one. I hope you're OK with that?" and Ella, joining in her laughter, assured her she was more than OK with it.

Then, leaving the difficult subject of Flick behind, she steered the conversation back round to Aminah; and as Aminah poured out her insecurities about her relationship with Sergei, berating herself for her lack of confidence and her self-destructive tendency to want to end it all before it was ended for her, Ella listened and responded as best she could, and gradually the heat left her face and she felt herself return to solid ground.

On the way home, as the car reluctantly clunked and creaked its way to number 22, Ella re-ran Aminah's take on the subject of Flick. It hadn't occurred to her before that she might see Flick as a surrogate daughter, but now she had to agree that was exactly what she was. Come to that, Aminah was probably a surrogate daughter too and so, to a lesser extent, were Arlene and little Jinty, with all their talents and insecurities and dreams and ambitions.

Which only left Harry Flood to categorise, she reflected as she reached the house and the car spluttered to what sounded like a terminal halt. She still wasn't quite sure what he was, but it certainly wasn't a surrogate Derek. He might bear a certain physical resemblance to him, but he was far, far more roguish - which was, of course, a huge part of his charm, and she pulled herself out of the car, checked there were no black cars on the horizon, and walked stiffly up the path.

As soon as she was in the flat she went straight to the living-room window to check again that everything was as it should be, and then she sank down on the red settee to watch the first pink streaks of sunset deepen above Arran's peaks and return to the subject of the relative roguishness of Harry and Derek.

Up until a few months ago, she'd have said that 'roguish' was the very last thing Derek was, that he was far too kind and sensitive and conventional for that. Recent events, however, had thrown that theory into doubt and now, bizarre though the idea was, she was forced to accept that the kind, sensitive, conventional Derek she'd thought she'd known had been replaced by someone entirely different.

For hadn't the evidence she'd acquired of late shown the Derek she'd left to be every bit as roguish as Harry Flood? And didn't that perhaps - just perhaps - give her the right to a tiny bit of roguishness herself?

18

That evening, Jinty pushed herself as far back in the big leatherette armchair as she possibly could and tried to concentrate on her poem, but it was no good. No matter where she sat in her bedroom or what she did to try to occupy her mind she could still hear, through the thin dividing wall, the awful sound of Nan calling Mam's name and then, when Mam didn't come, sobbing and sobbing as though her heart would burst.

When she'd got home from school she could see Mam had been crying too, because her face was blotchy and she had bright red rims below her eyes – or, more precisely - below her *eye,* because the other one was so dark and puffed-up you couldn't see its rim. And even though Jinty was aching to know what had happened that day, she hadn't asked. She never asked anything anymore, because asking only upset Mam and made things worse, so usually she ended up making her a cup of tea and then going upstairs out of the way.

Like Nan, Mam never drank the tea. Jinty knew when she came back down hours later it would still be sitting where she'd left it, cold and untouched, but as she emptied it down the sink she comforted herself with the thought that at least she'd sone *some*thing.

She'd propped the Commonplace Book, open at today's botanical drawing, on top of the chest of drawers, and now she got up and fetched it. Balancing it carefully on the window-sill where she could see the details of the leaves more clearly, she tried again to focus all her concentration on the poem she was trying to write.

Mrs Nwapa had been good at poetry as well as art. She'd told them she listened to poems while she was painting, provided of course they were good poems and read by someone with a nice voice, and she said it stimulated her imagination and steered it down hitherto unexplored pathways, so quite often, when they were busy at their drawings or their sculptures or collages, she'd take out a poetry book and read from it.

Jinty loved the feeling of having her hands busy with a paintbrush, or a stick of chalk, or a pencil, while Mrs Nwapa's words danced their way round her brain. Sometimes, the rhythm of a poem or its rhyming pattern would stick in her mind so fast that later, even hours later when she was in bed, she'd remember it. Then she'd make up her own poems, and sometimes she'd even set them to music and sing them softly to herself to make her fall asleep.

Not all poems had to rhyme of course, but Jinty preferred the ones that did, and Mrs Nwapa had shown them a good way to start to write a rhyming poem, which was to make a list of the main words and then, below, a list of all the words that sounded like them. She'd already started doing that at the back of her red notepad, and so far she'd printed 'leaves' in capitals and then, below, 'thieves' and 'heaves' and 'believes', but that was as far as she'd got. She knew roughly what she wanted the poem to say, which was to compare Nan's face, with all its wrinkles and furrows and fissures, to the beech leaves with their smooth greenness that changed to rough brown in autumn. But even though she kept looking at her drawing for inspiration, not one single line came.

Shabs was always talking about 'inspiration' these days. Since her little talk with Miss Ahktar she'd completely broken with Tracey Bell, and at first, when she'd told her she wasn't friends with Tracey anymore because she and her gang were 'time-wasters', Jinty had been relieved beyond measure. She'd assumed that now Tracey was out of the picture everything would go back to normal, but it didn't. Shabs had changed, and even though Jinty couldn't put her finger on quite *how* she'd changed, being with her felt like being with a different person.

She'd noticed it especially that Saturday. They'd met at the tree circle as they always did, and Shabs had brought cartons of orange juice and Jinty had brought crisps, and before they'd had their picnic they'd gone for a walk along the river and looked out for sticklebacks, but all the while Shabs was quiet and distant, as though the things Jinty wanted to talk about were no longer important to her. As though she'd outgrown them.

Shabs didn't, for example, seem to want to discuss their teachers the way they always used to, so when Jinty said she wasn't sure whether it felt good to have a male teacher at last or whether it was, actually, a bit of a disappointment, she just shrugged and said they'd have to wait and see. Neither did she want to discuss the possibility that Miss Blyth, despite her advancing years, might turn out to be just as wonderful as Mrs Nwapa but in a different way, and even when Jinty asked how the 'Teddy Bears' Picnic' show was shaping up, it evoked no dewy-eyed description of how amazing the stage set was going to be, or how beautiful and mysterious Shab's costume was, or how utterly dishy Aryan looked in his. Instead, Shabs had stopped walking and turned to Jinty with a world-weary expression.

"I'm beginning to realise how much I have to learn from Aryan," she said, and her voice was so soft and serious Jinty had to strain to hear it above the gurgling of the water. "I mean, it's not just about inspiration - though of course he does *utterly* inspire me - it's also about the complete dedication he has to his art."

She'd looked far into the distance then, beyond the river to where the trees were just showing traces of gold. "It's all about having a burning ambition," she went on. "That's what Aryan says. He says you have to accept you've been given a special talent, and then dedicate your life to being the very best you can possibly be at it, no matter how difficult that is." She turned to look at Jinty then, and Jinty saw that her dark brown eyes were so bright they looked as though they'd been lined with silver.

Shabs had walked away then, taking long fast strides, and at first Jinty ran to keep up with her. Soon, however, she realised that Shabs no longer wanted to be with her, and she gave up. She walked very slowly up to the tree circle, crawled inside the den, and ate both packets of crisps one after the other. They left her mouth salty and very dry.

It was dark by the time Jinty gave up on the poem and closed her notepad and, apart from the low murmur of voices from the television, the house was silent. Hungry now, she crept downstairs to the kitchen and found a tin of baked beans and a white loaf. She put two slices of bread into the toaster, washed a pan and tipped the beans into it, and when everything was ready she put it on a tray and took it into the living-room. Mam was sitting in her chair with a tumbler in her hand, glassily watching a film.

"The shop's given me the sack," she said, not taking her eyes off the television. "They say I'm too" – she paused for a moment, thinking – "un-re-lia-ble," and she said the word very slowly, syllable by syllable. Her chin was wet from the stuff in the tumbler and her eyes didn't seem to be able to focus. "And those bastards from Social Work say your Nan's to go into a home. They say we're not coping any more, and if things don't improve they'll have to reassess our situation ..."

Jinty cut a corner off the toast and steered it into her mouth, but it just lay there getting softer and softer and she wished she could spit it back out. "What's 'reassess'?" she said when she'd managed to get it down, and when Mam didn't answer she repeated the question, louder. "What's 'reassess', Mam? Does it mean me getting put into Care?"

But Mam wouldn't answer. She just shrugged and said she didn't know, that she didn't know anything anymore, and then she topped up the tumbler, and when Jinty asked again about the Care thing she told her not to shout, that she'd upset Nan and surely Nan was upset enough as it was.

Jinty cut off another tiny corner of toast, and as she pressed it to the roof of her mouth with her tongue she tried to imagine she wasn't in the dark little living-room with Mam staring at the television but in school, in the bright sunny classroom, at her table opposite William Law, with the botanical drawing beside her and Miss Blyth saying nice things about it.

'You know, Jinty,' she'd said this morning, 'you're an extremely gifted artist,' and then hadn't she gone on to talk about going to Art School? Hadn't she asked her if she'd like to do that?

She hadn't answered - hadn't even nodded – because she'd been so choked up inside she couldn't trust herself to. If she *had* answered, if she'd said what she was thinking, which was: 'Of course I'd like to go to Art School. I'd like that more than anything in the entire world,' she'd be bound to start to cry with the sheer frustration of it all, because how on earth could she ever do that? How could someone like Jinty McVey think they could study Art and become an artist? She didn't even possess a decent set of colouring pencils, and now Mam had lost her job there wouldn't be enough money to buy any. Going to Art School and becoming an artist was the sort of thing Mrs Nwapa did, and Miss Blyth did, and Shabs could do, if that was what she wanted. It wasn't something *she* could ever do.

She cut off a larger piece of toast and, not caring any more that tomato sauce was dribbling down her chin and ending up on the velour cushion, shoved it into her mouth and chewed it noisily, like an animal would chew. Then, abandoning the knife and fork, she ripped off mouthful after mouthful, and as she gulped the food down she looked over at Mam, asleep now with her mouth wide open and looking just like Nan, and she felt her head begin to pound, as though the inside of it was swelling like an over-ripe tomato.

What if Miss Blyth had thought she wasn't interested in Art? What if she'd assumed, because she hadn't said she'd like to go to Art School, that she didn't? That it wasn't important to her that she'd a talent for Art? And if that was what Miss Blyth thought, would she now lose interest in her? Would she not bother to praise her drawings anymore?

The over-ripe tomato in her head was pushing dangerously against the inside of her skull now and Jinty could imagine its skin splitting and stuff oozing out and drowning her brain. Moving the tray to one side and jumping to her feet, she went back through to the kitchen and stood at the sink, looking out at the darkness. There was a big moon in the sky, and she could see the grey shapes of the long grass that grew where once upon a time Nan had had her rose-garden, and beyond the grass the outlines of the trees she and Gramps had planted before they'd even had Mam. Then she let her eyes drift up beyond the canopies of the trees and, staring directly at the moon, picked out the dim shapes that might be craters, and the bright lines of light that might be who knew what? Moon rivers?

She stared and stared at the mysterious shapes, and as she did she felt the pressure in her head begin to ease, and as the moonlight trickled down into her brain it brought with it thoughts she'd never had before or, if she had, had never been able to put words to. It was like the feeling she sometimes had when a poem she'd been struggling with for ages began to come - as though the words and images that poured into her consciousness came from somewhere other than herself. It was like being full of light, that feeling; of being able to see properly.

And what she saw – what dawned on her in the moonlight – was that Shabs wasn't the only one who could be inspired and dedicated and have a burning ambition. *She* had a burning ambition too, and it was to go to Art School and become an artist, and as soon as that came clear she knew she *had* to tell Miss Blyth about it. In fact, she had to do more than that. She had to *show* her how inspired she was, and how dedicated she was willing to be, and in that moment she knew exactly what to do.

She'd pick flowers – lots and lots of flowers – and cover page after page of the Commonplace Book with drawings of them, and she'd take care to put all the dark shadowy bits in, and all the light bits, so that the petals and the leaves appeared to grow out of the page, and when she'd done enough drawings she'd show them to Miss Blyth, and tell her about her burning ambition, and ask her what she should do next.

She'd need coloured pencils of course, but she'd take them from school and be careful not to damage them, and afterwards she'd put them back, so that it was borrowing rather than stealing; and as for the flowers, she'd pick them from Miss Blyth's garden, just like Miss Blyth had done.

Miss Blyth's car was going into the garage tomorrow and she'd be walking home from school, so in the morning she just had to spin Mam some story about having to stay late at school, and then when the bell went give Shabs the slip and follow Miss Blyth home, which would be easy enough because of that bad leg of hers.

She'd wait till she'd gone into her house, and then she'd creep into her garden and pick the flowers. She'd run all the way home with them and put them in water, and every day she'd draw them, and if she needed more she'd go back for them, because by then she'd know where Miss Blyth lived. She'd know where Miss Blyth lived, so she could go there whenever she wanted and maybe – just maybe – one of the days she went, Mrs Nwapa would be there too, so she could show the drawings to her as well.

19

As arranged, a couple of mechanics from the local garage arrived bright and early on Tuesday morning to load Ella's car onto a breakdown vehicle and tow it away, and because it *was* so bright and early, and she was for once unencumbered by her usual bags and rolls of paper, as soon as she'd finished breakfast she set off for a leisurely walk to school along the sea front.

It was the first time she'd seen the streets so empty of people, and as she strolled along beside the sea with its soaring seagulls circling above her like children's toys dangling from invisible nursery ceilings, she scanned the houses on the other side of the road, trying to work out which one had been Gran's. She'd no memory at all of the house itself, and in any case all the houses that sat high above Largs Bay were rather similar, but she could remember the view. It was stamped on her memory as clearly as if it were yesterday that Gran and she stood at the window of the big front room and Gran pointed out the overlapping islands of Great Cumbrae, and Little Cumbrae, and the Isle of Bute, and the bluey-grey peaks of Arran looming behind them all.

They'd stand there together for ages sometimes, watching the ferries chug to and fro, and Gran would cling onto the handle of her walking stick with her red misshapen hands as she told Ella stories of marauding Vikings and the bloody battles the valiant Scots had fought against them. Sometimes, when she got particularly excited, two crimson dots would appear high up on her cheeks, as though she'd rubbed a finger on her lips then pressed on spots of lipstick. On those occasions, Ella would watch in wonder as, eyes gleaming and wild strands of straight white hair escaping from their usual neat bun, Gran waved the stick in the air like a battle-axe and vented her rage at the raping, pillaging Norwegians who'd dared to try and vanquish the proud Scottish people.

Ella had found Gran's tales of bloody battles and eventual victory immensely stirring, but even in the early days she was careful not to relay them to her mother. She was, of course, far too young to understand the politics of Scottish Nationalism, but very early on had somehow picked up her mother's antipathy towards it and knew, in the wordless way of children, that any mention of Gran's nationalistic leanings could jeopardise the longed-for summer visits - all of which gave Gran's storytelling a sense of danger and secrecy that greatly heightened its excitement.

A loud peal of church bells rang out the half-hour and, looking across the road, Ella saw she was standing directly opposite a rather imposing church made of red sandstone, and she crossed and stood on the pavement, looking up at the familiar flight of steps that led to its big red door. The door had four big black hinges, and all of a sudden Ella remembered those hinges, and how like the tendrils of giant plants she'd always thought they looked. The traffic was building up now and she knew she should hurry, but she couldn't resist standing for a moment or two longer, gazing up at the tall spire.

There was a large blue sign to the right of the door with 'St Columba's Parish Church' printed in white letters, but she already knew it was Gran's church, the one she attended every Sunday come rain or shine; and suddenly another memory appeared, vivid as a photograph, of Gran in her Sunday suit the colour of strong Ribena, and her matching velvet hat with its big stitched-on flower, sitting beside her, straight-backed as the pew itself. Moving closer to the noticeboard, she read the various bits of information printed in smaller letters and then, walking briskly now, hurried on to school.

The sun was warm, and Ella kept up a good pace, but no matter how fast she walked she couldn't rid herself of the strange coldness that had settled inside her. It was as though the sight of the church had made the marrow of her bones freeze, and when she reached the school and made herself a quick coffee in the staff room, she hurried along to the Black Hole and was relieved to find that Aminah hadn't arrived yet and she could be alone for a while.

Her lesson plan for the morning – an introduction to simple perspective for Primary Seven - was laid out in readiness, but when she tried to read it she found it impossible to take anything in, and eventually she stopped trying and sat back in her chair to sip the hot coffee and wonder what it was that was making her feel so uneasy.

It must have been connected with the church, because she'd been perfectly happy strolling in the sunshine along the front, and the cold feeling had only begun when she crossed the road and looked up at the big red door. But surely her memories of Sunday morning services with Gran in St Columba's were as happy as all the other memories she had of her summers in Largs? The sermons might have gone on too long and been incomprehensible and tedious, but nothing distressing had ever happened. Or had it?

Another image flashed through her mind of Gran, still sitting erectly in the pew, but this time, as Ella continued to watch, the image began to move and, slowly and stiffly, Gran turned round to face her. There was no blush to her cheeks now, and despite the layer of powder she always applied on Sundays, her face was gaunt and grey.

The bell was ringing now and Ella could hear the chatter of the teachers as they hurried round from the staffroom to bring in the lines of children, but the image of Gran was speaking to her now and, shutting the background noises out as best she could, she concentrated all her attention on what she was saying. Because now she knew what had chilled her through and through. It was the memory of what Gran had said to her that long-ago Sunday - the devastating thing she'd told her that had, in a single moment, changed everything.

The newly-unearthed memory tormented her all day, and even as she walked home in the sunshine it dogged her every step.

Once, she was so sure there actually *was* something behind her that, pretending to adjust her sandal, she took a furtive look back the way she'd come and could have sworn she saw, for a fleeting moment, the lower leaves of the hedge quiver as though they'd been disturbed. Forcing herself to stand still, she stared down the empty street, and when the leaves had stilled she told herself not to be so stupid, that it must have been a bird or a cat and, quickening her pace, she marched grimly on till she saw her car in the distance, spick and span and shinier than it had been for years.

During the evening the anxiety lessened, particularly after a meal and a couple of glasses of wine, but as soon as she went to bed the memory of Gran's chilling pronouncement returned, and when she woke on Wednesday morning she knew there was no longer any point in trying to push it back to where it had come from. She would have to face it, and hope that in the facing she could finally lay it to rest.

The previous morning, standing outside St Columba's, she'd noticed a poster about the forthcoming Harvest Thanksgiving pinned up beside the big blue church sign. It was decorated with brightly-coloured fruits and vegetables and announced, in large green letters, that all volunteers should meet at the church at ten-thirty tomorrow morning to set up the harvest table, which meant that the church would probably be open around ten.

She showered quickly and, after a breakfast she didn't want, loaded the washing machine with Flick's musty cushion covers and blankets and then, dressed smartly but demurely in her cream linen dress, with a wide-brimmed straw sunhat she hoped hid her face, she set off for the church.

When she arrived, the front door of the church was already open, and as she climbed the steps and entered the vestibule she felt herself shrink to the size of a six-year old, overwhelmed by the familiarity of what she saw and smelt. First there was the big marble plaque with the man's face on which, even with white-gloved hands, she was expressly forbidden to touch, and then, as she entered the church itself, the same smell of old books and polished wood she'd noticed in Wetherby's study.

She remembered the enormous organ too, whose ear-splitting chords were, Gran had assured her, all made by the hands and feet of the little man whose bald head was barely visible above the wooden balustrade, and the rows of stone pillars on either side, beside which she and Gran always sat, and the magical stained-glass windows she'd spent every sermon studying.

A little group of women had gathered in the nave, and as Ella headed for the most familiar window she took a quick glance back to check they were all absorbed in distributing the mound of fruit and vegetables laid out on the altar into a variety of wicker baskets. They did so with cheerful gusto, calling to one another and good-naturedly criticising one another's arrangements and, under cover of their camaraderie, Ella crossed to the side aisle and slipped into the pew she knew so well.

Nothing seemed to have changed in the fifty years since she and Gran sat side by side in that pew. The low cushion that covered the hard wood seemed still to be stuffed with unyielding horsehair, and there were still piles of red-covered, well-thumbed, hymn books like those from which Gran had sung lustily while Ella mouthed the occasional word she could make out.

There were the little metal brackets too, into which the tiny Communion glasses were clipped after the wine had been drunk – although that particular mystery was not something she'd ever been allowed to witness. She'd had to rely on Gran's explanation of how eating bread and drinking wine was a way of remembering the sacrifice Jesus had made for us poor sinners.

They were just 'symbols', she'd said when Jinty pressed for more information, and then she'd added that *some* people believed that when they were specially blessed they actually changed into his body and blood, and the idea had made the hairs on Jinty's neck stand on end. It was, if anything, even more thrilling than the Viking battle enactments and, as far as telling Ella's mother about it was concerned, every bit as illicit.

For a while Ella sat looking at the stained-glass window to her right which showed – the name popped unexpectedly into her brain - Mr Valiant for Truth from the 'Pilgrims' Progress', standing knee-high in a bright blue swirling river, and gradually she filtered out the background chatter of the women and pictured her Gran's trim upright form as, that morning, she'd turned towards her.

She'd never, ever seen Gran's face look so grey and grave, and long before she spoke – because in Ella's mind everything that morning happened in slow motion - fear had curdled her insides. Then Gran had bent down close, her lips tickling Ella's ears, and Ella strained to hear what she was about to say to her.

'I wish I could live to see you grow up, Ella,' was what she'd said, and then she'd stopped and gazed up towards the altar, and when Ella dared to look at her, she saw her face-powder was ribbed with tears.

The memory ran out then, and Ella could only imagine herself clinging to Gran's arm and asking her what on earth she'd meant, but no matter how hard she tried to relive what had happened next, she could call nothing more to mind. What she did, however, remember was that afterwards, on the way home to London, she'd been so desperate for reassurance she'd told her mother what Gran had said, and demanded to know if that meant she was going to die very soon.

Her mother's answer was lost in the mists of time too but, presumably, she'd explained that Gran was elderly and wouldn't be alive for ever and that, sadly, in the end, everybody had to die, but all Ella could be sure of was that after that there were no more summers in Largs and, from that day on, her little life was always slightly tinged with fear. A year later, Gran died.

Ella was nine then, and old enough to know she'd had nothing whatsoever to do with her death (which, her mother later explained, had been caused by a type of cancer of the blood), but even so, for years after, whenever she thought of what Gran had said, and how she'd gone on to tell her mother, she felt a stab of guilt, as though somehow if she'd acted differently, kept the secret to herself, things would have been different. And when, shortly afterwards, her migraines began, she linked them with the inexplicable dread and confusion and powerlessness with which the whole incident had filled her.

Her grief at Gran's death was numbing, and the migraines that followed, combined as they were with the onset of puberty, frightened her terribly, but the troubled time had one unexpectedly positive outcome which was that she and her mother became closer. Their relationship would never be as warm and carefree as her relationship with Gran had been, but it was as though a truce had been called, and because Ella's reaction to her loss was to throw herself into the drawing and painting she'd always loved, her mother became the provider of everything she needed, as well as her willing teacher. Later, however, when Ella began to paint in a way her mother disapproved of, the fragile bond between them broke down again and their rows were more violent, and more unresolvable, than ever. This time round, the only truce was her mother's death.

Ella sat watching the shafts of blue from Mr Valiant for Truth's river dappling her dress. The women at the Harvest Thanksgiving table were quieter now, and when she looked up she saw that the table was almost ready, and a few of them were making their way, in ones and twos, down the aisle towards the door. She knew she'd have to move soon, but an important question had begun to form itself in her mind, and it was so important she was anxious not to lose the thread of it; so she turned to face the window again and, for the first time, allowed herself to wonder why, all those years ago, her mother hadn't seen fit to tell her that Gran was seriously ill.

Did she simply not know, because Gran had decided to suffer in silence? Or did she know, but preferred to let Ella have one last carefree summer? Suddenly, it struck her as strangely significant that, in almost half a century, she'd never once thought of tackling her mother on the subject, and now, in the peace and quiet of the church, it dawned on her that her reason for not tackling her mother was the fear she always had that it would cause yet another blazing row.

Not only that, it also struck her that even now, her inability to deal with difficult situations head-on lay in those rows with her mother, in her lifelong dread of that anger of Veronica Blyth's flaring up and igniting yet another shouting match she knew she'd never win.

That was why she'd continued for years to paint roses in her claustrophobic little studio in The Moorings when she should have been telling Derek how frustrated she was. That was why she'd rented the flat in secret and scuttled off to Scotland, leaving him that pathetic note, instead of telling him what she was about to do and why. It was also why she hadn't put her foot down with Paul Wetherby and demanded to be told what exactly had happened to Felicity Hunter; and why, no matter what she did, she always, in the end, felt frustrated with herself ...

She was crying now, and for a while it was a relief to let the tears flow. Then, giving herself a little shake, she took a paper hankie out of her bag, rubbed it all over her face, and stood up, and as she was shuffling back along the pew she became aware of a figure standing in the aisle, almost as though in wait. Looking up, she saw the neat blonde bob and impeccably groomed figure of Caroline Flood, standing, stony-faced, holding a basket of what looked like Harvest Thanksgiving rejects.

"Well good morning, Ella" - Caroline shifted the basket so that it rested on her hip – "fancy seeing you here," and she stepped back to let Ella out but neither moved away nor changed her expression.

Ella looked down the aisle to where, through the church's open door, a sparkle of sea was just visible. "Good morning, Caroline," she said politely, and she took a few steps towards the door. Caroline, however, followed.

"I'm glad I bumped into you, actually," Caroline said, and she turned the basket round so that it blocked Ella's way, the movement causing a large and wrinkled parsnip to tumble to the floor. "There's something I've been wanting to talk to you about. Apparently, while I've been away looking after my sister, *you* have been seeing my husband," and she fixed her with a look of utter malice.

Ella opened her mouth to protest, but her throat had closed over and no sound came out. "I don't know if you're aware of what happened between Harry and Felicity Hunter, Ella," Caroline went on, "but suffice to say that, thanks to Miss Hunter's neurotic tendencies, there were extremely serious and unpleasant consequences. I would, therefore, strongly advise you" – she jutted her chin into Ella's personal space – "not to involve yourself any further with my husband, and on no account to ask him for any more favours. Do I make myself clear?" and she spun round and began to march towards the door.

For a moment Ella remained frozen to the spot, but then an almighty flash of red-hot fury seared through her body and, picking up the parsnip, she ran down the aisle after Caroline, took hold of her arm, and pulled her back.

"And I'll have *you* know, Caroline," she said, in the soft but threatening voice she usually reserved for errant children, "that I am not, in any way, shape or form, 'involved' with your husband, and I strongly object to your insinuations. I will continue to treat both of you with the same neighbourly respect with which I treat everyone else in the house, and I expect you to do the same. Do *I* make myself clear?" and, tossing the parsnip into the wicker basket with as much force as she dared, she tore her sunhat off her head and, head held high, walked out of the church and into the sunshine.

20

During September the summer faded so gradually into autumn that Ella, caught up as she was in her painting and teaching, hardly noticed the shortening of the days, and then one Sunday, after she'd put the final touches to the first 'Arlene in Flight' painting, she opened her phone to call Aminah to ask how Grace was, and realised it was the first of October.

The past month had been, with some noticeable exceptions, peaceful and productive. Arlene went to London for her castings and came back disillusioned and disappointed in the world of fashion modelling, and Ella made her a set of business cards advertising her services as an artists' model and asked Grace to display them in their gallery. She assured Arlene that if she built up a good client base of artists, word would soon get around about how flexible and expressive she was, and before long she'd be well on her way to affording the deposit on a premises for her tattoo parlour.

At school, work on the Commonplace Books went on apace, and whenever Mrs McMahon popped in and saw the children drawing their pictures or writing their poems and recipes, she gave Ella a little wink and said, loudly enough to be heard at the back of the classroom, that she trusted these wonderful books would be finished in time for the HMI Inspection in December. She said it in the tone of voice that clearly meant *not* being finished in time for the HMI Inspection wasn't an option and Ella, anxious to do her best for the school, gave her solemn word that they would.

It wasn't a difficult promise to make, because she and Aminah and the children loved the Commonplace Books project, and none more so than Jinty, who regularly took hers home to finish off this or that page, dutifully bringing it back the next week, safely in its plastic bag and always filled with immaculate work. Ella always made sure she took the time to look at whatever she'd drawn or written, and although Jinty seemed quietly pleased to be helped and praised, her old sparkle had faded, and increasingly Ella noticed she had a haunted, drawn look in her face. She no longer helped her in with her bags in the morning either, often appearing in the classroom when the register was being taken, looking half-slept and unkempt.

Often, she'd ask if she could stay in at playtimes to finish something off, and Ella was so concerned by how quiet and withdrawn she'd become she usually agreed; but even then, when they were on their own and Ella sat beside her and tried to engage her in conversation, she gave short answers and then clammed up, and as the month went on she drew and wrote less and less; in fact her favourite occupation became sharpening the coloured pencils, a task she did in complete silence, hunched over her table, her face pale and her eyes half-closed.

In the middle of the month there was another brief sighting of the 'paedophile' with the black car and the brown hat, and Mrs McMahon once again informed the police, but since no one had yet managed to spot his number plate, all they could do was say they had it on record, and that everyone should continue to be vigilant. To

Ella's relief, he hadn't appeared again outside her house, and she'd more or less decided she'd been mistaken. Black cars, after all, were common, and perhaps she'd imagined the brown hat ...

As for the neighbours at number 22, she continued to distance herself from Paul Wetherby as best she could, greeting him with neighbourly politeness when their paths crossed, and she avoided both Harry and Caroline Flood like the plague. The altercation with Caroline in St Columba's had shocked her to her core, and even though, at the time, she'd done the best job she could in denying any 'involvement' with Harry, whenever she thought about how staunchly she'd defended her innocence, it made her feel hugely uncomfortable.

No matter how fervent her denials had been, the fact remained there *was* something going on between her and Harry, as perhaps there had been something going on between Flick and Harry, and probably, before Flick, a whole array of other women who'd been captivated by his roguish charms. In fact, the more Ella thought about the whole affair, the sorrier she felt for Caroline and the more ashamed of herself she felt. For wasn't she every bit as selfish as the woman who had, miraculously, tempted Derek away from the straight and narrow? Wasn't she too a bit of a 'scarlet woman'?

Since then, she'd done her level best to push the whole business to the back of her mind, and because – presumably on Caroline's insistence – Harry had moved his hives away from her garden, she seldom caught more than a fleeting glance of him. Much to her dismay, however, her feelings for him remained the same, and there were still times when she couldn't stop herself from reliving the moment when they'd stood outside her door with the jar of golden honey, inches away from a kiss. And, increasingly guiltily, she often imagined what might have happened if she hadn't stepped away.

The only occupant of number 22 Ella didn't avoid was Maeve Oliver, and during those weeks she'd been pleased at how their friendship had blossomed into a nice comfortable pattern they both enjoyed. Maeve had had a key cut for her, and Ella liked the fact that she could drop in on her at any time and she'd stop whatever she was doing and make them both a cup of tea. They'd sit down together with the tea, and occasionally some home baking, and they'd talk about all sorts of things, but mostly about teaching and its various triumphs and challenges.

It felt, sometimes, like having a mother again, but an infinitely less judgemental mother than she'd ever had. Like Veronica Blyth in the years before her death, Maeve was sometimes apt to drift off into her own little world but, unlike Veronica, who often emerged from such episodes in a spitting rage, Maeve's little vacant times seemed to refresh rather than upset her. And when, occasionally, Ella talked to her about her painting, it was a blessed relief to know that she would never suddenly straighten her back, sit bolt upright, and use her venomous tongue to poison and paralyse whatever ideas Ella might have confided. In fact, Maeve was fascinated by the idea of the series, and she was also fascinated by Arlene, and would often lean out of the window and hand her a bag of whatever she'd baked because she 'needed fattening up'.

By mutual consent, they did not, however, discuss the other people in the house, and neither of them ever mentioned Flick, which made it all the more surprising when, out of the blue on the afternoon of the first of October, Maeve suddenly did.

It was the cat, Cally, who started it. Ella and Maeve were sipping tea when she slunk in and, after a few exploratory circuits of their legs, sprang onto the back of Maeve's chair and rubbed the side of her head in her hair. As she rubbed, she let out a series of high-pitched yelps, and when Maeve persuaded her down onto her lap, she gazed up at her and let out one long plaintive wail.

It made Ella laugh. "She sounds like a soprano in an opera who's about to die a terrible death!" she said, and Maeve smiled.

"That's my Cally all right, ever the tragic heroine. Did I tell you I named her after Calliope, the goddess of music? I got her from my son Nathan, and he always used her pedigree name, which was something atrocious like Hemlock Baby Face, but I soon got her to answer to 'Cally', and that's what she's been ever since."

Ella said no, she hadn't told her, and when she added that she'd never heard of Calliope, Maeve went on to explain. "One of her sons was Orpheus," she said. "You know, 'Orpheus in the Underworld'? and when he was young she taught him to sing and play the harp ..." She turned away then and stared out of the window, and Ella saw that her brow was knitted as though she was puzzling something out, and when she turned back the knots were gone and her eyes were clear and bright, as though a decision had been made.

"After I got Cally," Maeve said, "Flick gave me a painting she'd done of Calliope and Orpheus. I wonder, would you like to see it? I have it hanging in my bedroom," and she pulled herself to her feet and gestured to Ella to follow her out into the hall.

"Nat dumped her on me a year or so ago," she said as they walked together to the bedroom. "He just turned up on the doorstep, quite out of the blue, with the cat and its bed and a bagful of food, and said he couldn't cope with her any more and I'd have to take her, which has always, I'm afraid, been Nat's way," and she pushed open the bedroom door. Ella began to follow her in, but then Maeve changed her mind and, turning away from the door, went back to stand in the dark hall, twisting her hands together as though suddenly unable to decide what to do.

"Are you all right, Maeve?" Ella said gently, and for a while Maeve continued to wring her hands in silence. Then she spoke.

"Nat would be so cross with me if he found out I'd shown you Flick's painting," she said, and her voice was suddenly old and afraid. "He doesn't like me talking about Flick, you know. He says it just upsets me, and that I should forget about her" – she gripped Ella's wrist suddenly and squeezed it with surprising strength – "but I can't forget her, Ella. I really can't, and I don't see why I should either ..."

Unable to think what to say, Ella looked over Maeve's shoulder into the bedroom. It appeared to be very much smaller than her own, filled as it was with the same heavy furniture that cluttered the hall, and it was also much darker because the window was hung with trailing plants, but even in the poor light she could make out Flick's painting hanging above the bed.

"I don't want you to do something you're not happy with, Maeve," she said carefully, "but sometimes it's good to talk about people we've lost. I mean, coming back to Largs has brought back a lot of memories of my grandmother, and some have been very painful, but I'm still glad I've had them," and she took a small tentative step towards the open door. "Perhaps it would help you to talk more about Flick?"

She stood back then, allowing Maeve space, and was relieved when she slowly turned and led her inside. "This is the painting," she said and, leaning over Maeve's pillows,

Ella looked up at the now-familiar palette of glowing colours.

"It's called 'Calliope Teaches Orpheus Music'," - Maeve switched on the bedside light and pointed at the woman in flowing red robes seated in the foreground, playing a harp - "and you can see how tenderly she's showing him how to pluck the strings. Isn't it exquisite? I was so touched when she gave me it, you know. She said it was to express her gratitude for all I'd done for her, which of course wasn't necessary because I enjoyed every minute we had together, but still ..."

As Maeve spoke, Ella looked away from the foreground figures to the distant left of the painting, to the lake on which floated the now-familiar sorrowful little swan. "I've seen three of Flick's paintings," she said, "and they all have a sad swan in them. Have you any idea why? I mean, did she particularly like swans?"

Maeve rummaged around in her sleeve for a handkerchief. She held it to her face, in readiness. "I know why she put the swans in, dear, and if you like, I'll tell you. In fact, I'll show you. Shall we go back into the living-room?" and Ella let herself be led back across the hall.

"Flick had a little music group," Maeve said when she was back in her chair, "called *The Silver Swan*. There were three of them, a girl who played flute and a man who played lute, and Flick played harpsichord and she and the man sang. It was mainly madrigals they did, and of course 'The Silver Swan' was one of their favourites, hence their name. Have you heard of it, dear? It's by Orlando Gibbons and it's extraordinarily beautiful."

Ella picked up the little Madrigals book that still lay on the table by Maeve's chair. "I haven't," she said, "and I'm afraid I don't know anything about early music. Is 'The Silver Swan' in here? I'd love to read it."

Maeve nodded. "'It's actually for five voices, but I arranged it so that Flick could play the two lower parts on the harpsichord," and she took the little book from Ella, opened it at the place, and handed it back, and as Ella read about the swan who, mute in life, sang only at the moment of its death, she felt again the raw coldness of the autumn day.

"Those last two lines say it all, don't they," Maeve said and, closing her eyes, she began to sing:

Farewell all joys, oh death come close my eyes
More Geese than Swans live now, more fools than wise ...

For a while, after she'd stopped, the echo of the words hung in the air and neither women spoke. Then Maeve dabbed her eyes with the handkerchief and gave Ella the saddest of looks.

"That was how Flick saw herself, you know. As a swan, among geese," and she replaced the book on the table and sat for a while with her hand resting on the cover. Then, quite suddenly, she sat up.

"I wouldn't want you to think for a minute that she felt in any way superior to other people, Ella," she said firmly, "because it was quite the reverse. She was painfully shy and self-effacing and dreadfully insecure, almost as though she wasn't aware how very talented she was and didn't believe people when they praised her work. No, what I mean is she saw herself as an outsider, as someone who, no matter how many friends she had, never quite fitted in." She laid her head back on the cushion, and closed her eyes. "I believe she was afraid to become close to anyone," she said quietly, "and I always wondered whether something very bad had happened to her in the past, that made her unable to trust others."

Ella let Maeve's words sink in. "She must have been terribly lonely," she said, and as she spoke she pictured Lucy, sobbing at her reflection in the mirror, insisting she was fat, and ugly, and worthless, when all Ella could see was her fragile young beauty.

"She most certainly was," Maeve nodded. "And I often thought she deliberately exhausted herself with her endless painting and playing and singing so that she felt the loneliness less." She sighed a deep sigh. "I do wish I knew what happened to her," she murmured, and she closed her eyes but continued to speak. "At the time, when she went, I asked and asked, but those men would tell me nothing. They just kept telling me not to worry, and it made me so very angry," and she opened her eyes again and fixed Ella with a piercing look. "Have *you* any idea what happened to her, Ella? Has anyone said anything to you?"

Ella stood up and, bending, placed a light kiss on Maeve's powdery cheek. She could see the exhaustion in her face, and was angered by how lonely and frightened she looked, and how isolated. It also occurred to her to wonder why Flick herself had not seen fit to get in touch with her. Had something so bad happened to her that she couldn't even confide in Maeve?

"No one's told me anything either, Maeve," she said, "and I wish I knew that she was all right. If I ever manage to find out anything, I promise I'll let you know. And now" – she saw Maeve's eyelids begin to flutter and close and moved towards the door – "I'm going to have to go and do some work. Thank you very much for showing me the painting, and thanks for the tea," and she slipped out.

Back in her flat, she poured herself a glass of wine and took it to the studio. Later, she'd do an internet search for the madrigal and think more about the significance of its words, but for now she needed to take herself away from all the misery and back into the present. Dragging Harry's ladder out of the corner, she turned all her attention to figuring out how best to set it up for the next session. Arlene was due a week on Saturday to pose for the first 'Flying' painting and, despite the abundance of sketches Ella had made, she still needed to work out how exactly she was going to attach her to the ladder without the whole thing tipping up.

Sitting in the comfortable chair, she sketched out the various possibilities, and when she'd found the one she thought would work best she tore the page out of the drawing block and stuck it on the back of her easel where Arlene would be able to see it. Then she laid out her paints and brushes, and when everything was in order she sat back to finish her wine.

It was a calm evening, but even on the calmest day the beech leaves were never completely still, and as she watched them do their shivering little dance she noticed that their golden-yellow was already showing hints of brown, and the beech nuts that clung to the outermost branches were bursting out of their hard prickly shells. From time to time in the last days, she'd caught sight of a pair of grey squirrels, chasing one another through the canopy.

Her eyes were beginning to close when a sudden cracking noise from outside the window made her jump, and when she opened them wide again she saw that the leaves directly opposite the window were rattling together furiously. It was, of course, nothing but the squirrels, but somehow it still troubled her and she got up, lowered the blinds, and went off to prepare a meal. She was savouring her second glass of wine when, to her surprise, her phone rang, and it was Grace Nwapa.

Grace sounded immensely excited. "You'll never *guess* what I'm about to do, Ella," she announced, and when Ella said she couldn't wait to hear, Grace had giggled. "OK, so you know the baby's due early December? Well, believe it or not, the morning sickness has finally *finally* gone, so I've decided I'm going to have an exhibition! I actually had it all prepared months ago, but what with the sleepless nights and the throwing up I chickened out, and then yesterday Max said he'd had a cancellation and why didn't we just go ahead and launch it. The Private View's on Friday the twentieth of October. It's at two o' clock in the afternoon and I'd really love you to come. Will you?"

Grace paused for breath then, leaving enough space for Ella to say she'd be absolutely delighted to, and that perhaps she could also bring Arlene so that she could meet some potential customers, and Grace said of course she should, that it was a brilliant idea. They'd chatted for a while about the exhibition, and about school, and Ella was about to hang up when Grace shouted to her to wait a minute, that she'd just remembered something.

"You know your neighbour I said I recognised from somewhere?" she said. "Well, when I described him to Max he said wasn't he the dreadful little man who came to the gallery a year or so ago with Felicity Hunter and made the most awful scene, and of course then it all came flooding back. So anyway - don't forget to ask Max about it on the twentieth, and he'll fill you in on the details," and she was gone.

Ella sat back in the chair, and as she sipped the last of the wine she realised that her earlier sadness had been replaced by a pleasant buzz of excitement. In a couple of months, with any luck, her series would be ready to present to *Max James Fine Art*. All she had to do – apart, of course, from the rest of the paintings - was to find an appropriate title, and then she'd done it. She'd done what she came to Largs to do. And as for what had become of poor lonely Flick, it looked as though, finally, she was about to have a breakthrough; and since that breakthrough wasn't going to happen till the twentieth of October, she'd dismiss the whole sorry business from her mind till then.

21

Max James Fine Art was situated in an elegant corner of Glasgow's Merchant City and, unlike others galleries Ella had visited in the long-distant past, it was made up of several interconnecting rooms rather than being a single large space. The effect was one of cosy, intimate areas each with its own identity, and as she stood in the first gallery looking round at Grace Nwapa's exhibition she allowed herself once more to imagine her own paintings hanging there.

All around her, the great and the good of the Scottish art scene stood in their finery, admiring Grace's work, and as she tucked the inevitable stray strands of hair behind her ears and smoothed down her dress, she told herself over and over again that she had as much right as anyone else to be there, and that Aminah would arrive soon, and then everything would be fine. Smiling graciously at all and sundry, she helped herself to a tiny glass of wine then wended her way out of the main area and into one of the side galleries. To her relief, Aminah and Sergei had already arrived.

Aminah threw her arms round her and kissed both her cheeks, and then she introduced Sergei, who did the same, and then they all concentrated on looking in wonder at the exhibits. Here, in the smaller exhibition space, it was easier to take in the artworks than it had been in the crowded room next door, and Ella could see how strong the interaction was between Grace's pale grey sculptured heads and the huge, chaotic paintings behind, with their raw angles and vibrant, clashing impasto colours.

"The busts are really strong, aren't they," Aminah said, "and the paintings behind are so wild and expressive. They're meant to symbolise the characters' imaginations, you know. Grace told me …" She turned to look up at Sergei, and Ella noticed the scar, jagged as a lightning-streak, on his left cheek. "I've been trying to persuade Sergei to model for her. He has such a strong face, don't you think?"

"And a back-story to match," Sergei pointed out. "Let us just say, Russia is an interesting place in which to grow up," and he gave a wry smile. "I hear your model is coming tonight, Ella, and I would very much like to meet her, because I think Aminah is right. I should become a model," and he rolled up one of his sleeves, flexed his elbow, and struck a comic pose. "What do you think? Pretty damned good muscles, aren't they? I also have a very splendid bum," he added with a good-natured grin, "and I really fancy the idea of being paid to sit on it!"

Ella looked Sergei up and down approvingly and assured him he'd make an excellent subject, and she went off to the main gallery in search of Arlene, but there was no sign of her and she was about to go back when she saw Grace waving at her. Her hair was bright pink today, and she wore enormous silver hooped earrings and a skin-tight pink dress. Her bump was enormous and her brown skin glowed.

"Come and meet Max," she said, linking arms with Ella and leading her through to another gallery which was filled with large ceramic books lying open on plinths, their pages studded with exquisitely-detailed tiny figures and castles and trees. Behind each book hung a small painting depicting a fairy-tale scene, the bright palette and intricacy of which reminded Ella a little of Flick's work, and she was particularly drawn to one that showed a young black woman letting down her hair for a young man to climb.

"I see you like Grace's take on 'Rapunzel'." A tall man with a waxed moustache and a mass of grey curls detached himself from the far wall. He was wearing a silk cravat and a midnight blue velvet suit with a diamante brooch in the lapel, and he came towards them with his right hand outstretched. "It's a favourite of mine too," he said and he pumped Ella's hand warmly.

"This is Ella Blyth, Max," Grace told him, "Aminah's artist friend with the double-jointed Goth model, remember? You really must get her to show you her 'captive women' series – it's positively mind-blowing." She turned to Ella. "Have you got a title for the series, Ella? And how many paintings are going to be in it?"

"I'm still thinking about a title," Ella said. "I wondered about 'A Dream of Flying', actually. What do you think?" and she was starting to add that she hoped to do five paintings in all when someone waved urgently at Grace from the main gallery and, apologising, she hurried off.

Max gestured to a door on their left. "I wonder if I could have a quick word with you, Ella? It won't take a minute, and if we go in here no one'll disturb us," and he showed her into a small office. He fetched a white plastic chair for her, sat down behind the desk opposite, and poured himself a glass of water.

"Would you like some? I'm afraid it can get quite stuffy out there when there's a crowd." He held up the water bottle but Ella said she was fine, she still had some wine, and she waited for him to continue. Her palms were sticky now, and she was aware her face must be flushed and shiny.

Max leaned across the desk towards her. His smile was gentle and his eyes, a pale green with dark circles round the irises, were the kind of eyes she loved to paint. "Grace tells me she recognised your neighbour when she came to visit your studio," he said. "She seems pretty sure he's the guy who kicked up a stink here a couple of years ago when he came with Felicity Hunter, and I was wondering, do you know her?"

Ella's stomach gave the tiniest of spasms, and she was aware of not quite meeting Max's eye. She'd been looking forward to hearing whatever revelation he might provide, but now that the moment had come she was surprisingly nervous. "Not personally, no," she said. "I just live in the flat she once rented, but I've seen some examples of her work and I noticed one had your gallery label on it. And the guy who kicked up the stink is almost certainly Paul Wetherby, who's nice enough, but I'm not entirely sure about," and she took a gulp of wine.

Max pushed his chair back, opened a drawer in the white filing cabinet behind, and took out a sheet of paper which he handed to Ella. Flick's name and phone number were printed at the top, and below were two thumbnails, each with a title handwritten in black ink. One was 'Aristaeus and the Death of the Bees' and the other was 'Juno and the Peacock', and below the thumbnails was another title Ella couldn't make out. It was written untidily in pencil and then crossed out, and when she held the paper more closely she thought it said something like 'larger canvas', with a couple of question marks scrawled after it. Putting his hands behind his head, Max leaned far back in his chair and frowned over at Ella. "I have a problem with Felicity

Hunter," he said, and he waited in silence as she studied the document.

Ella looked closely at the familiar thumbnails, and as she examined their details she noticed tiny pinpricks of light beginning to flicker across her field of vision, and she prayed she wasn't going to have one of her headaches. In the past months she'd had more than usual, but so far they'd never developed into full-blown migraines. "I think I might like some water, actually," she said, and she reached into her bag for her painkillers. "Do you mind telling me what kind of a problem? I mean, if it's not confidential?"

Max handed her a glass and waited while she swallowed the tablets. "It's not exactly 'confidential'," he said, "but I'd sooner it didn't get out, if you get my drift," and when Ella assured him she'd be discreet he gave an audible sigh and went on.

"Felicity Hunter came to see me a couple of years ago. We'd been in discussion earlier in the year about the possibility of her having an exhibition with us, and she'd sent us these photos" - he nodded towards the piece of paper – "and I told her I liked them and to bring them in. She came a couple of months later with a smart-looking guy in a suit, and I remember saying to Grace afterwards that he reminded me of a Jehovah's Witness. Does that sound like your Paul Wetherby?"

Ella held onto the sides of her chair. The room was swaying slightly from side to side, and a small spot in her left temple was starting to pound. She tried closing her eyes for a moment, but it made the dizziness worse. "It does," she said. "And from the little he's told me I get the impression he and Felicity were close, though I don't know how healthy the relationship was. I certainly find him rather domineering. So anyway, what happened?"

"OK, well" - Max gave her a stiff smile – "that day Felicity brought three unframed canvases with her, two small ones and a larger one, all in bubble-wrap. She unwrapped the two smaller ones first – the ones she'd sent thumbnails of - and both of them were just the kind of thing I like in my gallery. Modern, but with a nod to antiquity, you know? Anyway, it was all going swimmingly till she started to unwrap the third, and that was when the shit well and truly hit the fan, if you'll excuse my French ..."

Ella's stomach gave a distinct spasm and she turned round to the door behind her, anxious suddenly for an escape route. To her relief, it had a notice on it that said 'Staff Toilet'. She took another sip of water and forced herself to breathe slowly and regularly.

"You could vaguely make out what was inside through the bubble-wrap," Max was saying, "and as Felicity turned it over to take off the tape the man caught sight of it, and it was then that the atmosphere changed completely."

He laughed then, a deep good-natured laugh, and shook his head slowly from side to side. "I can honestly say I've never, in all my years as a gallery owner, seen anyone behave the way that guy did. He grabbed the canvas out of Felicity's hands, stuck the tape back down, hissed something under his breath at her, then took hold of her arm and pulled her towards the door as though she was a naughty child. She was really upset, of course, and she kept trying to shake him off and take the painting from him, and the thing was, we were in the main gallery and all I could think of was getting the two of them off the premises before anyone came in. I actually thought I might have to call the police."

"What did he say when he hissed at her?"

"I don't remember his exact words, but it was to the effect that she'd only exhibit the painting over his dead body." He ran his hands through his hair, thinking hard, and then he smiled over at Ella. "That was it! 'Over my dead body', and then he went on to say that it was an 'affront to the senses'. Those were the exact words he used. I remember, because at the time I wondered whether a work of art being 'an affront to the senses' was necessarily a bad thing." He leaned over towards Ella. "Are you OK, Ella? You're very pale."

Ella shook her head. "I'm so sorry," she said, " but I feel a bit sick," and she glanced over at the toilet door again. "I'm afraid you'll have to excuse me," and, cupping her hand over her mouth, she stood up and ran.

When, five or so minutes later, she returned, Grace had arrived. She took her arm and steered her back into her seat, then handed her a fresh glass of water. "Take tiny sips," she told her, "and in between the sips breathe slowly and deeply in and out," and she began to rub her back in big gentle circles. "Trust me," she added. "I have a Masters in the art of vomiting," and when Ella assured her she felt a bit better she glanced over at Max. "I take it Max has filled you in on the Felicity Hunter debacle?" she said. "I only witnessed the tail end of it, but the way he treated the poor girl was awful."

Ella sat back in her chair and concentrated on breathing in and out. "So," she said when she felt calmer, "did either of you see what was on the canvas?"

Grace and Max exchanged doubtful looks. "I didn't," Grace said. "By the time I arrived it was all wrapped up and he had it firmly under his arm and was shepherding Felicity out, but you said you thought you saw something quite unpleasant, didn't you Max? Didn't you say there was blood and claws or something?"

"I had the impression of some kind of attack, yes," Max said slowly, "but I didn't get a close enough look to be sure. Anyway" – he picked up the sheet of paper and turned towards the filing cabinet – "I managed to give Felicity a sheet of gallery labels before they left, and I told her that once she'd had the paintings framed she should fill them out and stick them on the backs, then hopefully we'd have another meeting." He raised an eyebrow. "And I'm afraid that was the last we ever heard of her. I phoned her a number of times and left messages, but she never replied. I don't suppose you know what happened to her?"

Ella shook her head, and as Max slipped the paper back into the filing cabinet she said, "I've been trying to find out what happened to her ever since I moved into her flat, but it's been well-nigh impossible to get any information out of the neighbours. There's only one who's prepared to talk to me about her, but even that's difficult. They all call her Flick, by the way," she added, and then, as she followed Max and Grace to the door, she asked, "What was she like?"

"She was quite a striking woman," Max said as he closed the door behind them. "Small and slim and fragile, with pale skin and intensely blue eyes and long wavy red hair. Pre-Raphaelite, you know. After she'd gone, Grace said she'd love to paint her, didn't you Grace?"

"And how old?"

"I'd say late thirties, early forties. I mean, the day I saw her she was distraught, so she might have been even younger." He hung back as Grace vanished into the mass of people, then bent close to Ella. "I'd be grateful if you'd tell me anything you find out about Flick," he said quietly. "I mean, I don't want to sound melodramatic, but I do wonder whether something unpleasant might have been going on with her and Wetherby, and I've often thought I should have tried harder to find her."

He gave Ella an unexpectedly warm hug, and suggested that perhaps if she ate something she'd feel better, and he pulled a chair over and told her to have a seat and he'd fetch her some food. Then, as an afterthought, he took a thick glossy catalogue from one of the tables and handed her it. It was titled 'Fifteen Years of *Max James Fine Art*'.

"If you'd like to have a look at this," he said, "you'll see the kind of work we like to hang," and he hurried off towards the canapes.

Ella opened the catalogue. It had been so long since she'd interested herself in what was happening on the Art scene she'd no idea what to expect, and as she turned page after page her aching head began to spin with excitement.

There were exquisitely-painted images of dark-eyed sullen children in dream landscapes, their pale, almost luminous, faces pouting out malevolently from under hooded eyelids. Then there were digital prints in which twenties-style women stood on backgrounds of intricately layered plant forms, holding giant butterflies and birds; and vibrant redheaded women, their faces strong and impenetrable and their tattooed bodies wide and masculine, juxtaposed onto backdrops of vivid greens and turquoises.

Next came pastel studies of underwater swimmers in which the ripples and breath-bubbles were so accurately rendered it was hard to believe they'd been drawn with chalks, and these were followed by gloriously loosely-painted naked women, wild-eyed and witch-like, in poses so flagrantly sexual they took Ella's breath away.

The more pages she turned, the more possibilities opened up to her of who, in the future, she might meet, and how she might choose to paint. The headache forgotten, she gazed at benign, moonlike faces in dark impasto colours, their big eyes smiling out innocently at her, and mysterious figures, some naked and others gloriously robed, holding talismanic objects around which red arcane symbols had been superimposed.

Then, spread across two double pages, she was dumbfounded to see images of pale ethereal women in moonlit, dreamlike settings that were obviously drawn from Greek and Roman myths. There was even a 'Leda and the Swan', in which a naked red-haired Leda held the open-beaked bird solemnly aloft and observed it with a strangely dispassionate look. The paintings were so remeniscent of Flick's work in subject matter, style and palette, Ella felt sure they must have inspired it.

Closing the catalogue, she gazed into the distance, letting the wealth of images sink in. If this was the kind of art that was being made in Scotland, she had a great deal to live up to, and she felt her spirits sink a little as she realised how much she still had to do. Grace liked the work she'd done so far, but she'd only seen two finished paintings and there was no guarantee she'd like the series as a whole. She had to focus on finishing it, and making sure it was breath-taking and innovative enough to be accepted by both Grace and Max.

She must – *must* - push all the distractions of the past weeks to one side and direct every ounce of her creative energy to the rest of the paintings, and the thought made her feel so exhausted that, checking that no one was watching, she allowed her eyes to close; and, as she drifted off, an image of her mother came to her, as clear as day.

Veronica Blyth was standing at her easel, painting furiously with her big broad brush, a cigarette hanging loosely from the side of her mouth as it always did, and Ella watched her as she swept her screaming turquoises and almost edible pinks across the canvas, totally absorbed in the human-like forms that emerged, as if by magic, from the seeming chaos.

Then, without warning, Veronica stopped and turned towards her and, much to her surprise, Ella saw that her face didn't hold its usual disapproving expression. Quite the reverse, in fact. Her mother was smiling at her, and nodding, and holding a paint-smeared hand out towards her, as though inviting her to have the courage to lay aside her pride and fear, and come and learn from her ...

Max's voice made her jump. "These should do the trick," he announced as, with a little bow, he handed her a plateful of tiny pastry-wrapped savouries and a glass of sparkling water. Retrieving the catalogue, he stood smiling down at her as, suddenly ravenous, she steered one canape, and then another, into her mouth.

"So, what do you think?" he said. "Do we compare favourably to the London scene?" and when Ella, embarrassed now and covered in crumbs, hastened to assure him they most certainly did, he added, "Of course most of these guys show in London too, and beyond." Then he took her empty plate and gave her back the catalogue.

"Do hold onto this" - he smiled down at her and she thought he gave her the subtlest of winks - "and perhaps, one of those days, you'll let me see that series of yours?" Then he held out his hand for her to shake, and disappeared into the crowds.

Ella stood up. Her head felt a little muggy, as though she'd woken out of too deep a sleep, but as she wended her way towards the exit she was relieved to see there was no visual disturbance that would prevent her from driving home. In the distance she could see Arlene had arrived and was talking and laughing with a little group of people, but it was already well after three and she preferred to get home in daylight, so instead of going over to speak to her she slipped out into the street. Relieved to be alone and in the fresh air, she walked as quickly as she could back to her car and reached Largs in time to see a crimson sunset. She took another two tablets and sat back in the comfortable chair with the gallery catalogue on her knee, waiting for them to work.

It was almost dark now and the beech leaves were coppery in the last of the light. Despite the stillness of the evening, they seemed to tremble more violently than they ever had before, which must, of course, be those squirrels. The days were definitely cooler, and that drop in temperature would be driving them to search deeper within the canopy for their nuts, and as a particularly violent judder rocked the nearest branches Ella got up and closed the blinds. Then she sat back down again and drowsily turned the catalogue pages, and once again, she found herself thinking about her mother.

Her work wouldn't be out of place in Max's catalogue. It had always been well ahead of its time, and all of a sudden she found herself longing to see them again. One of those days, she'd dig out Veronica's old exhibition catalogues. One of these days, she'd take her paintings out of storage …

22

When Arlene arrived next morning for their session, she was in exceptionally high spirits. The launch, she told Ella as they walked upstairs, had been 'awesome', and she'd been 'completely blown away' by Grace Nwapa's work, but the best thing of all was that she'd garnered two definite modelling requests and one possible one.

"I'm starting both the definites next week," she told Ella breathlessly and at breakneck speed, "but I'm not sure whether I can do the other. I mean I'd love to, because it's this artist guy and honestly, he is drop-dead gorgeous. He's called Angelo, and he's Italian I think, or maybe Spanish, with eyes like deep dark pools and the sexiest little pointy beard. The trouble is he can only have me on a Saturday morning, and of course I'm committed on Saturday mornings, but anyway" – she skipped into the studio then stopped and stood stock-still, gazing up at the ladder – "Holy shit, Ella, what on earth's that? It looks like some torture device from the Middle Ages …"

"It does, doesn't it." Ella joined her at the foot of Harry Flood's twelve-foot ladder and together they stared up at it in silent admiration. About a metre from the top, Ella had inserted a curtain-pole which she'd lashed to the uppermost rungs with thick garden wire then draped with chiffon so that it cascaded down over the rungs, hiding their paint-daubed metal. "It reminds me of a crucifix, and that gave me what I'm hoping will turn out to be a good idea for the next pose." She turned anxiously to Arlene. "Are you OK about getting up there and hanging from it? We could put one of the small tables beside it to give you a leg-up?"

"'Course I'm OK!" Arlene began to peel off her clothes in readiness for the ascent. "Will I still have the chains?"

Ella cleared the nearest table and carried it over. "I'd still like chains, yes. Maybe we could have them hanging loosely round your neck this time, and in the next pose you could hold them up above your head in triumph."

She broke off then. "I'm sorry I didn't come and speak to you at the launch, by the way, but I got a bit stressed so I left early. I'm not good in crowds," she went on in answer to Arlene's quizzical look. "I mean, when I was your age I was absolutely fine, I loved socialising, but yesterday was the first time in over twenty years I'd been among so many people. Anyway" – she held out an arm to steady Arlene as she clambered up onto the table – "you managed fine without me, and I'm so glad you're starting to build up a client base. Mind you don't get your foot caught," and she stepped back and watched Arlene climb nimbly up, hook her arms round the pole, and hang limply with her head bent to one side and her eyes rolling heavenwards.

"I'm trying to look like those statues they had in the chapel when I was a kid," she explained, "of Jesus dying on the cross. Is that the kind of thing you're after?"

Ella viewed her from the easel. "Remember I'll be painting out the cross and making you appear to float in mid-air, so maybe make your arms and legs less rigid, and go for less 'agony' and more 'ecstasy'?" She adjusted the lights, picked up her camera, and took a few shots, then looked at each of them in turn. The pose was spectacular.

She took some more shots, and when she had the perfect image she began blocking in the main proportions of the composition. When she'd finished, she helped Arlene down.

"I'm very pleased with that," she said. "Thanks," and, leaving Arlene to dress, she went back to the easel, gathered up her brushes, and opened the blinds.

"I was wondering, Arlene," she said when they were standing side by side again, "if perhaps you'd like to come on Wednesdays instead of Saturdays for the next while? I've got more than enough material to last me a couple of weeks, so if you were to come, let's see" – she rummaged about on one of the tables and picked up her diary – "a week on Wednesday, that would give you space to see your new clients. Including" – she gave Arlene a wink – "sexy Angelo."

She looked at Arlene expectantly, but Arlene was staring out of the window and didn't answer. "Why are the branches rustling so much?" she said. "It's not windy, but they're bouncing about all over the place …" and when Ella explained about the squirrels and the beech nuts she gave her a dubious look.

"They must be squirrels in hobnailed boots then. Didn't you hear the sound of branches cracking? I'm sure I saw some bits of broken twigs falling …"

Ella followed Arlene's gaze. All was calm in the tree again, but she could see there were some broken twigs hanging ready to fall, and her stomach gave a momentary lurch. An image of the man in the black car popped up in her mind and she immediately dismissed it.

"It's just the time of year," she told Arlene firmly. "It'll have been a crowd of squirrels squabbling over nuts," and she picked up the camera and handed it to Arlene. "Aren't those last photographs I took of you brilliant? You know, I've had this camera for years and hardly used it, and I'd no idea it had such amazing clarity and depth of field."

Arlene looked approvingly at the photo on the screen. Then she turned the camera this way and that, reading the words printed on the case, and gave a low whistle of admiration. "This is one of the best digital SLR's I've ever seen. In fact the last time I saw one this good was at a photo-shoot with a professional photographer." She shot Ella a piercing look. "You do know they cost thousands?"

"Thousands?" Ella repeated. There was a sound in her head like a small heart beating very quickly. "I'd no idea. Derek gave me it for my fiftieth, and I thought it was maybe worth a couple of hundred, but *thousands* ... I can't believe it. Derek's my husband," she added.

Arlene passed the camera back. "The gentle, kind husband you left," she said. "Yes, you told me," and she took the little brown pay packet Ella handed her and left with a cheery wave. Ella sat back down and looked at each of the images again, choosing the ones to print out, and when she'd finished she continued to sit very still, nursing the camera in her lap, till it was well past lunchtime.

It was after two when Ella finished lunch, but even then she didn't feel like working. The business of the camera had shocked her, and she kept thinking back to that birthday, six years ago.

The day had been anything but joyful. Carys had taken the day off from her new high-powered job in Cheltenham and had arrived early in the afternoon bearing champagne and gifts, but there wasn't even a card from Lucy, and neither Ella nor Derek felt one bit like celebrating. They'd all drunk a great deal of champagne, and Derek had eaten a lot of Ella's birthday chocolates, and they'd both done their best to be jolly, but nothing could shift the utter gloom of it all; and now she found herself wondering if, even away back then, Derek had either already embarked on his affair, or was seriously considering embarking on it. Wasn't it the kind of midlife-crisis sort of thing people did to keep the blues at bay?

There had certainly been tell-tale signs, because as well as the prohibitively expensive camera, Derek had also presented her with an enormous bunch of red roses, tied with an over-large red ribbon, and wasn't that exactly the sort of thing men in the throes of guilt did?

She knew they did, actually, because she'd Googled it. She'd typed in 'Tell-tale signs your partner is having an affair' and sure enough, 'Gives more gifts than usual' was right up there, second only to 'Loses interest in sex' (which, to be fair, they both had at least five years earlier) and 'Takes more care over appearance'.

That birthday afternoon, she'd put the roses in a vase out in the hall, and as the weeks went by had taken a perverse pleasure in watching them open so wide you could see right down into their centres. Then, just as they began to drop their petals, she'd taken them to her studio and painted them in all their decrepitude, not missing a single detail of their progress towards death and decay; and all the while, as the new Millenium prepared to dawn and she painted this image of hopelessness, wasn't she having the first rumblings of anarchic thoughts?

At first these thoughts were too vague to be voiced but then, over the weeks, she began to give them words, and the words went something like, 'Perhaps it doesn't have to be this way forever. Perhaps I could change it. Perhaps, just perhaps, I could escape …' It had, however, taken her five more years to pluck up the courage to put her thoughts into action, and now the sobering realisation came to her that if she hadn't found out about Derek's affair she might still be in Highgate, painting roses.

Sometimes, you just had to force yourself out of your comfort zone. You had to do things that were out of character, things that scared you witless but were nonetheless worth doing and, dumping the remains of her meal in the kitchen, she ran into the living-room, checked that Wetherby's car wasn't in its parking space, then hurried into the hall. She unhooked both sets of keys from the hook, crept out onto the landing, and stood outside Wetherby's flat for ages, listening. Then, finally, she rang his doorbell, and when no one answered she rang again

She pushed the key into the lock, and then froze. This was utter madness, she told herself. She'd done it once, and that was bad enough, but to do it again was unforgivable, and very probably against the law. She had a key, so it wasn't technically breaking in, but it must at least be classed as 'trespass', and how would that look, if she was caught? Wetherby was unlikely to press charges, but what if he did? The General Teaching Council would certainly take a dim view of it. She could lose her job.

Taking the key out again, she turned and walked slowly back to her own door. She didn't immediately go in, however, but stood on the landing, listening again. Very faintly, from downstairs, she heard the soft sound of Cally's distant singing, and she pictured Maeve, sitting at her window, looking out at the garden hour after hour, wondering where she was, and how she was, and whether she was still alive.

It was what she, Ella, did every day of her life too - this awful, endless, wondering. Where Lucy was, what she was doing, whether she was ill and surrounded by strangers. Whether she'd died, and no one had told her and Derek because no one knew who she was. For all she knew, it was what Derek did too, and Carys; and it was torture. It was utter torture, and she had a moral duty to do whatever she could to spare Maeve from hers.

Suddenly resolute, she spun back round to face Wetherby's door. If the painting – the 'affront to the senses' - was in there, it must surely give a clue to what had happened to Flick, and, from what Max had said about Wetherby's behaviour in the gallery, she was more and more convinced it was. And if, for his own narrow-minded reasons, Wetherby had confiscated it, surely *that* was every bit as criminal an act as slipping into his flat when he was out and looking for it? Surely he had no right to have it in his possession? Not allowing herself another thought, Ella shoved the key into Wetherby's lock, slipped inside, and listened at the inner door for any signs of life. All was quiet, so she tiptoed inside and began to search.

The most likely place for the canvas to be was the big walk-in cupboard in the living room, but Ella decided to be methodical and look in all the other possible places first, starting with the hall. There was only one small cupboard there, and it was full of coats and hats and umbrellas, and she was about to go into the study when she noticed, lying upside-down on the hall table, a pair of small white shoes such as would be used for bowling, and two things struck her. One was that the shoes were certainly not Wetherby's, and the second was that it was out of character for him to leave them lying about like that, so perhaps he'd left in a hurry.

She took a quick look in the study and bedroom next, then hurried on into the living room and, taking care not to brush against any of the ornaments or soft furnishings, slid the cupboard door open, switched on the light, and immediately spotted what surely must be a painting, high up on the top shelf, wrapped in bubble-wrap. Standing on tiptoe, she edged it out a little and saw it had string tied round it, and there was a label attached to the string with its title on. Heart beating wildly now, she pulled it down and took it over to the window.

All along her intention, if she found Flick's painting, was to remove it as quickly as possible, unwrap it in the safety of her own flat, take photos to show Max and then, one Saturday afternoon in the future, nip back and replace it; but now that she had it in her hands and could see Flick's blurred and distorted image she couldn't resist loosening the tape and taking a little peek inside.

Laying the canvas on the green velvet settee, she read the title on the label: 'Leda and the Swan'. Then she untied the string, undid the tape, carefully eased off the bubble-wrap, and stared down at the painting; and as she took in its content, and realised the implications of that content, a feeling of disgust and nausea rose up from her stomach and she knew she had to be out of this flat, back in the safety of her own space, before she examined it further.

She grabbed the loose edges of the bubble-wrap, stuck them haphazardly down, then ran over to the cupboard to switch off the light and close the door, but as she turned to go she heard the sound of the gate being opened. Standing in the shelter of the curtain, she looked out of the window and saw Wetherby, in his straw hat and striped blazer, struggling angrily with the catch.

Her head was swimming with panic now, and her legs felt as though they couldn't move. Clasping the canvas tight to her side, she forced herself to make a dash for the door, and as she stepped out onto the landing she heard the front door open and then slam shut. Putting the canvas down, she fumbled in her pocket for her key, but her fingers were trembling and she couldn't get it to go into the lock, and for one terrible moment she wondered whether it was her key or Wetherby's.

The footsteps were on the stairs by the time she'd unlocked the door and pushed it open, and she picked up the canvas, hurled it inside and then, turning, smiled as bright a smile as she could muster at Wetherby and wished him a 'good afternoon'.

Wetherby barely acknowledged her greeting in his hurry to get inside his flat, and as she watched him take out his key she saw that his hat and blazer were wet. "Forgot my friend's bowling shoes," he explained as he opened the door. "Said I'd take them to be re-soled and what did I do but leave the blessed things behind, and she's due on in half an hour - if it dries up, that is. What a silly old duffer I am sometimes …" and he disappeared inside his flat.

Ella headed straight for the kitchen and poured herself a glass of wine. She took it and the painting into the studio, where she took off the bubble-wrap again and propped it up on the easel. She sank down onto the chair, took several mouthfuls of wine, and when her heart-rate had returned to some semblance of normality, began to study Flick's monstrous painting. And it was then that, to her utter horror, she remembered the string with its label, which must still be lying on the green velvet of Wetherby's settee.

23

"Oh my god, Ella" – Aminah gazed wide-eyed over her coffee-mug – "it sounds like one of those creepy horror films! So what happened next? Did he see the string?"

"Thankfully no. He didn't come out for ages, probably because he was getting a plastic bag to keep the shoes dry, and all the time I just had to sit there, quaking, waiting for him to ring the doorbell and demand his painting back, because no one else has a key so he'd know it was me who'd taken it. Anyway, eventually I heard his door slamming, and him thumping down the stairs, but honestly, Aminah, I was so scared I swear my heart stopped beating …"

"So then what did you do? Did you go back and remove the evidence?"

Ella smiled despite herself. "I didn't half! I grabbed the string of course, and then I was like one of these forensic scientists at a crime scene, searching for tiny bits of bubble-wrap and masking-tape I might have dropped, and stray hairs I might have shed in the heat of the moment, and I only went back home when I was quite sure I hadn't left a single incriminating detail behind."

"And then you phoned Max James?"

Ella took a couple of deep breaths, then sipped some of her coffee. Even here, in the steamy warmth of *Enzo's*, she could feel the chill she'd felt on Saturday afternoon. "As soon as I'd calmed down, yes, and I told him what was in the painting – that it was basically a very violent bestial rape - and he said something like, 'Ah well, that's 'Leda and the Swan' for you, isn't it,' and then he said he'd pop in on Sunday morning, and that's what he did."

She took her camera out of her handbag. "Do you want to see it? I brought it to show you, but you don't have to, if you'd prefer not," and when Aminah said of course she wanted to see it, she handed the camera to her. with a grim 'Brace yourself.'

As soon as she saw the image, Aminah's jaw visibly dropped, and as she examined the photo she kept giving little gasps as she spotted yet another gory detail.

"I didn't even know swans had claws," she said, "and the way it's been painted is so horrific. It looks as though it's ripping the woman's flesh to pieces, and she's just lying back taking it, and hasn't she got the weirdest expression on her face? It's hard to know whether she's in agony or whether she's actually enjoying it," and she handed the camera back to Ella. "Don't you think?"

Ella nodded. "Classic pornography, isn't it. The old 'women secretly long to be raped' thing. Apparently, Max was telling me, 'Leda and the Swan' was hugely popular in the nineteenth century, and he showed me a whole load of engravings around the theme of a swan making love to a woman," and she handed the camera to Aminah again. "See? Same pose. Apparently it was too shocking to indulge in erotic fantasies involving women and men, but women and swans was classical and therefore perfectly OK! "

Aminah peered at the old engravings. "I don't really mind these," she said. "I mean, they're a bit dodgy in the sense that a swan fucking a woman *is* a bit dodgy, but they're quite loving and tender, and I must say Leda looks like she's having a whale of a time. So is it one of the Greek myths then?"

Ella nodded. "The swan's Zeus, and actually one of the babies Leda bore to him became Helen of Troy. But what worries me is why Flick painted her version in such a shocking way. Every other time she paints a swan it's a sad little figure floating on a pond, and then all of a sudden she makes it this violent sexual predator." She leaned across the table and stared pointedly at Aminah. "And then she disappears and is never seen again. Surely now you have to agree something sinister's going on? Maeve Oliver's frantic with worry too," she added.

Aminah dabbed the sugar on her plate with her finger and licked it off, and when Ella repeated, "*Don't* you agree?" she put her elbows on the table and leant her chin on them. Then she bent forward so close her nose almost touched Ella's.

"By 'something sinister', I presume you mean some kind of horrible 'foul play'" – she drew air-quotes in the space between them – "but surely if someone in the house had done something awful to Flick, everyone would have known about it? And when she disappeared without trace they'd have contacted the police?"

Ella opened her mouth to protest, but Aminah went on. "Look, Ella. Someone came and cleared Flick's flat, didn't they? So someone close to her knew what had happened and now, presumably, they know where, and how, she is," and she reached over and her hand on Ella's.

"I know you're worried about this whole business, and so is your nice old lady, and you both want to get at the truth, but I honestly think you're getting into the realms of melodrama here. There's a logical explanation for Flick's disappearance that doesn't involve rapes and murders and decomposing corpses in attics," and she gave the hand a sugary squeeze. Then she stood up and took out her purse. "You know what I think you should do? Ask Wetherby. Take the painting back, apologise profusely for borrowing it, and say you've a right to know the truth, and so does Maeve. That's what I'd do. My shout, by the way," and she walked up to the counter and paid for the coffees.

Nothing more was said as they walked along the pavement to Ella's car, and when Aminah had hugged her goodbye she kept her hands on Ella's arms and gave her a concerned look. "I hope you're not cross with me for not quite believing you?" she said, and Ella shook her head.

"Of course I'm not cross, Aminah," she said. "You're probably right. I know I'm apt to let my imagination run away with me, and the most sensible thing would be to do what you suggest. I'll think about it. Promise."

Before she went upstairs to her flat, Ella popped in to see Maeve, and despite her assurances that she'd just had a coffee, Maeve insisted on putting the kettle on. While she was in the kitchen, Ella took a look round the room, and the first thing she found that interested her was a photo on the mantelpiece of a rather attractive young man with long dark wavy hair and piercing brown eyes that stared sullenly at the camera.

She picked it up, then headed for the piano and began to look at each of the photos in turn. Most of them were of choirs or people playing various instruments, and she edged each aside and finally found, right at the back, one that showed a group of three musicians performing in a church. She took it and the sullen young man over to the window and looked at each in turn.

The young man, she thought, might be Maeve's son although, with his dark eyes and rather aloof expression, he bore not the slightest resemblance to his mother, and after another cursory view Ella turned her attention to the three musicians.

Wiping the dust away, she looked closely at each in turn. On the left sat an earnest-looking man with close-cropped hair, gold-rimmed glasses, and a well-trimmed beard who was playing a lute, and next to him was a blonde girl with a flute. Behind them, seated at a harpsichord painted with gilded fruits and flowers, was a young woman who exactly matched Max's description of Felicity Hunter. She had finely-sculptured features and red hair tied up loosely in a ribbon from which little ringlets escaped to frame her face, and she was singing as she played. The expression on her face was one of utter joy.

"I've baked us some cinnamon buns." Maeve came back in and put a plate down on the coffee table. "I don't suppose you've eaten since lunchtime, have you dear? and I know you said the cakes in that café you and your friend go to aren't to your taste." She motioned to Ella to help herself while she went back to the kitchen to fetch the tea. "Shall I bring you a little cup of milk?" she called back from the door. "Help wash the buns down?" and when at last they were both settled, Ella tentatively held up the photograph of the dark-eyed young man.

"I hope you don't mind, Maeve, but I couldn't help seeing this and I was wondering, is he your son?"

Maeve gave a sad smile. "Oh yes, that's my Nat all right," and she reached over, took the photo from Ella, and studied it thoughtfully.

"I never thought I'd have a child, you know," she said at last, and it was a wonderful surprise when I discovered I was pregnant." She smiled over at Ella. "I was over forty, you know, and it had never happened before, so it seemed rather like a miracle," and when she went back to studying the photo, Ella noticed that her eyes had that glazed, unseeing look to them again.

"Nat was always rather shy and withdrawn," Maeve went on, "which I think must be the reason why he's never had a proper girlfriend." She turned the photograph round to Ella. "You can see he's good-looking, can't you, so I really can't think why. I used to think perhaps he was a homosexual, which of course wouldn't have bothered me in the slightest, but I never liked to ask, and he never volunteered the information," and, with a sigh, she laid the photograph, face down, on the table. "Since Flick went," she added so quietly Ella hardly heard her, "I hardly ever see him."

Ella nibbled the rim of her bun, giving Maeve as much time as she needed to talk about her son, but when she said nothing more she decided to risk another question. "I hope this won't upset you, Maeve," she said, "but is this the Early Music group you told me about? *The Silver Swan*?" and she passed the photo of the three musicians over to her.

There was another moment of stillness as Maeve looked at the photograph. Then she sighed into its silence. "Yes, dear, it is," she said. "We'd no idea at the time, but this was the last concert they ever gave." She held the photograph close to her face. "Don't you thinks Flick looks sublimely happy? She was probably singing 'The Silver Song', which I already told you was her favourite of all the madrigals."

She took a handkerchief out from her sleeve and dabbed her eyes. "I always felt Flick was too good for this world you know, and when she went away I knew I'd never meet anyone quite like her again."

She lowered her voice to a conspiratorial whisper. "After you left the other day, I remembered something. I have the leaflet for that last concert, and it has the minister's phone number on it. Perhaps you'd fetch it dear? It's in the letter-rack on the mantelpiece."

Ella walked over to the fireplace and leafed through the postcards and envelopes in the letter-rack. The leaflet was right at the back, pressed hard against the tarnished brass, and she took it out and unfolded it.

At the top was a sketch of a St Columba's Church, with its name printed above, and below was printed: 'Summer Evening Madrigals with *The Silver Swan,* Sunday July 3rd at 7.30 pm' and underneath was a phone number for a Reverend Michael Greer.

"May I borrow this?" Ella asked, and when Maeve nodded she folded the leaflet carefully and put it in her pocket. "I think I'll give the Reverend Greer a ring."

24

Jinty turned to a fresh page in her Commonplace Book and began to write, but she was so cold her brain felt frozen. When she'd got home she'd taken the duvet off her bed and wrapped it round herself, but it hadn't helped because the cold was somewhere deeper inside than a duvet's warmth could reach. It felt as though it was in her bones, and now there was something wrong with her hand too.

She put down the pencil and clenched and unclenched it, but it still wouldn't do what she wanted it to. Every time she wrote a word it gave a little jerk, as though it had a mind of its own, and the more she tried to hold the pencil steady, the more it jerked, so that the writing ended up looking the way your writing looked when you used the wrong hand. It scared her.

It was late afternoon on Wednesday, and earlier that day she'd witnessed something so awful she couldn't imagine ever telling anyone. She hadn't, in fact, found the words yet to properly tell it to herself, which was why she'd opened the Commonplace Book at the back page and written, in shaky capitals, the words: DIARY – STRICTLY CONFERDENTIAL.

If she could only write down what she'd seen, in her best writing on the lovely smooth white paper, then perhaps she'd begin to understand it; and the good thing was that, whatever she wrote, it would never be seen by anyone else because Miss Blyth had assured them the diary section would be private, and she'd told them to mark it clearly as 'conferdential' to make quite sure. She wouldn't, she'd added, read it herself either, and to prove it she'd given her solemn word, just like Mrs Nwapa had.

The trouble was that awful shaking in her hand, and she knew the reason for the shaking was the horrible mixture of fear and guilt she felt. Fear, because the act had been witnessed through Miss Blyth's window from the top of Miss Blyth's tree, which surely had to be the very worst form of trespassing, and guilt, because what she'd seen Miss Blyth was doing was too shameful for words.

Today was the third time she'd climbed Miss Blyth's tree. The first time was the trial climb on the day she followed her home from school, and the second was right to the top and had turned into a bit of a near-death experience. Today's climb could only be properly understood in the context of the first two climbs, so she'd decided the best thing to do was describe each climb in turn.

The first climb was easy to write about, in fact, if she'd been feeling better it might actually have been quite good fun. She'd called it 'Climb #1: The Trial', and it told how she'd followed Miss Blyth home.

Miss Blyth had, as expected, been very easy to follow, and in fact the hardest part for Jinty was forcing herself to walk more slowly than she normally ever would, but once she'd got into the way of it, it was fine. There was really only one sticky moment when, for some unknown reason, Miss Blyth suddenly stopped, swivelled round and, for one heart-stopping moment, stared directly back at Jinty.

Luckily, there was a big thick privet hedge growing alongside the pavement, into which Jinty had immediately thrown herself. Then she'd sat inside the hedge, as still as ever she could, with pieces of twig digging painfully into her neck, and leaves sticking up her nose and ears, and waited in fear and trembling to hear the dread sound of Miss Blyth's footsteps coming towards her.

She waited for ages, hardly breathing and then, when nothing happened, she peeped cautiously out and saw that Miss Blyth was bending down, doing something to her shoe. She withdrew back into the hedge and when she looked again, she saw her disappearing round a bend, and had to run very quietly after her, so as not to lose sight of her.

At last Miss Blyth stopped outside one of the big houses in Beech Avenue, and Jinty waited till she'd opened the gate and gone up the path before ambling casually up to the gate herself. She'd stared at the blue front door with its frame of bright red Virginia creeper and then, keeping a cautious eye on each of the big windows, began to walk up the path, but as she drew nearer to the door she saw there was an old woman sitting at the bottom left window, staring out and, side-stepping into the garden, looked around to see where she should go next. And it was then that she noticed, towering over her, the biggest, tallest, most magnificent beech tree she'd ever seen in her entire life.

She hadn't intended to climb it. Her mission, that time, had been to gather flowers to draw, but as soon as she set eyes on the tree, all that was forgotten. For this tree was, without a doubt, a first-class, five-star tree, and it would be criminal not to give it a go.

And it was indeed heaven to climb. The first branch, which grew almost at right angles to the trunk, was exactly the right height for her to reach up and grasp, and then, as she was hoisting herself up, her feet found a mass of wood just big enough for her to stand up and easily reach the next branch. Peering up into the canopy, she saw it was full of hedgehog-husked beech-nuts, and she pulled some and pushed them into her pocket. Then she stood up on the branch and, once again, there was the next branch, straight and strong and perfectly within arms-length.

It was getting late then, so she climbed back down and ran up the side of the house to the back, where she found two gardens separated by a path. One garden was neat and tidy and hadn't many flowers, and the other was untidy and full of them, so she picked a few, and then, right at the back of the untidy garden, she saw there were hundreds and hundreds of pink roses growing round a little sky-blue shed.

The roses would be lovely to draw so, glancing up at the top windows to make sure no one was watching, she picked her way through the weeds and gathered as many as she could carry. Before she left, she took a peek through the window of the shed and to her astonishment she saw there was a little chair, and a little chest of drawers, and all sorts of pictures, and cushions, and blankets. There was even a tired-looking teddy-bear and a faded pink floppy rabbit on the chair, and the whole thing reminded her of a house you might find in a fairy tale. She was certain that it, along with the nice untidy garden, must belong to Miss Blyth.

As soon as she got home she put the roses in water and, with the soft pink colouring pencil she'd borrowed from the classroom cupboard, made her first botanical drawing on a piece of Miss Blyth's nice thick white paper.

The account of the second climb she called 'Climb #2: The Discovery'. It took place on a Saturday morning while Mam was at the Dementia Unit arranging Nan's new room and Uncle Chris was away out with his mates, so she could stay all day if she wanted to. She'd climbed the first bit of the tree in double-quick time and then she went on climbing, and no matter how high she got there was always another convenient branch, and another, and another.

Eventually, of course, the branches became too thin for safety, so she sat down on the last weight-bearing one and peered out.

It was lovely in the tree canopy. The air was damp and smelt of autumn, and the more she sat, the more rustlings and scrapings she heard. There was the occasional bird-call too, and once she thought she saw the fuzzy tail-end of a squirrel; and every now and then, there was the dry shuddering sound of moving leaves when a stray little wind wheedled its way inside.

The branch was perfect too, warm and smooth and comfortable, and she slipped off her backpack, found the orange juice and Penguin biscuit she'd brought and, leaning back against the ancient trunk, half-closed her eyes.

She was as alone as anyone could possibly be, yet she must be so close to Miss Blyth's house she could almost reach out and touch it, and as she watched the golden leaves flicker all around her she realised that the cold empty feeling she'd had for weeks had gone. It had been sitting like a cold damp stone in the middle of her chest for so long she'd almost got used to it, yet now, sitting inside Miss Blyth's tree, she realised it had been replaced by something warm and safe and happy, and she wondered where exactly, in this beautiful big house, Miss Blyth was.

Carefully, she parted the branches, and when she saw nothing but more leaves she leant forward and parted more. Still she couldn't see where she actually was, so she edged herself a little higher, grabbed as much foliage as she could, and pulled it aside like two leafy curtains; and as she did, two things happened at more or less the same time. The first thing was that she tipped forwards, and the second thing was that, for one brief giddy moment, she saw, looking straight out of the window at her, a woman who was not Miss Blyth.

She could never remember what happened next because it was all a confused mix of crackling twigs and falling leaves and nothing at all to hold on to, and a light above her that was either the sky or the inside of her head. Then, quite suddenly, there was a thud and a sharp pain, and she was half-sitting, half-lying on solid wood. Clinging onto the branch, she waited till her breath returned to normal before carefully making her way down to the bottom of the tree.

She sat very still with her back against the trunk, waiting for the dizziness in her head to stop, and then she heard the front door click open, and Miss Blyth saying something, and then the door closed again and what sounded like one set of footsteps began to come nearer. The footsteps were light and skipping and quite definitely not Miss Blyth's, and as the slim, black-clad figure pushed open the gate, Jinty caught sight of its face and realised it was the same as the one she'd seen at the window; and at the very same moment she also realised that her backpack, and her juice, and her Penguin, were still at the top of the tree.

Jinty read the two accounts over twice. Written down like that, it sounded like an adventure you'd read about in a book and, because she'd been careful to leave big spaces in between the main parts of the story, there was plenty of opportunity for illustrations later. It would be fun to draw herself following Miss Blyth and having to jump inside the hedge, and then standing at the gate staring open-mouthed at the blue front door with the red Virginia creeper. She'd draw the fall too, with herself rolling over and over in mid-air, covered in twigs and leaves. She might even include a couple of squirrels running away in alarm, and end with the same two squirrels sitting together on the upper branch, eating her Penguin and drinking her juice.

The thought of the illustrations cheered her up and she couldn't wait to start, but she knew that before she did, she had to force herself to write 'Climb #3: The Chained Lady' because that, after all, was the whole point of the thing.

She printed the title and was relieved to find her hand wasn't so shaky any more, but then she realised that, for the first time in days, she was hungry. It was a nice, normal feeling and she went downstairs to the kitchen and found a can of curry-flavoured baked beans and a loaf of white bread. She put two slices of bread in the toaster and tipped the beans into a pan, and she was catching the toast as it popped up when the door banged open and Uncle Chris staggered in. He stood for a while, swaying to and fro and peering about, and then he shambled in and the kitchen filled with the stink of stale beer and unwashed trousers and cigarette smoke.

"A'right, Jinty lass?" He flung his jacket over one of the chairs, and when Jinty didn't answer he turned his back on her and began poking about in the saucepan with the wooden spoon. "Eatin' my beans now, are you?" he turned to grin at her. There was a frothy yellow plug of sputum in the corner of his mouth and the whites of his eyes were pink. "I ask you, what's the fuckin' world comin' to when a man cannae eat his own fuckin' beans …" and he opened the cupboards one after the other, then pushed past Jinty to the sink and splashed about wildly in the water.

"Where the hell's a' the plates gone? 'Ave you got the fuckin' plates?" and he made a lunge at Jinty, grabbing at the waistband of her jeans, pretending to look down inside them. "You got ony dirty plates down there, Jinty, eh? You bin hidin' the dirty plates inside yer knickers?" and he pulled her so hard she swung round and her head hit one of the open cupboard doors. For a moment she lost balance and stumbled, and as she fell he gave her a push.

He was above her then, slobbering down at her, and she felt her chest swell with fear and fury. "Get off me!" she heard herself scream. "Get your filthy hands off me!" and then she was kicking at anything she could find to kick – his arms, his crotch, his face – and her legs were like pistons, hammering away, gaining strength with every blow, and all she could think was that she'd passed the point of caring what happened to him. She was a wild animal now, and she'd kick that crotch of his till whatever horrors were inside were mashed to a bleeding pulp. She'd have bludgeoned him to death, if she'd had an axe big enough.

In the end, he gave up. Doubled over, he hugged his stomach and began to retch, and then there was a long liquid sound as he threw up into the corner where the bin was. Silent now, he lay there drooling, and Jinty saw that the drool was red and frothy. She stood up and, without a backwards glance, ran back up to her bedroom, where she threw herself into the big armchair and curled up into the smallest shape she could make.

25

Aminah lifted the witch-on-a-broomstick silhouettes off her desk and added them to the pile of bats on the floor. Sitting down, she pulled her chair over beside Ella's.

"I wanted to tell you the latest on Jinty before we go into class," she said, "just in case she's there, though I wouldn't be at all surprised if she doesn't appear again today. You know I told you about the 'Uncle Chris' guy being taken into hospital?"

Ella cast her mind back to last week. Her memory of Aminah's phone call was a bit hazy, and she suspected she hadn't given its details as much thought as she normally would because she was so taken up with the one she'd had with the Reverend Greer of St Columba's, and the one she'd had with Arlene about the dishy Spanish guy who, it turned out, even had a castle - a *real* castle with turrets and a moat - in Andalucía. "Yes, of course," she said. "Didn't you say he'd been beaten up at the pub?"

To her relief, Aminah seemed to find her response acceptable. "They're not sure where he was beaten up, actually. His attackers might have followed him home, because when they found him in the kitchen he was in such a bad way they don't think he could've walked there." She pulled an ironically sympathetic face. "Three ribs cracked, apparently, and a perforated lung. Anyway, he's OK and he's been sent home, but what I wanted to tell you" – she dropped her voice – "is that in the meantime Social Work have found Jinty a temporary foster home. Fortunately it's quite near here, in Fairlie, so she can get the bus in to school, but I dread to think how she must be feeling. According to her mum, she could've been in the house at the time. She might even have witnessed the attack."

"Why 'might'? I mean, hasn't she said anything?"

Aminah shook her head. "Nothing. I mean, she's hardly been at school, but when she does come she's completely withdrawn into herself. She appeared on Friday morning, but Gordon said she just sat there with her Commonplace Book open in front of her like a shield, and at lunchtime she managed to get on the bus and go home.

"Talking of which" – she raised her eyes to the heavens – "Maura wants all the Commonplace Books handed in to her by the last week in November so that she can make a start on the Parents' Night display. I know it seems like ages away, but it's actually only three more Mondays, so we'd better step on it this morning and get the Hallowe'en poems illustrated."

Ella looked at her watch. "It's only ten minutes till the bell rings," she said, and she piled the shapes into a box. "Let's talk while we're sticking these on the wall!" and they hurried along to the classroom.

"Why don't you come and see my studio one of these days?" Ella said as she handed a glue-smeared bat up to Aminah to stick on the orange frieze paper. "You could see 'Leda' in all its gory glory before I return it to Paul Wetherby and confess. What do you think?"

Aminah beamed down at her. "I'd love to! I'm not so sure about seeing 'Leda' up close and personal, but I'm dying to see your 'Flying' series. Actually, if it suited you, tomorrow afternoon would be good because I'm in Glasgow on a Day Release course at the Language Centre so with any luck I'll get away early. Would that be all right?"

"Tomorrow's perfect," Ella handed her up another gluey bat. "By the way, did I tell you about Bruno Glass?"

"Bruno Glass? No, you didn't. I'd have remembered ..."

Ella took a quick glance at her watch. Then, rather more urgently than before, she continued with her gluing. "Maeve finally opened up to me about Flick, and she gave me a leaflet about a concert she and her music group gave last year in St Columba's church. It had the minister's phone number on it, so I phoned him and he said the flautist had moved overseas but the lute player – that's Bruno Glass - lives locally. He wasn't allowed to give out his contact details, but he promised he'd give him my number. So now I just have to wait and hope Bruno's not taken a vow of silence like all the others."

Aminah stuck a bat on top of the large yellow moon. "I'm impressed," she said. "It sounds as though you're beginning to get somewhere," and as the bell began to ring she hopped off the table. "The Bruno guy's bound to know what happened to Flick," she shouted above it. "I mean, if you're practising and performing with someone you can't help but get to know them well. Sergei's in a rock band with three other guys, and the four of them are joined at the hip!"

She looked over to the table at the back of the class, and as the children filed in they both waited to see if Jinty would be among them. But when everyone had taken their places and Ella had handed out the pencils and the Commonplace Books, there was no thin little figure with turquoise spectacles and poker-straight hair sitting opposite William Hay, eager to start, and as Ella drove home that afternoon she couldn't get Jinty's face out of her mind.

It had rained all day, and as she peered between the windscreen wipers at the windswept leaves somersaulting across the streets, it seemed as though the last vestiges of summer were being blown away, and when she got home the studio was grey and dull too, and the gold almost gone from the beech tree. Its leaves hung drab and brown now, thin silvery lines of water gathering in their veins and tipping over to soak the leaves below.

Ella sank down wearily on the comfortable chair, kicked off her shoes, and gazed over at the easel. In this new painting, Arlene was hanging in mid-air with her arms stretched out on either side, and the gauzy material, instead of being draped over her in loose folds, stretched high above her, like great white wings.

The semi-nudity had come about accidentally that Saturday, when the chiffon garment slipped down and exposed one of Arlene's breasts. Lying on the translucent material, it looked as beautiful and delicate as a rosebud, and Ella asked her if she'd be comfortable leaving it there, and Arlene had laughed and said of course she'd be comfortable, she preferred to be naked anyway.

Ella had pulled the material further down, till the whole breast was visible, like Eurydice's breast in the painting Flick had given Harry Flood, and then she'd spent ages going up and down the ladder trying out different ways of positioning the chains round Arlene, but each time, when she went back to the easel to see how it looked, something was wrong.

Then she realised what it was. "The pose is great," she'd told Arlene, "but the light's awful. It was OK last time because it was still sunny outside, but today's so dull. Ideally, I'd love your skin colours to be in natural light," and immediately Arlene had said, "Why don't you open the blinds then? It's not as though we're overlooked."

Going over to the window, Ella had opened each of the blinds in turn, and as light flooded in she looked triumphantly up at Arlene. "That's *it*," she said. "Your skin tones are exactly right now, and the leaf shadows are much less intrusive now there's no sun," and she climbed back up the ladder and pulled the garment this way and that till its folds hung to her satisfaction.

She'd draped the chains round Arlene's neck then, letting them fall over her bared breast, and as she began to paint, she'd been conscious of exaggerating the billowing of the chiffon so that Arlene looked more and more like a butterfly breaking out of its cocoon; and now, as she looked at the painting again, a title suddenly came to her. She'd call this painting 'Metamorphosis 1', and the next – in which the chains were hardly visible any more - would be 'Metamorphosis 2'. Then the final painting, which would be the last in the series, would simply be called 'Flight'.

Feeling moderately accomplished, Ella padded through to the kitchen, put a frozen curry into the microwave, and began to gather her school things together, and as she was stacking her bags by the front door her phone rang and it was Arlene. She sounded much more solemn than usual.

"I don't know if you've seen today's Largs Chronicle?" she said. "One of my friends texted me to say Largs was n the news and had I heard, so I went on the web and some guy's written a big article about a paedophile who's been hanging around your primary school. There's a photo of the school and everything. Haven't you heard?"

A tiny shiver ran down Ella's back. "The Largs Chronicle?" she repeated. "But that's absolutely ridiculous. I mean, one of the teachers thought she saw a guy in a car hanging around during the summer, but anything else is pure speculation. Did the article mention anyone on the staff who'd been interviewed?" She paused. "Did it mention a teacher called Yvonne?"

There was a silence as Arlene searched through the article and then she said, "No, there's no actual name. It does mention the car though – apparently it was a black one - but all it says about where the story came from is 'a source on the staff who wishes to remain anonymous', and at the end it says, 'staff and pupils have been warned to be vigilant'. Anyway" – her voice brightened up – "whoever wrote the article's probably just trying to stir up a scandal because they've got nothing better to write about. I don't suppose there's much front-page news in Largs, but I just thought I'd let you know anyway," and with a cheery 'Take care!' she rang off.

Ella went into the studio and stood looking out of the window. A brisk wind was rustling the branches of the tree so that every now and then the ripe beech-nuts rapped against the rain-smeared glass like small insistent knuckles and, suddenly cold, she pulled down the blinds. Then, forgetting about the microwaved curry, she curled herself into a tight little ball in the chair.

It would be awful in school tomorrow. Maura would be beyond furious at the article, and of course she'd leave no stone unturned till she found out who the 'anonymous source' was, and meanwhile, the children and the rest of the staff would be constantly on edge. And if, as Ella suspected, that source was discovered to be Yvonne, the whole affair would be bound to split the staff into her supporters and her decriers. She envied Aminah her Day Release.

Eventually, she reheated the curry and took it, and a glass of wine, through to the living-room, and as she ate she found herself hoping that little Jinty, wherever she was, would stay well clear of the school tomorrow too. And long after she'd finished her meal she sat on the settee, picturing her, in a strange house full of people she didn't know, and so far away from her mother and grandmother they might just as well be dead.

26

Next day, Aminah arrived in the late afternoon, and the first thing she said as she wiped her feet on the doormat before stepping into the hall was, "Isn't it dreadful about that article?" and then "Was it awful at school?"

"It was appalling," Ella said as they climbed the stairs together. "You were well out of it, believe me. Yvonne was up there on her high horse, claiming she'd absolutely no idea the guy she'd been drinking with in the Scotia Bar was a journalist" – she raised her eyebrows and Aminah giggled – "and then Yasmin and Joanne started laying into her big style about being stupid enough to talk about school matters to *anyone* she didn't know, and by lunchtime you could have cut the atmosphere in the staffroom with a knife."

"And what about the kids?"

"Well, of course the older children had heard all about the article from their parents and older siblings so *they* started getting hysterical about paedophiles and talking as though there was one hiding round every corner, so Maura had to have an assembly and boy, did she call a spade a spade. She told them there was absolutely no truth in the article, and that no one was to get swept away by cheap sensationalist journalism, and if she heard of anyone who *had* got swept away, there would be dire consequences. She was magnificent, actually. Now, would you like a coffee? Or have you already got caffeine poisoning?" and she showed Aminah into the flat and waited while she undid her cagoule and handed her the dripping-wet garment.

Aminah laughed. "I'll manage another, and here's something for us to eat," and she handed Ella a white box tied with a yellow ribbon. "Don't worry, it's not jam doughnuts!"

Ella smiled and took the box, and then she pushed open the studio door and motioned to Aminah to go in. She'd put the 'Leda and the Swan' painting on the mantelpiece with its face to the wall, and Aminah headed straight for it. "So, is this *it* then?" she said, with another bright laugh. "The famous 'affront to the senses'?"

Ella began to turn the painting round and, as the image slowly came into view, Aminah's laughter faded. "Oh my goodness," she gasped. "It's even worse in real life. See how his claws have gouged great strips off the insides of the woman's thighs, and look" - she pointed up to the swan's head – "he's got blood all over his beak where he's pecked her lips. No wonder the Wetherby guy didn't want Flick to show it to Max. I mean, I always got the impression from you that he was a bit of a prude, but now I can see where he's coming from." A worried frown flickered across her face. "Why on earth would anyone paint a picture like this? Do you think Flick was mentally ill?"

Ella thought about it. "I certainly get the impression she was a very sensitive young woman, but now I'm beginning to think she must have been a bit unstable," she said. "You know, there's a shed in the garden that's kitted out almost like a kid's playroom, with soft toys, and pictures painted on the walls, and jars of sweets, and I'm guessing from what Wetherby said she spent a lot of time in there, chain-smoking. Ever since I found it, I've pictured her as rather naïve and childlike, which makes me wonder if this" – she nodded back up at the painting - "might have been a kind of cry for help? The woman has red hair, and so did Flick ..."

Aminah frowned again. "Are you suggesting she was raped and couldn't tell anyone so she painted a picture instead?"

"It crossed my mind, which is why I've been wondering whether confronting Wetherby is a good idea, and why I'm hoping the Bruno man gets in touch. And now, if you've had enough sexual violence" – she gave Aminah a wry smile – "I think we need that coffee, and while I'm getting it, why don't you have a look round?" and she gestured towards the walls.

Aminah turned round, and when she saw the paintings she clutched her cheeks and let out a long whistle of admiration. "Oh Ella, these are stunning," she breathed, and as she looked at each in turn Ella saw she was genuinely moved. "They're so strong, and yet so fragile and poignant. You can really feel the woman's pain at being constrained." She turned to face Ella. "And that was how *you* felt all these years, painting your safe pictures, in your safe marriage, in your safe house, was it?"

Ella picked up the cake box. She began to speak, then stopped, and when she tried again her words seemed to stick in the back of her throat. "That depends on your definition of 'safe'," she managed to say, and then she took the box into the kitchen, removed the ribbon, and opened it up. It was a carrot cake, with thick creamy icing and little sugar carrots stuck round the outside, and the thought of eating it made her want to gag.

Lifting it out carefully, she put it on a plate with a knife, and when the coffees were ready she put everything on a tray and went back to the studio. Aminah was standing by the easel, looking at 'Metamorphosis 1', and when she turned round Ella was distressed to see she had the guarded look of a child at school about to be given a serious talking-to.

"I'm so sorry, Aminah," she said. "I didn't mean to snap. It's just that what you said about my 'safe marriage' isn't true - but it's totally my fault you thought it was. I should have told you Derek was having an affair." She smiled apologetically. "I *was* going to ..."

Aminah looked crestfallen. "Oh my goodness, Ella," she breathed. "You poor thing," and she moved closer. "Will you tell me now?"

Ella paused before answering. "I'd like to, yes. I've never told anyone before, and if you don't mind listening I'd be interested to hear your opinion," and she turned carefully round and steered the tray towards the door. "Let's take our coffees into my posh minimalist living-room," she said, "away from all this nudity and crudity," and she laughed the tension away.

Aminah sat down on the red settee and looked round at the expanse of plain white wall and rich wooden floor. "It's minimalist all right," she said. "I'd love to have a room like this, completely uncluttered and with all that light pouring in. It's like taking a big breath of fresh air."

Ella put the tray on the coffee table and sat beside Aminah. "I love it too, and when I get time I'm going to paint the walls grey and make it into a little gallery. If I stay, that is."

Aminah looked aghast. "You're not thinking of leaving? Oh Ella, you can't. School would be no fun without you," and Ella smiled and shook her head.

"Don't worry, I don't mean move away from Largs. I just mean move out of this flat. I mean, it's perfect in so many ways, but the people are beginning to really get to me. Or should I say the *men* are. I keep wishing I hadn't given Wetherby my spare key," and she passed the cake to Aminah, who cut herself a thick slice.

"I suppose you could just ask for it back," Aminah said. "Or maybe you should get your lock changed? Would you like me to ask Sergei? I'm sure he could do it in a few hours," and when Ella thanked her and said she'd think about it, Aminah took a large bite of cake and spoke through it. "You were going to tell me about Derek's affair …?"

Ella made a show of brushing away the spray of crumbs on her chest. "OK," she said. "I'll try to make it brief," and she took a mouthful of coffee, sat back, and composed herself. "About a year ago, I overheard him on the phone a couple of times, talking to a woman called 'Jen', and for various reasons I knew right away Jen wasn't a colleague. His tone of voice was much too intimate, you know, and in any case I know most of his colleagues' names and I'd never heard him talk about a 'Jen'."

She stopped and, grateful for Aminah's patient silence, gulped down some more coffee. "At first, I told myself not to be stupid, that Derek wasn't the kind of man to have a lover, but as time went on there were other things too. He started to take an interest in his clothes, which he hadn't for years, and he began to wear after-shave, which he never had, and when he started bringing me flowers and little gifts I was certain he was hiding something."

She looked down into her mug and spoke very quickly. "Anyway, one night when he was away on a business trip I trawled through his emails, and I found an incriminating message." She stopped abruptly and looked up anxiously at Aminah. "Do you think that was an awful thing to do? I mean, it struck me as awful at the time, but I was beside myself with worry …"

Aminah shook her head violently. "Oh Ella, honestly – of course it wasn't an awful thing to do. Your partner was cheating on you, for God's sake. Anyone who does that relinquishes all rights to privacy. So was the email from Jen?"

Ella shook her head. "No, 'Jen' was the subject. The email was from Carys, my oldest friend. She was actually Derek's friend originally, and she's our daughter's godmother. It was obvious from the email that she and Derek had been talking about me, and it said something like, 'I really think you should tell Ella about Jen. She has a right to know'. So then, you see, I knew for sure, and I was completely, utterly, devastated and, for some reason I don't understand, terribly ashamed too," and, close to tears, she sat back in the settee and closed her eyes.

For a while Aminah was silent. Then she said, "So that was when you decided to leave him?" but Ella snapped her eyes back open and shook her head.

"No," she said emphatically. "It definitely wasn't. I'd been wanting to go long before I found out about Jen, but finding out was the catalyst I needed, and that night I wrote the first draft of the note I'd leave him. I told him I found my life in Highgate suffocating, and that I needed to develop my art and I couldn't develop it there, and I ended with the sentence: 'And since I know about you and Jen, our marriage is merely a sham.' Was that overly brutal, do you think?"

Aminah smiled. "It was a statement of fact," she said, "and I'm sure I'd have said something similar. And is that the note you ended up leaving?" and she raised her eyebrows in surprise at Ella's sudden laughter.

"God *no*!" she said, shaking her head at the memory. "I wrote dozens of notes, and some were short and to the point, and others went on and on, and in the end they all ended up in the bin. Then, the night before I left, I drank hell knows how many glasses of his best brandy and wrote the final version." She picked up her mug and gulped the last of it down, and then she sat in silence, trying to order the chaos of her thoughts.

"I thought about leaving out the bit about Jen actually," she said at last, "because I didn't want to give Derek the gratification of thinking that was why I'd left, but in the end I put it in. At least, I think I did. Maybe I didn't. To be honest, I can't remember. Anyway" – she leaned over to touch Aminah's arm – "thank you for listening, Aminah. It's done me good to get it all out in the open."

For a while they both sat in silence, looked out of the window. The rain had stopped and a weak sun was shining, and in the distance the lights of the ferry were just visible, chugging its way over to Cumbrae, looking like a little floating castle.

Eventually Aminah spoke. "I think you were very brave to leave, Ella," she said, "and I'm so glad you did. I mean, just look at the art that was inside you, bursting to get out! And as for Derek – maybe it was kinder to leave him a note, rather than the two of you have a huge row and say a lot of things you'd regret afterwards." She bit her lip. "I must admit, when I left *my* nightmare man, I did it by text, which is arguably the most cowardly way of all," and she stood up and gave Ella a sheepish grin. "I suppose I'd better get home," and she stood up and walked out into the hall.

"You're not taking a bus home tonight, by the way," Ella said as she helped her into her cagoule. "It's far too wet," and when Aminah protested she fetched her keys and marched her downstairs.

Later, when she was back home and sitting down with a bowl of soup, her phone beeped and it was a text from Bruno Glass, saying he was sorry he hadn't contacted her sooner, but he'd been abroad, and that he'd be taking part in a concert in St Columba's church at 1.30 on Sunday the 5th of November if she'd like to meet him there.

She texted back her thanks and said she'd look forward to that, and then she finished her soup and padded through to the kitchen for a refill, and as she ate it she reflected that, for the first time in ages, her mind was relatively clear of worries. The only troublesome thing (apart, of course, from the constant nagging concern about Jinty) was the problem of what to do with 'Leda and the Swan', and with a bit of courage that was easily enough dealt with. As soon as she'd finished the soup, she'd wrap it back up in bubble-wrap, replace its label, and put it into the cupboard to be delivered, at the earliest opportunity, from whence it came.

Then she'd pull down the blinds, sit back in the comfortable studio chair with her feet up on the stool, and think about what she'd do tomorrow. Because tomorrow, it occurred to her suddenly, was rather a special day ...

27

Next morning, quite early, Ella's doorbell rang and when, rather warily, she opened the door Paul Wetherby was standing there clutching a small bunch of Queen of Denmark roses and a large colourful object she couldn't identify.

Her first thought was, 'How could he possibly have known it was my birthday?' and for a moment the idea was so bewildering she couldn't think of a thing to say, and it was only when he announced, "The very last of the roses, and some Bramley apples, fresh from the tree," and thrust the large object at her that she realised it was simply a coincidence and stepped back to let him in.

"Shall we take them through to the kitchen for a better look?" he said, and he followed her through and waited as she deposited the large object – which turned out to be a set of plastic filing trays like the ones children used at school – on the work surface, and put the roses in a mugful of water.

"I'm sorry the apples aren't in a conventional drying rack," Wetherby apologised, "but I only have one and it's been such a bumper year it's filled to overflowing. I've wrapped each apple individually in a sheet of newspaper," he went on, "and if you put them in your shed to complete the ripening process you'll have delicious apples in the winter. I do hope you'll enjoy them."

Ella was so moved by his thoughtfulness she was tempted to tell him about it being her birthday, but instead she thanked him and said she was sure she'd enjoy the apples very much, and would he like to come in for a coffee. He smiled and accepted, and as she filled the kettle she felt an unexpected rush of warmth at his unexpected kindness.

"This 'paedophile' affair is most terribly concerning, isn't it," Wetherby said when they were both settled on the settee and Ella had cut him a slice of Aminah's carrot cake. "I imagine it must be making life difficult at your school? I mean, how does one instil caution in children without frightening them to death?"

Ella watched him take a tentative bite off the edge of the carrot cake. "School's fine," she assured him. "We have a very good head teacher who won't allow any hysteria to develop, but it doesn't help when the press are making such ridiculous assumptions. I mean, we don't even know for sure there *is* a suspicious man lurking about, let alone a paedophile. For all we know, the guy who was seen could have been a travelling salesman who went to the wrong address," and she steered the conversation back to apples, and when, after a good ten minutes, Wetherby had exhausted his wide knowledge of the various varieties and their relative attributes and had finished off his cake, she stood up and led the way to the hall.

"Thank you again for the roses and the apples," she said as she opened the door. "It was a lovely surprise, and very kind of you to think of me. I must say," she added on a sudden impulse, "everyone's been very kind and welcoming to me since I arrived. I mean, Maeve's forever baking me things, and Harry's given me honey from his bees, and now you with your apples," and she stopped and watched his reaction.

For a while Wetherby looked awkwardly at the floor, and when he looked back up she saw his face had reddened. "Of course we're kind to you, Ella," he said, and he stretched out a hand as if to touch her shoulder, then pulled it back again. "We all miss Flick, you know, and in a way you've taken her place and we want to make sure …"

He stopped then and, leaving the sentence hanging, took a step out onto the landing. Pulling his keys out of his pocket, he started to walk across to his flat, but Ella followed him doggedly out, and for one wild moment she considered fetching the 'Leda' painting and getting the whole matter over and done with there and then. "Make sure what?" she asked. "What is it you want to make sure of?" and she continued to stare at him, silently demanding an answer.

"We want to make sure that you are not taken advantage of," he said, and he spoke stiffly, choosing his words with care, "because I am afraid there are people in this house who are not entirely to be trusted."

"Which people?" Ella said quickly, but as soon as the question was out she saw Wetherby's shutters come down and suspected that, once again, she'd gone too far.

Taking a step backwards, he inserted the key into his door. "I'm afraid I have no proof of anything" - he sighed a very audible sigh – "and it would, therefore, be quite wrong of me to name names. I only know what Flick told me, but Flick, I'm sorry to say, was what they call an 'unreliable witness', so all I am prepared to say is that certain people in this house should be treated with the utmost caution."

He pushed the door open, but before he stepped inside he turned back to Ella. "Which I have every confidence you are doing, Ella," he said, and he smiled an avuncular smile at her. "From what I know of you, you seem a most sensible and discerning woman who would not be easily swayed by mere masculine charms," and with that, he turned and scurried inside.

For a while, after Wetherby had gone, Ella stood on the landing and turned over what he'd said. By 'certain people in this house' he must of course mean Harry Flood, and since Caroline had more or less told her the two of them had been having an affair, it was clear Wetherby blamed the whole business of Flick's disappearance on Harry. And though it was reassuring, and oddly flattering, that he considered Ella sensible and discerning, the bit about not being easily swayed by mere masculine charms struck an uneasy chord.

The memory of standing here with Harry had a faraway quality to it now, as though it was a daydream rather than something that had actually happened, but if she was brutally honest with herself she was still not quite immune to those masculine charms of his. In fact, she reminded herself as she went back to the studio, there were still times – in the evenings, usually, as she sat in the window watching the darkness roll in, or when she was in bed - that she still allowed herself the guilty pleasure of fantasising about him.

There were two fantasies, and both began in the same way. In each, it was a warm summer's evening and she was pottering about in Flick's shed, sweeping out leaves or looking out of the little window at the roses, when she'd hear footsteps outside and look up and there he'd be, leaning in at the door, smiling in at her and asking, with a roguish wink, if she'd seen the state of the shed roof.

There was a bit of a problem with it, he'd tell her. The roofing felt was starting to come away, but she wasn't to worry because, if she waited a minute, he'd fetch his ladder and have it sorted in two shakes of a dead lamb's tail.

At this point, the two fantasies diverged. In the first, Harry would go and get the ladder and start to hammer on the roof, and she'd sit on the little chair below with the picture of Leda and the Swan on her lap, feeling the whole shed shudder at each stroke; and when he'd finished he'd reappear, face glistening and streaked with dirt and, without a word, take her in his arms and kiss her so hard on the lips her insides liquified. He'd kick the shed door closed then, and undo the buttons of her dress, and she'd fall backwards onto Flick's blankets and let him stroke her breasts and put his rough hands up inside her skirt.

In the second fantasy - which, of necessity, took place when Caroline was conveniently out - she'd point out that he didn't have his ladder any more, that he'd lent it to her, and then lead him round to the front door and up the stairs and into the studio, or the bedroom, or the living-room, and they'd make love in any number of inventive ways, depending on the location. Often, that second fantasy would take even more exciting turns than the first one, because now there was the ladder, and the chiffon, and the long silver chains, with all their erotic possibilities.

Lately, though – and particularly after the altercation with Caroline - these fantasies had made her feel increasingly guilty, and even though that guilt hadn't entirely stopped her indulging in them, she found herself wondering now whether today's little revelation might mean the end to it all.

Because Wetherby's warning had alarmed her more than a little, and it forced her to wonder just *how* 'roguish' Harry Flood might be. Could he be a bully? A sadist? When she'd been frightened by his bees, had he actually revelled in the boyish delight her fear gave him?

Pushing the uncomfortable thoughts aside, Ella went over to the big cupboard and slid its door open. Today was her birthday, and she was damned if she was going to spend it worrying about Harry Flood. She'd do what she intended to do - what she did every birthday - and, reaching up to the highest shelf, she took down the pink-and-white box she knew was right at the top. She lifted it carefully out, carried it over to the chair, removed its two elastic bands, and took off the lid.

A dozen or so cards slid onto the floor but, precious though they were, she didn't rush to pick them up. Instead, she knelt on the floor beside them and, tipping all the others out, spread them so that each card had its own space. Then, as she did every year, she counted them.

There should have been thirty-two birthday cards in the box, one for every year Lucy had sent one, but of course there weren't, and Ella searched for the very first one, which was a crayoned scribble made when Lucy was two years old, underneath which Derek had printed 'Happy Birthday Mummy' in blue biro. It was, Derek had assured her, a portrait of herself, and for a while she gazed at the wobbly lines that were her legs and arms, and the half-completed orange circle that must be her face. Then she gathered up all the toddler cards and, laying them to one side, began to sift through the others.

She held each card up to the light in turn, examining its detail and marvelling at how, over the decades, the words 'Happy Birthday Mummy, love Lucy' had progressed from separate letters to joined-up script, through neatly cursive hands to the looped flamboyance of early teenage years, to culminate in the near-illegibility of deeply-troubled and rebellious teens.

The cards were handmade up until the time Lucy left school, and by the time she was nine or ten their complex designs were as skilfully drawn and shaded as the ones in Jinty's Commonplace Book, and Ella smiled as she remembered how fiercely proud she'd been to see the obvious artistic talent her little daughter possessed. In the first two frenetic University years those handmade cards had given way to well-chosen images bought, no doubt, in local art galleries, but in Lucy's third year they were replaced by cheap, flimsy things with crass pictures of flowers or puppy-dogs, and their hastily-scribbled greetings became hardly decipherable. Then, they stopped altogether.

For years, as life descended into an endless nightmare of desperate phone calls from flatmates to say Lucy was sick, Lucy was missing classes, Lucy was staying out all night, there were no cards; and then, more chilling than any of that, there was the call that told them Lucy had gone. The police had been informed, and for weeks, Derek and Carys had driven round and round the streets of London, searching among the mounds of stinking blankets that barely covered the homeless and hopeless, while Ella waited in Highgate for them to phone to say they'd found her, or they hadn't found her, and wondering which news was the more difficult to bear.

Eventually, Lucy was found living at Centrepoint under an assumed name, but she refused point-blank to see them or talk to them, and at that point, to preserve her sanity, Ella closed her mind to the possibility of any hope, shut herself inside her tiny studio, and painted rose after rose after rose.

Then, two years ago, a miracle happened. A brown envelope arrived bearing a stamp with a brightly-feathered bird on a scarlet hibiscus flower and 'Papua New Guinea' printed below. It had a faint fragrance that might have been frangipani, and Ella's hands had shaken so much she could hardly manage to tear it open.

She'd been rapturously happy to get the card, and so had Derek, because not only did it mean Lucy was alive and living some kind of life again, it also meant she was somewhere warm. At first, Ella had put it on the bedside table where she could smell it as she slept, but after a few days she'd replaced it in its envelope so that it wouldn't lose its scent. Now, pulling it out, she once more ran a finger lightly over the rough paper and the smooth creamy-white flower before holding it to her nose and breathing in the remnants of frangipani sweetness.

She didn't have to open the card to know what was written inside. 'Happy Birthday Mum,' Lucy had written, and the letters were, for the first time in years, carefully formed in dark, confident, black ink. 'I hope you and Dad are OK,' she'd added, and then she'd drawn a smiley face, but there was no address, no phone number, and nothing but the greeting to give Ella hope that Lucy, at last, was well.

For months after the card arrived she'd hoped for something more – a phone call, an email, a text – but nothing came, and the next birthday, when nothing arrived, she wondered if she'd dreamt the whole thing, and only the roughness of the card and its lingering scent reassured her she hadn't. And now, as she shuffled all the cards back into a flat pile and, keeping only the Papua New Guinea one out, shut them back in their box, it suddenly struck her that perhaps, this year, Lucy had sent one. Perhaps there was another rough brown envelope lying on the hall carpet in Highgate.

There might be. Lucy might have missed last year because she was travelling, or perhaps mail from Papua New Guinea sometimes went missing. This year, she might well have gone to the market in some other exotic location and chosen another card, with another flower and another faraway smell, and this time, when she wrote the greeting inside, she might even have included a contact number.

If a card had arrived, one thing was sure - Derek would immediately have phoned Carys to tell her that her goddaughter was safe and well; and, without another thought, Ella took out her mobile and did a Google search for hotels in the Cotswold area. Shaking with excitement, she very nearly threw caution to the winds and booked a room for that very night, but then she stopped herself. If she was to go and see Carys it was vital that, when they met, she was calm and composed, and could give a well thought-out account of precisely why she'd left Derek. The last thing she wanted was to be arriving on Carys's doorstep in an emotional state and getting all mixed up and saying the wrong things so, taking a deep breath, she booked a three-night stay in a hotel just outside Cheltenham, starting next week, and then she contented herself by fetching one of the suitcases from the cupboard and taking it into the bedroom.

She packed her walking boots and two warm jumpers, and then she put in her thermos flask too, because when she arrived in the Cotswolds she wouldn't immediately contact Carys. She'd take some time to do a bit of walking in the hills, planning all the things she was going to say to Carys when she met her, and in exactly what order she'd say them.

One thing was sure, though. When she *did* meet Carys, she wouldn't just ask her whether Lucy had sent a card. She'd also tell her she knew about Jen, because the more she thought about it, the less sure she was that she really *had* put that sentence at the end of Derek's farewell note. And when she'd done that, she'd go on to ask her some very direct questions.

28

It had poured all morning, but when Ella had finished packing and went back into the studio to have her lunch she saw that the rain had stopped and there were even a few tentative shafts of sunlight shining on the burnished copper of the beech leaves.

She washed down her cheese and ham sandwich with a small celebratory glass of wine, and by the time she'd finished the sky had cleared to a clean bright blue, so she made herself a quick cup of coffee, put Lucy's card on the mantelpiece, took her walking boots back out of her case, and set off for a refreshing walk

The air had an autumnal smell and the pavement was plastered with leaves and strewn with beech-nuts, and as she walked briskly along Beech Avenue she noticed that the pain and stiffness in her hip had almost gone. Relishing the new feeling of strength in her legs, she turned right into Gogoside Street and, almost running now because the downward slope was so steep, followed the course of the Gogo towards the sea.

The river itself was hidden from sight by trees and bushes, but the rain of the past days had deepened its waters, and its wild gurglings and roarings were louder than she'd ever heard them before. The sound excited her and filled her with energy, and when she reached the main road she decided not to head back towards the town and get herself another coffee, but turn left instead and head out of Largs along the Fairlie road, in the direction of Haylie Brae.

A couple of weeks ago, when she'd driven down the Brae on her way back from Grace's launch, she'd noticed a large cemetery on her right, and at the time it had occurred to her to wonder whether Gran might be buried there. If she was – and surely even her solidly unsentimental mother had erected some kind of monument to her memory? – it would be nice to know where her grave was. If she found it, she could put flowers on it at special times like today, and Christmas Day, and Gran's birthday in March.

She walked along the busy main road till she came to the junction where the road went on to Fairlie, then rounded the bend and strode up the steep slope towards the cemetery gates. When she reached the gates, her calf muscles burned from the effort of the climb and, leaning against the wall, she stood for a while, surveying the vastness of the graveyard. It was hard to see just how far it stretched, because there were so many trees and bushes punctuating its paths and creating private little islands of calm where, presumably, the bereaved could sit and think about their loved ones.

At the furthermost end, near the high boundary wall, the grounds rose even more steeply. The view from up there must be breath-taking, but for a while Ella wended her way slowly between the gravestones, moving closer from time to time to read their inscriptions. Then, when her legs had recovered, she began the upwards climb, past plain crosses and Celtic crosses, moss-covered obelisks and cloth-covered urns, and roofed, pillared structures like tiny Greek temples till at last, at the cemetery's highest point, she reached the high stone wall behind which the forest began.

There was a huge bank of red marble memorial slabs there, each slab dedicated to a different member of what had clearly been an important and affluent family, and behind, almost touching the wall, what looked like a small mausoleum with thick walls set with carved pillars. Ella peered in through the bars of the locked gate, expecting to see some kind of casket, but the mausoleum was empty and its floor covered with soil and leaves and empty beer cans, and as she backed away from it and turned to take in the stunning sea view she heard, behind her, the sharp gunshot noise of cracking wood, followed by a loud flapping as a flock of black birds rose untidily into the sky, cawing in alarm.

She swung back round towards the source of the noise and looked up into the canopy, but the only movement she could see was the slight trembling of leaves the birds had left behind. Then she heard more cracklings, softer and lighter this time, as though someone was creeping around on the other side of the wall, and as she held her breath and continued to listen she saw, peeping over the top, a small pale dirt-encrusted face with turquoise spectacles and wild hair hanging in long rats' tails.

Warily looking this way and that, it clambered up onto the wall and scanned around like a frightened animal, and then, for just a split second, it glanced down at her and immediately bolted away, skipping from tree to tree like a sure-footed, denim-clad, monkey. Mesmerised, Ella stood watching it jump from one sloping branch to another and then, with a final death-defying leap, vanish into the shelter of the trees.

"Jinty!" she called as the footsteps faded into the forest's darkness. "Jinty! Please come back!" and she ran up to the wall and stood on tiptoe, looking for a place where she might be able to climb over. But if Jinty heard her calling she didn't come back, and no matter where Ella looked the mass of wall towered high above her, with no broken-down areas low enough for her to reach.

Defeated, she turned and gazed over the expanse of graveyard and down to where Great Cumbrae glowed deep purple. The sun was just touching the horizon now, spilling its orange-gold reflection onto the waves, and soon the road to Fairlie would be pitch dark and dangerous for a child to walk. Taking out her mobile, she phoned the police, and when she'd given them all the information they asked for, she half-walked, half-ran down to the gates and back to Gogoside Road to begin the long climb home.

As soon as Ella arrived home, she put the rather superior frozen chicken curry she'd bought herself into the microwave and opened a similarly superior bottle of Merlot, and as she watched the curry rotate she was more and more tempted to phone Aminah and tell her about seeing Jinty. In the end, however, she decided not to.

If she phoned Aminah, she'd run the risk of letting her imagination run away with her as usual and over-dramatizing the whole affair, so it was better to wait till tomorrow morning, by which time Jinty would probably have found her own way home, and as she savoured her birthday meal she thought about this tendency of hers to over-dramatize things. She'd always been aware of doing it, but since arriving in Largs she'd become more and more conscious of it, as though the new place, with its broad golden horizons and wide bright vistas, had given her new eyes with which she saw more clearly the anxious child she'd been, and the over-sensitive woman she'd become.

Could this over-sensitivity of hers have been the reason she and her mother had so often been at loggerheads? She'd always blamed her mother of course, but perhaps it was she, Ella, who was partly to blame for the endless bitter arguments. If she'd been confident enough in herself to listen to Veronica's advice, instead of always jumping to the defensive and seeing it as unkind criticism, what might she have learned from her? What kind of fearless artist might she have become, if she'd dared to experiment when she was younger?

And as the first mouthfuls of Merlot cleared her head, she wondered too if that same over-sensitivity, that lack of self-confidence, could also have been one of the reasons she and Derek had drifted so far apart. It was almost certainly why Carys had trailed the backstreets of London with Derek while she stayed at home, safely and miserably holding the fort.

She'd changed, though. In these past months, since coming to Largs, she could feel she had. She was far less apt, even when stressed, to go off the deep end. That afternoon in the cemetery, for example, although her heart had pounded in her chest, she hadn't been over-dramatic when she'd spoken to the police. She'd remained calm as she explained that Jinty was in a vulnerable state and should not be out alone so late at night. She hadn't mentioned how dreadfully thin and filthy she'd looked, and she certainly hadn't mentioned possible paedophiles on the loose; and when the police had assured her they'd contact Social Work and check with her foster parents that all was well, she'd quietly thanked them. So now, having done everything she could possibly do, she deserved to give herself a pleasant birthday evening.

She raised her wine glass to drink herself a toast, and then the thought came to her that, actually, there was no reason for her to spend her birthday evening drinking on her own, so she recorked the wine, took Lucy's card off the mantelpiece, fetched the jam jar with Wetherby's Queen of

Denmarks, and ran downstairs to Maeve's door, and when Maeve opened it she announced it was her birthday and would she help her celebrate. And when Maeve said she couldn't think of anything nicer, took the roses, and ushered Ella in, she noticed to her delight there was a delicious smell of baking in the hall.

She followed Maeve into the living room, which was lit by a number of lamps with pink beaded shades that, combining with the flames from the gas fire, gave it a warm, rosy redness. "You must be psychic, dear," Maeve laughed as she coaxed Cally off the chair opposite hers and motioned to Ella to sit down. "I've just baked a batch of cheese scones, so sit yourself down and I'll get us some glasses," and she went over to the sideboard and came back with two large crystal goblets.

"Why don't you pour," she said, "and I'll go and get the scones. And mind and only give me a half-glass. I'm unsteady enough on my pins," and, walking carefully behind the cat, she went off to the kitchen.

Ella sat down. She put Lucy's card on the coffee table, with the frangipani flower facing Maeve's chair, and poured a little wine into one of the glasses. Then she filled the other to the brim, and when Maeve came back with a plateful of scones and a glass butter dish she held the goblet up so that the wine glowed in the light. "Here's to another year older," she said, and when Maeve had sat herself down they clinked glasses.

Maeve picked up Lucy's card and held it to her nose. "What a beautiful card," she said. "It looks and smells terribly exotic. Is it from someone special?"

"It's from my daughter Lucy," Ella said, "but it didn't come today," and she smiled away the apologetic tone of her voice. "I'm afraid she's been a bit" - she swallowed three mouthfuls of wine, one after the other - "wayward over the past years, but I'm really hoping she's settled down enough to send me one this year."

Leaning over, Maeve put a hand on Ella's knee. "I always thought there was something making you sad, dear," she said, "but I never liked to ask. I hope you don't think it was because I didn't care," and Ella, giddy with wine, sat back with relief and assured her that of course she didn't.

"I'm going to Cheltenham next week to meet a friend who might be able to tell me if Lucy's all right," she said, and then, because Maeve was still looking at her with infinite concern, she added, "It's a long story, but the nub of it is I've left my husband, so if a card comes it'll be in London with him," and she sat back to watch Maeve's reaction.

For a long time Maeve continued to look down at Lucy's card in silence, opening it to read its greeting then closing it again to admire the flower. Then she took a tiny sip of her wine, and when she looked up her expression was a bit like the one Gran had worn when she'd said she wished she could live to see Ella grow up.

"Children are often wayward," Maeve said, "and when they are it breaks one's heart. Usually, in the end, they find their way again, and I do hope your Lucy finds hers, because it's most terribly sad when they don't," and then she gave a too-bright smile and replaced the card on the table. "I love the name Lucy. Who does it come from?"

The question took Ella by surprise. "It was my grandmother's middle name. She lived here all her life, and I used to spend my summers with her, but I've just realised I've no idea what her first name was," and, sitting back, she closed her eyes in concentration.

"Would you believe it?" she said, opening her eyes again and staring at Maeve. "I can't for the life of me remember! I mean, I was only nine when she died, and I suppose I never heard anyone call her by her Christian name. People at church called her 'Mrs Henderson', and so did the home help, and my mother would refer to her as 'Mother' or 'Ma', and somehow I never ever thought to ask what her actual name was ..." and she broke off, aware that the wine was making her talk too fast.

"I was looking for her grave today, actually. In Haylie Brae cemetery. Is your husband buried there?"

To her surprise, Maeve took an audibly large gulp of wine and pulled an expression Ella had never seen her wear before. "Oh, Joseph's buried there all right," she said, and the edge of anger in her voice matched the unfamiliar expression on her face, "but the only time I've seen his grave was when they put him in the ground.

"I picked a gravestone though" – she took another mouthful of wine then dabbed her lips primly with a handkerchief – "a nice plain white marble slab with his name and dates in gold lettering and enough space underneath for mine. I didn't want anything slushy or ostentatious ..."

Her voice faded away then, and Ella saw that the vacant look was back in her eyes and she was staring out at the dark garden. Sitting back in her chair, she waited for the moment to pass, and when it did, and Maeve spoke again, she was surprised to hear the longing in her voice.

"You know, dear," she said, "there are times, when I'm here on my own, that I find myself drifting away back into the past and wondering what would have happened if I'd done things differently."

She drained her glass and set it carefully back on the table. Then she leaned over towards Ella.

"I could have had someone else, you know," she whispered. "I could have left Joseph, and gone away with a man I really loved, but I didn't. I told myself it wouldn't be fair on Nat, who was only a child at the time, but the real reason, if I'm honest with myself, is that I was too afraid of change. And often, now, I find myself wondering what would have happened if I had. How very much richer my life might have been."

She snapped her back suddenly straight. "I'm glad you've had the courage to change your life, Ella," she said. "It's what life's about, after all. Isn't it?" but before Ella could find words to frame an answer she flapped her hand dismissively, waving the topic away like a bothersome fly.

"So," she said, "presumably your mother would have erected a memorial to your grandmother and the site will be in the records? It would be easy enough to find out where it is."

Ella smiled despite herself. "My mother was a bit unconventional," she said. "I'm hoping she did, and that it isn't ostentatious either, because my mother could be quite an ostentatious woman, and Gran would have hated anything showy. Anyway, I'll make enquiries when I've more time," and she drained the goblet and then, aware she was now extremely tipsy, took a large bite of cheese scone.

"By the way, I meant to tell you, I contacted the minister at St Columba's and I've had a reply from a man called Bruno Glass. Do you know him?"

Maeve's face lit up. "Of course I know him, now you say his name. He was the lutenist in *The Silver Swan*, and such a pleasant and talented young man. I always wondered, you know, whether he and Flick were – now what is it they call it these days? - an item. So, did Bruno tell you anything about Flick?" and, despite herself, she gave a little yawn.

"It was just a text, but I'm going to see him next month and I'll let you know what he says. And now" – she glanced over at Maeve's flickering eyelids and, standing rather unsteadily, picked up Lucy's card – "I really must go and let you get ready for bed. Thank you so much for the scones and the company," and she bent down and kissed each of Maeve's cheeks.

Back in the studio, she replaced the card on the mantelpiece. She took the 'Leda and the Swan' painting out of the cupboard and, after a few moments' reflection, put it in the hall beside the door. If she hadn't drunk so much she'd have taken it to Wetherby's door there and then, but as it was she'd do it tomorrow, and then all her affairs would finally be in order and she could go to Cheltenham and face Carys with a clear head.

29

On Monday, when Ella arrived at school, it was clear that the impending HMI inspection, coupled with the furore over the 'paedophile' article, had successfully dampened any excitement the children might have been feeling about tomorrow's Hallowe'en party.

The air was positively electric as Mrs McMahon marched round the school, assessing the quality of wall displays and checking that every record of every child was perfectly up to date, and that any glaringly bad pages had been removed from their exercise books. In that spirit, she'd also asked Ella to check all Primary Four's Commonplace Books, finish those that weren't finished, and deliver those that were to her office immediately.

"The trouble is," Ella confided to Aminah in the privacy of the Black Hole, "I told the children they could have a diary section, and I promised that if they marked it 'Confidential' I wouldn't read it. But now that Maura's putting them out on show for all and sundry, how can I *not* read them? I mean, would *you* trust a Primary Four to put in full stops and take new paragraphs?"

Aminah looked up from the sheaf of language reports. "It's a tricky one," she agreed. "I mean, you can hardly tape the sensitive pages shut" – she raised her eyebrows hopefully at Ella – "or can you?"

But Ella shook her head. "We'll just have to be honest," she said, "and tell the children if they're worried about something personal being read, they've got this morning to get rid of it. Talking of which, I wonder if Jinty's going to turn up today. I saw her last week, just as it was getting dark, climbing about in the woods by the cemetery, and I reported it to the police."

Aminah frowned. "That's really worrying. She hardly put in an appearance last week, and when she did she was so withdrawn she might just as well not have been here. I wonder if there's a problem with the foster home ..." She picked up a pile of Commonplace Books and checked through them. "Hers isn't here. She hasn't taken it away with her, has she?" and she looked over at Ella. "She has, hasn't she?"

Ella pushed the door open and took a step outside. "I'm sorry, Aminah," she said. "She was so keen to work on it, and she's usually so conscientious. I'll tell Maura and say it's my fault, and I'll tell her about seeing her last week too," and she rushed off.

The bell began to ring as Ella came back out of Maura's office, and she hurried round to the classroom to join Aminah, who was watching the children file in. "Maura's just phoned the foster home," she told her. "The foster mum's called Barbara, and she's terribly worried about Jinty. Apparently she's been sneaking out a lot, and coming home at all hours. She did eventually come home that night, but it was very late and she was covered in mud and refused point-blank to say where she'd been."

She dropped her voice to a whisper as, right at the end of the line, a bedraggled and miserable-looking Jinty trailed in, carrying neither her schoolbag nor the plastic bag with the

Commonplace Book inside. "Maura's arranging for Zareen to do a visit this afternoon," she told Ella, "and I'll ask her to try and get the Commonplace Book while she's at it," and they both went in to start the lesson.

From time to time throughout the morning Aminah tried to coax Jinty to speak, and when that yielded nothing Ella went to her table and tried to engage her in conversation, but each time she did Jinty put her head down and let her hair hang over her face like a greasy brown curtain, and it was clear that if she'd seen Ella in the graveyard, it was the last thing she wanted to talk about.

Finally, when the children were filing out for lunch, Ella took her very gently by the arm. She bent down and confronted her with what she'd seen and asked her, as forcefully as she dared, if there was anything she'd like to tell her. But Jinty simply stared at the floor, and Ella was forced to let the matter drop and hope that the home visit revealed more than she could elicit.

All day she continued to worry, and when, early that evening as she was tidying up in her studio, Aminah phoned, she wasn't at all surprised to hear the worried tone of her voice. "Jinty's done another runner," Aminah said breathlessly, "but this time she actually kicked Barbara and bit her arm, and then she ran off and said she wasn't coming back. She's reached some kind of crisis point, don't you think? I mean, I wouldn't have thought she was capable of violence, would you?"

Ella breathed in, held the breath, then breathed out again. "I think everyone," she said quietly, "is capable of violence. Has anyone any idea what caused the row?"

"Apparently she came in after school and went straight to her room, and then all of a sudden she started screaming at the girl she shares with, accusing her of stealing something, and then she came flying down the stairs and out the door. Barbara chased her of course, but you know how fast she is. She could be anywhere."

Ella looked out of the window. "It's almost dark," she said. "And it's absolutely pouring ..."

"Of course they called the police right away," Aminah was saying, "and they went from house to house, but there's nothing much they can do in the dark so the search party'll have to wait till first thing in the morning. Maura's organising one too, and she wondered if you'd be willing to join it. Would you?" and Ella said of course she would, and she could stay all day if need be, because the afternoon would be taken up with Hallowe'en parties.

"See you tomorrow then," Aminah said. "And I hope you've got a good raincoat!"

A light but steady rain fell on Tuesday morning as the search party, headed by Shabana's mother, Selena Akhtar, gathered outside the school and, following the map Shabana had drawn the previous evening, headed out of the playground. As they walked down towards the Gogo river, several police cars passed them, and when one of them stopped Selena showed the two officers the map, and they assured her they'd send a car up to join them.

Most of the search party had equipped themselves with canes or walking sticks, and when they left the school they fixed their eyes on Selena's tall figure and hurried to follow her long lithe steps. She was easily a head taller than Ella, and as she struggled to keep pace with her she felt the nagging ache in her hip return.

"Apparently there's a tree circle where they used to meet on Saturdays," Selena said as they crossed the road and headed up the hill. "They'd made a den there, and they used to have picnics in it and go down to the river to look for sticklebacks."

"Is the tree circle anywhere near the Haylie Brae Cemetery?" Ella asked, and when Selena nodded she said, "I saw Jinty around there last week, just as it was getting dark. Heaven knows why she was in the woods so late ..."

Selena raised her eyebrows. "She'd have been to the den. According to Shabana, since her grandmother was taken away she's been spending more and more time there. I suppose it's a kind of womb-like space that makes her feel safe, though it must be very damp and cold at this time of the year. Anyway, Shabana's certain that's where she'll have gone, and I've packed a good torch so we can take a look inside." She glanced back at Ella and slowed to match her steps. "Shabana's sick with worry, you know. She keeps saying it's all her fault ..."

"Her fault? What on earth's given her that idea? I mean, I know they'd had a falling-out, but I thought they'd made it up?"

But Selena shook her head. "They had made it up, but I wouldn't say they were back to being friends. Not like they used to be, anyway. Shabana's quite a bit older than Jinty you know, and this past month or so she's really grown up, but poor little Jinty hasn't." She slipped a hand under Ella's arm to urge her on. "If anything, Jinty's become even more of a child. Are you OK, by the way?" and she nodded towards Ella's leg. "Is it arthritis?"

Ella grinned. "Bad hips run in our family, as they say. My mother was quite disabled by the time she was seventy. I'll be fine if I keep moving."

The houses, Ella noticed, were becoming larger and grander the further up the hill they climbed, and when they were almost at the top Selena signalled for the search party to stop while she consulted the map. Then she pointed up the hill. "See the green space between those two villas?" she said. "We're going to cross it, climb over the fence to where the forest begins, then turn right, and the tree circle's about a hundred yards further on. Fan out as best you can, and walk slowly, keeping your eyes peeled for any signs of Jinty – sweetie wrappers, hair ties, that sort of thing," and she led the way up.

"I know this is all strictly confidential and you're not allowed to comment," she said as she helped Ella over the fence, "but I'm convinced there was abuse going on in that home, and that's why Jinty's been retreating more and more into her little fantasy world ..." she stopped suddenly and turned as, from the bottom of the hill, a thin, wavering voice called her name and a solitary figure, lightly clad, came trudging through the pouring rain towards them.

"Oh no," Selena sighed. "It's Jean McVey, and just look at the state of her," and, peeling off her raincoat, she climbed back over the fence, ran down to wrap it round Jinty's mum's shoulders, then led her up to join the searchers. In the distance, Ella saw the blue light of a police car as it drove up to join them.

Jean McVey was skeletally thin. Her hair was plastered down to her scalp and her face was covered in scabs and old yellowed bruises, and when she began to speak her breath came in short painful gasps. "The polis told me I shouldnae come, but how can I no' come? I cannae jist sit at home when ma baby's out there," and she burst into tears and threw herself into Selena's arms; and when the police arrived and suggested they drive her back home she clung on even tighter.

Selena took the policewoman aside and pointed up towards the forest. "We're pretty sure Jinty's taken shelter in a den up there, so maybe you could just allow Mrs McVey to come with us while we look? I'll take her home afterwards, if we don't find her," and when the policewoman nodded she took Jean's arm, helped her over the fence, and together they picked their way through the undergrowth to where, dug deep into the bank and covered with a sheet of corrugated iron, was the mound of leaves and branches that was Jinty's den.

They all stood aside and waited as the policewoman slid the corrugated iron away, crouched down and, putting her head inside, called Jinty's name. When there was no answer, she crawled inside, and they could see the glow of her torch as she swung it from side to side, but a moment later she reappeared, shaking her head. "She's not there," she said, "and it doesn't look or feel as though anyone's been there recently," and as Jean gave a strangled little cry she took her arm and, assuring her they'd keep on searching the forest, led her over to Selena.

"Let's all get home and dry off," Selena told the search party as they headed back to the fence. "We're best out of the police's way. Mrs McMahon's having posters made with Jinty's photo on, so this afternoon we can stick them up round the town," and she stopped and looked up into the sky to where, away in the distance, a couple of helicopters were heading towards them. Then she headed down the road with Jean clamped to her side, the bedraggled little band of searchers trailing dismally behind them.

Ella drove home and stripped off her sodden clothes. She put on her dressing-gown and ate some soup, and as she was finishing Aminah called to say Zareen had managed to retrieve Jinty's Commonplace Book, and that she'd leave it in the Black Hole for Ella to take away and inspect, just in case there was anything she'd prefer HMI didn't read. Much relieved, Ella sat back and closed her eyes, but she couldn't settle, and less than an hour later she was back at the school picking up a sheaf of 'Missing' posters and collecting the Commonplace Book.

As she put the book safely in the car and the posters in her backpack, the air above her clattered with the noise of the helicopters circling above the rooftops, every now and then wheeling round and hanging in the air, like dragonflies on the hunt. She fought her way out through the hysterical sea of tiny witches and wizards and Incredible Hulks, all clamouring to know where Jinty was, and had the paedophile got her, and was he going to kill her, and as she gave her assurances that everything was being done to find her, and the less said about paedophiles the better, it occurred to Ella that the best place for her to spend the afternoon was the cemetery. It was obviously one of Jinty's favourite haunts and, with its empty crypts and woody nooks and crannies, it was surely an ideal place for a child to hide. Shrugging the backpack onto her back, she set off for Haylie Brae.

The rain had settled into a thick grey mist that dripped from the trees and seeped insidiously through her raincoat, and by the time she reached the empty mausoleum by the boundary wall she was chilled to the marrow.

Leaning her back against the wall, she looked down over the expanse of cemetery, straining to spot any movement among the gravestones, but seeing nothing. Even the sea was invisible, its islands enshrouded in mist, and for a while she walked back and forth beside the wall, bent double, searching for anything that might give a clue Jinty had been there. Then, away in the distance, she heard the sound of voices calling, and when she looked down the slope a line of police men and women were emerging out of the haze, sticks swinging from side to side as they methodically searched every inch of the ground.

Straightening up, she began to trudge back down to the cemetery gates and out, and when she reached the Gogo bridge she went into the supermarket, handed in a couple of posters, and – rather guiltily – nipped round to the Drinks section and found a bottle of Sloe Gin with which to ply Carys. That accomplished, she worked her way round the shops and cafes until all the posters were delivered, then walked very slowly back to school. With a heavy heart, she drove home through the gathering darkness.

It was well after four when she arrived back, and as soon as she'd tucked the gin underneath the jumper in her case and changed out of her damp clothes she went into the studio and phoned Aminah who, in the world-weary voice of one who has partied with children all afternoon, told her there was still no news of Jinty.

"It's looking quite bad, Ella," Aminah said, and then, after a pause, "You don't suppose there really *is* a paedophile, do you? I mean, we're all comforting ourselves by saying it's just Yvonne being attention-seeking and the journalists looking for a good story, but surely if Jinty had a choice she wouldn't stay out this long, not in this weather? If she couldn't face the foster home, surely she'd go to her mum's house? It's quite near the den, at the bottom end of Gogoside Street."

Ella walked over to the window and pulled up the blinds. Paul Wetherby's car, she noticed, was parked outside, and as she spoke to Aminah she walked out into the hall.

"I literally cannot bear to think of someone like that having her," she said as she picked up the Leda and the Swan painting. "I mean" – she heard her voice falter – "if it turns out she's been taken by a sex predator, I don't know how any of us would cope. Do you?" and she listened to the silence at the end of the line as for a moment they both imagined the unimaginable.

"If she hasn't been found by tomorrow night," Ella said, "I won't go to Cheltenham. I'll cancel the hotel," and when Aminah protested she needed the break and that there was, in any case, nothing more she could do, she remained adamant. "I couldn't, Aminah. It wouldn't feel right. But anyway" – she took her keys off the hook – "we have to keep optimistic. Try not to worry too much, and I'll speak to you tomorrow." Then, clamping the painting firmly under her arm, she went to Wetherby's door and rang his bell.

"I hope I'm not disturbing you, Paul," she said, "but there's something I need to tell you," and when he gestured to her to come in she walked briskly into the living room where a pleasant-looking woman with short spiky grey hair and wearing a pale pink trouser suit was sitting on the settee sipping what looked like sparkling white wine.

"This is Lynn," Wetherby said. "Lynn, this is my neighbour Ella Blyth," and when he turned back to Ella his face was as pink as Lynn's suit. "Lynn and I were just having a little glass of bubbly," he went on. "Would you like to join us?" and when Ella, prickling with embarrassment, apologised profusely for intruding and said it was nothing important and she'd come back some other time, he insisted she stay. He watched Ella lean the painting against the chair and sit down, then hurried over to the sideboard to fetch a glass, and Ella got the impression he was rather pleased to show each woman off to the other.

"Ella teaches at the school where the little girl's gone missing," Wetherby explained to Lynn as he poured Ella's bubbly, and they both made sympathetic noises and asked her the usual questions, which Ella answered as best she could. Then Wetherby stood up, walked over to Ella's chair, and picked up the painting. He examined it front and back, then and gave her a pitying look.

"You really are determined to find out what happened to Felicity Hunter, aren't you, Ella?" he said. "But I have to say I would never have thought a professional woman like you would be so desperate for information they'd stoop to breaking into someone's flat and removing their property," and he turned to Lynn and shook his head despairingly. "You see what I mean, Lynn? This is what happens when one gets involved with drug addicts," and as Lynn shook her head too and made sympathetic noises, Ella felt like a child again, hauled up in front of the teachers for some heinous crime. Fury seethed in the pit of her stomach.

"So was Flick a drug addict then?" she blurted out in what she knew was far too loud a voice. "Is that why you covered up her rape?" Putting down the glass, she stood up. Her heart was pumping hard now, and she knew she should make a dignified exit before she said something truly awful, but now she'd started, she couldn't stop.

"Is that what happened, Paul?" she went on, and she stepped right up to him, took hold of the painting with one hand and held on hard. "She was raped, and because she knew no one listens to drug addicts she painted what had happened instead" – she took a long shuddering breath in – "and when you saw what she'd done, rather than reporting the rape to the police you decided she was just another useless junkie who deserved everything she got, so you took the painting from her and refused to let her hang it in a gallery. Is that what happened?" She gripped the painting with both hands and gave it a hard tug. "*Is* it?"

She was about to pull again when she realised that Wetherby had already let go. Stepping back, he turned to Lynn, shrugged his shoulders, and sighed, and when he turned back to Ella his face wore an expression of defeat.

"No, Ella," he said wearily. "That was not at all what happened. Flick would never have taken illegal substances. But as for what *did* happen, I only know what she herself told me" - and now he gave her an almost pleading look – "and as I have already explained to you, I cannot make allegations without being completely sure of the facts. I have a moral obligation to protect the innocent."

He began to walk towards the door then, moving his arms back and forth at her as though shepherding her, and the painting, out. "One thing I can tell you, however" – he held the door open – "is that, at the end, Flick herself wanted the painting destroyed. By that time she was in a state I can only describe as psychotic, but even so she realised it was an aberration, and she gave me it and asked me to dispose of it. I have never felt able to, however. It seems wrong to smash it up, or burn it …"

They were in the hall now, and Ella noticed he snibbed the door and closed it before moving out onto the landing with her. His face had paled, and for a while he stood catching his breath, and when he spoke again she saw the side of his lip was trembling a little.

"I'm sorry, Ella," he said. "I must apologise for losing my temper just then. It was quite, quite wrong of me, and I hope you can forgive me?" and when Ella, suddenly tearful, said of course she could, that she'd hardly behaved impeccably either, he smiled a relieved smile.

"I've been wondering for a while, actually, whether you might consider disposing of the dratted thing for me in an appropriate fashion?" he said. " I mean, perhaps you could paint it over and replace it with a more edifying image? Then Flick's painstaking work would still, in a sense, exist, but no one but us would know it was there. I really would be eternally grateful," and when Ella said she'd give it careful thought, he put a hand awkwardly on her shoulder and thanked her.

Ella took the painting into the studio and dumped it in a corner. The tearful feeling had subsided, but she was still overwrought and achingly tired, and though it was high time she ate something, her stomach felt like a small hard knot of anxiety. The only way to calm herself down was to move.

Fetching a cloth and a pail of soapy water from the kitchen she rushed from room to room with a bin bag, cleaning and tidying and emptying wastepaper baskets, and when the flat was suitably purged she heaved the bag over her shoulder, took the keys and torch from their hooks, and went downstairs.

As had become her habit of late, she crept past the Floods' flat, and when she was safely outside she tiptoed round to the bins and switched on the torch, and as she dumped the bag in the bin, she felt relief flood through her.

Things, she told herself firmly, weren't so bad. She'd solved the problem of the 'Leda' painting at last, and made some sort of peace with Paul Wetherby, and as for Jinty, she was a resourceful little girl and would surely have found somewhere dry to shelter for the night. She'd probably reappear tomorrow, and then the trip to Cheltenham could take place as planned. This time on Thursday night, she could be soaking in a big hotel bath, looking forward to a day on her own, far away from police cordons, and clattering helicopters, with all the time in the world to figure out exactly what she'd say to Carys.

30

When Jinty had run away from Barbara's, she'd had no earthly idea where she was running to. It was as though her brain had shut down, or relocated itself in her feet, and all she could do was follow them, but as she reached the outskirts of Largs she realised that, of course, her feet were taking her to Miss Blyth's house.

The Social Workers had her Commonplace Book. Barbara hadn't admitted it, even when she'd kicked her and bitten her, but Jinty knew they had. They'd come that afternoon, and now the book was gone, so they must have it. They were forever poking their noses in where they weren't wanted, always thinking they knew what was best for people. Well, they'd really done it this time. They'd well and truly ruined her life now, *and* they'd ruined Miss Blyth's.

When she'd reached number 22 she saw Miss Blyth's car was parked outside. She crept through the gate and, from the shelter of the beech tree's lower branches, checked the windows – particularly the ground floor one where she'd seen the pale old woman, and the upper right one that was Miss Blyth's studio. The old woman wasn't there, and the blinds were safely down in the studio, so she climbed up till she reached the wide branch where her backpack still lay.

To her surprise, the carton of juice was still there too, lying beside it, but the Penguin had vanished. That would have been the squirrels.

Jinty sat in the tree till it was almost dark, drinking the juice in slow sips and trying to decide what to do next, but no matter how hard she tried she couldn't. She was wet through and frozen stiff and something bad had happened to her brain. It had gone all grey and woolly and she couldn't seem to find her thoughts in it. She had to calm herself down, tease out the thoughts, put them in a neat, orderly line …

She looked out at the curtain of leaves around her. It wasn't as thick a curtain as before because a lot of the leaves were missing, so now she could see patches of sky, and the patches were not blue but pink. She kept on staring at the surprising pinkness and the dark shadows of leaves around it, and as she concentrated all her thoughts on the colour, and the shapes, and the sharp moist tree-smell, the woolly thoughts grew clearer till at last she could put them in the order they should be in.

The first thing she must do was tell Miss Blyth she was sorry. She was sorry for following her home, and then she was sorry for climbing her tree and spying on her, and most of all she was sorry she'd written it all down in the Commonplace Book.

The apologising, however, was the easy part. The hard part was how to deal with what she'd seen Miss Blyth do. Because it wasn't just about liking to touch other women's boobies, was it? That just meant Miss Blyth was a lesbian, which was perfectly OK because Shabs had told her all about how lesbians didn't fancy men, they fancied women, and Jinty quite liked the idea. In fact, the more she thought about it the more she thought that actually, *she* didn't fancy men either. She didn't like the way they acted and she hated the way they smelt, and she definitely didn't fancy being married to one and sleeping next to him for the rest of her life.

But it wasn't about Miss Blyth being a lesbian, was it? There was the ladder, and the chains Miss Blyth had wound round and round the lady's chest, and that scream on the lady's face you couldn't hear but you knew was there.

And then there was the paedophile, who might have picked up the lady when Miss Blyth was finished with her, and even though she hadn't actually seen the lady get into the car, she'd seen the driver and it *was* the paedophile, it definitely was, because Mrs McMahon had said he had a big black car and a brown hat. And the more Jinty thought about Miss Blyth knowing the paedophile, the more helpless and frightened and confused she felt, and the more she knew that there was no point in wondering what to say to her. She just had to ring the doorbell, and when Miss Blyth came to the door, she had to trust the right words would come.

The pink of the sky had darkened to purplish-grey now and the rain was beginning to fall, and when she crept up to the blue front door her legs felt like rubber. Standing on tiptoe, she groped about among the leaves for the doorbell, but she couldn't find it and now a light had come on in the window to her left and two people – a woman with long dark hair and the old lady – were moving about inside. Bent double, she ran round to the back of the house and up the path between the two gardens to the little blue shed that looked as though it had come from a fairy-tale and, after a quick check of the house windows, she slipped inside.

It was very dark in the shed, and even when she pulled back the curtains she could hardly make out a thing. For a while she groped about blindly, not even knowing what she was trying to find, and then she opened the drawers in the chest of drawers by the chair, and in the second drawer she found a bunch of candles tied together with string.

She went on stirring the drawer's contents and found some small tins, and in one of the tins there were boiled sweets, all stuck together, and in another there was a box of matches. Prising one of the sweets off, she popped it into her mouth, and then she lit two of the candles, sat them carefully on top of the chest of drawers, and pulled off her wet clothes; and as the shed filled with yellow light she saw there was a little chair in the corner with a folded-up blanket on top.

There was a cushion on the chair too, and leaning against the cushion was a tired-looking teddy-bear and a faded pink floppy rabbit that looked for all the world as though they'd been sitting there forever, just waiting for her to arrive. Propping the rabbit up on the trunk beside the chair where she could see it, she wrapped herself in the blanket and, hugging the bear close, looked around.

In the flickering candlelight, the shed was an enchanted place. Pinned to the wall above the trunk were scores and scores of picture postcards, and as the candlelight grew she saw they were reproductions of famous paintings. There were some abstracts, and she recognised one that was made up of squares painted red and blue and yellow, because Miss Blyth had shown them one just like it the other week. She'd told them the artist's name, but Jinty couldn't remember it, so she eased the drawing-pin out and read the back. It was Mondrian, and when she looked further along the row she saw there was another painting she knew - the pointillist one by Seurat, with the river and the monkey and the girl who looked like Shabs. The paintings made her feel at home.

Sleepy now, she put the cushion on the trunk and lay down, and as she lay there she saw there was a stack of plastic shelves on the floor, just like the ones they had at school. She took her glasses off and cleaned them on the cushion cover and when she put them on again she saw that the shelves were full of crumpled-up newspaper, and she swung herself off the chest and took one out.

To her amazement, there was an apple inside – a golden-coloured apple with specks of red. She took a bite, and as the soft sweetness filled her mouth she turned towards the door and, as if by magic, there, flying across the wall, were two huge swans with golden crowns on their heads. One had a crown set with blue stones, and the other had a coronet studded with pink heart-shaped jewels.

Jinty clambered back up onto her lumpy little bed. She closed her eyes and, as she drifted into sleep, she pictured herself on the back of the swan with the pink coronet, soaring over mountains and valleys and forests and streams till at last she was above the ocean and could see, far below her, tiny islands, and tinier ships, and whales that blew fountains of foam into the air. The apple fell out of her hand and thudded onto the floor, but the sound didn't wake her, and she slept till morning.

When she woke up she had no idea where she was, and for a while she lay, rigid with fear, wondering where on earth Social Work had put her now. Then she saw the little window with its pink gingham curtains, and the two flying swans with their golden crowns and, gradually, it dawned on her she was in Miss Blyth's enchanted shed.

She eased herself off the trunk, opened the door a crack, and peered up at Miss Blyth's flat. The curtains in the big windows were still drawn, and the smaller window to their left was still in darkness, so she put on the Wellingtons (which, amazingly, were only marginally too large for her) and slipped out. She trudged through the long wet grass to the back of the shed to pee, and as she did she saw there was a big bramble bush there, still heavy with fruit. There was also a water butt, and after she'd washed her hands and face and glasses, she gathered two big handfuls of brambles, and took them back to the shed.

Her backpack was lying on the floor by the chair and, with some difficulty because the buckles were wet, she opened it and felt inside. There was a giant bar of Galaxy chocolate, and with a shock of guilt she remembered back to that Saturday morning when she'd been alone in the house while Mam was away organising Nan. She'd found the Galaxy in Mam's secret hiding-place at the back of the kitchen cupboard behind the spaghetti hoops, and as she packed it she'd thought that it served Mam jolly well right if she lost her chocolate. It served her right for not being there.

Sitting in the little chair, Jinty ripped the wrapper off and took a bite. The chocolate tasted a bit mouldy but she pushed in three brambles, also mouldy, to join it, and that made it better. The taste of the chocolate made her think of Mam, and she closed her eyes and imagined Mam with her arms wrapped round her, telling her she was the most precious thing in the world. 'You're ma wee guardian angel, Jinty,' she always used to say. 'I'd be lost without you, so I wid.'

What was Mam doing right now, alone in the house? Or, worse, in the house with Uncle Chris, doing the same thing to Mam as he'd try to do to her? She'd fought him off, but Mam wouldn't. For months now she'd stopped fighting back. Jinty heard them often through the wall, him shouting rude, horrible things to her in that awful rasping voice, and her sobbing and begging him to let her go. It got so bad sometimes that Jinty wished she could claw off her own ears, or stick hot rods inside them so she'd never hear again.

There was a law against doing the kind of things Uncle Chris did to Mam, but Mam would never tell the police, and if no one told the police he'd go on and on doing them. *She* had to tell. That was another thing she had to remember to tell Miss Blyth, so that Miss Blyth could tell Mrs McMahon, and Mrs McMahon would know who to tell next.

There was, of course, yet another possibility, but that possibility was too nightmarish for words. Because maybe Uncle Chris *wasn't* there. Maybe Uncle Chris was dead. She'd watched from her bedroom window as the ambulance people took him away, and she couldn't make out if he was still breathing, so perhaps she'd killed him. From the look of the pink froth on the floor, she might well have done, and that meant that, on top of everything else, she was a murderer. And that was something she wasn't at all sure she could tell anyone.

Jinty lifted the blanket and cushion off the trunk and looked inside. There were more blankets, and underneath the blankets were sheets of white paper and lots of coloured pencils. There were books too, one with beautiful photos of birds, and one called 'Myths of the Greeks and Romans', which had a sheet of paper sticking out from one of its pages, and when she took the paper out she saw it was a pencil sketch of a woman in a see-through dress, chained to a rock. The woman had one of her breasts hanging over the brim of the dress, just like Miss Blyth's chained lady had, and as Jinty read the legend of Andromeda and studied the sketch she began to wonder if maybe – just maybe – she'd got it all wrong. Maybe there could be another explanation of what she'd seen through the studio window ...

Could it be that Miss Blyth *wasn't* helping the paedophile do horrible things to the lady? The lady had, after all, been smiling when she came down the path towards the gate; in fact, she'd actually been skipping, and then didn't she even turn round and wave? You didn't smile and skip and wave if you were about to be driven away by a paedophile, did you?

She took out a piece of paper and some pencils and began to copy the picture of Andromeda, and as she shaded the folds of the dress she ran over in her head the very last thing she'd written in the diary section of the Commonplace Book.

She'd written it the day she'd seen that story in the paper about the paedophile, with the awful headline 'Monster in Our Midst?' and a photo of the school gates. She'd decided not to go to school that day because Mam wasn't well and the house was a worse mess than usual, and she'd noticed the paper lying on the hall floor and had picked it up. She'd read the article, and as she did the seriousness of what she'd seen Miss Blyth doing began to dawn on her.

She'd gone up to her room then, and written the diary entry, but what had she actually written? She'd done several rough copies on bits of scrap paper, but now she couldn't remember which version she'd decided to copy into the book. Whatever it was, if the Social Work people bothered to read it, they'd have to take it to the police, and the police would be sure to arrest Miss Blyth.

Jinty finished off the Andromeda picture and pinned it up beside the Seurat, and then she opened the book of birds and drew one of a bird of paradise with its wings outstretched. The sun was coming out now and shining through the window, and the pink roses were bobbing about in the breeze like little fairy people, and she found a pair of rusty scissors and some string in one of the drawers and cut the bird out. She hung it from the ceiling and it looked really nice, so she drew another, and another, and hung them up too, until a whole flock of brightly-coloured birds flew this way and that above her head.

She was hungry then, so she took one of the jam jars she'd found in the chest of drawers and fetched some water from the water-butt. She ate two of the apples and a very small piece of Mam's chocolate and then she stretched out on the trunk with the teddy-bear in her arms and watched the birds sway slowly to and fro above her.

This evening, when it was dark, she'd have a rummage through the bins and see if there was anything there she could eat. She'd also pick some of the beans from next door's garden, and gather beech nuts from the foot of the tree, and later on she'd light the candles and read some more Greek myths. It was like being on holiday, safe in her very own little house with no grown-ups shouting through the walls and no children barging in to bother her.

Perhaps, after all, she'd wait a bit before she talked to Miss Blyth. Perhaps she'd leave it till tomorrow, or the day after that. The Social Work people probably wouldn't bother looking at the Commonplace Book anyway - they'd be far too busy putting grannies into Homes and children into Care. So, when you came to think of it, there was really no great rush.

31

When Arlene arrived next morning Ella asked her if she'd mind keeping her clothes on and having a seat while she made them both a coffee.

The night before, once the flat was spick and span, she'd drunk some wine then slept for hours, but her dreams were a jumble of steep hills and dark tunnels and rivers in spate and, over-laying it all, the overwhelming feeling of trying desperately to find something that was lost.

In the strange language of dreams, that lost thing felt like a treasure of some kind, but as she'd padded through to the kitchen to make herself a calming mug of cocoa, she realised it wasn't a treasure in the sense of gold and jewels. It was Jinty, and Lucy, rolled into one.

Her hip had ached and her head was sore, and as she watched the milk rotate in the microwave it looked a bit blurred, and she wondered if it was the beginnings of another migraine. She made the cocoa, swallowed two paracetamol, and made her way back to bed, and as she was passing the window she thought she saw, for the briefest of moments, a small bright light flash on and off in the garden.

Leaning over the sink, she peered out of the rain-streaked window. Then she wiped the window with the dishcloth and peered again, but she saw nothing more and, telling herself it must either be the migraine or a reflection of the bare kitchen bulb, she went back to bed with the cocoa and slept fitfully till morning. When she got up she saw the rain had stopped and a weak sun was shining, but her head still pounded and she was as exhausted as ever.

"What happened to your leg?" Arlene asked as she took the coffee. "You can hardly walk," but Ella shook her concern aside.

"It's just the old hip thing. We spent yesterday searching for Jinty, and there was a lot of climbing up hills and bending double under bushes. It'll be fine in a couple of days if I take it easy."

Arlene's face clouded. "Does anyone know why she ran away?"

"I'm not really supposed to talk about it, but the family was in crisis and she'd been put into Care. I suppose she wanted to be back with her mum, but she didn't run home so I don't really know."

Arlene was quiet for a while, and then she said, "I ran away when I was fourteen. My mum's boyfriend was playing silly buggers with me and one day I just snapped and did a runner. That's how I got into drugs actually" – she looked down into the coffee – "and while I'm at it I might as well tell you I sold sex to pay for them."

She looked anxiously over at Ella, but Ella smiled back at her and patted her on the arm and assured her she was pretty well unshockable.

"So how long's Jinty been gone?" Arlene asked.

"Two nights now. The police have asked at the Nursing Home where her grandmother is, and we've put up 'Missing' posters, but so far there's been nothing and you know what they say - the longer she's gone the less likely it is she'll be found unharmed. I should be searching again today, but with this ruddy leg I'd just hold people back. Her mum, of course, is completely devastated."

Arlene nodded. "It's always the mums, isn't it. Mine broke her heart over me, and for years, when I was being such a bloody nightmare, we didn't speak. We're fine now though," she said, and she gave a little laugh. "Thank goodness she's the forgiving sort," and, turning, she waved over at the finished paintings.

"I can't believe how much you've done since I was last here," she said, and she stood up and looked closely at each. "These are *so* cool, and I love the roses, how they're pouring down on me and catching in the chiffon. They're quite – what's the word? – 'wanton'," and she turned round eagerly. "Don't you think?" and as Ella stood up too and went to her easel, she began to peel off her clothes.

Ella picked up the length of chiffon she'd folded away behind the easel and held it lightly in her arms. It felt like holding sea-spray. "Absolutely," she said, "and there's going to be dozens of them in the last painting - in your lap, on the ground, falling through the air, everywhere.

"I'm calling the series 'The Dream of Flying', by the way, and I'm hoping it'll express our longing to take flight and escape from our troubles," and as she draped the chiffon over Arlene she let her hand rest for just a moment on her shoulder.

"In this final painting you and your chains are going to be floating in space, with you scattering roses into the air, so I'd like you to just sit back in a nice relaxed position, with your knees slightly apart. I'll paint the roses and the chains later, so just have your hands open with the fingers spread out," and she waited as Arlene relaxed into the pose. "And now, how about you do me your best 'wanton' expression?"

For a while there was silence as Ella sketched in the first loose composition lines and then, when the drawing was almost finished, she said, "I'm going away tomorrow to visit an old friend, and I was wondering if, when we're finished, you'd change the SIM on my phone? I tried last night, but it was too fiddly for me," and when Arlene was dressed again, she handed her the phone and the old SIM card.

"So" - Arlene deftly changed the cards - "where are you going?"

"Cheltenham. My friend lives there and I haven't seen her since before Christmas. Her name's Carys, and she's my daughter's godmother. I always felt she was closer to Lucy than I was, actually. Lucy and I never got on terribly well, I'm afraid," and she took the phone Arlene held out.

"Does Carys have children?" Arlene asked, and the question took Ella by surprise.

"Oh no," she said quickly. "In fact, as far as I know, she's never had a partner, not that she's ever spoken of anyway. In fact, when I come to think about it, I've always thought of Carys as not really having a sexuality," and she handed Arlene her little brown envelope.

"She must have a sexuality," Arlene said matter-of-factly. "Everyone's got a sexuality, even children and old people," and she dropped the envelope into her backpack and walked to the door. "I hope you have a nice time in Cheltenham, and your hip gets better, and I really hope they find Jinty and she's OK," and she ran off down the stairs and out.

That afternoon, as Ella unwrapped the 'Leda and the Swan' painting and propped it up on the easel she recalled her surprise when Arlene asked if Carys had children, and wondered why she'd reacted so strongly to the question.

Carys being a mother was surely not such a bizarre idea and nor, come to that, was her having a sexuality, yet in all the years she'd known her she'd never, ever, thought about either of these things. In fact, the more she thought about them now, the more she realised how little she did know about her, and as she squeezed out a large mound of Titanium White and began to drag the first brushstrokes over Flick's terrible swan, she thought about the mystery that was Carys.

'Stolid' was the word that always sprang to mind when she thought of her, which was, she supposed, a combination of 'solid' and 'steady' and 'stoic', and of course Carys was all these things, which was why she'd been promoted time and again till her status with the company was way above Derek's, and she now had a hugely important job in leafy Cheltenham; and as Ella smeared a thick white line over Leda's contorted features, erasing her tortured scream forever, she recalled once more that awful Christmas visit.

Carys must have known all about Derek's affair, and she and Derek had doubtless talked about it when they were alone together, and the idea of their subterfuge made Ella feel both foolish and furious, and as she swept the brush back and forth over the canvas she found herself wondering whether visiting her *was* the best way to find out if Lucy had sent a card. It was certainly very unlikely that their meeting would be a relaxed affair.

She squeezed out more paint and covered over the last vestiges of the painting, then stepped back to check she hadn't missed anything. From certain angles you could still make out vague shadows of the forms underneath, but Flick's paint marks were so smooth and uniform that even with a single coat they hardly showed. When she got back from Cheltenham, she'd give it two or three more coats, and then it would be ready for a new image, and the more she thought about it, the surer she was of what that image would be.

The police helicopter thrummed overhead as she scraped the paint off her brush, and shafts of light flashed across the blinds, lighting up the room. Her plan was to have an early night and get up around seven to miss the morning rush hour, so after she'd eaten she wheeled the case to the door in readiness for the morning, then phoned Aminah to give her the new mobile number.

It had been a grim phone call. The atmosphere in the school was, Aminah said, more subdued than anyone could ever have imagined, and in the afternoon the children had been shepherded into the hall to watch a cartoon while an emergency staff meeting was held to discuss such harrowing matters as, in the worst case scenario, grief counsellors for both staff and children.

"Please don't cancel your trip," Aminah urged Ella. "Quite honestly, you're best out of it, and I promise I'll phone you if there's the least little bit of news."

Ella made her way slowly to bed, but in the end she did nothing but toss and turn and finally, at six thirty, she got up. It was still pitch dark, and she boiled water for coffee and filled a thermos, and as she was throwing the teaspoon into the sink there was another flash of light down in the garden.

Leaning close to the pane, she looked down, and this time she saw, quite distinctly, the shed door open and a small figure carrying a candle picking its way carefully behind the shed and disappearing into the bushes. She ran to the bedroom, phoned the police, then flung on her dressing gown and slippers and crept downstairs.

She knew she shouldn't go into the garden and open the shed door. Both the garden and the shed had probably already been designated as crime scenes, and when the police arrived they'd no doubt swathe them in blue and white tape like they'd done in the cemetery. She knew she should wait till they arrived with their various bits of equipment, and let them deal with the whole matter professionally.

But they hadn't actually *said* not to open the door, had they? They hadn't told her she must wait in the house till they came. And it was, after all, her shed ...

32

Jinty was sick and tired of the shed. She'd read all the Greek Myths, memorized the back of every single postcard till she knew the artists' names off by heart, *and* their dates of birth and death, and she'd hung up so many flying birds she could hardly move without getting tangled up in their wings.

In addition, there was no more paper left to draw on, the apples were eaten apart from three rotten ones, and she had the mother of all tummy-aches. Worst of all, though, Miss Blyth was cross with her. She was *extremely* cross with her, because even though she'd definitely seen her the other night, she hadn't bothered to come down to check she was all right.

Jinty didn't know exactly when Miss Blyth had seen her, because all the days had got mixed up, but she remembered it was the day of the terrible rain and that it had been quite late on. She'd opened the door to go for a pee and there Miss Blyth was, in the kitchen window, staring straight down at her, and the kitchen light was on so Jinty could see her quite clearly. In fact, she saw her wipe the window with a cloth or something, and her face was all creased up the way it got in the classroom when she was giving someone a row.

It had given Jinty a bit of a shock, seeing Miss Blyth like that, but in another way it was an immense relief because now Miss Blyth knew she was here and she'd come and find her, and then she'd be able to tell her how sorry she was about everything, and about what Uncle Chris had done, so that he'd be arrested and she could go back home to Mam.

She'd been thinking quite a lot about Uncle Chris, actually, and what she'd done to him, and she was feeling a bit better about it because she'd decided that if she *had* killed him, it had been an accident which didn't, after all, make her a murderer; so all that had to happen now was for Miss Blyth to come and everything could be sorted. But hour after hour passed, and she didn't.

To begin with, Jinty comforted herself with the thought that it was just because the rain was so heavy, and the minute it dried up she'd come running down. She'd maybe even bring her a hot drink and a biscuit, but as darkness descended and the rain finally stopped, there was still no Miss Blyth.

It made Jinty feel sad and very confused. Surely no one could be so angry as to leave you in a freezing cold shed with no food? Surely Miss Blyth, who was the nicest person she knew, wouldn't do that? And as the hours passed she began to allow herself to think that maybe, after all, she'd been mistaken. Maybe Miss Blyth *hadn't* seen her. Old people, after all, had quite tricky eyesight. Nan, bless her, could be staring straight at her knitting and at the same time ask you where it had gone, so if that was the case with Miss Blyth, there was nothing for it but to take her courage in both hands, walk up to the blue door, and give it an almighty thump.

She'd do it tomorrow, for sure. She'd have to, because the tummy-ache was getting worse and without the apples there was nothing else to eat unless she raided the bins again. She'd done that twice, and the first time she found the back end of a loaf of bread and the second time a baked bean tin with four beans in it, and when she'd eaten both finds they'd made her feel even sicker.

The runs were the real trouble. No sooner had she gone than she had to go again, and of course she'd no toilet paper, so each time she had to wash herself with cold water out of the water-butt, which was miserable; and as she settled herself down for another night she made a solemn promise to herself that tomorrow would be her very last day in prison. Tomorrow, she'd escape.

That night, the pains in her tummy were dreadful, and no matter how small a ball she curled herself into, and how hard she hugged herself, she couldn't sleep a wink. It felt as though there were tiny but immensely strong hands inside her, gripping her fast and twisting her this way and that, and the twists started off quite small and then gradually got stronger and stronger till they forced her to rush outside and relieve herself. Then for a short while it wasn't quite so bad, but no sooner did she feel herself dropping off to sleep than the tiny hands were back, twisting more and more viciously.

In the end she gave up on the idea of trying to sleep, and she lit two candles and opened the Myths book at the story of Pandora's Box, but when she got to the bit where Pandora opened the lid of the beautiful carved box and set free all the ills of the world, her tummy gave an almighty heave and she had to run outside again.

It was still dark, so she took one of the candles with her, which was comforting when she was walking but a bit of a fiddle when she was washing herself at the water butt, and when she got back inside she felt marginally better. Without taking her shoes off, she curled up under the blanket and took a last look at the illustration that showed gremlins and pixies and tiny horned monsters flying triumphantly up into the sky, and then she blew out the candles.

She took off her glasses and closed her eyes, and she'd just nodded off into a complicated dream in which she was running away from some large and indefinable evil when, without warning, the door burst open and the shed filled with blinding light.

Red panic seared through Jinty's brain. She groped for her glasses but couldn't find them and, as a large shadowy hand reached out through the strings of the flying birds to grasp her, she shot off the bed and, still half-asleep, pushed the shape away with all her strength. It gave a humanlike moan then fell with a sickening thump, but Jinty no longer cared. Her head was filled with paedophiles who wanted to do her unspeakable harm, and evil flying demons from whom she must escape and, without a second glance, she jumped over the shape and ran out into the garden.

On down the path she went, tripping over plants and stubbing her feet on stones but never stopping till she reached the beech tree, and even though, without her glasses, she could see nothing but a dark blur, she climbed grimly up, her feet remembering every branch, while around her the wail of police sirens grew steadily louder.

Then, quite suddenly, the sirens stopped, blue lights flashed, and heavy footsteps ran along the pavement and up the path, and, pressing herself hard against the big comfortable branch, Jinty breathed in its mossy scent and listened to the confusion of voices below.

The confusion went on for what seemed like an eternity and then, gradually, it calmed down and Jinty began to make out separate voices. Raising her head a fraction, she listened hard. She was wide awake now, and slowly, as she separated out the voices and realised they were all talking about her, the magnitude of what she'd done began to dawn on her.

There was a man's big deep voice demanding to know how long ago she'd run off, and a woman's soft steady voice asking which way she'd gone, and then another woman's voice, tearful and tremulous, saying she was most terribly sorry, she knew she shouldn't have opened the shed door, she should have waited, and with a rush of utter dismay Jinty realised that the tearful woman was Miss Blyth, which meant *she* must have been the dark shape in the shed who'd fallen with the sickening thump.

Then the soft steady voice asked Miss Blyth if she was sure she was all right, and wouldn't she let them take her to hospital, and at the same time the big deep voice was asking to see the shed, and then all the voices began to move away, and Jinty laid her cheek back down on the furrowed trunk and wished with all her heart she was dead. Because of all the unforgiveable things she'd done, what she'd done tonight was the most unforgiveable, and she didn't even understand why on earth she'd done it.

Why had she run away like a mad thing? Why hadn't she taken a big deep breath, put on her glasses, and seen who it was? Poor Miss Blyth probably got a bigger fright than she did, and now Miss Blyth was badly hurt and it was all her fault. Everything – *everything* – was ruined, all because of her.

Then an even more dreadful thought came to her. Maybe Social Work had already given the Commonplace Book to the police, so they knew Miss Blyth chained ladies up and touched their boobies, and now that they'd found out she also kept little girls locked up in her shed, she'd be sure to be arrested and thrown into a prison cell ...

The voices were coming back now, but they were so faint Jinty couldn't make out words, and then the front door opened and closed and all was still, and she knew, from all the cop programmes she'd watched with Mam and Uncle

Chris, that the police would be in there telling Miss Blyth she need not say anything, but anything she did say could be used against her in court.

After they'd done that, they'd put handcuffs on her and lead her down to the police car, and as she got in the back, one of them would put a hand gently on her head so she wouldn't hit it on the rim of the door and claim later it was police brutality. And then they'd drive her away to the station, and that would be that.

Jinty couldn't bear to see any more. She couldn't bear to witness Miss Blyth's handcuffed walk of shame, and she couldn't bear to hear the car drive her away, and even though she wished she was brave enough to climb down and tell the police the whole thing was her fault, she knew she couldn't because her head was so sore and dizzy she wouldn't be able to find the right words. Not only that, her stomach was in agony again and she urgently needed the toilet. She had to – *had* to – get back to the shed and the water-butt.

By now the lights had come on in both ground floor flats, but if anyone was watching her she wouldn't have seen them - and in any case, what did it even matter if they *were* watching her? What did anything matter anymore? Doubled over with pain, she ran round to the shed, threw herself into the mass of grass and brambles, and when she was finished and washed, she felt her way back into the shed.

She lit one of the candles and looked all over for her glasses, but she couldn't find them, so she lay on the trunk watching the flying birds soar round and round in their tangled little circles, and eventually she heard the sound of the front door banging, and a car engine starting up, and then the police car, with poor Miss Blyth inside, roared away into the dawn.

Jinty blew the candle out. She ran down the garden, out into the street and down the hill, and she didn't stop running till she reached the school. Leaning against the railings, catching her breath, she peered in at the familiar playground, grey and sinister in the moonlight, and then, out of the corner of her eye, she saw something flapping against the railings. She walked up to it and stared at it, blinking in disbelief.

The flapping thing was a poster, and when she moved nearer she saw it had the word 'Missing' at the top in big thick capitals, and below there was a little girl in a blue blazer with poker-straight hair and turquoise glasses sitting slightly crookedly on her nose. Below, in red, important-looking, letters, was printed 'Jinty McVey', and below that there was a lot of small print and a phone number.

Jinty stood looking at the poster for ages, trying to make sense of it. She knew the photo well enough – it was the last school photo she'd had taken, and she could still remember the day, just before the summer holidays, when she'd smiled the big wide smile for the school photographer. It had been quite a nice photo, and when she'd taken it home Nan said she was a proper young lady now, wasn't she Jean, and Mam agreed and said she certainly was, she was a proper credit.

Suddenly, even though it was still pitch dark, Jinty felt as though everyone in Largs could see her and, forgetting her aching tummy, she spun round and away, as fast as her shaky legs would carry her. Along the dark pavement she ran, careering from side to side, narrowly missing the parked cars, arms straight out on either side, like wings, until she came to the big road, where she wheeled round to the left and began the steep climb up towards the cemetery.

Her head was so dizzy now, and her legs shook so much, she could hardly climb the slope up to the big wall, and it was as much as she could do to clamber up onto the roof of the mausoleum then creep along the overhanging branches and as, finally, she trailed through the forest towards the tree circle she kept tripping on grass tussocks and bramble bushes. Once, when she fell so hard it knocked the breath from her, she lay on her back, staring up at the lightening sky, wondering if she'd ever make it to the den.

She had to do the last bit on her hands and knees, and when she saw that the corrugated iron had been pulled away she crawled over the muddy entrance and wormed her way as far inside as she could go. It was quite dry in there, and it smelt as it always did, of earth and leaves and mould. Lying hard against the back wall, she listened to the faint soughing of leaves and creaking of branches and, now and then, the scrape of a mouse and the distant call of an owl.

She'd no idea what to do next, or where to go, and she no longer cared. All she was conscious of was her grumbling tummy, and her tongue stuck to the roof of her mouth like a lump of sandpaper, and the feeling of being safe at last, deep down within the earth, where not a soul knew where she was. Curling up like a fox in its lair, she closed her eyes and slept.

33

It took the police less than an hour to reach the den. Ella had been quite insistent that was where Jinty would be, and since the whole area was already swathed in blue and white tape and the female officer had been there before, their powerful torches soon found it again.

The minute Ella got the news that Jinty was safe and well and recovering from her dehydration in hospital, she texted Aminah, and Aminah immediately phoned her back. For a while they said the same things over and over again, and once they'd finally exhausted the topics of how utterly relieved they were, and how long it might take Jinty to recover, and where she'd go when she *had* recovered, Aminah broke the news that the reason *she* hadn't been asleep was that, earlier that evening, Grace had gone into labour.

For a while after the call, all Ella could do was sit numbly in the studio, letting it all sink in. Then she limped through to the bathroom and surveyed the damage to her left temple and was relieved to see that, despite a sizable lump surrounded by deep purple bruising, the skin hadn't broken and her eye, though bloodshot, remained more or less open.

Amazingly, it was still only half past ten, and Ella wheeled the suitcase into the studio and sat looking at it, considering whether she should, after all, drive to the Cotswolds. Not to visit Carys of course – that was out of the question now she looked as though she'd been mugged – but simply to escape for a couple of days, and as she weighed up the various pros and cons it occurred to her that Jinty's Commonplace Book was still in her backpack in the hall.

She fetched the book, took it out of its plastic bag, and leafed past the botanical drawings, and the poems, and the recipes for Apple Crumble and Eve's Pudding, till she came to a page marked DIARY - STRICTLY CONFERDENTIAL.

She began to read.

Climb #1 The Trial, the first entry began, and then it went on: *I followed Miss Blyth home from school. She was dead easy to follow on account of her limp ...*

Heart fluttering now, Ella read quickly through the rest of the entry, then turned to the next page and read on. Liquid kept swimming over her eyes, blurring Jinty's words, but she blinked it away and scanned past careful illustrations of the house, with its blue front door and red Virginia creeper, and the long descriptive passages about the tree and how excellent it was to climb, till she came to the next entry, which was entitled *Climb #2: The Discovery.*

That entry had hardly any words at all, but was told as a kind of strip cartoon, and its movement and energy was as stunning as any Ella had seen in a professionally-published children's picture book.

One set of illustrations delighted and horrified her in equal measure. The first showed Jinty, backpack on her back, clambering grimly upwards, and the second showed a smiling Jinty sitting on a broad branch unpacking a carton of juice and a biscuit. The third, which took up an entire page, was Jinty tumbling through the air, her mouth open and a long *H-e-e-e-elp!* snaking in and out of the leaves, while two terrified squirrels dropped their beech nuts in alarm and dived for cover. Despite herself, Ella found herself laughing out loud.

Then she turned to the next page. Its title was *#3 The Chained Lady,* and as she read through it and grasped its significance, her laughter died, and she realised she would certainly not be travelling to the Cotswolds today.

I climbed right to the top of the tree, Jinty had written, *and I saw Miss Blyth chaining the lady up. The lady looked quite happy and she had one of her boobies out and Miss Blyth was touching it. I think Miss Blyth must be a lesbian, which it is all right to be, but chaining up ladies is defenately not all right ...*

Ella read the entry to the end. Then she pulled herself out of the chair and made herself a strong coffee. When she'd drunk it, she fetched a craft knife and very carefully cut out each of the 'Diary' pages, and then she went down to the shed and disentangled ten of Jinty's flying birds.

She slid the diary pages and five of the birds into a large manilla envelope, wrote Jinty's name on the front with the word 'Personal' underneath, and packed the other five birds in her suitcase. Then she dragged herself wearily to bed and, at three o' clock that afternoon, she drove to the hospital.

She showed the nurse in charge her school identity card and explained who she was and, very briefly, why her face was injured. Then she told her she had something to give Jinty which, she thought, would ease at least some of her recent burden of worry, and the nurse led her to the private room where Jinty lay. Her eyes were half-open and one of her arms was attached to a drip, and she was surrounded by instruments with tiny pulsing lights.

"Just a couple of minutes please, Miss Blyth," the nurse told her, and she pressed a hand against her back and smiled. "I'll be right outside, if you need me," and she left the room. Clutching the strap of her backpack, Ella looked down at Jinty. The first thing that struck her was that, for such a little girl, her face had aged terribly.

She was desperately pale, and her hair had been brushed tightly back off her face, emphasising the sharp angles of her cheekbones. Her glasses, their bridge stuck with a piece of surgical tape, sat on her nose at an even more rakish angle than usual, and when Ella eased herself down onto the chair beside her bed and gave her the brightest smile she could manage, Jinty didn't smile back.

For a long time neither spoke, and the only hint of how Jinty was feeling was the brightness in her eyes and the deep knot of anxiety on her brow. Then she whispered, in a voice so small Ella could hardly hear her, "I'm terribly sorry, Miss Blyth. I'm terribly sorry about your face, and about looking in your window, and everything …" and her eyes filled so quickly to overflowing it was like a small tap being turned on.

Ella handed her a tissue from the box by the bed and, as Jinty wiped her tears away, she assured her that she was perfectly all right, and that it was her own silly fault for taking the law into her own hands, and that she hoped *she* was all right. She waited to see if Jinty wanted to say anything else, but though she bit her lip and sucked her cheek and seemed on the point of speaking again, she didn't, so Ella bent down and took the manilla envelope out of her backpack.

"This is for you, Jinty," she said, and she pushed the envelope under the hand that didn't have a needle in it.

Jinty made no move to open it. "Is it a card?" she said at last, and Ella took another envelope out, small and white this time, and, laughing, told her that no, it wasn't a card, *this* one was a card, but wasn't she going to open the big envelope first?

Slowly, and with a look of great suspicion, Jinty opened the manilla envelope. She pulled out its contents and looked at each page in turn and, as she slowly realised what they were, she gave Ella a quizzical look.

"I'm so, so sorry, Jinty," Ella said, "but I broke my promise and read your diary. I had to, because other people were going to read it and I didn't think you'd like that. I didn't show it to anyone else, or tell them what you'd written," she added quickly, because now Jinty's face had crumpled and she was beginning to cry again. "Do you understand?" and, to make quite sure she did understand, she repeated very slowly, "No one but me has read it." Then she leant a little closer.

"One day, when you're better," she whispered into Jinty's ear, "I'll explain all about the chained lady, and you'll see it was all right. But for now, just believe me that it is. It's just what mad artists like you and me do …"

The nurse had opened the door a crack and was looking in with some concern. "It's fine," Ella assured her, and she glanced down at Jinty, who gave a tiny grin. "Can we have just a couple more minutes, please?" and the nurse nodded and slipped back out.

Ella bent over Jinty's pillow and pushed some stray strands of hair to one side. "You're going to go to Art School when you grow up, Jinty," she said, and she made her voice sound firm and teacher-like, as though she was giving an order that must be obeyed. "Mrs Nwapa and I will make quite sure you do. And maybe, one day, you'll write stories and illustrate them, and then you'll be rich and famous," and when Jinty gave another tiny grin and, pushing the manilla envelope safely under the covers, closed her eyes, Ella tiptoed out.

The traffic on the way home was heavy, and when Ella arrived back at number 22 it was after five and almost dark. She made herself coffee and a sandwich which she took into the living room, and when she'd finished she stretched out on the red settee and lay staring up at the ceiling, concentrating on the overwhelming feeling of relief she felt, and wondering how the throbbing pain in her face could possibly be almost pleasant.

She was gathering up her mug and plate when the sound of a car engine made her turn and look out of the window and, by the light of the streetlamp, she saw a car driving very slowly up to the gate. It was a black car, and the driver was a man wearing a brown hat with a small brim, and as Ella held her breath and watched, the man heaved himself out of the driver's seat, pulled off the hat to reveal a tousled mop of grey hair, and stood for a moment or two, peering up at the front door.

Putting down the dishes, Ella took her phone out of her pocket and was about to dial 999, but then she stopped, looked back out, and let the phone drop onto the settee; because as the man walked towards the gate she saw that something was very, very wrong.

The man was opening the gate now and looking directly up at her, and as Ella continued to watch, she felt the hottest of all hot flushes envelope her. For the man's face and figure were strangely familiar, and as, with big, stolid footsteps, he strode up the path towards the front door, she realised it was not a man after all. It was Carys.

34

Holding her head very still, Ella made her way carefully down the stairs, and when she reached the hall and saw Carys's tall figure silhouetted against the stained glass she hurried to open the door, anxious that Harry Flood might look out and demand to know what the devil had happened last night.

Seeing Carys standing there in the dark was nothing short of uncanny. It was as though a being from another life had landed on her doorstep, and all Ella could do was stand, staring at her, while Carys, uncharacteristically lost for words too, screwed up her eyes and peered in at Ella. Then she pushed the door further open, and said, in a voice that seemed to echo all round the hall, "What in heaven's name's happened to your face?" at which Ella threw the door open, pulled her in, and motioned to her to be quiet and follow her upstairs.

"Sorry, Carys," she whispered as she led her up, "but we've had a bit of trouble lately and I'd rather not disturb the neighbours again," and she showed her into her flat where they both stood, in the brightness of the hall, gazing at one another.

Ella was shocked at how much Carys's appearance had changed in the past months. Her face was the same broad-featured, almost peasant-like, face she'd known half her life, but her hazel eyes seemed smaller, as though they'd sunk slightly into their sockets, and she seemed altogether older and thinner and more dishevelled than she remembered.

Her shoulders too, which she'd always held proudly erect, were rather stooped, and her normally ruddy complexion was pale and rather sallow, and for a while they continued to stand very still, neither knowing whether an embrace was, under the circumstances, appropriate.

"Are you all right?" Carys said at last. "Have you had an accident? Have you been attacked?" and as Ella assured her she was absolutely fine, that she'd just had a silly fall, and showed her into the living room, she added – crisply this time - "Do you have the slightest idea how worried Derek and I have been about you, what with all this paedophile stuff going on? The television's been full of it. And why in God's name haven't you replied to my texts? I must have sent a dozen of the bleeding things …"

Silenced by the sudden barrage of questions, Ella indicated the settee, but even when Carys was sitting, arms crossly folded, she didn't trust herself to speak. Part of her felt she should be apologising, but part of her absolutely didn't, and as Carys continued to sit, staring up at her in silent disapproval, she felt the apologetic part evaporate, leaving behind a residue of pure, blind, fury.

"*You've* been worried?" she said, struggling to keep her voice low and measured. "Have you any idea how your stalking has worried *me*, not to mention the staff and children in my school?" She didn't look at Carys, but directed her words to the middle distance and, much to her surprise, her voice didn't waver, and when Carys didn't immediately respond she added, a fraction louder, "What I can't understand is why you didn't just come and talk to me, when you'd obviously worked out where I was? What was the point of all that ridiculous skulking around?"

She looked down at Carys then, at her bedraggled hair and crumpled raincoat and big brogued feet planted firmly on the nice wooden floor, and saw that those broad shoulders of hers had sagged even more.

"Oh Ella," Carys said wearily, "it wasn't *my* idea to 'stalk' you, as you put it," and she shrugged off the raincoat and folded it over the back of the settee. "Believe me, if I'd had any say in the matter I'd have let you get on with it. You knew what you were doing, after all. You made your reasons for leaving very clear in your note."

At the mention of the note, Ella's stomach give a tiny flip. "Then why didn't you? Why didn't you just let me get on with it?"

There was a tangible pause, then Carys straightened her shoulders and raised her head to its usual proud position. "I *did* let you get on with it, Ella," she pointed out. "I've been letting you get on with it for four very long and difficult months, and during that time I've checked up on you a total of, let's see" – she looked up at the ceiling, counting – "four times. And believe me, there were plenty of things I'd rather have been doing."

"But *why*? What was the point of it?"

"The point of it, Ella, was Derek of course," she said, and now her voice was quivering with the effort of concealing her emotions. "And I hope I did it discreetly because - and let's be quite clear about this, Ella - I did *not* 'stalk' you. I merely did my utmost to keep a very dear friend from going out of his mind with worry."

A sudden vision of Derek, out of his mind with worry, flashed through Ella's head, but Carys hadn't finished. "You're covering a maternity leave, I believe? For a Grace

Nwapa? Whose husband Max owns two rather elegant art galleries?" and when Ella's jaw dropped she frowned knowingly. "It really wasn't very difficult to find you, you know. You left a Seavale Primary syllabus on the desk in your studio, and of course the great thing about a job like mine" – she gave Ella her first, albeit grudging, smile – "is that my spies are everywhere."

She turned away and, still smiling, took a look round the empty room. "This is very" – she paused just long enough to be annoying – "minimalist," and then, patting the space on the settee and softening her voice, she said, "Why don't you sit down, Ella? You look as done in as I am."

Leaving as wide a distance between them as possible, Ella perched on the edge of the settee. "You must have known when you wrote that note," Carys was saying, "that Derek would let me read it …" and as Ella half-listened she pictured her suitcase in the bedroom, with the half-bottle of Sloe gin buried between her jumpers.

"It may surprise you to learn that I was relieved to hear you were finally going to develop your art," Carys went on, "but what I can't understand is why you left in such a theatrically childish way? Surely, if you'd discussed it with Derek, the two of you could have come to some sort of compromise? Derek cares very deeply about you, you know. Did you ever, in all this wild flight of fancy of yours, stop to think about him? Or was it an act of supreme selfishness?"

Ella forced herself to take slow breaths. Then, speaking as calmly as was humanly possible she said, "Derek may care very deeply about me, Carys, but he knew, and so did you, that the marriage was a sham and I'd little option but to leave it," and as a sharp pain stabbed above her temple she glanced towards the door, wondering if there was any tonic water in the kitchen to go with the gin.

Carys looked askance at her. "I haven't the foggiest idea what you're talking about, Ella," she said. "The marriage may not have been love's young dream any more, but it wasn't a 'sham'. 'Sham' implies deception, and Derek's as honest as the day's long," and she gave a disparaging little snort and stood up. "Where's your toilet?" she demanded. "I've been driving for hours," and, following Ella's directions, she stomped angrily off.

As soon as she heard the bathroom door close, Ella dashed through to the bedroom. She unzipped the case and fished out the gin and then, making more noise than was necessary, she rifled around in the kitchen cupboards till she found a half-empty bottle of tonic water, and poured generous portions of gin into two mugs.

Then, remembering that at some point Carys would be required to drive, she poured most of the gin from one of the mugs into the other, topped up both with tonic, and took a very large gulp of the strong one. When Carys reappeared, she handed her the one that was mostly tonic.

With a disapproving sniff at the contents of the mug, Carys sat back down. Giddy with nerves now, Ella swallowed another large mouthful, and as the alcohol hit the inside of her head she stared down at Carys and braced herself.

"If Derek's as honest as the day's long," she said, "then how, may I ask, do you explain Jen?" and she sat down triumphantly, savouring her moment of triumph.

The triumph was short-lived and, in years to come, whenever Ella recalled the next few moments they were accompanied by the same gut-clenching mix of shock and shame and red-hot embarrassment she'd felt when Carys first answered her question. It was as though a moment in time had been photographed, in glorious technicolour, and gone on to become, and forever remain, one of the most cringingly humiliating moments in Ella's life.

It had taken Carys quite a long time to frame her answer, and as she did Ella watched her expression change from bewilderment to anger and then back again. Finally, she'd drained her mug of gin-laced tonic, looked down into the empty mug, and then back up again at Ella.

"You didn't think …? I mean, you couldn't possibly have thought?" and then she stopped and started again, and this time she gave each word its own distinct space.

"You didn't actually think Derek was having an affair with Jen?" she said, and when Ella, cheeks burning, said nothing, she repeated, "You didn't think that, Ella. Please tell me you didn't?"

She waited while Ella slowly nodded, and for a brief moment seemed almost on the point of laughter. Then, serious again, she said, "Oh Ella, what an imagination you've got," and, smiling and shaking her head in disbelief, she put her big hand on Ella's knee and gave it a not-unfriendly squeeze.

"Jen's not Derek's *lover*, you idiot," she said. "She's his counsellor. Her full name is Jennifer Dunmore - Dr Jennifer Dunmore - and he's been seeing her for a year or so, and personally, I've noticed a big improvement. I mean, we know he's always been rather emotionally 'bandaged', shall we say, but he's gradually learning to confront his feelings and express them. It took a great deal of courage to admit he needed help, you know, and he did it because of you."

Inclining her head, she looked into Ella's down-turned face. Then she put her big arm round her and squeezed her tight. "Poor you," she said. "You must have been terribly upset. I do wish you'd talked to us about it, instead of taking off like that," and before Ella could protest, she added, "I know, I know, the 'taking off' was all to do with your art, so please don't get back up on your high horse. In fact" - she sprang to her feet – "why don't you show me what you've been painting? I'd love to see it!" and they took their mugfuls of gin into the studio, where Carys couldn't have been more lavish in her praise.

"You know who'd really approve of these?" she said when she'd admired each of the paintings, and when Ella said she didn't, but probably not Derek, she laughed. "Lucy, of course. She's crazy about women's rights. She'd go an absolute bundle on them. And there's someone else too who'd like them, but if I tell you who you'll hit me …" and she gave Ella what could only have been described as a devilish smile.

Ella tensed. "Who?" she said, and Carys took a deep breath.

"Your mother, of course. These are just up Veronica Blyth's street. She was all for daring, convention-defying, feminist art, and your endless puppy-dogs and roses frustrated her no end."

She looked tentatively at Ella. "Oh come on, Ella" – she gave Ella's arm a playful little punch – "you must admit I'm right?"

Ella thought about it. "Maybe you're right about the 'daring' and 'convention-defying'," she conceded, "but I'm not so sure *my* art is strictly 'feminist'. I mean, yes - I've chosen to depict a woman escaping from the chains that limited her, but being enchained isn't exclusively the fate of women. There are men who are equally constrained and need help to take flight," and she gave Carys her best confrontational look. "Surely you must agree?"

Carys smiled. She gripped both of Ella's shoulders and squeezed, and then she let go and drained her mug.

"Yes, Ella," she said. "I surely must," and, laughing, she turned towards the door. "And now, might I suggest that, as it's a horrible night and we've both had a highly emotional day, I spend the night on your settee?" and when Ella said of course she might, and it would be nice to toast her birthday, however belated, she handed her the empty mug.

"Right," she said, "that's settled. Now for God's sake get me a decent drink," and she went down to the car to fetch her overnight bag.

In the kitchen, Ella managed to find two matching glasses, still wrapped in newspaper. Feeling suddenly wildly festive, as though today really was her birthday, she emptied crisps and olives into bowls, and as she set them on a tray with the gin and what was left of the tonic, it occurred to her that the pain in her temple, though still throbbing vaguely in the background, no longer troubled her. It was, in fact, like an old war wound, bravely won and to be endured with pride, and when she and Carys were sipping their almost-neat Sloe gins, she said, "Please don't tell Derek what I thought about Jen. I'll take time off school and go down on Monday and tell him myself. Perhaps you'd let him know about my face, though, so he doesn't get too much of a shock?"

Carys said she'd do her best, but it would make her task easier if she herself knew what had happened, and when Ella had told her the story (with some editorial omissions) of Jinty and the shed, she said all the right things; and as the evening drew to a close Ella, in a great rush of magnanimity, insisted that she should have her bed, to which Carys gratefully agreed.

"By the way, I almost forgot to tell you," she said as Ella wished her goodnight and pulled the bedroom door shut, "Derek said a card arrived for you. From Papua New Guinea …"

35

Next morning, despite the gin of the night before, Carys was up with the lark, and by eight o' clock she'd set off back to Cheltenham, leaving Ella to creep back into the warmth of her bed and sleep till midday.

When she did eventually wake, her face felt like a large throbbing balloon, and when she examined it in Flick's swan mirror she was horrified to see that it looked very much worse than the day before. There were shiny dark bags under each eye now, and the left lid had swollen so much she could hardly make out the eye at all, and after she'd taken a long shower she felt more than justified in phoning the school to say she wouldn't be in next week.

After she'd taken note of Ella's various infirmities, the secretary asked her to stay on the line, that Mrs McMahon would like a word, and after a long conversation during which Maura thanked her for all she'd done in the search for Jinty, she insisted she take as much time off as she felt she needed, and they would see her when she felt able to return.

She also told her, in the strictest confidence, that after her visit Jinty had told the nurses everything that had been happening at home and they'd contacted the police, who'd placed Uncle Chris in custody. There was, furthermore, to be a high-level meeting with Social Services next week after which, it was to be hoped, Jean McVey would receive the support she needed to rebuild her life, and in the meantime Jinty had given her solemn word she'd return to school next week and work extra hard to make up for the time she'd lost.

Euphoric with relief, Ella took a late breakfast into the studio and sat in the comfortable chair watching the birds hop from branch to branch of the almost-bare beech tree. The 'Leda' canvas was still too wet for a second coat, and her brain was far too addled to think about doing sketches for the new series, so she decided she'd spend the day clearing what still needed to be cleared before deciding what she'd take with her to Highgate.

One thing that definitely needed to be removed before she left was Harry Flood's ladder. After the 'flying' paintings were finished she'd moved it into the hall, and every now and then she'd thought about buying the duck-egg blue paint and starting to paint the bedroom, but now she was no longer sure she wanted to make any more improvements to the flat. In fact, after Carys's revelation about Jen, she was no longer sure of anything. The only thing she *was* sure of was that there was a birthday card from Papua New Guinea waiting for her in The Moorings, and at the thought of it a surge of energy rippled up her back and propelled her into the hall.

She ran down the stairs to the Floods' door, where she gave herself a minute or two while her breathing returned to normal before ringing the doorbell. Then she stood, still rather breathless, wondering which of the Floods she would least like it to be answered by.

Surprisingly, it was a relief when it was answered by Caroline, and as soon as she saw Ella she clasped her cheeks, gave a horrified gasp, and asked her what on earth had happened to her; and when Ella put it in a nutshell, then explained about the ladder, Caroline took her gently but firmly by the arm and pulled her inside.

She mustn't, Caroline assured her, give the ladder another thought, and she most certainly mustn't contemplate returning it herself. They had a key to her flat which Flick had given them and which they'd been meaning to return, and as soon as Harry got home she'd send him up to collect the ladder and give her back her key.

Right now, however, the top priority was to get that face of hers treated, and as she rhymed off the bewildering list of substances with which she intended to do that - arnica, frankincense, wormwood, St John's wort - Ella, somewhat mesmerised both by her unexpected kindness and the depth of her arcane knowledge, allowed herself to be steered through to the lemon-coloured living room which, she could almost swear, still smelt of home-baked bread.

Half an hour later, her stomach comfortably full of hearty vegetable soup and – yes – home-made bread, her face smelling like a cross between a perfumery and a medieval apothecary, and her pocket filled with plastic vials and instructions on how to apply their contents, she climbed back upstairs. Almost asleep on her feet, she lay down on her unmade bed to let Caroline's herbs and unctions work their charms.

It was almost dark when Ella woke up and, resisting the temptation to check on the progress of her face, she changed into her nightclothes, put on her dressing gown and slippers, and padded through to the kitchen to think about a meal. She turned on the oven, took a bag of frozen peas and a packet of fish fingers out of the deep freeze, and as she was arranging the fingers on the grill pan she heard a small scraping noise coming from the hall and shuffled out to investigate.

A key was being turned in the lock and, to begin with, she wasn't at all concerned because she was sure it was Harry come for the ladder. She did feel a certain annoyance that he was letting himself in rather than ringing the doorbell, but then perhaps he thought she might be sleeping and didn't want to disturb her, and she was on the point of calling out to him when the door opened, a strong torch was shone inside, and a long-haired woman wearing a pale-coloured sweatshirt and jeans crept in.

Apart from the kitchen light the flat was in darkness and, flattening herself against the wall, Ella watched in growing alarm as the woman made her way, somewhat erratically, round the hall and then, with a final cautious look around, slipped into the living room.

She watched the torch beam sweep around, bouncing from wall to wall, and it was obvious she was searching for something; and when, muttering angrily under her breath, she came back out and headed into the studio, Ella was so paralysed with fear she couldn't think of a thing to do other than stay in the shadows and watch.

Feverishly, she searched her aching brain for where she'd put her phone, but even that alluded her, and as the torch began to sweep around her studio she was torn between the wish to escape and the need to protect her precious work.

The woman had closed the front door behind her, but if she was quick she could make a dash across the hall, slip out onto the landing, and raise the alarm. Paul Wetherby was probably at home, and Caroline certainly was. If she did that, however, if she left the woman in her studio, what might she do? There was something about the way she was acting – her erratic movements, her incoherent mutterings

– that made Ella wonder whether she might be under the influence of something, and if she was, there was no knowing what could happen. When Lucy was high, she often became destructive, both to herself and her possessions. This woman might suddenly take it into her head to damage her paintings ...

Keeping her eye on the swaying torch beam, Ella inched her way out into the hall and carefully turned the handle of the front door so that it was open a fraction and any noise would be heard by the rest of the house. Then she crept to the studio door, held onto the frame, and put her head cautiously inside.

The woman had opened the cupboard door, and as she shone her torch from one shelf to the next her breath came in short and ever more angry rasps. Then she reached up and started to pull things down from the top shelves, and as the pink cardboard box hit the floor and Lucy's cards tumbled out, Ella's fear changed to anger.

She watched the woman bang the cupboard door closed, and as she turned and swept the torch beam round the rest of the room, her face was momentarily illuminated, and in that moment Ella knew, or thought she knew, who it was. She walked into the studio and switched on the lights, and, smiling encouragingly, she took another few steps in. As she did, she put both her hands behind her back, like she'd often done with Lucy, to let her know she was safe.

"Would you like to tell me what you're looking for, Nathan?" she said, and she spoke softly, as though to a wounded animal. "Or may I call you Nat? Nat's what your mum calls you, isn't it? And I'm a very good friend of your mum," and she dared take another step so that, if need be, she could reach out and touch him.

Like a schoolboy caught in the act of mischief, Nathan looked around furtively, as though planning his escape.

Then, muttering something Ella couldn't catch, he made to run for the door, but before he could reach it Ella slammed it shut and stood with her back against it. And as, trembling from head to toe, he stood staring at her through pinpoint pupils, her mind once more flashed back to Lucy, and she knew there was little point in trying to communicate with him. His physical body might be in the room with her, but his mind was in some other strange and distorted dimension, and his dark eyes, though they stared wildly at her, saw only his own crazed version of reality.

"Mum said you were away," Nathan Oliver mumbled. "I'd never have come if I'd thought you were here. I never wanted to frighten you ..." and then he began to sob and speak at the same time, his voice so quiet and hoarse Ella couldn't make out what he was saying; and when she asked him to repeat it she thought she heard, in the midst of all the incoherence, the word 'painting'.

"You're looking for the 'Leda' painting, aren't you, Nat?" she said, and then, hearing heavy footsteps running up the stairs, she added quickly, "Could you tell me why, please?"

For a second Nathan opened his mouth as if to speak, but before he could the studio door burst open and Harry Flood ran in. He took one look at Ella's bruised and battered face and then, with a furious howl, threw the whole weight of his body on top of Nathan's slight form, and Ella watched in horror as he took hold of the lapels of his jacket and shook him so hard his feet almost left the ground.

"Stop it, Harry!" she shouted as Nathan fell. "It wasn't him. He didn't hurt me," and as, deaf to her protests, Harry continued to glare down at Nathan, she grabbed his jacket and pulled at his flailing body. Harry's anger, however, was too strong for her and eventually, in desperation, she ran out into the hall, picked up the ladder, dragged it across the floor, and hurled it blindly at both of them.

There was a crash and then an eerie silence as both men lay crumpled together. Then Paul Wetherby's door burst open and, running in, arms flapping, he stood, viewing the scene in utter horror. Assuring him she'd not been attacked, Ella marched over to the easel and picked up the 'Leda' canvas, now thankfully touch-dry.

"Look!" she said, as all three men stared vacantly at the white rectangle. Nathan's eyes were wide open now, and he seemed suddenly completely present.

"Look at this," Ella repeated more softly, "because this is what you're all fighting over, isn't it? This is what the whole business with Flick was about" – and she pushed the canvas first into Nathan's face and then into Harry's – "but it's nothing, is it? It's nothing any more. It's just a harmless blank canvas," and she waited as Wetherby lifted the ladder and Nathan and Harry picked themselves up and stood, red-faced and looking for all the world like two miscreants in a playground brawl.

Harry was the first to recover his voice. "Can I see that more closely please, Ella?" he said, and he took the canvas and turned it this way and that, while Nathan, following his movements, gazed at it too. For a while, as Harry peered at the canvas, Nathan stood beside him, silent and trembling, and Ella wondered whether perhaps he could still see, in his mind's eye, the details of Leda's anguished face, and the swan's razor-sharp beak, bloodied by her flesh. When he spoke, his voice was perfectly sober.

"Bruno Glass said they'd use it against me in a court of law," Nathan said. "He said it was proof I'd raped Flick" – he looked first at Wetherby and then at Ella, eyes pleading to be believed – "but I didn't. I didn't rape her, honestly I didn't. I'd never have hurt her. I loved her, and she loved me," and he shook his head, as though trying to summon up the truth of what had happened. "She said we'd get married one day and …"

Bristling with anger, Harry took another lunge at him. "Why don't you just admit what you did?" he growled. "You got high, and you forced yourself on her, and now you can't even remember what happened because your mind's in such a bloody mess. And look what you've done to poor Ella's studio," and he looked over at Wetherby, appealing to him for support.

The support was not, however, forthcoming. "If you truly examine your conscience, Harry," Wetherby said quietly, "I think you will be forced to admit Nathan was not the only one who took advantage of Flick's trusting nature," and he took a deep breath. Then he opened his mouth to speak, but Ella had heard enough. Opening the door, she held it wide.

"I'll be talking to Bruno Glass tomorrow," she said, "and I'm sure he'll tell me the full story so, for the moment, I'd be grateful if you would all leave," and she watched as Harry took a key out of his pocket, laid it on the table, then picked up the ladder and, with a final sheepish glance at her, followed Wetherby out.

Nathan began to trail miserably away too, but before he reached the door Ella took hold of his arm. "Tell your mother I'll see her very soon," she told him softly. Then she touched the side of his forehead gently with her finger. "You're bleeding a bit," she said. "Perhaps you'd tell your mum you tripped over the cat?" and when Nathan nodded and, smiling timidly, assured her he would, she closed the door behind the lot of them and made her way to bed.

36

Next morning, Ella rose late and spent the time before Bruno's concert making final preparations for tomorrow's journey to Highgate.

She took everything back out her suitcase and re-packed, making sure Jinty's birds were safely underneath her palette at the bottom, and the tube of Titanium White and the brushes were in a plastic bag out of harm's way, and when the suitcase was sitting by the door in readiness for the morning, she fetched the white canvas and propped it up against it. Then she took her wedding and engagement rings out of her jewellery box and eased them onto her finger, and after a light lunch she set off for St Columba's.

When she reached the bottom of the stairs Harry Flood was standing by the front door. He had dark circles under his eyes, and his face was more lined than she remembered it being, and it occurred to her he might have been standing there for a while, listening out for her.

"I'm sorry, Harry," she said as he opened his mouth to speak, "I've got an appointment and I'm already rather late," and she opened the door and began to walk down the path. Harry, however, walked with her, and when they reached the gate he held it closed.

"Ella, please," he said, "I have to speak to you. Just listen for a minute and then I promise I'll bugger off," and when

Ella repeated that she hadn't the time, nor indeed the inclination, to listen even for a minute, he released the gate but followed her doggedly out and onto the pavement. Keeping her eyes firmly fixed on the middle distance, Ella strode off.

"Caroline's leaving me," she heard Harry say as he trotted along behind her. "She thinks I've been unfaithful but honestly I haven't. And I was wondering if you and I" – he side-stepped awkwardly in front of her, barring her way – "I mean, could we possibly have a proper chat? There are some things I have to tell you."

Ella barely concealed a sigh. "Not now, Harry," she said. "*Please,*" but even when she fixed him with a look she hoped bordered on the desperate, he didn't make the slightest move to leave her be. Then he gripped her by the shoulders and she could feel the trembling in his hands.

"I promise you, Ella," he said, "the affair with Flick, it wasn't an *affair,* as such. I swear it wasn't. I was only trying to help her," and he squeezed her shoulders in time with the words, as though pumping them into her.

"I'd realised by then that Nat was an addict," he went on, "and I could see the two of them were on some terrible downwards spiral. I was worried to death about Flick, and I was frightened for Maeve too. I mean, Nat was always a disappointment to her, but if she found out about the heroin, it'd be the last straw, " and he let go, put both hands behind his back, and needlessly tucked in his shirt.

Ella clenched her jaw. She longed to believe him as much as she longed to walk away and leave him behind, but a question niggled insistently enough to make her stay. It was a question she'd been asking herself, on and off, since the incident with Nathan Oliver, and part of her needed to know the answer, and part of her dreaded knowing.

She spoke very softly. "I have a problem believing anything you say, Harry," she said, "because you've already lied to me," and she watched his face change from indignation to bewilderment.

"Lied to you, Ella?" he said. "When? When have I ever told you a lie?"

Ella pulled down the brim of her sunhat, hiding from him. "When you showed me 'Aristaeus and the Death of the Bees', I asked you if Flick always put a swan in her paintings and you said you didn't know because you'd only ever seen the 'Aristaeus' one. But that wasn't true," and she began to walk away, knowing he'd be bound to follow. "You'd seen 'Leda and the Swan', so why didn't you tell me you had? What did you have to hide?"

She kept her head down, watching the brown leather of her shoes as they thumped down on the pavement, and as they both picked up speed Harry's words came out in short bursts.

"I didn't want to burden you with the details of what happened to Flick, Ella. You'd only just arrived and you were getting on so well with Maeve" - he was alongside her now and she could see his expression was grave - "and I wanted it to stay that way. I'm sorry. I should have realised you were the determined sort and you'd keep at it till you found out the truth."

Unexpectedly, he stopped. "I'll get out of your hair now," he said, "and I dare say Bruno Glass will fill you in on all the bits I've missed. And please accept my abject apologies," he added with a boyish grin, "for any inappropriate behaviour I might have been guilty of in the past. Sure and I can be an awful one for the old impropriety."

Ella smiled despite herself. "I'm going away for a while," she said, and she placed her left hand on his arm so that the diamonds of her engagement ring sparkled between them, "but when I'm back and the dust's settled, maybe we can have another chat?" and when he'd nodded and turned away, she set off down the hill towards the bright rim of the sea.

The fresh breeze felt good on her battered face, and when she reached the church she joined the line of people walking through the arched doorway. She kept her head self-consciously down, and when she got inside she didn't head for Gran's seat beside Mr Valiant for Truth as she'd have liked, but tucked herself into the darkness of the back row.

When everyone was seated, a choir performed an anthem and then two young women sang with guitar accompaniment, and finally Bruno Glass was introduced, and as he got up from the pews to take his seat Ella peeped out from the shadows to see the familiar bearded, bespectacled face from Maeve's photo, and was reassured by his calm presence.

Before he began, Bruno told the audience how sorry he was that *The Silver Swan* was no more and that, for the moment, he was forced to perform alone. Then he picked up his lute and sang, and as his sweet tenor voice filled the church Ella listened to its purity and clarity and was entranced.

After two more songs he introduced his final piece, which he dedicated to the two absent members of the group, and as the church filled with the sound of Flick's favourite madrigal about the dying swan, Ella remembered how lovingly Maeve had sung it to her all those weeks ago; and when the concert was over and everyone but Bruno had left, she crept out from her dark corner into the brightness of the nave.

"You must be Ella. Hello!" Bruno laid his lute into its case and walked towards her with his hand extended, his long limbs loose and a big open smile on his face. Still holding her hand, he led her to the chair he'd vacated then fetched another, and when they were sitting side by side he said, "I hope you don't mind me asking, but are you all right?" and Ella laughed and assured him that, despite appearances, she was perfectly OK.

"Thank you for agreeing to see me, Bruno," she said. "I didn't know Flick personally, but I've lived in her flat for several months and I almost feel I do. I hope you don't think I'm an awful busybody?"

Bruno shook his head firmly. "Flick made a strong impression on everyone she met, so I'm not surprised you feel you know her. I mean, she was terribly shy and self-effacing, but somehow people were drawn to that." He took off his gold-rimmed spectacles, ran his hand over his face, and sighed. "Men, in particular, were drawn to it. Anyway, what was it you wanted to know?"

Faced with the direct question, Ella took a moment to frame her response. "I want to know where, and how, she is," she said, "and I also want to know why she painted a picture of herself being brutally raped. One of the men in the house told me you'd threatened to use it in a court of law?" and she sat back in her chair to await Bruno's response.

He was clearly upset now, and Ella thought she detected anger too in his gentle features. For a while he sat, head bowed, fiddling with the legs of the spectacles. Then he put them back on and gave her a frank look.

"First of all," he said, "Flick is, as far as I know, alive - though where, or how, she is I'm afraid I couldn't tell you. At the time of her breakdown, I was told her sister came and took her away, but they left no forwarding address, and

I can only assume Flick has her own reasons for not being in touch.

"As for Nathan Oliver and the hideous painting, I believe, in the heat of the moment, I did threaten him with some kind of legal action, but you know, Ella" - he gave her a look she could only have decribed as 'anguished' - "I was at my wits' end. Flick was making no sense at all, and Nat was as high as the proverbial kite, and I think I just wanted to sober him up so that he realised the gravity of the situation.

"Realistically," he went on, "a painting would never hold up in a court of law as evidence of a violent crime. And anyway," he added before Ella could ask, "Nat's not capable of anything like that. He's a heroin addict of course, and a hopelessly erratic character, but from what Flick said he was devoted to her, and I'm pretty sure she loved him too" – he paused, frowning – "as far as Flick was capable of loving any man, that is …"

Ella let everything sink in. "So," she said at last, "Flick had problems with relationships?" and Bruno raised his eyebrows and gave an ironic little laugh.

"She was forever forming relationships with men and then, as soon as things began to become physical, she panicked. I'm sure something dreadful must have happened to her in the past to make her so morbidly afraid of intimacy, but if I ever tried to probe she'd get terribly upset and clam up. My partner's a psychologist," he added, "and he's pretty sure there's serious childhood trauma there."

"So the swan who's raping her isn't Nathan," Ella said. "It's her father, or uncle, or something?" and when Bruno nodded and shrugged a 'maybe', Ella could see his eyes were slick with unshed tears.

"Before she moved to Largs," he explained, "Flick had never lived on her own. She'd always been with her sister, and she was very dependent on her, but the sister was about to get married and Flick decided it was time to live independently. She'd heard we were short of a harpsichordist, so she moved to Largs.

"For a while, everything was fine. She was perfect for *The Silver Swan*, and she threw herself into that and her painting. Then she met Nathan and fell for him, and she just couldn't handle the relationship." He gave a long sigh. "I watched her unravelling, and there was nothing I could do to stop it. I felt so utterly useless."

He took his glasses back off and covered his face with his hands, and Ella leant nearer.

"I suppose the strong emotions brought her latent terrors to the surface," she said. "And perhaps, because she couldn't talk to anyone about her fears, she painted them instead. She needs psychiatric help," she added, "doesn't she?"

Wiping his eyes, Bruno nodded. Replacing his glasses, he looked towards the door, where a man was gathering up abandoned leaflets from the pews. "She does," he said, "and I only hope she's getting it," and he stood up and went over to where the lute lay in its open case. He covered the instrument over with red velvet lining, tucking it in all round as though it was a baby. Then he closed the case and locked it.

"I haven't given up hope though," he said, and he turned and flashed a smile at Ella. "I still believe one day I'll go into an art gallery and see her work hanging on the walls, where it should be."

He picked up the lute case, and they walked together down the aisle. "What about Harry Flood?" Ella said. "Do you think he made a pass at Flick and frightened her?" but Bruno shook his head.

"I think he was as concerned as I was about her relationship with Nathan and was trying to be protective.

There may have been the odd bit of innocent flirting, because Flick was a flirt and Harry, as you no doubt know, is a charmer, but I'm sure there was nothing more. I only bumped into Harry once," he added, "and he struck me as a very decent sort."

He stopped then, and gave Ella a serious look. "Look Ella," he said, "I'd hate you to think I'm trivialising the upset these men caused Flick, but believe me" – he took her hand and squeezed it hard – "if she'd been attacked in any way I'd have known about it, and I'd have gone straight to the police."

They both stepped out onto the church steps and for a while Bruno stood, brows knotted, staring out to sea. "I wish I knew where that painting was though," he said, "because I honestly don't think it should be out there. Even Flick was ashamed of it at the end, you know."

Ella leaned close enough that their shoulders touched. "It's not out there," she said. "Not any more. And one day I'll repaint the canvas with the painting that *should* be 'out there'. Which reminds me, do you have a photo of Flick?" and, taking out his mobile, Bruno assured her he had several dozen.

"I took a whole load of both the girls last year, for a publicity leaflet that never happened," and he handed the phone to Ella. Flick's face, with its pale skin and green eyes and sensitive expression, smiled shyly out at her from its frame of auburn hair.

"Tell me which ones you'd like, and I'll email them to you," he said, and he dug about in his pocket again and gave her his business card. "And of course, when Flick finally decides to contact me, I'll be sure and let you know," and, carefully avoiding her wounds, he kissed her lightly on the cheek.

"Loving that frankincense fragrance of yours, by the way," he laughed. "Very seasonal!" and, with long loping strides, he was gone.

A milky sun shone through cirrhus crowds as Ella turned away from the town and headed up towards Haylie Brae. There were still a couple of hours of daylight left, just time for one last-ditch attempt to find Gran's grave, and as she rounded the corner and headed up to the cemetery, she began to plan the painting with which, one day soon, she'd replace Flick's 'Leda and the Swan'.

The original painting had been in landscape format, but this new version would be a portrait, so once she'd completed her layers of white she'd turn the canvas and paint Flick's head and long slender neck as she looked shyly out into the middle distance. Then, coiled round her shoulder and looking protectively down at her, she'd add as benign and empathetic a swan as she possibly could.

It would be the first painting of her second series, and even now, as she walked through the cemetery gates and headed upwards towards the boundary wall, she began to see, in her mind's eye, a host of other paintings on a similar theme: women with brightly-plumaged birds in their hands, or clutching their hair, or gripping onto their clothing, or flying beside them.

Arlene could pose for her again, and Aminah too, and of course it needn't be exclusively women. She could make Sergei, with that sensitive, battle-scarred face of his, fly with a great flock of doves ...

She'd do six or seven paintings, maybe more, and then she'd paint the living-room grey and hang them, and the first series, on its walls and invite Grace and Max to come and see, and maybe - just maybe - they'd give her a solo show.

When she reached the top of the cemetery she stood looking at the strands of blue and white tape that flapped from the trees and down onto the mausoleum roof, almost expecting Jinty's freckled face to pop through the branches and smile its toothy smile at her.

Turning, she began to work her way slowly and methodically back and forth along the paths, bending now and then to study a gravestone, and wondering once again what kind of memorial Veronica Blyth would have chosen for her mother. She walked across the upper level then down to the next, where she wended her way in the gathering dusk between slabs and obelisks and crosses, scanning each lichen-encrusted inscription.

The cross, when Ella found it, was so much smaller and plainer than any of the others that its very simplicity made it stand out, and it was in such a prominent place she wondered why she hadn't seen it before. Moss-covered with age and neglect, it rose from its little mound of rocks to stand with its back solidly to the sea, and when she bent down to examine it more closely, she saw there were rough lines carved into its surface so that it looked like rough-hewn wood taken straight from tree to carpenter. The stonemason had even carved, where horizontal and vertical met, a row of large square-headed nails.

Kneeling, Ella read the inscription. *In loving memory of my mother, Elizabeth Lucy Ferguson, born 2nd March 1884, died 4th April 1959*, it said, and for a while she traced the letters round and round with the tip of her finger, saying Gran's name – *her* name - over and over to herself.

She'd stood up and was about to turn and go when she noticed that lower down, almost entirely covered in moss, something else was written, and when she knelt and picked the moss away to reveal the rest of the message Veronica

Blyth had instructed the mason to carve, she felt her body stiffen.

Beloved grandmother to Ella, the letters spelt out, and as she read them she felt her chest expand and fill with a lightness she'd never felt before.

Stepping back from Gran's grave, she gazed over to where the sun's last blood-red rays spilled out over the silver water of the Firth. The sky overhead was almost dark now, and the air smelt of wood smoke as, in the distance, bonfires began to be lit and the first fireworks cracked.

Soon they were whistling into the sky, whooshing up then disappearing with small sizzling sounds, their brightness illuminating the entire graveyard with a strange electric light. Then there was a much louder roar as a huge rocket seared up from the direction of the harbour, and when it had arched its way across the sky it seemed, for a moment, to stop in its tracks just above Ella's head.

Leaning back, she watched as, with a series of muffled pops, the head of the rocket exploded into bright red, then green, then blue lights, each of which sprayed out like drops of water in a fountain before dying and, with tinkling little sounds, falling to earth. Rocket after rocket was launched, their lights spewing up then crossing and mingling till it seemed the whole sky was transformed into one immense dazzling cavalcade of colour.

Her hands resting on Gran's cross, Ella watched the display till it ended, leaving the air heavy with smoke. Then she stepped away from the grave and began, very slowly, to walk back down through the graveyard, and when she reached its open gates she quickened her pace.

Hugging herself close against the cold, she followed the harbour lights, and the smell of wood-smoke, down to the sea and home.